T0285271

Acclaim for
ESTUARY

"Sometimes you just need to check speculation at the door and sink into an utterly absorbing tale, taking you to a dreamy place (Italy), introducing you to fascinating people (time-travelers) and casually learn about a time period you might not know much about (medieval). Diving into the deep end of this first book in the Oceans of Time will bless you with a refreshing 'break read,' as well as a restorative opportunity to consider how families are sometimes uniquely brought together by God . . . a theme close to my heart. I'm eagerly anticipating book two!"

— TRICIA GOYER, bestselling author of 80 books,
including *A Daring Escape*

"*Estuary* will whisk you away into a richly woven world of danger and beauty—and sweeping romance. Full of twists and intrigue that will keep you turning pages, this riveting tale delves into the ties of family that span centuries and the parts of ourselves we discover in long-forgotten places. Fans of the original River of Time series—as well as new readers, diving in for the first time—will discover charm, heart and courage brought to life in a breathtaking new way. This spellbinding novel a must-read. Highly recommended!"

— KARA SWANSON, Christy Award-winning author of
Dust and *Shadow*

"Lisa Bergren weaves a beautiful story in this unique time jump novel. Medieval Italy provides the backdrop with knights, battles, and strong women. A definite recommendation for both those who love her River of Time series and fantasy."

— MORGAN L. BUSSE, award-winning author of
The Ravenwood Saga and Skyworld series

"Fabulous and utterly satisfying! *Estuary* is a glorious return to Bergren's much-beloved River of Time series. Beautiful portrayals of love, betrayal, and courage are as gorgeous as the Italian countryside in which they're set. This story will delight Bergren's longtime fans and have new readers searching caves for that portal back to medieval Italy to meet the infamous She-Wolves of Siena. Nock your arrows and get ready to ride—this is one story you won't want to miss!"

— **RONIE KENDIG**, award-winning author of the Droseran Saga

Estuary

Books by Lisa T. Bergren

The Oceans of Time Series
Estuary

The River of Time Series
Waterfall
Cascade
Torrent
Bourne & Tributary
Deluge

River of Time California
Three Wishes
Four Winds

The Remnants Trilogy
Season of Wonder
Season of Fire
Season of Glory

The Gifted Series
Begotten
Betrayed
Blessed

View more of Lisa's books
at lisatawnbergren.com

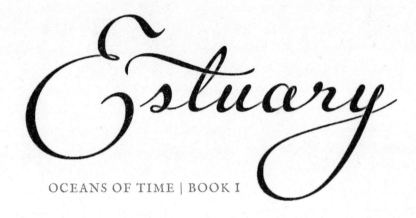

Estuary

OCEANS OF TIME | BOOK I

LISA T. BERGREN

Estuary
Copyright © 2023 Lisa T. Bergren

Published by Enclave Publishing, an imprint of Oasis Family Media, LLC

Carol Stream, Illinois, USA.
www.enclavepublishing.com

All rights reserved. No part of this publication may be reproduced, digitally stored, or transmitted in any form without written permission from Oasis Family Media, LLC.

This is a work of fiction. Names, characters, places, and incidents are products of the author's imagination or are used fictitiously. Any similarity to actual people, organizations, and/or events is purely coincidental.

ISBN: 979-8-88605-046-2 (printed hardcover)
ISBN: 979-8-88605-047-9 (printed softcover)
ISBN: 979-8-88605-049-3 (ebook)

Cover design by Kirk DouPonce, www.DogEaredDesign.com
Typesetting by Jamie Foley, www.JamieFoley.com

Printed in the United States of America.

For my beloved River Tribe,

who never tire of tales from Toscana.

I so appreciate each and every one of you!

PROLOGUE
Luciana Betarrini

In all my daydreams about time traveling to medieval Italy, none included being in a wagon, bouncing over cobblestone streets, with my hands tied behind my back. And yet there I was, my bound brother behind me, and the Perugian crowds calling us all sorts of foul names in an ancient form of Italian. Some threw rotting fruit at us.

Seriously. Rotting fruit. I thought people only did that in movies.

But I've gotten ahead of myself. You probably want to know how two modern college kids ended up in medieval Italy, before the Medicis and da Vinci were around, and a little after the Black Death had killed every third person in the country.

I blame it on my brother, Domenico.

Nico was a bit obsessed with our Betarrini relatives, to the point of convincing our dad that we should spend the summer as volunteers in the refurbished Castello Forelli, a big tourist attraction in Tuscany. He won Dad over by claiming it'd be "educational" as well as a connection to our lost Italian relatives. Not that Dad cared much—only what it cost. But Nico was totally convinced he had a lead on some medieval treasure. An ancient scepter and miter of some corrupt pope who'd sheltered with the Medicis for a time. And he had it in his head that if we could just bop back in time, he'd find a way to nab it.

Admittedly, The Great Betarrini Disappearance Mystery was all the clan—the few we were connected to—could talk about last Thanksgiving. My dad's uncle and that side of the family gathered on the Jersey shore every year, and once in a while, I accepted their invitation and made Nico go with me. We'd never really had extended family connections, but for some reason, last year, all the commercials showing big, happy families had made me push Nico to bail on Dad in LA—who never made a turkey dinner but preferred to take us out—so we could hang out with Uncle Vinny and his five kids and twenty-plus grandkids. It was always a madhouse being with them, but they did their best to include us.

I could still see Uncle Vin—Dad's eighty-year-old uncle—lifting his bear-paw hands as he said, "If you ask me, somethin's off. Ya know, beyond the obvious. Ben must've gotten on the wrong side of the wrong family, and *that* family made ours disappear."

"But, Uncle Vin, I don't think they disappeared," Nico said excitedly, pacing in his agitation on the chilly, wind-swept beach. "There are many stories among families, passed down for generations, about two Betarrinis—the She-Wolves of Siena. They married two of the Forellis. Cousins. And together, they led the Sienese in battle, and not just once. Repeatedly. It's all over the Internet."

I rolled my eyes. Nico was forever researching on the Net, chasing mysteries. The family closest to us stared at him, half amused, half alarmed—like he'd gone off the deep end.

"Couldn't those She-Wolf Betarrinis be any of our ancestors?" I asked.

"Potentially," Nico allowed. "But I found an article from a librarian who interviewed old people to record stories passed down, generation by generation, and she mentioned Gabriella and Evangelia Betarrini specifically. And there's a statue in Chianti depicting two women, one carrying a sword, the other a bow. Don't you remember Lia winning all those state competitions? Didn't we wonder if she'd beat everyone at nationals?"

I winced, feeling one of my migraines beginning to form. Couldn't he just give it a rest?

Uncle Vinny shrugged his ham-like shoulders and peered at Nico from beneath his bushy, gray-black brows. "The girls obviously had the talent in their blood. We Betarrinis inherited many fine attributes from our ancestors," he said, proudly looking around at the others. "And Ben and Adri were always neck-deep in history stuff. It's only logical that they encouraged their daughters to do things like that. Ya know, like our ancestors. Maybe they got onto those same old tales and named their daughters after them."

"But what if they didn't just encourage them?" Nico asked. "What if they didn't get kidnapped or murdered, Uncle Vin? What if they found some way to go back in time? What if they weren't named after those ancestors, but *are* those ancestors?"

Uncle Vinny frowned. "Do I need to smack you upside the head, son?" He collared Domenico's neck and pulled him closer for a big, wet kiss on the cheek. He grinned at all of us. "This guy," he said, pointing at my brother, "always with an imagination run amok!"

The family had laughed and turned away from the bonfire on the cold beach to retreat to the warmth of the house and dinner. Only Nico, Uncle Vinny, and I were left. But I knew Nico wasn't done; I'd tried to convince him myself. I was curious if an older relative would have better luck.

"I'm serious, Uncle Vin. It's not all in my head," Nico persisted. "I really think there's a chance . . ."

All trace of a smile left Uncle Vinny's face. He waved a meaty finger in my brother's face. "Now listen to me, Domenico. I'm gonna tell you this just once. Just once. Don't go nosin' around in that mess. Mark my words . . . if four Betarrinis disappeared, more could after 'em. I've lived enough life to know it smells like the mob."

If our parents had been around and heard all that had happened, they would have probably sided with him and nixed our summer-trip plans then and there. But Mom had died three years ago of cancer. And Dad? Well, Dad hadn't been a real part of our lives since we were in Pre-K. Our only connection with him was pretty much a monthly deposit in our checking accounts to cover college expenses. Our Nona had helped raise us, but she was gone now, too, buried the year after Mom. And the rest of our extended family just chalked it up to Nico's latest conspiracy theory.

After all, two years ago, Nico had been pretty darn sure that aliens had built the pyramids.

I had to admit that there were reports that Ben Betarrini's wife and daughters had shown up on his archeological dig last summer, and then they'd all disappeared. There was an open investigation, missing persons reports, an episode of "48 Hours"— everything you'd expect if two prominent scholars and their kids vanished. After his alien obsession waned, Nico had gone all Internet detective with the missing family, and he'd turned up this evidence of an ancient Gabriella and Evangelia Forelli. But most of our family assumed what Uncle Vinny did; given Adri and Ben's passion for history, Gabi and Lia had simply been named after ancient relatives . . . and that something very bad had happened to them last summer in Tuscany.

Authorities found their car not far from Castello Forelli, along with Ben's cell phone and wallet, euros and credit cards still inside. If they'd not been robbed, they'd been kidnapped. But with no ransom request, well, we all pretty much thought they'd been murdered. There was speculation that Ben or Adri had discovered something valuable—and some bad guys had demanded they hand it over. It was awful. The only saving grace was that none of the family had ever been really close with them. They were always elsewhere in the world—usually Italy—too busy to show up at any reunion. So while it was sad, it was kind of a distant-sad sort of feeling for us.

Uncle Vinny thumped Nico three times on the back in what was his customary gesture of affection and smiled at me. "You kids comin'? Turkey must be done, and this fire's not keeping off the chill." He grunted, already trudging on arthritic hips up the dunes toward the house.

"We'll be there in a minute," I said. I crossed my arms and stared at my twin, who dumped sand on the fire, smothering it. The wind blew his wavy, dark hair about his handsome face.

"Look, I know it sounds crazy, Luci," he said, looking up at me. "But what if . . . what if it's not?"

"Okay. Let's just go there," I said, a bit irritated he still wouldn't let it rest as I shivered in the cold wind off the Atlantic. My head was throbbing now. "Let's go *all* the way there. Let's say our cousins *did* find some sort of time-travel portal. Let's say they did become the She-Wolves of Siena," I said, tossing up my own hands in exasperation, finding it hard to believe that we were actually having this ridiculous discussion again. "What does that have to do with us?"

"What does that have to do with *us*?" He ran his hands through his hair. "Only everything. *Luciana.*" He turned and rested his hands on my shoulders. "It means we have famous ancestors. Not even ancestors," he corrected himself excitedly. "Cousins, who found a way to time travel! What if we could too? Do you know what that would do for my Medici treasure hunt? I could be instantaneously five hundred years closer to the find of a lifetime!"

I folded my arms a bit more securely. "Nico, they *disappeared*. They did not come back. If they found a way to time travel, they obviously couldn't find a way to return."

"Or they came back for Ben and then chose to stay. Students at Ben's site said Gabriella, Evangelia, and Adri were all in medieval costumes. Why?"

I didn't have an answer for that. There really was no logical answer. "Maybe they'd been invited to a medieval reenactment or something and wanted to include Ben."

He lifted a brow. "You know nothing like that was happening.

And if it were, why wouldn't Ben have been dressed for it too? Why hustle Ben into the Jeep and drive off so fast?"

"Maybe it's like Uncle Vin says. The mob was after them."

"Or maybe they were rushing back to a time tunnel. Maybe there was some sort of urgency . . . to get back to it before the star gate closed down or something."

I sighed and shook my head. I hated that he was piquing my interest. Making me start to believe a tiny bit of his theory. It *was* super weird that they'd shown up in medieval gowns.

He shook me a little. "Don't you want to know more? Deep down, aren't you as curious as I am? What if we just go this summer and see what we find out? Go work at Castello Forelli? With us being fluent in Italian, and you being a medieval history major, we'd be in."

"There have to be tons of kids who apply."

"But not many who speak fluent English as well as Italian. Plus, we have my good looks going for us." He gave me his best smolder-look, cocking one dark brow.

"You think that'd do it, huh?" I said, rubbing my temples.

"Uh-oh. Migraine?" He shifted behind me and began rubbing my shoulders, knowing it sometimes helped a little. And probably trying to butter me up. Nico was insufferable when he became obsessed with something like this. I knew if I said no, he'd launch a full campaign to win me over. And he could be relentless.

"C'mon, Luci. Surely a history major can't resist this. We can go check out Ben's last site—see if we find any clues about where they went. Interview people. Discover tidbits others might have overlooked."

I narrowed my eyes at him. What did he really want? He was an econ major. Did he really think this was his get-rich scheme? Time traveling to Italy and finding a hidden treasure from the Medicis? Even if he did locate it—*What am I thinking? Am I really giving his crazy idea a chance?*—I doubted the Medicis would just let him take it and run. That family was famous for being ruthlessly protective of what they believed was theirs.

"You really think we could follow them straight into the Renaissance?"

"Yes! Think about that. We could pop right into the center of Michelangelo's world!" He tilted his head. "C'mon. If nothing else, we get a summer in Italy. How bad could that be?"

I looked at the others through the big window, laughing and milling about, serving up delicious food. As they were our only real semblance of family, I'd been thinking about joining the annual summer reunion too. But as much as they invited us to come every Thanksgiving and Fourth of July gathering, we never really felt a part of them. More like orphaned kids they had to include, since we went to college nearby.

And I couldn't deny that it'd be kinda cool, spending a summer in a castle. I'd seen all the pictures on Nico's phone. It looked romantic. Definitely Instagram worthy. And it'd be nice to spend more time with Nico. We'd kind of gone our separate ways at NYU. Who knew what would happen to us after graduation next year? We might end up on opposite sides of the country. With his big dreams—even in different countries.

"So if I agree? If we head to Tuscany this summer, volunteer at the *castello*, you'll give it a rest until then?"

"Yes! Yes!" he cheered, picking me up and swinging me around.

"All right, all right," I said, laughing and shoving him away.

We trudged up the dunes to the warm house, and I smiled—despite the now-piercing pain in my head—thinking that it did really kind of sound like a fun adventure.

But now, as a rotten apple hit my chest with a thud, juice splashing up my bare neck, I wasn't smiling. And if I'd had a pounding headache last Thanksgiving, now I had a doozie that felt like someone was slowly twisting a screwdriver into both temples at once.

"Nico?" I asked over my shoulder.

"Yeah?" he returned, shifting his back against mine. He tensed when a big man followed behind the wagon, yelling at us, his face twisted in a sneer of disgust and rage.

"How are we gonna get out of this?"

He was silent.

And you have to know this: my brother was never silent.

He has no idea.

Even worse . . . neither did I.

1

TILIANI FORELLI
Summer 1372, Toscana

When he rode around the bend, I drew my bow taut, aiming at the man's jugular. He was handsome, but not overly so. Two or three years my senior. But this was my soil, not his, and alarm echoed through me, seeing the Paratores' family color—crimson—across his mount. I'd cut my teeth on the tales of how the Paratores had sorely abused my mother and aunt. Heard tales of their scarlet banners once waving from the castello ramparts, as well as scarlet tunics on enemy soldiers.

And now one of that clan had dared to come here, twenty-some years after they'd been sent back to their fellow Fiorentini forever. On a black destrier, a warhorse.

"You trespass, sir," Giulio said. His sister, Ilaria, was at his side, looking regal and equally fierce, no trace of her usual dimples in view.

The man paused and casually drew himself up. His hands remained loose on his reins. He did not look at me, but rather around at Castello Greco, as if mentally calculating its value. "I do not trespass."

"I believe you do," Giulio responded curtly. Ilaria's hand moved to her dagger and slid it from her belt. She could hit a target from thirty paces.

I glanced at my cousin Fortino then back to the visitor. Mayhap the man was lost. "This is Greco land, under Forelli protection,"

I said, edging forward on my gelding with a gentle squeeze of my knees. "*Sienese* territory."

"It has been Sienese," he returned, looking me over slowly. A slight smile edged his lips and lit his green eyes, as if he liked what he saw. "But at long last, it shall be returned to her proper lord and master. Me. I am Aurelio Paratore, Cosimo's heir."

Sensing no mortal threat, I lowered my bow and gazed at him in confusion, and then up at the restored walls of Castello Greco, once Castello Paratore. Guards, alerted to our confrontation, were gathering on the alure above us. My gelding, Cardo, shifted beneath me, sensing my unease. "I am Lady Tiliani Forelli. These are my cousins, Fortino and Benedetto Forelli."

"And I am Lord Giulio Greco, and this is my sister, Lady Ilaria." The muscles in his jaw grew taut. "Those are our men on the parapets," he said, waving upward. "They guard her, as they've guarded her for decades now. You have no further claim on this estate. And even if you believe you do, you are outmanned, twenty to one."

I edged closer to the interloper, as did Fortino. The young man swept aside a lock of sandy-brown hair from his eyes and looked at me again. That same wry smile danced behind his gaze. "There is much to discuss. Much you all have apparently not yet learned. Might we retire to Castello Forelli to converse?"

I swung my bow over my shoulder. He was surrounded. What was there to fear? And why did he direct his questions to me, rather than Giulio? Or Fortino? "As you wish," I said slowly, resolving to let my father sort it out.

"M'lady! He is not alone!" cried a guard from the corner tower above us.

"Be at ease! Be at ease!" called Paratore, lifting an arm as the Forelli guards all scurried into increased alert, bows instantly pulled taut. We all had done the same, circling the interloper. He raised his second gloved hand in surrender. "'Tis only two men and our squire who accompany me," he informed us calmly.

"They shall not draw their weapons. We come in peace. They waited a moment only to see if you would welcome me in kind."

He gave a whistle, and two men and a young squire, also mounted, eased from the trees and into the yard that opened before Castello Greco's gates. One—with wide, brown, slightly sorrowful eyes—briefly caught my attention. He was arrestingly handsome. Familiar, somehow. Had we met before?

But that was impossible. The Fiorentini and Sienese did not mix.

"When my captain, Sir Valentino Valeri, thought that he had glimpsed you on patrol, m'lady," Paratore said, again directing his comments to me, "I could not resist the urge to make your acquaintance at once."

"Surely you realized, sir, that your name would not engender any good will," Ilaria said. "No Fiorentini is welcome." Guilio's father, Lord Rodolfo Greco, had died while battling them. Their mother had lived for a time in the castello, before remarrying.

"Clearly," was the reply. "And yet I wanted to see this place for myself. To know if it was worth the fight." He peered about and then casually crossed his hands as his eyes settled again on me. "It appears suitable."

I shifted, a shiver of foreboding running down my back. Why me? Because when he uttered those words, it was as if he was saying *I* was as suitable to him as the castle.

I frowned. My father would straighten this out, in short order. There had been two decades of relative peace between the Fiorentini and Sienese, but tensions had risen of late. Papa had only just returned from Firenze, sent there by the Nine on a mission to attempt to build further bridges between the two republics. Mayhap this was a result of those diplomatic missions. I knew I could not disrupt them.

"Come, sir—"

"*Lord* Paratore," he corrected.

"Lord Paratore," I repeated, understanding then that I faced the eldest heir of the Fiorentini clan. "We shall introduce you to my father and uncle." I wheeled my gelding around, eager to pass him off.

"I have met your father," he called, as we all moved into a trot. "Only this past week."

I glanced back at him. "Be that as it may, he shall decide what to do with you now. We are guardians of this land," I said, gesturing to Ilaria, Fortino, and the other knights about us. "And as far as we are concerned, you are trespassers. My uncle and father shall sort it out."

"As you say, Lady Tiliani," said the young man. The note of humor in his tone made me grind my teeth, as well as his presumptuous use of my first name. What secret was held behind those green eyes?

I settled my split skirt across Cardo's back, glad for the leather breeches I wore beneath when I noted Paratore—and his men—glancing my way with continued interest. The breeches kept me from having to overly fuss with my skirts. But I knew Papa preferred that I at least attempt to look like a lady, even if neither Ilaria nor I utilized the socially favored sidesaddle.

Giulio and Ilaria—as well as my cousins, Fortino and Benedetto—rode in pairs before and behind me. They were my best friends, as well as my ever-present guards. More brothers and sister to me after all these years, helping ease my loneliness after my own younger brothers had died.

Our group made our way down the well-worn path, past the ancient, mounded Etruscan tombs, to the river that had once marked the boundary between Paratore and Forelli land. I glanced over my shoulder at the group behind me. Without orders, the silver-haired Captain Cillini and seven knights from Castello Greco now followed behind our visitors, ensuring they remain as peaceable as they claimed, as well as effectively setting up a barrier wall between these interlopers and Castello Greco.

But I felt no tension from Aurelio Paratore. He still had the hint of a smile on his lips, as if he knew some secret that I should surely be in on by now. But it was the sad-eyed, handsome knight behind him that sent a little flutter through my heart when our gazes met. He looked at me with such intensity—almost quiet warning—that I glanced away with a start, my mind whirling. What was this? What truly compelled these men to wander so far south? What unspoken mission?

A mile farther, and we reached Castello Forelli at last. It felt like it took twice as long as usual.

"Hail, Sir Forelli," called Frederico, one of our most senior knights and the chief gate guard, to Fortino. "'Tis well?" His eyes turned to sweep across the three newcomers who accompanied us.

"All is well," my cousin returned. "We found three visitors at Castello Greco who wish to speak to my father and uncle." He waved over his shoulder, not honoring them with even a glance. "One claims to be Lord Aurelio Paratore."

Frederico was clearly startled by the name. "Open the gates! 'Tis our patrol and another from Castello Greco!" He looked back and continued shouting, "Send word to Sir Luca and Lord Forelli—they have visitors, a Lord *Paratore* among them."

"Open the gates!" the call was repeated inside. As was their custom, the gates remained shut each morning, until the various patrols returned from their scouting missions, to assure that all was well across the vast Forelli holdings. And for the first time in many months, we had something significant to report, as well as visitors of interest, sending the guards into swift motion.

The teeth-grating sound of metal against metal always made me inwardly flinch, but I remained still as they waited for the bolt to be removed and the twin tall, wide gates to swing open. I nodded to Ilaria and Giulio, and they led the group inward. Inside, six of our knights stopped Lord Paratore and his two men. Wordlessly, they took the visitors' visible weapons. How many others did they carry at their belts, beneath those fine, red-embroidered tunics? But what mischief could they manage in the midst of sixty armed men inside our walls?

Some of those men emerged from the Great Hall, the runner having spread the word. As a groomsman came to take my reins and another came around to offer a hand as I dismounted, I saw my aunt and uncle—Lord Marcello Forelli and Lady Gabriella—emerge from the west tower stair, presumably fetched from the solarium, where they often spent their mornings. My father, Luca Forelli, emerged from the Great Hall and edged over to my uncle's side, his customary stance as the captain of his guard. Mama was not to be seen.

Giulio and Ilaria stepped back, as did Paratore's men, giving the group a modest bit of privacy. But Fortino and Benedetto, as family, remained beside me.

"M'lords, this is—" Fortino began.

"Welcome, Lord Paratore," Papa interrupted with a small, but strained smile.

"Sir Luca," Aurelio returned.

I paused, jolted by the familiarity in both their voices. Aurelio had spoken the truth—they had met in Firenze.

Papa stepped forward, took Aurelio's shoulders, and swiftly kissed him on either cheek. The two men were about the same height. Papa's hair was like mine, ash-blond, streaked with a little gray, while Aurelio's was sandy brown. "Welcome to Castello Forelli."

"*Grazie mille,*" Aurelio said, returning his kiss.

I tried to catch Papa's eye. But he—who was forever giving me sidelong winks and silly faces to try and make me laugh—refused to meet my gaze. I glanced at my mother, who had finally appeared at Zia Gabi's side. And what I saw in her expression sent a wave of foreboding through me. She appeared as confused—and alarmed—as I was.

"I expected you in a fortnight," Papa was saying to Aurelio, his tone a bit tight. "What brings you here this day?"

"Forgive me, m'lord. Anticipation at all that was promised upon our last meeting fair demanded I come at once." His eyes shifted around the group and settled on me. "I found I must ensure that all was . . . suitable, before our negotiations concluded."

All that was suitable. Was it true? Had Papa given him the castello?

"Tiliani," Papa said, turning to me and taking my hand in both of his. "Would you and Ilaria like to visit your quarters to freshen up after your ride? You can join us and our guests in the Great Hall."

Confusion continued to make my mind swirl. Papa never sent me away without a report from our morning patrol. And our patrol had produced this man—these interlopers! Surely he did not expect me to leave now. Something was askew. Desperately askew. And why just Ilaria and me?

"Papa, what is this?" I asked under my breath, drawing him a quarter-turn away. I glanced to the young Lord Paratore. "Why is he here?"

Mama came forward and took his other elbow, her blue eyes clearly full of the same questions.

Lord Paratore coughed. We turned back toward him. "Forgive me, m'lord." He stepped closer, his hands crossed on his chest as he gave Papa a slight bow. "I have placed you in an awkward position, pressing my suit before you had the opportunity to inform my lady."

Pressing his suit? He was staring at me. *As his lady.*

"Inform me?" I asked, turning further to face him. As I might an opponent. "Of what?"

"Tiliani," my father warned, hopelessly trying to stay a flood.

"That you, the most highly sought-after daughter of Siena," Aurelio took my hand from my father's arm, making Papa stiffen, "are my intended bride."

He bent over my hand, regal in every move, then slowly drew erect. "For the good of Siena," he said loudly, looking about at the crowd that had gathered, "as well as to ensure the ongoing peace with the mighty Republic of Firenze, our houses are to be joined at long last."

LUCIANA BETARRINI

When we flew into Tuscany, I still thought time travel was nothing but a far-fetched dream. And eight weeks in, we had settled into the daily life of running Castello Forelli, welcoming tourists, giving them tours of the castle from the parapets to the dungeon, adopting our medieval roles, and conversing with our visitors, all while remaining in character. It was so immersive that even Nico finally seemed to set his wild imaginations aside and focus on the blessings of our summer here in the lovely Italian countryside, as well as how to make the castello more profitable.

It was he who cajoled the manager into securing realistic bows, arrows, swords, and shields, so the men could pretend to be training as knights, while the women worked on their archery skills in the forest outside the castle. When such antics immediately improved the reviews on the tour web sites, our manager gave him a raise and brought in experts to train us in hand-to-hand combat, as well as how to craft bows and arrows and properly shoot them. Then he restored one of the outside forges and brought in an ironsmith to craft swords, arrowheads, and horseshoes. The castello's traffic boomed. Nico was made an assistant manager and given another raise.

I was not given a raise, but I didn't care. I was happy. I was in beautiful Toscana, where I could flirt with handsome, olive-skinned college boys with more *machismo* than I cared for in a real boyfriend back home but found charming and different here. The girls were friendly, too, curious about American life, pumping me for perspective and answers on everything from politics to pop culture.

Fat grandmothers from the nearby village volunteered to sit in corners here and there, darning socks and stitching up dresses that we actors would wear. And when their husbands came to collect them at the end of the day, they did so with old ceramic bottles of *grappa* that the manager provided them as payment. They would all sit, chatting for a while, as golden streams of sunlight filtered through the crenellated wall above, just as they might have in medieval times. A cook and a sous-chef were hired to make authentic medieval food in the kitchens—food that we actors, our manager, and the guy in the ticket booth all ate around long tables in the Great Hall as visitors looked on.

I was living out medieval history—or at least a semblance of it—and loving every minute. But as the weeks wore on, my twin started to get restless. "This is close enough to time travel for me," I told him at lunch that day. "This summer is everything you promised me it'd be. And, bonus—there's something about what we're eating . . . or maybe it's the lack of stress . . . but I'm only getting a migraine twice a week now. I've heard gluten-intolerant people can eat pasta here because it's non-GMO. Maybe my migraines are tied to GMOs. Or all the preservatives we have in our food back home."

"That's awesome, Luce." But his tone was flat as he stuffed a wooden spoonful of soup in his mouth.

"C'mon, Nico. We knew it was kind of a long shot," I said. He'd spent weeks trying to come up with some new clue on the Great Betarrini Disappearance. It seemed to me he'd tried nudging every brick in the castello, like he thought if he pulled one out, a magic time-travel portal would appear.

"*You* thought it was a long shot. I hoped . . ." He let his next spoonful of soup drip back into his ceramic bowl.

"Hoped for what?" asked Milana in English, from across the table. She was a cute, voluptuous, lighter-brown-haired girl, intent on bettering her English this summer by jumping into our conversations.

"Hoped for a date with the cutest girl in the castello," my brother said easily, with his trademark sidelong smile. He met her gaze and lifted one brow.

I resisted the urge to roll my eyes.

"What do you think? Picnic dinner on the hilltop at sunset?" he asked. More of our companions tuned in, realizing what was happening. The two had flirted for weeks.

"Absolutely," she said, her cute dimples deepening as her color rose.

The two kept stealing glances at each other through the rest of the meal, even as they spoke to others.

Whatever, I thought. At least she might get him off the whole time-tunnel obsession.

He'd chased a hundred different theories. Quizzed every single person in the castle at least three times to find out all they knew. Interrogated the ticket booth guy—but he didn't know who had manned it last summer, when our relatives had disappeared, nor did our manager, new to the job himself. Nico had talked to the local police, even a detective, using our name—and overstating our relationship with the missing people—as rationale to inquire.

Ben's archeological site, not far from the castello, was now overseen by a Dr. Manero, and the man seemed to think of all Betarrinis as vermin. He seemed *glad* they'd disappeared, sniffing in disgust and irritation as he arrogantly ordered us away and returned to his tent. And when Nico tried to ask some of the junior workers on site about last summer, we were ushered off the premises.

"If there was something to find, the cops would have by now," I told him, as we left the Great Hall and headed toward the gates. We slept in two long bunkhouses behind the castle—women in one, men in the other.

"Yeah, I'm not so sure. Remember that American girl they

framed for murder?" he returned under his breath. "The cops aren't all that awesome here. Or trustworthy. Maybe they're getting paid off by the . . ." *M-O-B*, he mouthed silently, as if the ancient walls around us were bugged.

"Maybe you're better off concentrating on Milana," I said with a wink. "You might get farther this summer on a relationship than any medieval get-rich scheme."

"Yeah," he said ruefully. "The only medieval wealth I'm seeing right now is what we're making for the owner of this thing," he said, gesturing to the castle walls. We hadn't met the owner. Rumor had it the current Forelli family lived in Roma and rarely came to the "country."

"Milana *is* pretty cute. Just your type."

He gave me a sly smile. "That she is. And she thinks Americans are hot."

As we walked, I hid a smile. It was good to be with Nico this summer, sharing this amazing experience. When would we get such a chance again? He was my closest living relative, and in many ways, we weren't just the nucleus of our family, we were pretty much all of it. Dad hadn't bothered to reach out to us in weeks. I'd sent a postcard to Uncle Vinny, but hadn't heard back.

I wanted to stay close to my brother, and that was going to get progressively harder in the years to come. Hopefully this summer would cement our relationship forever, so that no matter how long we were physically separated, we would always be emotionally close. And if it took a summer romance with an Italian girl to keep him focused on the here and now, so be it.

While Nico headed out for his sunset date with Milana, I agreed to accompany two of my friends, Teresa and Flavia—college girls from Roma—into Chianti. They were bent on eating non-medieval food for once—something lighter—and checking out the local guys. I went along for the ride.

We settled under an eve outside a trattoria as the sun set over the vineyard below us. We perched on tall barstools around a tiny table and enjoyed a glass of local wine, while chowing down on an appetizer of pecorino cheese and gooey date spread on crisp crostini. We were engrossed in sharing gossip about other staff members at the castello when I overheard him at the next table.

"Te lo dico io, loro erano lì," he said. *"Impegnativo li porto subito al sito archeologico."* I *tell you, there they were, demanding I take them to the archeological site at once.*

I froze, trying to pretend I was listening to my friend go on about why Matteo was so lame for dropping her last week, but all I could focus on were the guys behind me, rattling on in Italian.

"They really were in medieval costumes? Just like you told that reporter?" asked the guy's friend, in Italian.

"It was very odd. They wouldn't take no for an answer. Not that I really wanted to say no. Because those girls were beautiful, especially the blonde. The brunette was all hunched over in pain, like she had appendicitis or something. But I had a job, you know. And my boss didn't want me leaving my post."

It was him. It had to be him! The ticket booth operator from the castello. The one who had given my cousins a ride to Ben's site.

I took a hurried gulp of wine and swallowed wrong, coughed, drew my friends' attention for a moment, but once they knew I was okay, resumed dissecting Matteo and all his inadequacies.

"I never heard about this part before. So you took them to the site?"

"Yes. They said there was a doctor there. I was taking them to the clinic, but they insisted there was a doctor on the dig site."

"What were they like? What did they talk about?"

"Only words to hurry me along. Hurry, hurry, *hurry.* They were in a terrible rush. Like it was a life-or-death thing."

"Do you think it was the appendicitis?"

"I'll just say this . . . watching Gabriella get out of the car, I don't think she really had appendicitis."

"And so you got to the site and . . ."

"They told me to wait and started looking for the doctor. But it was Dr. *Betarrini* they were after. The woman's husband. The girls' dad. Not a medical doctor, but an archeologist."

"And so they met up with him . . ."

"That was the oddest part," he said. "They just stood there, staring at him like he was a ghost. And then they threw themselves at him, crying and laughing at the same time."

"Who knows with Americans. They can be crazy."

"I don't know. I've tried to figure it out a thousand times since."

"They said nothing more to you?"

"Nothing. They just ran and got into Dr. Betarrini's old Jeep."

"*Strano.*" Strange.

"*Molto strano.*" Very strange.

They started to move into another conversation, but I could wait no longer. I rose and moved to their table. *"Mi scusi,"* I said, apologizing for barging in. The three guys leaned back to check me out, then a bit farther to check out my friends, who had paused to see what I was up to. I ignored it and pressed on. "I couldn't help overhearing. I am Luciana Betarrini. You've been talking about my relatives."

The guy's eyes widened, and he quickly raised a hand. "Listen, I meant no offense," he said in Italian.

"None taken," I hastened to reassure him. "I am really glad to have run into you. My brother and I wanted to ask you what you knew. We're here for the summer, and we're hoping to find out more about them, of course. For the family's sake."

"Of course," he said, losing a bit of his bravado. His brown eyes searched mine. "It is very sad. About them disappearing and all."

"It sounds like you did what you could to help them. Do you mind if I get your name and number?" I handed him my cell, ignoring his friends sharing a raised brow, like this was some sort of come-on.

"Text me anytime," he invited, handing back my phone with a small smile. I saw his name, Renato, in my contacts. "I work, but I'm available most nights."

I nodded and smiled too. *"Grazie."* I turned to go, but then paused. "Hey, can you tell me anything about where their Jeep was found? The police would not say."

"Oh, sure," he said with a small shrug. "All the locals knew, though they kept it out of the papers. They found it half a mile from the castello."

My heart picked up its pace. "Do you know exactly where?"

His smile slipped a bit, and his eyes seemed troubled. "It was weird. It's a seldom-used road that really leads to nowhere."

I could read between the lines. He thought what the police thought, what our Uncle Vinny thought—they'd parked their Jeep in a remote location, attempting to escape someone who pursued them. They'd either been successful, so successful no one in the world had yet caught up with them . . . or their enemy had, disposing of their bodies where they might never be found again.

"Do you know the name of the road?" I asked.

He shook his head. "It has no name."

"At all?"

"The old people call it *Vecchio Modo,*" he said.

"Like they do all the old roads," laughed his friend.

Vecchio Modo. *The Old Way.*

The wheels in my head started turning. "Can you tell me where it is?"

"That'd be hard," he said, frowning a bit at my intensity. "But I can show you." A hint of a smile returned to his lips.

But I had more on my mind than flirting. "Tomorrow? Meet me at the castello at 5:30?"

"Sure," he said, his smile broadening. "I'll pick you up then."

"Thanks. I really appreciate it," I said, turning away. *And so will my brother.*

2

TILIANI FORELLI

I stared in shock at Papa, Aurelio Paratore's words echoing through my mind. *Intended bride. For the good of Siena.* Both of my cousins looked at me with horror.

"Luca, tell me you did not . . ." Mama whispered, "not without—"

But he lifted a hand to her, then to me, and cast a furious look at Aurelio. "You did me a disservice, sir. You were to give me a fortnight to prepare my women."

Aurelio straightened. "Forgive me. I thought . . ."

He pretended ignorance. But with one furtive, warning glance from his captain, Valentino, I knew this was exactly why he had surprised us. To discover my true feelings. His chances. The lay of the land.

But this was *our* land. I was a daughter of Siena, tried and true.

A daughter of a She-Wolf.

And the Fiorentini were more often foe than friend.

I swallowed my fury and frustration and awaited my father, as did my mother before me. I'd learned to do as she did. She had never led me astray. And in matters with my father, it had come to aid me time and again.

"Tomasso," Papa called, motioning to the servant. The slim man hastened over. "Please see Lord Paratore and his men to the guest quarters in the east wing and attend to their needs."

"Yes, m'lord." Tomasso waved to a groomsman, who would see to the visitors' mounts, then gestured for the men to follow him.

"We shall look forward to you joining us for our noon meal," Papa said to Aurelio.

Lord Paratore swept his cape over his shoulder, and in tandem with his men, gave us a genteel bow. Before they rose, we were off, heading toward the tower that led to the solarium—one of the few places in the castle where we could speak in relative privacy. I could feel the tension rolling off Mama, a tension that only heightened my own. Zio Marcello and Zia Gabriella followed behind us.

As soon as the turret door closed, Mama and I both started speaking, but Papa hushed us. "You shall wait until we reach the solarium," he said, brooking no argument. He climbed the steps before us, clearly not rushing, and I cast a furious glance at Mama. But in her eyes, I read a hint of warning. Worse, a hint of worry.

My heart pounded. Was there no fighting this? I followed behind her, watching the sway of her skirts and slight train before me. Up two flights of stairs we went, then down the hall to the solarium, with its tall windows set with creamy quartz to let light through. I noted Papa did not open one, as he customarily did, but bent to light a few candles instead. Clearly, he did not want anyone to overhear what he was about to say.

Neither Mama nor Zia Gabi waded in as I expected, with indignant protests. After all, it was Cosimo Paratore who had nearly killed them all. Instead Mama methodically poured us each a goblet of watered wine before we all took a seat. Zio Marcello elected to stand.

"He is Cosimo's second cousin, heir to what remains of their estate in Firenze," Papa began, glancing to his cousin as if seeking reinforcement. "Upon our meeting a week past, we were introduced. In spite of our previous experiences with his clan, I thought the young man was not without merit. He is part of the new generation, looking for new opportunities for themselves beyond making war. And yet on that front, he has proven himself in battle, helping Firenze fend off attacks from Milano. He is in line to serve with the Grandi."

The Grandi—Firenze's ruling council, like Siena's own Nine—of which Papa was one. As Zio Marcello had been before him.

Mama sat down and leaned forward. "And you believed that a young man who was 'not without merit' was enough for our daughter."

Papa rubbed his chin—stroking the golden-brown stubble there—and heaved a sigh. "Evangelia, Tiliani is two-and-twenty, well past marrying age. And to date," he said, his voice rising, "every one of her few suitors has been found wanting."

"Not a one has stolen my heart as Mama stole yours," I said quietly. "Or as Zia Gabi stole Zio Marcello's. Is it so wrong to wait for one such as each of you found?"

That stilled them all for a moment. My uncle and father shared a brief, discomfited glance.

"Were you not once promised to another, through no doing of your own?" I asked my uncle.

He took a slow sip from his goblet before replying. "I was. But 'twas different. Our families had long been friends. It was understood, from the time we were children."

"Did you not allow Fortino to choose his own intended?" I pressed, thinking of the lovely Anna Cavani of Lucca. The two were to wed next summer. "And will you not allow Benedetto the same honor?"

My uncle's jaw twitched, but he said nothing.

"And yet you and Papa have promised me to the clan who has long been our foe. As a surprise."

He looked at me. "When I was promised to Romana Rossi, it was to strengthen our family's ties to Siena. Solidify protection for this very castello in which you've become a woman grown. Only your mother's and aunt's heroic actions could have done more for us." His face grew earnest. "But *mia dolcezza,* your father and

I never wish for you to go through what they had to in order to survive."

Survive? Were we truly worried about our survival? I glanced at Mama. While I had spent my whole life preparing for battle, little more than skirmishes had transpired. But from the stories, I knew Mama and Zia Gabi had nearly died, several times over. When Marcello spoke of what they had gone through for our family's sake, for Siena's sake, he did not do so lightly.

"What might this union do for us now, with Firenze?" Papa blew out his cheeks and leaned back against the horsehair-covered chair. "Do you not know, Tiliani? Can you not see?"

I swallowed hard at the need and hope in his voice.

"This would not only strengthen our standing in the republic. This could bring peace between our republic and *Firenze*. 'Twould not solely benefit us, here at Castello Forelli or Castello Greco. 'Twould benefit all. No more battles, nor war."

"We have not been at war for years," I said.

"But this could help ensure that Siena never goes to battle against Firenze again," Papa said. "'Twould also give us sufficient power to stand against Milano, Perugia, or others who continually threaten us. Unite us all against Spain. Increase our trade. Wealth. 'Twould not only be us who might gain, but everyone in the republic. Both our republics. Hundreds of thousands of people."

My throat constricted. Hundreds of thousands of people relying on me? How could one marriage, one union, bear such fruit?

He glanced at Mama. She set aside her goblet and rose, moving in agitation to the window and fingering the silk-corded lining at the neck of her dress. Why was she not speaking against this? Or Zia Gabi? They had always taken my side. Maintained that who I married was my decision alone.

"How close was he to Cosimo Paratore?" she asked.

"Mama . . ." I began in horror. Was she truly considering this?

"His father is Umberto Paratore, Cosimo's first cousin, who had been in line to inherit lordship of the palazzo in Firenze and other estates. Upon Umberto's death last autumn, he became heir. Aurelio never knew Cosimo."

"Mama—"

"Ceding rights to Castello Greco to the Paratore clan would do a great deal to heal the rift between our republics," my uncle said.

"And bring the enemy right to our door again," Zia Gabi said, speaking for the first time.

"Or they could be an extension *of* our family, guarding our gates as fiercely as we would ourselves," he responded evenly.

I shook my head. "What of Chiara? Giulio? Ilaria? Castello Greco belongs to them."

"And yet they choose to reside here, with us. They are our family now, and they seem quite content. Siena shall compensate them for the castello, granting them a fair fortune. They could build their own manors. Become merchants. 'Twill be a blessing to them."

"This cannot be happening." I met Papa's gaze. "I do not love him. I do not know him!"

Mama slowly turned and knelt before me, taking my hands in hers. And in all my years, I'd never seen her kneel before anyone. "Might you not endeavor to get to know him a bit, at least? See if he might appeal to you in time? If we wish Castello Forelli to stand forever, if we want future generations to continue to abide in this place, Tiliani, Siena must find some way to build bridges with the Fiorentini, rather than continue to antagonize and defy them."

My eyes searched hers. Mama, Nona, and Zia Gabi had always seemed to have an uncanny sense of intuition—as if they could see the future—and I'd learned to trust it when she spoke in this manner. If she thought it important, how could I not?

But a Fiorentini? In all my life, I'd never considered it.

I paused.

"I shall give him a chance," I whispered.

And yet as I uttered the words, it felt as if I had already pledged my oath to bind my hand to his forever.

LUCIANA BETARRINI

Nico was out late with Milana, so I didn't catch up with him until the next morning in the castello courtyard, as he sparred with Raul, the tallest "knight" in our cast of characters. They used crudely carved wooden swords—as did the other four pairs about them—for this exercise, as had the knights of old. For the actors, it was a warmup for the second time they sparred in the afternoons, practicing moves until they were rote, so that when they picked up actual steel blades for their afternoon "act," they didn't harm one another. Still, as the summer wore on, every one of them seemed to gather their share of nicks. Raul had taken one blow that required six stitches; that's when he decided he favored Nico as his sparring partner.

Nico took to the sword with ease. Years of our own sparring in jiu jitsu—something Mom had insisted we learn when she found out we wanted to attend NYU—had prepared him well to judge his opponent and anticipate his next move. The gift of the art was that it never relied on strength, luck, or chance, only calculated skill. We'd taken it a step further in our senior year, training in Krav Maga. Between the two, I felt pretty safe on the streets—though I always kept a small knife in my pocket at night. But it also granted me a settled sense, physically. When I began training, I gained a *centeredness*, easily able to pivot and respond at a moment's notice, as well as a sense of power and confidence.

I could see it in Nico now, too, even against his taller, bulkier opponent. I sat back and studied his moves from the shadows for a while before Raul caught sight of me. He hesitated, and Nico used the moment to turn and bring the wooden sword around and across his belly, making him bend in half with an audible *oof*, even though Nico slowed at the end.

"No fair, man," Raul complained in heavily accented English, panting. He couldn't be too hurt—given the padded shield he wore to cover his chest and belly. But it likely stole some of his breath. "Your sister distracted me."

"Can't blame me for using a distraction to my advantage," laughed Nico, patting his friend on the shoulder. Together, they tossed their practice swords to a pile. "All's fair in love and war, right? A warrior can't take his eyes off his opponent. Let that be a lesson to you, big man."

Nico threw his arm around my neck like a victor leaving the field, and I couldn't resist. I grabbed his wrist, planted my feet, and wrenched him up and over my shoulder, landing him flat on the ground. He stared up at me in wide-eyed surprise, the dust billowing up around him, as Raul hooted a laugh. Others around us joined in.

I grinned as I placed my foot on his chest. "A warrior can't take his eyes off his opponent. Nor should he relax too readily in the company of 'friends.'"

Nico grinned and grabbed hold of my ankle and leg. Too late, I realized my mistake. I tried to wrench free, but he held tight. "The only reason you're not on your back yourself, little sister,"—I was his *little* sister by five minutes—"is that Signora Toroni would have my hide for ruining your gown. Now let me up."

I relented and offered him my hand.

Appearing to relax, he grabbed it with both of his. But before rising, he placed a foot on my chest and sent me over his head and onto my own back.

"Nico!" Raul hurried over to me and helped me up, awkwardly helping me dust off my skirts. "That is no way to treat a lady!"

"Ha!" said Nico, wiping his upper lip of sweat. "That's my *sister*. And make no mistake, she's a two-stripe purple belt in

jiu jitsu. I only narrowly beat her out in our last competition—
which has eaten her up since. But trust me, she is as lethal as she
is pretty."

I shook my head and brushed off my hands, swallowing
a grimace. I wanted to deny it, but it was true. It had always
irritated me that he'd come in first at the regional tournament our
sophomore year of college, and I'd come in second. Although he'd
been competing with the boys, and me with the girls, I'd always
wondered . . .

I looked down at my dusty skirts. "What of Signora Toroni?"

"I figured it was worth the ten lashes," he said lightly, giving
me a wink. "Or a dock in my pay if I had to pay for a seamstress."

"You knew Dona Morelli would fix it for free."

"Maybe."

"Are you all right, Luciana?" Raul asked, still hovering about
anxiously.

"Oh, yeah. I'm fine, fine," I assured him. "I only need Nico for
a sec. Sorry to interrupt." It'd become a much bigger interruption
than I had intended . . . trust Nico and me to start sparring like
puppies. We'd always been like that. Physically trying to best each
other since we were little. Mom had seen it and figured we'd be
naturals for the martial arts. We had been. We started with Tae
Kwon Do as littles, then went to the more intense jiu jitsu in high
school, once we had our hearts set on attending NYU.

I could feel Raul's eyes follow us all the way to the turret door.
I'd figured he had a thing for me. He always seemed to linger a
second too long as he said good-bye to my brother when I came
around. But he also seemed like he might not be the sharpest
knife in the drawer . . . or at least, he had a hard time coming
up with something to say when I was around. But he was super
sweet. And the way he'd rushed to my defense was kind of cute.

"So Raul thinks I'm a distraction, huh?" I whispered as we
climbed the curving steps for a word alone on the wall above.
Nico and I looked fairly different facially—his was somewhat

square while mine was oval—and while his hair was dark and wavy, mine was a bit lighter, with some golden-brown streaks.

"That dude pretty much likes everything about you."

"On the surface, maybe," I said dryly. "We haven't really had a discussion."

"Yeah, well, Raul's a good guy. But he's more of a physical sparring partner than a mental one." He shot me a glance. "And I know you want both. But don't crush his summer-romance dreams yet, will you? It'll be a sad day when he finds out he doesn't have a chance."

"So you want me to lead him on."

"No, no. Not that. But what's the harm of letting the poor guy dream a little dream? It's not like we'll be here forever."

"True." We only had another six weeks before we had to return home.

Or we might be in another place. Another time.

I shook my head as if to shake my thoughts back into line. Meeting Renato, hearing him talk about that night he drove Gabriella and Evangelia and their mom to the site . . . he had clearly been rattled. And finding out the Jeep was parked in such an odd place . . . Was I really beginning to believe it? That the Betarrinis might have disappeared into another time? If we went looking along that road, would we find their portal?

Or just their bodies?

Surely the police had searched every square foot of land for miles about. The worldwide interest had been fierce. Regardless of their potential lack of CSI skills, they'd have done their best. But if no bodies had been found, where had they gone?

Nico had taken me to Greve in Chianti to study the bronze statue at the center of the piazza, depicting the She-Wolves of Siena. Evangelia was in skirts, on horseback, arrow nocked, bow drawn, as if aiming. Gabriella was on the ground, also in skirts, but feet askew, looking in the same direction as her sister—a sword in two hands and held aloft. Standing there, I'd felt a shiver run down my spine. A shiver of recognition. A shiver of belief.

Now we'd reached the top of the stair and came out onto the wall, the hot summer sun beating down on us, the heat radiating from the stones. All around us, the thick woods crowded closer. In the distance, we could see rolling hills, and peeking out from two miles away, the ruins of another castle. We turned the corner, hovering in the meager shade of the turret. Nico reached up and pulled a twig from my hair, a memento from our skirmish. We shared a brief grin.

"Okay, you have my full attention now," he said, flicking it over the side. "What's up?"

I bit my lip, aware how he might react. "Last night in Chianti, I ran across last summer's ticket-counter dude. His name is Renato, and he knows where the Betarrinis left their Jeep."

Nico grabbed both my arms in excitement and leaned closer. "Are you *kidding* me?" His eyes widened. "That's amazing, Luci!"

"I know."

"Did he tell you where?" He let go of me and brushed the hair back from his face.

"He couldn't. The road has no name other than The Old Way. But he said he could show me tonight."

Nico huffed a laugh. "Used those golden-brown eyes on him, did ya?"

I fluttered my eyelashes and gave him a sidelong look. "Why, I have no idea what you mean."

"I assume he doesn't know I'm coming along as a chaperone."

"No," I said. "I wanted him to actually show up."

"Fair enough. We can buy the guy a pizza to ease his pain."

"He was cute enough. Maybe I'll go out with him again some other time."

"And crush poor Raul's dreams?"

"Maybe. If we don't catapult back to medieval times."

He sobered and studied me. "You're kind of getting into it now, aren't you? There really is no other explanation," he added.

"Unless they came up against some really bad guys and those guys whisked them off in a helicopter."

"Or buried their bodies somewhere no one has yet found."

We stood there, staring out into the forest and hills, wondering if that was what lay ahead of us. Finding the four bodies of our dead relatives.

"So," Nico said, clapping his hands together, snapping me out of my reverie. "Tonight?"

"Five-thirty. Dress for hiking. I'm assuming we might be doing some bushwhacking."

"Bushwhacking and searching for a time-travel portal? Sounds like the best kind of date ever. But what will we do with Renato?"

"Leave Renato to me."

3

TILIANI FORELLI

I rose with the sun, aware that today was my first full day with Lord Aurelio Paratore.

"*Dio, dammi la tua grazia, misericordia e guida,*" I muttered. *Lord, give me your grace, mercy, and direction.* I swung my legs to the side of the bed and ran my fingers through my hair, then my palms across my face. 'Twas a prayer my papa had taught me from his friend Tomas, a priest he had once known, the predecessor of our current chaplain, Padre Giovanni, a kindly old man. *The truest Christian I have ever known* was how Papa described Tomas once. It had stuck with me. And his prayer had become my own morning petition. If I could find a measure of the Almighty's grace to cover the sins of another as it did my own, mercy for the undeserving, and direction for the future, mayhap I might find happiness and contentment with all whom I encountered.

And mayhap even with Lord Aurelio *Paratore.*

The name had always been synonymous with a curse in our household. And now? Did my parents truly believe I might become a Paratore myself and all would be well?

Grace, I repeated silently, as I feared I might need to a hundred times this day. *Mercy. Direction.*

Clearly my parents were clinging to hope. Certainly they had not yet moved through grace and mercy. After all that Cosimo Paratore had done? Made them endure? Cosimo may well have been a renegade among the Fiorentini, but his people had not sent him away in disgrace for how he had abused my family; they had welcomed him with open arms and sent him back to the front lines to fight us again. Aurelio's father may not have been close to Cosimo. But the same blood ran through both their veins.

I rose and went to the window, unlatching it and swinging it open, staring out at the pink hue of sunrise on the horizon as the cool lavender-scented air washed over me, sending goose bumps rising. I gazed out at the countryside and considered . . . if our roles were reversed, if it had been *my* uncle who had been so cruel and *I'd* been sent to Firenze to win Aurelio over, how would I feel? Surely this was not only his idea. I was certain there were as many family members and friends urging him onward as there were around me. Republics as mighty as ours were not unified by crafting a flimsy rope bridge—nay, it would take a great, stone-arched monument that could withstand flood. And great stone bridges were built by many hands.

'Twasn't fair to hold Aurelio accountable for the sins of a distant cousin—a cousin whom Papa said he'd never met. Why should I assume he was anything like him?

Grace.

It irked me how he had surprised Papa and Zio Marcello. All of us. His bravado irritated me further. But mayhap 'twas his own defense, to enter enemy territory as if he already owned it. Mayhap he had to believe it in order to act as a man ought.

Mercy.

I yanked my hair back and wove it into a quick braid. We were to meet in the Great Hall to break our fast. But I was far too agitated to meet him yet. What I needed was a quick ride. To the far hill, where my ancestors and Zio Fortino and little brothers had all been buried, along with other faithful friends and servants over the years. There, high on the hill, looking back at the castello, I oft found a settling that my soul craved. There I might find direction too.

I yanked on some tights, quickly tied a rope belt around my waist, and then dropped a shirt over my banded breasts and a tunic over it. Papa favored me wearing proper gowns, but at first light, he often looked away if I wished to take a quick ride in the manner of men. He knew it was far easier, and if the villagers or nobles were not yet out and liable to take notice, he elected not to take note either. Especially since he knew that Mama and Zia Gabi much preferred to do the same.

I hurried down to the stables, happy to see but a couple of servants had yet risen. Cook was just now entering the kitchen to stoke the fires. I had a good hour yet before others rose and began to make their way into the Hall. With luck, I could get to the stables, brush down Cardo, go for a ride, and return with only seeing three or four people. That was Papa's preference. If I was going to do this, I had to do it swiftly and quietly, or I might be waylaid. With a potential suitor on the grounds, everything felt a bit more tenuous.

"Good morning to you, m'lady," a deep voice said to me as I entered the stables.

I jumped, hand to my chest, as surely as if Captain Valentino Valeri had come at me with a sword.

The captain laughed—a pleasing, low sound—and leaned an elbow on the wall his gelding shared with my own. "Forgive me. I gave you a fright."

I did a double take. The young captain was quite handsome when he smiled. "Nay, 'tis my own fault. I usually have the stables to myself at this hour. I assumed . . ."

"As did I," Valentino said, turning back to his horse to continue his brushing. "I favor a ride in the morning, before my lord has need of me. And saddling my own horse gives our squire another half-hour's sleep, which the boy needs."

"I favor a ride before the whole world has need of me," I muttered. And then I looked up, wondering if I'd uttered it aloud.

The man stilled a moment as if he'd indeed heard, then resumed his brushing as if he had not. *A man of discretion,* I surmised. And his care for their young squire moved me. Early morning light streamed through the stable windows, catching the wide curls of his hair, brow, and thick lashes as he turned to look my way. "Do you need aid to saddle your mount?"

"I do not."

He held my gaze. "And you intend to ride out alone?"

"I do. Siena is at peace and has been for some time. Nor do I go anywhere unarmed."

"As is wise," he said with a nod, throwing a blanket across his mare. "But even the daughter of a She-Wolf could be overpowered."

I threw a blanket across Cardo's back, too, then turned for a saddle. "I would like to see them try." I reached beneath the gelding's belly for the strap, pulling it taut.

"As brave as you are beautiful, then," he said, tossing his saddle across his mare. We both paused a moment—him likely thinking he ought not have voiced that thought, while I hid a smile. I liked the sad-eyed captain. There was something soulful and honest about him. It gave me hope for Aurelio. I sensed a man such as he could not serve another who was not somewhat decent.

That spurred a thought. "Captain Valeri, would you serve as my guard this morning?" I asked. I might learn more about Aurelio during a ride than I would in person over the course of the day.

He paused after belting his mare's saddle and rested his arms on it, peering over at me. "I thought you desired a measure of solitude."

"I did. But now I see I might gain from a measure of companionship." I lifted my foot into the stirrup and swung up into the saddle. "Ride with me if you wish. I leave it to you."

With that, I moved out of the stables and to the gate, which wordlessly opened for me, the guards well accustomed to my dawn rides.

For a good distance, I thought myself alone, that Captain Valeri had elected to move in a different direction, not rising to my subtle challenge . . . mayhap afraid of the subtle flirtation in it too. For that *had* been flirtation, I acknowledged. What had I been thinking? Did I wish to fray the barest beginning of a weaving between Lord Aurelio and myself?

But then I saw him on the next hill, echoing my movement, matching my pace. Giving me space, privacy, breathing room, but accompanying me too. When I slowed, he slowed. When I sped up, so did he. He did not look my way, directly, just kept me in his peripheral vision. I smiled, even as my hopes of finding out more about his lord died.

It wasn't until I climbed the hillside to my family's gravesites that he moved to join me. I paused as the sun fully cleared the far, eastern hills and streamed across the dew-covered fields and vineyards with golden light, closing my eyes, feeling it warm my face. I lifted my palms partially toward it. *Grace, Lord. Mercy. Direction. May yours be mine.*

For a moment, 'twas only the Lord and me. But in seconds, I heard the creak of the leather of his saddle, the gentle sound of his mare's hooves on the loamy earth. Felt his eyes on me.

I opened my own and looked his way.

He stared at me with that sad, soulful gaze. His eyes seemed to belong to a man's thrice our age. What had he seen, experienced that had so aged his soul, while leaving his complexion youthful, his body strong?

"May I ask what you were thinking about as you closed your eyes?" he dared.

"I wasn't thinking. I was praying." I paused. "Well, 'twas a thought. But I made it a prayer." Curious, I said, "Do you pray, Captain?"

He smiled, and I liked the crinkles that formed at his eyes. "Every time I go into battle, and every time I come out."

"Not in between?"

He pursed his lips and glanced to the sunrise, crossing his

hands on the saddle horn before him. He looked my way. "Seldom between."

"Why?"

"I do not see the need. Unless I am about to greet my Maker or thank him for not greeting me as of yet . . ."

"Ahh. You miss a great deal, then, about your Maker. You should meet with our chaplain while you lodge with us. I think you'd find Padre Giovanni most agreeable." I set out, climbing the hill, leaving my gelding to graze, and felt him on my heel. "What of your lord?" I asked. "How often does he pray?"

"He attends mass every afternoon," Valeri said.

"As is required by the Grandi?"

"As he has done all his days," he returned.

It surprised me, this. *Grace,* I reminded myself.

"And does he give alms to the poor?"

"Alms and more. He supports an asylum for the mad and infirm alike, an asylum his father built."

Again, I was surprised. *Mercy.*

Mayhap Cosimo's blood did not run through Aurelio's veins after all.

I paused before my great-grandparents' gravestones, lying side-by-side, as were my grandparents, and then my Uncle Fortino's, with a depiction of him in knight's armor, hands grasping his sword. Too young and taken too soon to have a bride buried beside him. But not as young as my brothers—their graves marked by two small stones.

"Your relatives?" he asked quietly.

"My great-grandfather," I nodded to his gravestone, "the one who built our castello. And my grandparents, dead before I could ever know them." I gestured to Fortino's grave. "My uncle, sacrificed in the battle between us and the Fiorentini." Then to the stones. "And my little brothers, taken by plague and an accident."

A silence fell between us. I looked to the rising sun, realizing my time was growing short. I would soon need to return and don a proper gown and break our fast with my intended. Walk and tour. Mayhap go for a ride. Would it feel as easy as it did with his captain?

We stood there a moment, and again, I closed my eyes, feeling the warmth of the summer sun on my cheeks like a whispered welcome to the day. I gradually felt the captain's gaze upon me and saw him hurriedly glance away and look outward. "So all of this is Forelli land."

"As far as the eye can see," I said, pointing to the east. "Out to those far hills in the distance, that's Perugia." Then I pointed north. "And to those mountains, north of Castello Greco, that's Firenze."

"Must be a fair burden, being the farthest outpost in the republic."

I smiled. "Elbows and shoulders take the brunt of the blows in battle, for certain. 'Tis been a blessing that times have been peaceful of late. Not like they were when my parents were young."

"True," he said, nudging a rock with his toe. "But I hear tell 'tis not likely to last," he said, looking outward again. "This union with my lord . . . it could provide you needed support and spare you a fair bit of grief."

"Oh?" I asked, the quirk of a smile on my lips. "Did he send you here to tell me that?"

Captain Valeri looked down at me with those wizened, warm eyes. I wished he would smile again, but he was utterly sober. "Nay. M'lord knows not that I am here." Speaking of it seemed to make him more aware. "I best return. He may have need of me."

"By all means." I inclined my head.

He hesitated, as if reluctant to leave me behind.

"Captain," I said, "I will remind you that this is my land, and I oft take a daily morning ride. Alone. The knights on the castello alure keep one eye on me, as well as the horizon in all directions."

"Yes, m'lady," he said, mounting up. With one more searching look, and a glance to my bow and quiver of arrows, he rode off.

I had to admire his fine form. Clearly, he was a man who had spent years in the saddle. He moved as if one with the horse. His shoulders were wide and strong, his waist narrow, his legs steady.

But as he grew small in the distance, his words came back to me. *I hear tell 'tis not likely to last. This union . . . provide you needed support. Spare you grief.*

From whom? From what?

And what, exactly, made Captain Valentino Valeri's eyes so unaccountably sad?

LUCIANA BETARRINI

Renato was not very pleased to see Domenico at my side when he pulled up outside the castello. But with Nico's customary charm, and a rueful smile and shrug from me, he gradually warmed up on the short drive. It helped when I mentioned that we were so grateful that we wanted to buy him dinner. And he visibly relaxed when I casually mentioned that maybe we could score some time alone later in the week for just the two of us.

But when he turned the corner, our short trek became even shorter.

"Whoa," he said, braking so fast the tiny Peugeot sputtered to a stall.

Before us the forest had been cleared, and there was a temporary barrier across the road, a small tent beside it.

"This wasn't here before?"

"No," he said, staring in wonder. "Not at all. This is nothing like it was."

Beyond the gate, more was going on. There were a bunch of cars, Jeeps, and trucks. Tents with *Societa Archeologico dell' Italia* emblazoned on the side.

"You haven't heard anything about this?" Nico asked, edging between our narrow front seats from his cramped perch in back.

"Nothing. No one knows about this."

Two armed, military-type guys had left the tent and were walking toward us, waving us forward.

"Uhh, should I . . ." Renato said.

"Yeah," Nico said. "Let's see what they say."

Renato turned the key, and the Peugeot rumbled to a reluctant start again. We edged forward, and I saw that Renato's knuckles were a bit white, so hard did he cling to the steering wheel. I was nervous too.

"*Regazzi vi siete persi?*" asked a middle-aged soldier, peering down at us. *Are you kids lost?*

"Maybe," Renato said, with a half laugh, in Italian. "I was just taking them to Vecchio Modo. We thought we'd have a hike and a picnic, watch the sunset. I thought that it was here."

The man's friendly expression faded, and he placed a casual hand on the top of his gun. "That may have been what they used to call that road," he said, continuing to speak in Italian. "But now it's a protected archeological site. You understand . . . if word gets out, we'll have all sorts of interlopers, which could damage it before Dr. Manero has enough time to fully study it. We need time to determine how we best protect it before granting the public access."

Manero. The same jerk who had taken over Ben Betarrini's dig site.

"*Cosa hanno trovato?*" Nico pressed. *What'd they find?*

"I'm not privileged to discuss that," the soldier said, his face becoming stony. "I suggest you turn around and steer clear of this area. No civilians are allowed entry without a special pass."

"Oh. okay. We didn't know," Renato said.

The man straightened. "Just find another place to picnic. And don't talk about this in town. I don't need any other visitors out this way."

"Got it," Renato said. He stepped on the gas, reversed, shifted, and we moved down the road, both Nico and I staring through the rear windshield at the guard—an armed guard—and then sharing a long look. What kind of archeological site required an armed guard? Manero's other site in the next valley—co-opted from Ben Betarrini—hadn't required one. Or was it more than an archeological site? I felt a tingle. Could they have really found a star gate or something?

We didn't encourage our driver to take us to another hilltop. Instead, we persuaded him to take us to Chianti and a good Internet signal. We pulled into a small taverna, not very crowded yet. We hurriedly settled at a small table and ordered drinks and *appertivo*, all rapidly navigating our phones.

"*Hanno bloccato tutto il traffic aereo,*" Renato said in puzzlement as he scanned the text before him. *They blocked all air traffic.* "It's still blocked, for three square miles, under military orders." He frowned and continued to scan.

"That's how no one knew of this," I said. "In searching for the Betarrinis, they must've come across that site."

"Whatever it is," Nico muttered, studying at his phone.

"The tents said Societa Archeologico dell' Italia," I said, looking them up. "So it's not like they discovered uranium or defunct WWII bombs or something."

"No," Nico said. "It has to be something of historical significance. Renato, are there any rumors of old ruins in that area?"

"Ruins?" he repeated blankly, dragging his eyes from his screen. "Not that I've heard of. *Tranne . . .*"

"*Tranne?*" Nico and I repeated together. *Except for?*

"My friend's great-grandfather. He used to run sheep and goats through those woods. He always said there were some sort of ancient mounds back there." He leaned back on his stool and looked from my brother to me.

"Ancient mounds," I repeated. "Could he have meant tombs?"

He shrugged. "My friend always thought it was a ruse, a way to get him to come and help with the herds. He never looked."

I turned back to my phone and quickly looked up *Etruscan tombs* and clicked on *images*. Scrolling through, I finally found what I was looking for. "Like this?" I held up my screen for him to see.

"I don't know," he admitted in English.

"Your friend's great-grandfather. Is he still alive?"

"Last I heard."

"Can we go see him?"

"What—tonight?"

"Yes, yes," Nico and I echoed each other.

A wary smile stretched across Renato's face. "You know who you two remind me of? Your lost relatives. What's with all the urgency?"

"The urgency is that the last known location of our relatives is now a sealed-off site," I said.

"And we want in," Nico said.

Renato lifted his hands. "I don't want any trouble."

"I get that," I said. We didn't want him in the middle of this either. "But please," I reached out to cover his forearm with my hand, "can you introduce us to this man? Then we'll take it from there."

"I don't know," he said hesitantly. "I don't want to bring any trouble to my friend's family either. Those guys back there were serious."

"It will be our secret," I said. "All we want to know is what that man saw. What could be behind that gate."

"And that will be it?"

"That will be it." *For you. For us, it may be just the start.*

He heaved a sigh and then gave a quick nod. "Let's go now. The old man will likely soon be asleep."

4

TILIANI FORELLI

My parents invited the whole countryside to a feast three days after Aurelio and his retinue had arrived. I knew they were surrounding me with the villagers I had come to love through my growing-up years, and clearly, they'd invited in our closest friends from Siena, seeking to put me at ease, as well as win their support for this potential union. But when I went to my quarters and saw the gown Mama had set out for me to wear spread across the bed, I slowly backed up until my shoulders hit the stone wall.

'Twas a thing of beauty. Worthy of a bridal gown, truly. A vibrant blue with a deep, wide neckline and tight, long sleeves that came to a point at the wrist. An ample skirt with many gathers, and a bit of a padded bump on either hip to accentuate my womanly curves. Incredibly intricate embroidery in a black thread along the hem. My hand went to my chest, and I fought for breath.

I was a woman of two-and-twenty, no mere pup at her mother's teat. And yet in that moment, I felt like my family was casting me to sea without benefit of neither sail nor anchor.

As if she sensed my need, Mama knocked softly on my door. I knew it was her by the way she tapped twice, paused, then once more. Silently, I opened it.

She stood there, every inch of her a lady. Dressed in her finest purple gown, her hair expertly wound by her maid in an obedient plait. Would I ever be the lady she was? Could I do this? My last few days riding with Aurelio, talking with him, even sparring with him had been pleasant enough. But there was no spark. Nothing like I'd heard of love.

I shook my head slowly. "You ask me to do the impossible."

She scurried in, glancing backward, as if making sure no one else had heard, then shut the door. But before she shut it entirely, Zia Gabi had a hand on it and edged inside.

I took a deep breath. Did I have the strength to face them both? And yet, if they both asked it of me, could I not trust it? Because they clearly were here, together, to ask *something* of me.

Mama brought a chair to the side of my bed, and Gabi another from the corner. Giacinta came to the door to assist me with my gown, but the two of them assured her they could see to my needs. Mama drew me behind the screen to unlace the bodice of my day dress.

She indicated the basin and cloth. "Clean the dust from your face, your arms," she said gently, leaving me to my bath.

From the other side of the screen, Zia Gabi raised her voice. "Tiliani, you know we want the best for you."

"I do," I returned in measured fashion, wringing out the cloth in the lavender-scented water and watching golden drops—reflecting in the candlelight—return to the basin and disappear in the pool. Becoming one with it. Was that what I was? A droplet destined to dissolve into the larger pool? Adding my effort to theirs for the greater good?

I rubbed the cloth across the back of my neck and down my chest, feeling the refreshing cool evening air across my damp skin while waiting for them to speak again.

"My dearest girl, 'tis past time we tell you something," Mama said.

I slowly straightened. "Yes?"

"Can you come to us?"

I rounded the screen and went to them in my underdress,

wondering what might be of such import that they had come to me now, here. Taking Mama's outstretched hands, I sank to the edge of the bed.

"When we were younger than you," Mama said, "a great deal was asked of us."

"Yes," I said. "I know."

"And now we must ask a great deal of you," Zia Gabi said, sitting on the bed at my other side.

"By marrying Lord Paratore."

"If he eventually captures your heart, it would be good for the republic," she said. "But also benefit your family. And the castello," she added. "And the people who depend upon us."

"In what way?" I dared, looking from my mother's face to my aunt's.

"In a way that will affect all," Mama said, "forever."

"Forever?" I echoed. "How so?"

"Tiliani, what we must tell you is a secret so grave, you mustn't tell a soul," Zia Gabi said.

"Very well," I said slowly. Out in the courtyard, we could hear the musicians begin strumming a familiar tune. Men laughing.

"What we have to say might seem far-fetched, but 'tis the truth," Gabi said. "God made a way . . . there came a time . . ." Her words trailed off and she looked to my mother.

"*Mia dolcezza*," Mama said, looking directly in my eyes. *My sweet.* "There is a reason we are so different than any others you know in Toscana. We are not from here. We are not from this place at all."

I knew all of this. "I understand. 'Tis your Norman ways."

"Nay. We are not from this . . . *time*," Gabi said carefully.

I looked at them, bewildered. "What do you mean?"

"We are not from this time," Mama repeated, holding firm to my hands. "We are from the future. God opened a portal in the tombs near Castello Greco." She leaned closer, a shining intensity to her blue eyes. "And we came through."

I tried to swallow, but found my mouth dry, wondering if I'd heard her right. But with the expression on each of their faces, I knew. *I knew.*

So much became clear. Why they were so odd among Toscana's women and matriarchs. Why they never quite fit, like pegs not cut right. Why men often grumbled that they were more like men than women, half admiring them, half distrusting them.

The first question formed in my mind. "From what time are you?"

"About seven hundred years in the future." Mama's words were steady.

I drew in a quick breath.

"We're getting older, Lia," Zia Gabi said, in her angst, lapsing into their Norman-talk, though I only understood a portion. "And we must give you and your cousins every edge we can find."

Mama took a long, deep breath and resettled her hands around mine. "We know that we ask much of you." Sudden tears came to her eyes. "Lord Cosimo Paratore was someone we loathed and would never wish to face again. But his young cousin, Aurelio . . ."

She looked to Zia Gabi who said, "He seems altogether his own person."

"And you think this union is worthwhile." My mind searched for the rationale, back and forth, settled, like a bumblebee hovering over just the right flowering sprig. "Because if I do not agree," I said slowly, realizing the only answer, "we shall all pay a cost."

They sat, unmoving, affirming my guess.

"What-what sort of cost?" I stammered.

"The destruction of the castello," Zia Gabi said, sorrow in her voice. "Mayhap the demise of all future Forellis."

Mama rose and strode to my high, narrow window, alight with sunset's golden apricot glow. "The Republic of Siena shall stand for almost another two hundred years, but those two centuries shall be stormy. And in 1555, she shall fall."

I stilled. 'Twas impossible. The castello? Well, castelli were oft taken and retaken. But the republic?

I thought back to the bustling city. Her masses, coming and going from the gates. Il Campo, teeming with fishmongers, ceramicists, glass blowers, silversmiths, butchers, and more. Little children chasing pigeons, sending them fleeing to the ramparts. Ladies in fine dress, parading about. Knights, marching in formation.

To say nothing of the countless villages that surrounded Siena and our own castle.

The republic, no more?

"Are you certain?" I whispered.

"Absolutely," Mama said, turning to look at me. "Which is why this match is so fortuitous. And yet the last thing I wanted was to make this your responsibility." She came over to me and knelt again at my feet. "Truly, this remains your decision, Til. We shall not force you to do anything. But if there were some way, if Aurelio softens your heart . . . might you give it a chance?"

I rose, even as my head spun among the swirl of facts. My mother and aunt were from a different time.

The She-Wolves of Siena were so different, so remarkable, because they were *from a different time.*

I was different, because of them.

The image of a dust storm rose in my head, filled with leaves and dirt and tumbleweeds . . . a veritable maelstrom. But one thing centered it.

The She-Wolves were asking something of me. Something vitally important.

And if they were asking it, my only logical answer was . . . yes.

LUCIANA BETARRINI

We donned our darkest clothes the next night. I wore black jeans and a mock turtleneck, and the soft, long black boots I wore each day as we performed archery shots for the crowds. I'd wound my hair into a bun, so it wouldn't catch on any branches or brush. Nico wore a black T-shirt and leather jacket over his darkest blue jeans. He wore a new belt at his waist and short, black leather boots.

"How much trouble do you think we'll be in if we get caught?" I asked, as Nico tossed a pack in the backseat of a castello car and opened the door for me.

He hovered there as I clambered in. "A lot. We might lose our jobs here. We might get booted out of Italy. It might even be an international incident. A news-media event." He paused. "But can we really do anything but this?"

I bit my lip and shook my head, even as I glanced up at Castello Forelli. I'd be sad to lose the rest of the summer here. It had been even cooler than I could've imagined. But this chance to potentially find out what had become of the Betarrinis? Even if it was confirmation of their deaths?

I felt like we owed that much to the family.

And there was the tiny fact that Nico would drive me absolutely bonkers if I didn't agree. Deep down, I knew he'd go alone if I didn't go with him. Together, we were stronger. And smarter. Even if my head was already throbbing in pain.

Something Mom used to say came back to me as we drove away from the castello and hopped on the highway for a bit. *We always regret the things we might've done more than the things we did. Even if it was a mistake.*

I hope you're right, Mom, I thought, as we turned on the road that led up into the hills. I still missed her and thought of her nearly every day. Did Nico? We seldom talked about it. I know he got angry when he thought of it. About the futility of her fight against the cancer. How the chemo treatments had really robbed us of her in that last year of high school, a year we really needed her. How Dad didn't bother to come home until the funeral.

Nico had been convinced that if Dad had stepped up, offered to pay, Mom might have sought better treatment. Or at least considered a visit to the leading cancer centers in the country for a consult. But while Dad was willing to cover expenses for anything we wanted to do—from camp to college—he seemed to wash his hands of Mom when he left home.

I thought it was what drove Domenico to want to establish wealth at an early age. Find his own security, outside of relying on Dad. Be able to provide for himself, for us. I worried about it. What would that pressure, that desire, lead him to? And what might he miss, by focusing so much on it?

He pulled off the road and into the woods on a small spur, until our vehicle was hidden from the main road that led to Vecchio Modo. "I think this is as far as we'd better go," he said.

"Agreed," I said, hopping out.

He pulled out his phone and opened a GPS map of the area. "We're about here," he said, pointing. "And we need to get up here. It's about a mile, maybe a mile and a half. Will you be okay in those?" he asked, looking at my boots.

"I will," I said. They weren't hiking boots, but I wore them for hours each day during my archery stint.

He opened his pack and handed me a flashlight, while slinging a headlamp around his neck. I slid the flashlight into my back pocket. I saw he had two water bottles in the pack, as well as some bars. We set off at a brisk pace, tracing the line of the road, but gradually gaining elevation, separating from it. I took note of landmarks as we went. Odd clumps of trees, a craggy cliff, knowing if we returned at a run, I'd want to know where I was. My blood pulsed in my ears, every cracked stick and clump of a boot seeming louder than it actually was. I wanted to at least get to a viewpoint so we could see if the tumuli were there, as the old man described. Twelve mounds, mostly buried by centuries of soil and brush, several of them open at the top, presumably by grave robbers through the years.

"No one had any interest when I was a boy," he had said. "This land is full of such mysteries, with each generation building atop another. My neighbor found Roman mosaics in her field. Another an Etruscan tomb beneath a corner of his field." He'd shrugged. "Since my father could not find anyone who seemed interested, I did not think it worth mentioning."

"But it was your land," I'd said to him. "And the Societa Archeologico confiscated it?"

"No, it was my good fortune," he'd returned. "They purchased it from me." He'd given us a toothy grin. His days of running sheep were long over; clearly this had become his retirement fund.

"Bet you they bought it for far less than it was worth," Nico had muttered to me in English, even as he smiled and nodded, as if happy for the old man.

Especially if it's a site capable of eventually bringing in tourist dollars, I thought. Nico had done the calculations at the castello. Even with all the expenses in upkeep, staffing, and utilities, he figured the absentee Forellis cleared several thousand euros a day. "Not bad for a biz you don't have to be present to run," he'd said. "And a way to keep the old family estate from disintegrating."

I'd looked up and around at the castello then. It was sad that there was not a Forelli to be found among the staff that summer. They all apparently had better things to do. The boss had told them they went to the finest schools and summered with people "in a different league" than all of us. I'd pictured yachts out of Marseilles. Golfing in Scotland. Trekking in the Andes.

What had the Forellis been like back in the heyday of the castello? Had the Betarrinis really met them, married some of them? And how was I even thinking that any of this was possible?

I shook my head and concentrated on following in my brother's footsteps, making as little noise as possible, especially as we neared the site. My headache was building, making me feel nauseous. Or was it nerves? He slowed and waved me down. Hunched over, we crept closer, until we were on our knees behind a massive clump of wild lavender. Fat bees buzzed around us, the warm streams of the setting sun casting a golden glow across the purple tips and sage-colored leaves. I usually loved the smell of it . . . but tonight, along with the pine about us, the decay of fallen leaves beneath our feet, it made me feel a little more sick. *Do not throw up, Luciana. Do not throw up!*

I focused on the waning activity below us. There were indeed twelve mounds, five of them excavated down to their foundations. A dozen tents were in a group on the far side of the compound, one clearly an open mess tent, where people were gathering for dinner around long communal tables. About twenty people sat there, laughing and talking, each dressed in dirt-smeared T-shirts, emblazoned with the Societa Archeologico dell' Italia logo on the back.

"Too bad we couldn't score a couple of those shirts," Nico whispered.

"That would have helped," I agreed. "But think how tired we are, working at the castello all day. These guys will be the same. We just need to wait for dark, and they'll be out."

Adrenaline was keeping me going tonight. Usually by seven o'clock, I was counting the hours until I could go to bed. Being with people all day and the physical work—hauling water, periodic kitchen duty, cleaning, shooting arrows, leading tours—took it out of all of us.

Nico pulled a small pair of binoculars and studied the site carefully, then handed them to me. "Counting from the right, it seems like most of the work has been done on the first three tombs."

I nodded. There was a hole in the top of a few of the tombs.

"Getting inside will be risky," I observed. "What with the entrances being on the same side as the tents."

"And, if they have a guard on duty, he'll be walking along that side."

"With the open domes, we might be able to get to one from this side and take a look inside from the top, ducking for cover when the guard comes by again."

Nico nodded. "Or we could even drop inside."

"What if they're deep? They look pretty tall. How would we get out again?"

"We crawl to the entrance, wait for the guard to get to the far end of the line, then steal out," Nico said. "We can wait until the middle of the night, if we have to. There's no moon tonight."

I lifted a brow. He'd thought to check. That was smart. I'd been too consumed with the thought of breaking and entering—and the potential repercussions—to stop and think about that. *We're better together,* I thought again.

I brought the binoculars to my eyes. "Did you see anything that might indicate they found a body?"

"No. I think there'd be a police presence if they had. Don't you?"

I handed the binoculars back to him. "Yeah. Looks like a regular ol' archeological dig to me."

"Agreed." He slid the glasses back into a case and into his pack. "So now we wait."

5

TILIANI FORELLI

Ilaria came to my door, knowing I would not wish to enter the courtyard without her at my side. Giulio was with her. Ilaria, a few years younger than I, and Giulio, a year younger, served me as both guards and siblings, much like my cousins. Between the four, I thought I might be the most protected woman in our valley. My cousins were protective because I was both female and I'd lost my brothers. The Grecos—because we were inextricably bonded since birth, and they'd always served as my guards. Their elder sister, Chiara, assisted my grandmother with her healing work, and treated me like a little sister. There had been a deep bond between our mothers, even after Alessandra remarried. When she died, my mother took in her children as her own. We were kin.

They both smiled at me as I opened the door wider, letting them see me—really see me. Giulio took a step back and swept his short cape over his shoulder, bowing in exaggerated fashion. "M'lady, you are a—"

"Cease," I said, shaking my head with a laugh. "I shall receive enough idle praise this night." He and Ilaria knew I loathed being in such finery. It was simply so . . . confining. But goodness, Guilio was arresting. I took in his handsome visage as a sister might—feeling a little smug and proud about it, rather than fancying a true attraction. My mother always said he was the image of his father, Rodolfo, with his straight, almost black hair and dark-blue eyes.

He pulled back his shoulders and offered his arm, arching one dark brow. "It is not idle praise. Aurelio will be a fortunate man if he wins your heart."

I placed my arm on his and felt Ilaria hook her arm through my other. Together, we moved down the castello hallway, hearing the merriment outside.

"How do you fare with such a thought, my friends?" I asked, looking from one to the other. "The idea that Castello Greco might again become Castello Paratore? How does Chiara feel about it?"

I felt the muscles of Giulio's arm tense, while his face remained passive. Ilaria visibly swallowed. While she was the daughter of another man, she was included in the Greco inheritance. "We had a long conversation with your father and mother," Giulio said. "They have cared for us all our lives and will continue to do so, as will your aunt and uncle. None of them would make such a decision lightly."

"Indeed." I glanced at Ilaria, dressed in a dark green gown, her hair in a lovely, plaited knot at the back of her head, sweet curls dancing around her heart-shaped face.

"We trust them," she said simply. Her lovely eyes were the color of the rich soil farmers turned up each spring. Her skin the tawny brown of the hillsides come autumn. And her words urged me to do the same. *Trust.*

The last days with Aurelio had not been objectionable. He was polite, refined in his manner. Appealing in form, and I had to admit an attraction to the startling green of his eyes. Fastidiously clean, smelling of linen and lavender. And yet well acquainted with his sword, giving me a good run when we sparred, while irritating me when he pulled back in deference to my femininity. My mother and father had long trained our knights to give me and Ilaria no quarter; they knew well that women who trained for battle would not be granted quarter on the field. But Aurelio had not been taught the same, I reminded myself for the hundredth time.

Grace, Tiliani. Mercy.

"Ready?" Ilaria asked, her hand on the door. From the sound of it, hundreds of people reveled in the courtyard outside.

"As ready as I shall ever be," I muttered.

Giulio reached across to pat my arm. "Strength, dear friend. Chin up. Shoulders back," he said, repeating words my mother and aunt often had said to us.

I smiled up at him, impressed again by his visage. He routinely drew the attention of every girl in the republic. But while he was utterly self-aware, he did not let it go to his head. I'd wished more than once that we could find our way to love, but it was hopeless; growing up together, it never felt right to pursue anything more than friendship. He had a way of drawing people together, even between his sisters.

While each of the siblings had been fathered by different men, they were firmly tied as kin. His older sister Chiara was quintessentially Tuscan in her looks, with her long, curly hair, golden-chicory skin, wide, nut-brown eyes, and dark lashes. But she was dedicated to my grandmother and never encouraged a man's interest. At thirty, she was well past marrying age. Ilaria, who was a head shorter than I, was fiercely strong and perfectly capable on the battlefield between her belt full of daggers and her bow. Her desire to follow in my mother and aunt's footsteps as a She-Wolf had quelled any man's interest, so she, too, was alone. The four of us shared that . . . the way we had been raised made us somewhat inaccessible to our fellow Sienese. We were considered odd. Off-putting.

So mayhap this union with Aurelio was truly my only way toward what I also wanted in life . . . a husband. Children. His ardor did not seem cooled by my skills as a warrior. He seemed intrigued. *Grace. Mercy. Direction. Please, Lord.*

I did as Giulio directed and drew myself up. Ilaria opened the door, and we were immediately in motion. People turned to us as we walked, nodding at us in greeting. There were many I knew, and with some surprise, I saw that there were many I did not. I prickled with surprise. *Fiorentini.*

Aurelio's people, I tried to remind myself, but my muscles tensed in a wave of alarm.

"Steady," Giulio said in a low voice, leaning his head toward mine. "M'lord would not have invited them had it not been strategic to do so."

"Indeed," I said, forcing a smile and continuing to move through the throngs to Aurelio's side. Once there, he turned to fully face us and gave me a most genteel bow—perfectly executed—and smiled at me as he rose. He offered his arm, and Giulio took my hand and gently placed it atop Aurelio's. Together, we turned to face my uncle as he climbed atop a step, and then a large cask, to stand above the crowd, which gradually quieted. "My friends, my friends, welcome."

Zio Marcello looked about at the crowd, as did I. Every torch was lit, and standing, wrought iron candelabra holding massive beeswax candles were dotted across the courtyard, illuminating many faces.

"'Tis been nigh unto a century that so many Fiorentini have been welcomed behind our gates," he said, raising his goblet. "But 'tis our hope"—he nodded at my mother, father, and aunt, then us—"that this is the dawn of a new era."

I found my cousins, Fortino and Benedetto, finding comfort that they—and all our knights—carried daggers beneath their tunics, while a great pile of weapons by the gates indicated that the Fiorentini had been disarmed. My parents had welcomed these people into our sanctuary; they would not allow them the opportunity to overtake us. I, too, wore a dagger strapped to my calf. And I was certain that Ilaria carried at least four.

"We have all lost loved ones over the years, even land," my uncle called, so all could hear. "But change must incorporate mutual benefit and glory for all. Let us move forward from here on as friends, standing together against others who might wish to see us fail at forming this new union."

"*Salud*, Lords and Ladies Forelli!" said Aurelio loudly, raising his goblet of wine, and he handed me another, so I could join in the customary toast to their health.

It warmed me, and surprised me somehow, that the Fiorentini used the same, customary address. Mayhap they were not as different as I had always thought.

"Salud!" echoed the crowd, many of them raising their own goblets.

Tomasso edged toward my uncle and Zio Marcello, whispering in his ear. "All is prepared for the feast," my uncle called. "Please, my friends. Let us sup together and celebrate our newly forged friendship." He gestured everyone inside to the Great Hall, even as servants finished setting up many additional tables in the courtyard to accommodate the numerous villagers. Servants passed us with two whole roasted hogs, steaming meat pies, and crocks of soup to serve them.

We moved inside the hall, and I looked up in surprise. Lengths of gold and crimson cloths had been stretched across the rafters in alternating fashion, arcing and creating a tent-like, festive atmosphere. I stiffened. *'Tis as if this is the marriage feast itself.*

Aurelio turned slightly toward me. "Are you well, m'lady?" he asked, his green eyes quizzical. In this light, I could see his sandy lashes and brows were tipped with a golden blond, as was his hair.

I forced a smile. "Indeed."

"Your family has honored us," he said, leading me down the center of the hall to the dais. My aunt and uncle were seated in the center, on the other side, my father and mother to their left. Clearly, we were to sit to their right.

He paused to allow me room as we moved single file around the end of the table, then pulled my chair out for me. I took my seat and smiled formally at the room, meeting the gaze of many Sienese nobles, who raised their goblets in greeting, as I did in turn. He sat down beside me and filled my goblet from a small crockery pitcher before us.

"It displeases you?" he asked quietly, as Giulio and Ilaria sat down across from us.

"Nay. 'Tis a lovely gesture," I said, looking up and watching as the fabric moved in the breeze each time someone came through the door. It reflected the torchlight below. "I merely think it might be putting the cart before the horse."

"I see."

I glanced at him. "I am not against this, Lord Paratore," I said, gesturing toward him and back. "But I shall not be rushed."

He held my gaze and took hold of my hand before I could put it to my lap. I stilled as I felt the warm strength of his fingers, the command of his touch. Then, never dropping my gaze, he lifted my hand to his lips and slowly kissed my knuckles.

A shiver ran down my arm, but not in an unpleasant way. I felt others pause and hush around us, but refused to be the first to look away, even as I felt the heat of a blush rise on my cheeks.

"Mark my words, m'lady. I shall not allow anyone to rush you," he said, while I gently pulled my hand from his at last. "Ever."

He seemed so earnest, and I appreciated his promise a great deal, but found it all a bit overwhelming. Hurriedly, I took a sip of wine, cursing my trembling hand. Did he note it? The man seemed to note everything about me. Did he know that few men had dared to kiss my hand? That no one at all had dared kiss my lips? I practically sighed in relief as Giulio and Ilaria began asking Aurelio questions, subtly sizing him up for themselves.

Captain Valentino Valeri sat across from us, next to Giulio. He briefly introduced the rather plain—but elaborately dressed—Lady Palandri, of Firenze. His own intended? Her small, dark eyes perused me overlong, likely curious to see a daughter of a She-Wolf in person.

But in moments, I surmised the two were mere acquaintances. She must be a daughter of a Grandi, to be honored so. The table filled with alternating groups from Castello Forelli, several other members of the Nine, and nobles from Firenze. The food—roasted game hens and steaming piles of cream-covered vegetables—came then on trenchers, along with crocks full of savory soup.

Chiara was now asking Aurelio of his education—he had been schooled in Firenze but attended university in Bologna for four years, studying literature, philosophy, history, and politics before returning last year. I envied him that . . . four years to sit at the feet of scholars. While my parents had brought in private tutors for us over the years, much of what we knew had been taught to us by my parents, aunt, and uncle. Which made more sense now that I knew what I did about them. Mayhap my mother and aunt were even more educated than the best tutors.

"Which was your favorite subject?" I asked him, finishing my last bite of delicious, stewed meat.

"History," Aurelio said definitively. "I believe it beneficial to study every great society and government through the ages. Then we might find the best route forward ourselves."

My grandmother had been listening intently. "There are some who say that those who do not remember the past are condemned to repeat it," Nona said.

"Indeed, m'lady," Aurelio returned, full respect in his tone. I appreciated that he not only honored my family, but seemed to genuinely enjoy them. What had his parents been like? I thought about his father and his relationship with Cosimo. Mayhap they had rarely conversed.

"'Tis well and good to know history and endeavor to not repeat mistakes. But do you believe we might actually not do as our ancestors did?" I asked, taking a sip from my water goblet. "After all, do we not struggle against the same sins? Greed, pride?"

I caught Captain Valeri's small smile of admiration. "Mayhap if we endeavor not to fall to the siren's call of such sins," he said, "we might forge an entirely new sort of government."

"That is not government," Aurelio said with a laugh. "That is heaven. But I would not object to a heavenly society. To the hope of heaven!" He lifted his goblet.

Captain Valeri tipped his goblet against his lord's and smiled. His teeth were fairly straight, if a bit crowded. And his lips were lush—wide and welcoming. Catching myself before he noticed, I hurriedly looked away.

Outside, the music began again, a subtle invitation to come and dance beneath the stars.

As soon as Zio Marcello and Zia Gabriella rose, dismissing us all, Aurelio was on his feet, offering me his hand. "I have waited all night to dance with you, m'lady," he said in my ear as he passed close by me at the end of the table. He stepped forward and then reached back to assist me down the two stairs, conscious of my ample skirts and the dangers that lay within their potential tangles. If I were to fall, it would be considered his failure.

The idea of it rankled me, and yet I could not help but feel grateful and honored by his keen attention. And as we walked down the Great Hall, I liked the solid assurance of his arm, the way he held himself erect, shoulders back, head high, just as my mother had taught me.

I felt the warming hint of both grace and mercy simmering in my heart. Was the wall between us beginning to crumble?

We moved as one to the center of the group of dancers and joined in a merry folk dance that the villagers were halfway through. Once done, my father leaned in to speak with the musicians, and the villagers moved off to the side as the nobles formed lines to introduce a more refined dance that began with women on one side, men on the other, then divided into groups of eight, then four, then two.

By design, my partner was Aurelio when we were in pairs. He took my waist firmly with his left hand. Then, in tandem with the music, edged past me, hooking my waist again with his right, his green eyes never leaving mine. He took my hand in his and with a press to my hip with his other, turned me beneath his arm, made a quarter-turn himself, and turned me again. Four times I twirled, leaving me a bit breathless and dizzy when I finished.

"Steady, my friend," he said in my ear, as he held me close an instant before the dance ended and he stepped away to bow.

My friend. I appreciated that he did not yet call me "my sweet" or "my love." He had understood me when I said I did not wish to rush. And yet why did I get the sense that he was handling me? Maneuvering? As if I were but a piece upon a chess board?

"Save me another?" he asked, lifting my hand to his lips and again kissing my knuckles as he bowed. "I fear there are many others who wish to dance with the lovely Lady Tiliani this night. Reluctantly, I must share."

And indeed there were. I danced with one after the other. Nobles from Siena, as well as friends from neighboring castles. Giulio. Even my cousins, Benedetto and Fortino. Benedetto was but a year older than I, but he acted as if I were a toddler on his heels, furiously protective and asking me many questions about Aurelio and how he was treating me. His elder brother Fortino was more distant, casually interested in my thoughts over this "Fiorentini infiltrator."

Then Captain Valentino appeared before me. "M'lady," he said. "My lord has asked me to claim this dance."

"Oh?" I said, cocking my head and searching the crowd for Aurelio. He had left some time ago with a group of young men, disappearing back into the Great Hall.

"He sends his regrets that he has not yet returned to claim another himself."

"How kind," I said wryly.

"His delay is my gain," he said valiantly. He lifted his hand, and I set my palm against his. Only the constant dancing had kept me warm enough. But as the music began again and I circled Captain Valeri, and then he, me, I thought there was something warm about everything in the man. From his gaze to his touch.

I could feel the heat of his palm through the fabric of my gown at my waist. Felt the warmth of his breath as I passed beneath his chin. The warmth of his arm as he lifted it and brought me back around. And if Aurelio had not dropped his gaze throughout our dance, Valentino practically locked me in his.

What was it about the man that made me feel so thoroughly known, even though we barely knew each other?

While Aurelio was attentive and careful in his interaction with me—as if playing the part of the attentive lover—I felt as if Captain Valeri somehow already understood me. As if we had known each other for years, not days.

Why could it not have been him that Firenze sent? I thought.

Catching myself, I abruptly halted and stepped back, even as others continued to dance around us.

"M'lady?" the captain asked, frowning.

Giulio was there, then, noticing my dismay. Ilaria beside him. Consternation lined their expression, and they looked to Captain Valeri as if he had offended me or made some inappropriate advance.

"Nay, nay," I said to them, waving down my guardians. "All is well." I forced a smile before others around us lent us further scrutiny.

I gave the man a slow curtsey. "Captain Valeri, I believe 'tis time to say good night. I fear I have . . . overtaxed myself."

He nodded once, sweeping an arm across his chest and bowing. "I pray 'tis not I who overtaxed you."

"Nay. 'Tis simply the culmination of a momentous day."

With that, I gratefully took Guilio's arm, and he escorted me toward the turret, wordlessly assuming I meant to retire, Ilaria right behind us. But it was Valentino Valeri's eyes—those warm, wise eyes that missed nothing—that I felt all the way.

6

LUCIANA BETARRINI

The camp was totally quiet—and most lights out—when we carefully made our way down the hillside to the nearest tomb, the second from the right. We'd watched the bored guard for half an hour. Most of the time, he hung out at the far end, ducking behind a tree to look at his phone for fifteen minutes at a time. It was perfect.

There was one main camp light—mounted to a tree above the mess tent—that cast slivers of light across the hillside and grounds. Three of the sleeping tents still had lights on, but their occupants' shadows had ceased moving, so we figured they were reading, chatting, or had fallen asleep with their camp light on. When the guard again idled down to the far end, and the glow of his phone lit up his face, we scrambled up the stone face of the rounded tomb, pausing at the entrance on top.

I pulled my flashlight from my back pocket and, lowering it inside the tomb, aimed it toward the back and cautiously clicked it on, watching the guard the whole time. He didn't look up.

Nico gasped. "Look," he whispered.

I glanced down and my eyes widened. From our research on the Betarrinis, we realized that this was a crazy-beautiful find. The frescoes—even in this tomb that had been exposed to the elements for decades, if not centuries—were spectacular.

"Want to get inside?" Excitement filled his hushed voice.

I nodded. I had no idea what was in the other tombs, but we were here, now. Maybe this would give us an idea of what might be in the others. Plus, I was too nervous to stay out here, where the guard might catch a glimpse of us and sound an alarm. My heart was pounding, thereby making the pain in my head all the worse.

"Shine your light on the ground so I can see where I'm landing," he instructed. Taking one more look at the oblivious guard, Nico lowered himself to his belly, then dropped to hang from the edge, then with a soft thud, to the bottom. I watched as he gaped, looking around. "Luci, throw me my pack and get *down* here."

I tossed him my flashlight and then did as he had, easily dropping the last four feet to the dirt floor. Side by side, we did a slow three-sixty, careful to keep my flashlight beam from going through the open entrance. Nico bent and scrambled to the igloo-like entrance and carefully peered down to where we'd last seen the guard.

He returned. "Still texting," he reported. He brought his headlamp up. "Here, I'm putting this on. It's a softer light. Switch off yours."

I did as he suggested, finding relief in turning off the beam that might expose us. His softer, wider light might be mistaken for an archeologist's lamp—less like a burglar's furtive, narrow stream. Together, we moved past the brightly colored frescoes depicting people feasting together, others shooting boar, a group of figures—a family?

"See anything that indicates the Betarrinis were here?"

I shook my head.

"What about anything that might be a reference to time travel? An hourglass? A sundial?"

"No," I said, looking at every image as we made our way around the circular room again, wondering if any of them had double meanings. "What about this sun and moon?"

He paused and drew closer. "I don't see anything special

about it. And I think they're pretty typical as fresco elements."
We moved on, past the images of a feast and a boar hunt again.
But then we paused near two handprints.

"Huh. That's weird," he said, hovering over my left shoulder.
"I've never seen handprints in all the Etruscan fresco pics we
looked at. Have you?"

"Not that I remember."

He did what I'd thought about doing. What I'd been drawn
to do . . . but resisted. He raised his left hand and put it on the
slightly larger print. He pulled back fast, his lips parted.

"What?"

"It's-it's hot."

"What?" I wasn't sure I understood him.

"It's *hot*," he repeated.

"You're crazy." I reached up to the right one, matching my
fingers to the ancient's, wondering about the person—or people—
who had made them. But then it was my turn to draw back, stunned
by the heat that met my palm. "Whoa. Nico, what-what is that?"

"I don't know," he muttered, putting his hand on the print
again. I put mine up to the right too. "It makes no sense. There is
nothing behind this wall but stone and air. There couldn't be any
geothermal source . . ."

That was when I felt it. Almost a fusing of my flesh to the wall
as it heated. The room began tilting, as if I were getting dizzy.
"Nico . . ."

I felt his right arm go around my waist, and I reached out
to wrap my left around his, trying to steady myself. Distantly, I
thought I should remove my palm but then felt as if I needed the
anchor—as though in releasing it, I might collapse to the floor.

I tried to call out to my brother, but my words seemed
swallowed, engulfed, drowned. I looked up to the ceiling and
watched the stars above us swirl into a maddening stream that
seemed to circle around the globe in mere seconds, forming
glowing arcs like a thousand meteors of varying intensity. Day

came and went in the briefest flashes of light, and eventually, all was dark, the opening above us gone. I wondered if my skin was now fused to the wall. If I pulled it away now, would my skin go with it? But my panic was rising. Something frightening and powerful was happening. Something so beyond us, it terrified me.

It was then that I felt the pull at my waist, and together with my brother, we fell to the floor.

We laid there in the dark for several seconds, gasping for breath. "Nico?" I reached out to touch him, panicking for a moment that I was alone. I held my breath until I felt the reassuring, warm mound of his chest.

"I'm here," he said, panting. "Luciana, what just happened? Was it . . . could that have been . . ."

I knew what he was not saying. "Time travel?" I stared upward. "Well, we're here in the dark," I said slowly, "no stars above us. I'm assuming that means that we went to a place before that opening in the roof was created." But my own thoughts seemed nonsensical to me.

"Or the guard discovered us and has trapped us," Nico said.

"Do you really think that's what happened?" I asked. "Did you feel that? Under our hands?"

"Yes," he said gravely.

"Does your headlamp work?"

I heard the click of him trying it several times. "No. It's been knocked out. What about your flashlight?"

I rolled slightly to my side and fished out the slender cylinder from my pocket. I tried to switch it on. "No luck."

"Curiouser and curiouser," he quipped, using one of our mother's favorite lines from *Alice in Wonderland*. I felt him sit up and did the same. "If we fell away from the wall, then the entrance should be to our right. Let's crawl there."

I set aside my flashlight and moved down the tunnel, comforted to see the warm glow of daylight at the end of it, even if there appeared to be a large stone in the way. My heart stilled. "Nico, why is it daytime?"

He did not answer. I reached the stone and pushed, but it didn't budge. I put my shoulder to it. "No luck. It's too big."

"Here. Let me try."

We squeezed past each other, and he tried with his shoulder, too, then leaned to one side and used his legs to push. I leaned over his legs and shoved with my hands. The stone—really a big disc—gave way then, falling flat and cracking in half on a stone beneath. I winced. If any of the archeologists were about, they would be furious.

But as I blinked in the soft, morning light, so familiar from our days at the castello, and yet not . . . I realized how foolish my thoughts were. I scrambled the rest of the way over Nico's legs, ignoring his grumbles, and got to my feet, gazing about in shock, torn between horror and wonder.

Nico rose beside me, and we turned in a slow circle. Golden flags streamed from both Castello Forelli's corner towers . . . and from a nearby castle—what had been ruins in our own day. But the flags were different than those we had known and hoisted ourselves. Considerably longer and narrower, waving in serpentine fashion in the morning wind. "Nico . . ."

"I know, I know," he said, his expression matching all that I felt inside. But then his eyes lit up, and he grabbed hold of my arms. "Luci, I think we did it. We did it! Did what the Betarrinis did! We're here! Back in the time of the Renaissance!"

I looked back at the tomb, noting the undisturbed dome, as well as the others, all partially buried by dirt and foliage. None of them had been excavated. There were no archeological tents. "How?"

"We are here! Back in time!" he exclaimed, hands on his head. "It's true. It's really real."

"Is it? Or are we in some sort of weird twin dream? Some joint hallucination?"

He reached out and ran his hand over the tomb. "Feel that."

I followed his lead, running my hand over the rough stone.

He turned to me. "Feel this," he said, gently slapping me.

"Harder," I demanded, wondering if I was still dreaming.

He obliged, of course, as brothers do, and I felt the sting and resulting warmth at once.

Not dreaming. I winced and held my cheek.

"You asked—"

"I suggest you not strike the lady again," growled a voice to our right.

Together, we wheeled in surprise, not having heard anyone approach. Two knights, on horseback, dismounted and strode toward us, hands on the hilts of their swords. Four others rode up behind them and divided, wordlessly flanking us on either side.

"I am Lord Aurelio Paratore, and you are trespassing on what is soon to be my land." His green eyes slowly moved from my boots to my shoulders and then over my brother, taking in our clothing, stitch by stitch, so different than his own. The clothing on them, I couldn't help but study myself—from soft, handcrafted boots, to the leggings, to the tunics. His was embroidered with a purply-red, matching the cloth beneath the saddles of their horses. "You are grave robbers?" he asked.

"*Ladri di tombe? Noi?*" I blurted. *Grave robbers? Us?*

"No, we are not," Nico returned. "We are travelers and stumbled upon your tombs. Forgive us. We shall be off your land and on our way. We did not mean any harm."

"We are unarmed," I said. "And see? We have taken nothing from the tombs." I spread out my hands.

The man's eyes lingered on me. No doubt he'd seldom seen a woman in pants. Or likely any shirt this clingy. I regretted not wearing my costume from the castello. But then, who knew that Nico had actually been right with his wild imaginings? That it looked like it was actually possible to travel through time?

Renato's story of the Betarrinis in their medieval gowns came back to mind. "Please," I said. "We are seeking our family. We are Luciana and Domenico Betarrini. Might you tell us where we might find Benedetto or Adri Betarrini? Or Gabriella or Evangelia Betarrini?" I held my breath and glanced toward Castello Forelli, hoping the name-dropping would give us the edge we needed.

Lord Paratore and the larger knight at his right shared a long look, then returned to us.

Or were these guys against the Betarrinis? Judging from their statue in Chianti, and folklore, the sisters had more than a few enemies.

The shorter Paratore, the one with green eyes, came between me and the castle and glared down at me. "You shall go nowhere but the magistrate in Firenze. He shall decide whether you shall be tried for grave robbing or witchcraft or espionage." He sniffed. "You have the look of Norman spies, in what you wear," he said, giving us a dismissive wave.

"We are not," I said, squaring my shoulders.

"M'lord," tried the man beside him.

But Paratore ignored him. He dismounted and strode over to me until he was six inches away, staring down at me. Nico stepped closer, but I lifted a slow hand, silently urging him not to do anything rash.

"We are perhaps guilty of trespassing. But it was inadvertent. Simply let us go, and we shall be off your land as fast as we can walk."

The man put a hand on his belt. "Trespassing itself is reason for punishment."

"We must speak to the Betarrinis," Nico insisted. He moved as if to start walking toward Castello Forelli.

Without warning, the knight turned and liver-punched my brother, making him fall to his knees in pain. I rushed over to him, glaring at the man. Nico partially picked himself up, eyes wild with fury and confusion and a barely controlled desire to retaliate. I held on to him. We were outnumbered and unarmed.

"You do not have the right to approach Lord Forelli," Paratore said. "There is a sennight between me and my lady formalizing our union. And nothing—*nothing* shall get in our way. No interloper. No visitor. No unrest. And from what I have experienced, newcomers frequently sow unrest." He raised his voice. "Take them! Quickly, before the Forelli patrol discovers us and complicates matters."

Men moved in on either side of us. We shifted back-to-back and crouched, hands open, arms preparing to defend ourselves as we'd been trained to do. A knight reached for me first, grabbing my arm. I turned into him and rammed my elbow up under his chin, sending him stumbling back. The other grabbed my other wrist, and without thought, I turned and grazed him with a roundhouse kick to the head. He backed up and stumbled over the first, landing hard on the ground.

I looked to my brother. One knight had his burly arms around his chest, but Nico had rammed his head back, bloodying his nose. As the second prepared to strike him, he kicked his opponent. The first immediately dropped him, belatedly realizing Nico had used him against his companion.

I helped Nico up as Lord Paratore and his Number Two advanced on us, swords in hand. The other four rose and flanked us again, looking infuriated.

I thought we were done for, but another group on horseback arrived, and this time, there were women among them. My heart leaped. Gabriella? Evangelia? The women and one of the men carried bows, the others, swords.

"M'lady," Lord Paratore said to the young woman in front, a beauty with long, dark-blond hair pinned in a knot at the nape of her neck, her eyes an ethereal blue. "There is no need to trouble yourself here. I have it in hand."

"Undoubtedly," she said, though her tone belied her disbelief. She eyed us from head to toe, then noted the Paratore knight dabbing at his bloody nose, another cradling an injured arm. "Who are they?" she asked. Her beautiful tawny gelding danced beneath her.

"No one but grave robbers," he said. "Pretending to be kin of yours."

The young woman's eyes moved back to us. "Oh?"

"Yes, m'lady," Nico said, stepping toward her. "We only wished to—"

Paratore swung his sword about and stopped just shy of his neck. "Speak not," he gritted out between his teeth.

Nico didn't argue, only concentrated on the girl. He sensed what I did—she was our only hope of rescue.

Before he could threaten me, too, I blurted, "I am Luciana Betarrini. This is my brother, Domenico. We are in search of Benedetto, Adri, Gabriella, and Evangelia Betarrini."

The woman stilled her dancing horse and again surveyed our clothes. "What reason do you seek an audience with them?"

"We have come . . . a great distance. We are kin. I believe it best if we leave it to their ears alone."

"A likely story," Paratore scoffed. "How many come to your gates, m'lady, claiming kinship?"

Her eyes moved to the tomb behind us. "You found them here?" she asked Lord Paratore, moving her mount closer to him.

"Yes, m'lady. From what I hear, they are not the first to search these mounds for treasure." He lowered his voice. "With your father and uncle away, allow me to assist. Firenze is well versed in dealing with such troubles."

"And you believe Siena is not?"

Ooo, he's getting on her nerves, I thought hopefully.

He paused. "From here we are closer to Firenze than Siena," he said carefully. "My men shall bind them and escort them to my magistrate. After all, if everything progresses as we hope, this land shall soon be Fiorentini territory."

"And yet it is not *yet* Fiorentini territory." She leveled her gaze at him. "You assume much."

He swallowed hard. "It was my understanding that we *both* assumed what is likely to come."

"Assumption is a poor habit." Her horse continued to step side to side, sensing her agitation. "Do you count your chickens before they hatch, m'lord?"

"Nay, m'lady. Hear me. This has taken a turn I had not imagined," he said, lifting a placating hand. "With your menfolk away, I only thought I might spare you—"

"You thought to spirit these people away? People who claim to be kin? Did you not think that we might benefit from at least knowing of their arrival? Their claim?"

"I clearly acted in error," Lord Paratore said at last.

"Clearly," she returned. "Bring them," she said to her companions with a wave.

Without hesitation, one of them edged his mare forward and reached for my arm. "M'lady?"

I paused, not certain what he intended—pretty distracted by my *dang, he's hot* reaction—but then I saw it. Grabbing hold of his burly left arm to the elbow and stepping forward quickly, I used my momentum to swing up and behind him, even as he did most of the work. The horse shifted left and right after I landed, getting used to my added weight upon her back, and I tightened my grip on the man. I had only been on a horse once or twice in my life, and it seemed way higher than I remembered. Or maybe Tuscan horses were crazy-tall compared to normal horses.

"I am Lord Giulio Greco," he said. He was about my age, but the dude was built. All muscle. He'd seemed to lift me without really feeling a hundred of my hundred-and-forty pounds. "My lady's protector. I shall not let you fall."

"Grazie." *Thanks, buddy. I'd rather not come all this way and break my neck.* I took a breath. "May I . . . may I ask your lady's name?" She didn't look like any of the pictures of Evangelia, but she resembled her.

He paused as if everyone ought to know who she was. "You truly are from a great distance, are you not?" he asked, glancing down at my pant-covered legs.

"You have no idea," I muttered in English. "*Sì,*" I said louder.

"That is Lady Tiliani Forelli," he said with an admiring nod to the beauty at the front of our troops. "And behind us is her intended, Lord Aurelio Paratore."

I hesitated over that, remembering her terse words, their stilted conversation. "They do not seem . . . I mean, it does not appear that . . ." How did one say in medieval-speak that Til didn't seem all that into Lio?

Giulio seemed to catch my drift. "You have the way of it," he said quietly. "But at times, one must do what one must for the good of the republic."

I didn't like the sound of that. It reminded me of the men who threatened to take me to their republic, Firenze. Off us. Make us disappear. *Talk about gangsters . . .*

I glanced back to see if they followed and found my brother on the back of a mare behind us, trying not to crowd an archer with straight, dark-brown hair escaping her braid, and a wild, earthy beauty about her. Nico always had a thing for the earthy, Italian girls. And this one was even cuter than Milana. And he was of course already chatting her up, making her smile.

"Lady Ilaria Greco escorts your brother," Giulio said, sensing my turning. "She is my younger half sister and an able horsewoman."

Two more riders met us at a juncture in the road, introduced as Fortino and Benedetto Forelli. Excitedly, they scanned our group, inquiring of Tiliani just what was going down. Two others came from the other side. More scouts, I surmised, reporting to Til as part of what appeared to be a morning patrol. From what I could gather, all was well in the land—except for us.

Lord Paratore trotted past us, up to meet with the group and listen in on the report, leaving his men behind. I glanced back and one gave me a laser-beam glare. We'd showed them up and somehow made their lord look bad. I gripped Giulio a little tighter as the horse danced beneath us.

Giulio gently patted my hands, and I tried to relax, realizing I was upsetting his horse. Then, when the horse did not settle, he briefly rested a commanding hand on my thigh. "Pardon, m'lady. But try not to squeeze," he said. "My mare is leg-trained."

His hand returned fully to the reins, and his attention to the horse. I had no choice but to let my legs go all floppy and grip him all the harder around the waist. A hot blush rose up my neck and cheeks. I was so glad he couldn't see me. Could he feel the heat radiating from my face? Seriously, it felt like a solar flare. And what did *leg-trained* mean?

I eyed the bow near his left knee, the sword in a sheath near his right. Now it made sense. They had horses they could control with their legs, freeing their arms to shoot.

I thought of the statue of Lia and Gabi in the piazza and my mind wandered. Could they have truly come here and influenced the course of Castello Forelli? The way they rode horses and went to battle? The course of the entire Republic of Siena? Were we influencing their impact even now or was this just the way of things in this era? I'd read up on the constant warfare but really hadn't thought about specific tactics and what it would be like in person.

Giulio glanced back at me as the horse settled. "Are you well, m'lady?"

"Oh yes," I said, forcing myself to take a breath and ease up on my death grip around his waist. The guy was probably having a hard time breathing. "I am . . . I am simply not used to horses. In the city . . . in the city, we simply . . . walk."

"And from which city do you hail?" he asked curiously.

I hesitated. Why hadn't Nico and I come up with a cover story?

Because I hadn't really thought any of this possible.

Part of me still didn't. Maybe I was dreaming and I'd wake up and all of this would be some distant, crazy memory. Or maybe I wouldn't remember it at all.

One of the men whistled from up by Tiliani and waved his hand in a circle, saving me from Giulio's question. Instantly, we were off, and I had no more time to think of dreams or cover stories.

Because I was holding on for my life.

7

TILIANI FORELLI

I was torn. Half of me was consumed by rage that Aurelio had
either elected to make a decision for me or thought he could
keep it from me in total. And the other half was consumed by
wonder. These newcomers had to be like Mama and Zia Gabi and
Nona . . . time travelers.

It was plain enough by their dress and their slightly odd accent.
And what I'd seen the girl do in fending off the knights . . . she and
her brother were adept in hand-to-hand battle, using techniques I
had never seen—with no weapon but their own physical prowess.
I could already sense the dissatisfaction rolling off of the Paratore
knights and had noted Aurelio's twitching cheek muscle. They'd not
only failed at carrying out his orders, they'd been held at bay by two
unarmed opponents—one of them female.

Raised by my mother, and at Zia Gabi's knee, I had seen
firsthand how most men managed such situations. The knights
of Castelli Forelli and Greco were well used to women among
their ranks. Chiara had trained alongside the boys from the very
beginning, and Ilaria and I followed behind her, years later. No
favor was ever granted to us because we were female. But others
from Siena and farther afield had forever cast us curious looks,
never quite accustomed to the idea of women among the ranks,
let alone fighting beside them.

Not that they complained once they saw what Ilaria and I could do. She-Wolf pups, we were called. Or Little She-Wolves. 'Twas an honor to follow in my mother and aunt's footsteps. And I was determined to not allow Aurelio Paratore to get in the way of our progress.

While I could never ascribe to assuming my father's seat among the Nine—that would not be allowed—I wanted a husband who would listen to me and my ideas. Represent me in places I was not allowed. Value and respect me for more than how I might run a household or warm a bed or bear an heir. Look me in the eye when I spoke. Fully respect and see me. Like my father did my mother. Or Zio Marcello did Zia Gabi.

Like Captain Valeri had at me, in the stables and on the dance floor.

Valentino Valeri. He had not been in the stables this morning, as I'd hoped. It had startled me, recognizing my disappointment as I saw the empty stall. Had he used his knowledge of my early morning ride to encourage this impromptu, early-morning patrol of Aurelio's along borders he already mentally claimed?

I'd seen them ride out from the castello just as I reached the neighboring hill. I was only thankful that a feeling of foreboding had urged me to turn back and go after them. I was still trying to tamp down my fury when Aurelio rode up alongside me.

"I beg your forgiveness, m'lady," he said. "I truly only meant to lift a load from your shoulders. Patrolling our borders is something my men and I can readily do."

"When and if they become your borders to patrol," I said evenly.

"Indeed," he said, tucking his chin. "But can you blame me, truly? Wishing to see what was once Paratore land? If our roles were reversed, would you not wish to ride what had once been Forelli territory on the map?"

I had to give in to his point. "Mayhap."

He gave me a small, tentative smile.

"But Lord Paratore—"

"Aurelio, please," he said ingratiatingly.

"Aurelio," I said with a sigh, not inviting him to call me by my first name. "You should know that I enjoy patrol duty. I have been on patrol since I was but twelve years old, and I aim to continue doing so, regardless of whether I wed or not."

He was silent, weighing my words. Moreover, likely weighing his response. 'Twas particularly important at this juncture. I knew it. As did he.

"You wish to continue patrol duty even if you wed?" he repeated, his tone carefully devoid of emotion.

"I do. And more." I gave him a long stare. "If we go to battle, I shall be with my cousins and men. With Ilaria and Lord Greco. We are stronger together, having trained together since we were babes."

He started to shake his head slowly, as if fighting an inner battle. As if his head said, *My wife shall never* . . . but also said, *But if she insists* . . .

"Aurelio, I am the daughter and niece of the She-Wolves of Siena," I said, lifting my chin. "I shall never be set aside or put on a pedestal. I shall not wait in a castello as my men go to fight in my stead. I shall be at the front of the charge. Surely you considered this before you came to contend for my hand."

He stared stoically ahead as we trotted ever closer to the castello. But then he visibly brightened. "I confess that I do not favor the idea of my bride going into battle," he said. "But in our union, I have hope there shall not be battles seen for generations."

I nodded at this. At least he was not duplicitous in his response. He did not wish to see me in the fray, but he would not forbid it. And what he noted was what kept me from immediately sending him home to Firenze—a political union for the good of my people.

Because the promise of generations ahead enjoying peace was all that my parents wanted. And the future of Castello Forelli and Siena appeared to depend on it.

LUCIANA BETARRINI

As we all rode in to the castello courtyard, Lady Gabriella froze and then visibly paled. I recognized her immediately, despite the fact she had aged a good twenty years from the most recent photographs we'd seen. "Tiliani, escort our guests to the solarium, please," Gabriella said, looking quickly to Evangelia, who had just emerged from the Great Hall.

I watched as she took stock of all who had witnessed our arrival—and likely what we wore. Her brown eyes moved to the parapets, around the courtyard. Guilio neatly dismounted and then turned to me, arms up.

"Oh," I said, wondering if I ought to tell him to not worry, I had this, then figuring it might not be kosher for an escorted woman to dismount alone. "Grazie." I pulled my leg across the back of the horse and he took my waist in his hands, then eased me to the ground. It would have been a graceful move, steady and sure, but I was awkward and antsy, trying to get to ground and away from him before he was ready. We nearly bonked heads as he straightened, and as he released me, I took a half-step back, catching myself even as he caught my arm.

"M'lady?" he asked, those gorgeous blue eyes searching mine.

Never had I felt more unsure of myself. More *out of place*. But there were good reasons for that. "Grazie," I assured him, pulling my arm away. "*Sto bene.*" *I am fine.*

He gave me another searching look, but then turned to look about at the others.

Gabriella approached and pulled Ilaria and Giulio aside to share a few words. The pair set off at once, clearly sent on some errand. Evangelia came closer, wringing her hands.

I was having a hard time handling my surprise—almost

shock—at seeing the Betarrinis. First, really seeing them, in the flesh. Second, recognizing that they were not young anymore, as we had expected, but rather women in their mid-to-late forties. Tiliani looked familiar because she was clearly Evangelia's *daughter*.

How was it possible? They had only disappeared the year before . . .

My mind stuttered as I began making the mental calculations. If they'd been gone a year in our present and lived twenty or more years in this time, what was happening for Nico and me?

"If you please," Tiliani said, gesturing for us to follow her.

"Lord Paratore," Gabriella spoke from behind us. "Kindly take your ease in the Hall. You must be weary after your ride. I shall send Tomasso with some refreshments."

Although walking as if in a daydream, my mind still struggling with the reality of it all, I swallowed a smile. The meaning was clear in any century. He was not welcome to follow.

Tiliani approached a turret door, and a knight opened it for us.

I looked back to find Nico. His expression was filled with amazement, yet there was triumph there too. We followed Tiliani up two flights of circular stairs, her aunt and mother behind us. I realized that in modern times, these stairs were far more dilapidated than they were now, worn down in places by thousands of feet over hundreds of years. As we went down the hallway, I kept peeking into doorways, marveling at the furnishings, mentally comparing it to how the castle was kept in the future.

Marcello and Luca were away somewhere, it seemed, which was probably why the Paratore lord thought he'd take the whole man-of-the-house role and handle us.

But as we took a seat in the solarium, the women who faced us did not appear to be women who needed a man to handle things. Gabriella stood in the center of the room, Evangelia on one side, Tiliani on the other. An older woman came from around a desk in the corner—Adri, I realized, now in her sixties, but still regal and beautiful. As soon as the door was shut, Gabriella leveled a gaze at each of us. "Tell us, quickly," she said in English, the first we'd heard. "Every detail."

"Of course," Nico said. I admired his calm tone. "But we have questions of our own."

"As we can well imagine," Evangelia said with a small laugh.

Nico carefully explained how we were related, in case they doubted it, as Lord Paratore had intimated others might attempt. It didn't take long for them to understand there would be no way for us to know such things unless we were who we said we were. Not that they really doubted at all. Our American English and our clothing were convincing and clearly answered key questions.

Gabriella moved to the window and opened it, as if needing some fresh air. "'Tis been some time since we have had other . . . relatives join us here."

I took that in. "There have been others?"

Evangelia nodded. "Two brothers. From the future."

"Brothers? So time travel . . . this ability seems to be shared among Betarrini siblings."

"Indeed," Gabriella said, gesturing to the two of us.

"You said the brothers came from the future," Nico said. "You mean from the *future*-future? Beyond *our* own time?"

"Yes," she said.

"What happened to them?" I asked, trying to wrap my head around this new concept.

"We assume they returned to their own time," Gabriella said. "They did not return."

"After they were nearly killed," Evangelia added, "it was hardly surprising."

"People in this time do not look favorably upon those who move among the tombs," Adri put in. "They're a superstitious bunch."

Nearly killed. Was that what would have happened to us if Lord Paratore had succeeded in spiriting us away to Firenze? In all our imagining medieval times, that had not been a possibility we'd entertained. Clearly, it was obvious that Nico and I had not spent enough time imagining potential hazards or how we would handle them, despite my education.

"You did travel through Tomb Two, did you not?" Adri asked.

Tomb Two, I repeated in my mind. "You mean the second one with the opening? Yes, by placing our hands on the prints. Is that how you got here too?"

Gabriella and Evangelia shared a look, but Adri stared only at me. "So the site still stands? Is it active?"

Nico lifted a brow and crossed his arms. "You could say that. A guy named Manero is excavating it and more. It's on lockdown with armed guards and everything."

That brought Adri to a halt. "Manero."

I nodded tentatively. "He's in charge of Ben's site too."

"Figures," Gabriella said in English. "That guy co-opts everything you go after, Mom."

"And yet this time, because we left *before* I found it," she said, rubbing her forehead, "when we went back to get Ben . . . that it truly was a new discovery." She sighed, crossed her arms and gave her daughters a rueful smile. "It is just as well. Maybe they'll learn all I wished to."

"Or maybe they've figured out that there's something there that has to do with our disappearance," Evangelia put in. "Why else have armed guards?"

"Did they see you enter the tomb?" Gabriella asked warily.

"No. No one saw us," Nico said.

Ilaria and Giulio Greco arrived then, each carrying clothing.

"They are indeed our kin," Gabriella informed them. "And you are to protect them as you would any of us."

"Yes, m'lady," Ilaria said, and both she and Giulio bowed their heads in deference.

"Thank you. Will you two please stand guard at the door?"

Dismissed, they filed out and quietly closed the door behind them.

Gabriella, Evangelia, Adri and Tiliani moved closer so we could speak in lower tones. "Tell us why you have come," Gabriella said.

I glanced at Nico.

"Curiosity mostly," he hedged, not mentioning that he hoped to make a quick buck by scoring some treasure. "Your unusual appearance at Ben's site a year ago—dressed in medieval gowns—and then your *disappearance* made headlines around the world. There has been a global search on for months for any trace of you. Ben's Jeep, with his wallet and cell still in it, made it all the more mysterious. But then I found some references to two famed women," he said, looking them in the eye, "named Gabriella and Evangelia Betarrini."

"And he found a statue in Chianti," I said. "It's called the 'She-Wolves of Siena,' based on local lore. One holds a bow, the other a sword. The old stories say the She-Wolves were famous warriors named Gabriella and Evangelia Forelli, who led the Sienese in battle after battle."

"Our uncle thought you were just named after them," Nico said. "Given your parents' passion for history and all."

With one look at them, we knew that wasn't how it went down. "You actually went into battle?" Nico asked.

"More than once," Gabriella said, sitting down in her chair.

"To say the least. But it has been some time," Evangelia added.

"There is nothing more? No other historical notations of us?" Gabriella searched our faces.

"No. But then, there is little that survives from this era," I said. "Other than oral tradition. Or sometimes historical sources conflict."

"It is really weird," Nico said. "With all that survives about the Renaissance, the Medicis . . . we really thought we might find more about your family, if you were here. But I read everything I could and there was nothing."

"Domenico," Adri said gently, "this is 1372. A century before the Medicis rose to power or the Renaissance came to be."

Nico's mouth opened, and he sat heavily back in his chair. It was like watching a cartoon, his get-rich-quick scheme exploding in a cloud above him. As if the Medicis would just let him cruise in and grab the papal treasure anyway.

Evangelia leaned forward. "But Castello Forelli survives as of yet, in your time?"

"It does. It's in good shape," I said. "We work there. Well, we *were* working there. As tour guides and cast members and stuff."

They exchanged half smiles.

Nico's brow furrowed. "Was it not in good shape at some point?"

"In our time," Gabi said, "when *we* first traveled, back in the present, it was but rubble."

I frowned. "But Castello Forelli . . . it's been a tourist stop for at least ten years. And reconstruction isn't part of the tour talk."

"Because it's 'always' been in reasonable condition," Lia said meaningfully.

"So . . . you're saying we can change the future?" Nico asked, his eyes shifting back and forth, trying to understand.

I rubbed my temples, sure all of this would bring on the worst kind of headache . . . and then paused. I'd had a killer one when we dropped into the tomb. But since we'd arrived, I'd been fine. *Maybe my brain simply can't handle anything more than processing all of this . . .*

"We believe we can change some things," Lia said. "We have not yet ascertained to what extent. We're hoping we can affect physical change—like for the castle—but not harm people. Or potentially future people. Our goal is to survive, assist. Not harm."

I glanced at Tiliani, some things beginning to make sense. The chatter about Firenze. The land. Paratore's posturing. Her resistance. They were being thrown together because the Forellis were counting on that union to survive?

No, I thought. For *Siena* to survive. Because in time, I knew Firenze would conquer her. So they were after some sort of peaceable transition.

But in orchestrating that, what else would change? And was it truly possible to not affect people in the process of changing everything else?

8

TILIANI FORELLI

I regretted not being able to answer Giulio and Ilaria's silent questions as I passed them. We had few secrets between us, but even my cousins did not yet know the tale of how our mother and Zia Gabi came to be in Toscana. I had only been told because they needed me to understand why they supported this union with a Paratore.

My friends fell in behind me, following me down to the yard. At the base of the stairs, I turned to them.

"I wish I could tell you," I said. "But 'tis for the good of all that the secret remains with us."

"Tell us one thing," Ilaria said evenly. "Are they spies?"

"They are not."

"But what of their odd clothing?" she pressed.

"And their fighting prowess?" Giulio asked. "I have not seen such technique. If not spies, from where do they hail? Why are they here?"

"They are from Britannia, here to inform my aunt and mother of a Norman inheritance. Being prepared to fight appears to run in our blood . . . and has undoubtedly served them well while on the long journey here."

He did not respond, but I could feel his doubt.

I thought back to how my aunt and mother had instructed the twins, making them repeat what they'd said. Neither Domenico nor Luciana knew French, so they suggested an English home. "You are from the Cotswolds," Mama had specified. "Not London, nor anywhere on the coast."

"If anyone has sailed, we do not want questions to arise," Zia Gabi interjected.

"You have come to find us because there is an inheritance. Our Norman grandfather has just died and left us a sum of money. Relatives there—"

"In the Loire Valley," Gabi supplied.

"Told you where to find us," Mama finished.

"And so now that we have found you, your inheritance can be sent," Nico had nearly chanted.

"And you two may return home."

Mama obviously thought they would wish to do so at once.

"But what if . . ." Nico began. "What if we wish to stay a while?"

Mama had stilled. "This is neither a safe place, nor a safe time."

"Is any place?" Luciana had asked. "Any time? Truly?"

"There is plague here," Mama said. "It rolls through every few years. Nothing like 1348 or '52, but—"

"There was a recent pandemic at home," Luciana said. "A modern plague, of sorts."

That brought them up short.

"It had variations and mutated easily. It will be with us forever, like a new cold or flu bug, but it was lethal for some."

"Well, be that as it may," Mama said after a moment, "there is unrest here. Battles. Wars."

"As there are in our time. China and Russia—" Nico began.

"No." Mama shook her head vigorously. "This is a time of hand-to-hand combat. And while we have enjoyed a time of relative peace, Firenze appears restless of late. Umbria, too, specifically Perugia." She glanced at me again, and I knew what she was thinking. If only I would marry Aurelio, we might avoid sliding into war again . . . at least on one of our borders.

But as I listened to them share stories—history—I could not

help but feel that no matter how long time went on, people remained the same. People would forever be driven to acquire more land, achieve greater status, more wealth. And if they could not find it within their own borders, they would seek it in their neighbors' lands.

"Why do these travelers not have horses?" Giulio said.

"Nor men?" Ilaria added.

"They were robbed," I said, returning to the story my mother and aunt had concocted for them. "And they are not adept with horses."

"Indeed they are not," Giulio said with a snort. I'd seen him struggle with Luciana behind him.

"Will they be returning home now that they have ascertained Lady Gabriella and Evangelia's whereabouts?" Ilaria asked.

"I do not know."

"Are you so eager for them to depart, sister?" Giulio said, casting her a curious look. "I myself would not mind playing guide to Luciana. And I saw you laughing with Domenico."

"I certainly was not."

"You were!"

I sighed as they devolved into the debate and banter that marked most of their conversations.

"I was not. I merely found him . . . intriguing. Different."

"Speaking of men . . ." Ilaria said, looping her arm through mine as we passed Aurelio's knights, still sparring with our own. By now, every single one had untied their shirts at the neck or pulled them off altogether. Sweat shone on their finely muscled torsos as they continued to parry, block, turn, and strike, my cousins among them. "What of Captain Valeri?" she dared in a whisper.

"Captain Valeri?" I whispered back, my eyes darting to Aurelio, even as he sparred with Valentino.

"He is very Roman, is he not? With that aquiline nose, those broad shoulders and narrow waist? He looks like the statues of old. And while I have a special place in my heart for a man with curls, you have always favored men with soulful eyes."

"I do not know of what you speak."

"You do. You only mean to remain true to where your parents wish your heart to go."

I cast her a furious look and shook her loose. "You do not aid me, friend, by suggesting otherwise."

She crossed her arms and faced me. "'Twould not bother you unless you had thought about it."

Giulio turned and closed our small circle. "Say the word, m'lady, and I shall send Paratore on his way."

I bit back a smile. "You would enjoy that, would you not?"

"For history's sake," he allowed, "I wouldn't mind. But rest assured, Ilaria and I shall do what you bid. We will willingly give up our birthright if it serves the Forellis and Siena best. But you, m'lady, are our principal charge. If you ask it of us—"

"It shall be done," Ilaria declared.

"I could not ask for better friends," I said to them both. "Thank you."

"Then you are not yet certain of Lord Paratore?" Giulio looked in the man's direction, just as he feigned and struck Valentino across the belly with his wooden sword, making the man bend over in pain.

"Nay. There is much yet to discern and discover."

"Or is it that you're not yet certain of Valentino?" Ilaria teased.

I gave her a dark look and glanced around. She'd been a bit loud with that question, and the last thing we needed was for anyone else to overhear. But as I watched Aurelio take the man's hand in his and share a laugh as Valentino straightened, I wondered anew about my disappointment that morning when I discovered the captain wasn't in the stables.

But it didn't matter what I thought—or felt.

Aurelio was the only viable suitor present, and I had to find some way to fully open my heart and mind to him. Or at least, see if I could. That was all my mother and aunt had asked of me. I knew, deep down, they would not force me to marry him. But I also knew they would not have agreed to this potential union unless it truly, *truly* would be a help to us and Siena at large.

"I do not know how long the Betarrinis will remain in our keep," I said. "But in case they decide to stay for a while, 'twould be in their best interests to train them on several fronts. Mama and Zia Gabi would like them to become proficient in rudimentary horsemanship, sparring, and dancing. And they've asked us to see to it." I smiled. From what I'd seen, neither would likely complain about this assignment.

Guilio cocked a brow and pulled back his head. "Dancing, eh? They do not dance in Britannia?"

"They likely have learned different dances than our own. And with the gathering in Siena on the horizon, Mama assumed they'd like some training in advance."

"I would not mind dancing with Domenico," Ilaria said, with a dimpled smile. "While he lacks skills on a horse and I can easily best him with my short sword, he has other . . . skills."

I returned her smile. "*Skills*. Yes. Not to mention he's rather handsome." I turned to Guilio. "And you? Do you object to this task before you, training the lovely Luciana?"

"Well, nay," Guilio said slowly, digging the toe of his boot into the dust and twisting, "as long as you do not have need of us, m'lady."

"I need you to do what I have described, while I concentrate on getting to know Lord Paratore a mite better. 'Tis convenient for all of us, yes?"

They both nodded, clearly pleased, just as I saw Aurelio call an end to their sparring and reach for his shirt. "Good. Off with you, then. Find the Betarrinis and report to me of your progress when we sup this eve."

They followed my gaze to Aurelio and moved to do as I bid.

Before I could think further about it, I followed Aurelio to the stables, thankful when Captain Valeri turned with the other men to the barracks instead. I would catch Lord Paratore alone and avoid the keen scrutiny of the captain.

I smiled a little as Aurelio laid a gentle hand on the shoulder of their young squire, Rocco. It had given me pause when I first learned the boy's name, as he shared it with my late brother. But many were named as such in Toscana and I shook it off. Aurelio and the boy disappeared into the dark doorway, and I followed, thirty paces behind. Once I reached the stables and my eyes adjusted, I found them in the stall with Aurelio's black destrier, Renzo. Aurelio grabbed a brush and was showing the boy how to work out the knots in a horse's tail.

I leaned against the gate. "Our groomsmen could see to that for you."

He looked up in surprise and smiled, and I had to admit that he had a nice smile, revealing even, white teeth with a charming small gap between the two in front. It was much different than the superior, secretive smile he'd first given me upon meeting.

"Undoubtedly," he returned. "But Rocco will be best served by training on all fronts. A knight doesn't always have a groomsman— or a squire—to see to his mount." He handed the brush to the boy and gestured to the horse's tail, then stepped closer, clearly wondering why I had come.

"How many times have you had to brush out your own mount?" I asked, skeptical that it had truly ever occurred.

"More than you might imagine," he said, with no trace of guile. "Last year, my men and I served on the northern border, defending the republic from Pisa's advances. We lost enough men that every servant stepped forward to serve in the fight alongside us. 'Twas every man for himself when it came to finding food or caring for our mounts."

I took that in. I'd heard it had been a fierce fight that had gone on for several months—and during the coldest, wettest part of late winter. We had spoken of it around the Great Hall fire upon more than one occasion, thankful that it had been Firenze's fight, and not our own. But I had to admire Aurelio in that too. Clearly, he was not all the pampered prince I'd judged him to be.

"Are you here to see to your own mount, m'lady?"

"Nay," I said. "But I shall saddle him in a moment. I wondered, Lord Paratore, if you would care to join me on a secret mission."

"A secret mission?" He lifted a curious brow. "I am intrigued."

"When I was a little girl, Cook showed me a secret gooseberry patch. She believes the first crop of berries might be getting ripe as we speak and said if I went and fetched her enough, she'd make my favorite pie."

Aurelio nodded, holding back a smile. "That sounds like the most delectable sort of mission possible." He swallowed and then laughed. "I already salivate at the thought of the sweet and sour."

"As do I," I said with a grin. "Mayhap you and your squire would like to accompany me?" I could not yet make myself utter the boy's name.

"But m'lady," he paused, his lips twitching, "then we shall know the location of this secret patch."

I nodded gravely. "'Tis a test to see if you can keep such momentous knowledge to yourself, or if you are loose-tongued. If I can entrust you with this, mayhap I might entrust more to your care."

We smiled at each other, then, until I turned away. I moved toward Cardo's stall and reached for his saddle blanket, unhooked the gate, and went in, speaking in the low tones that quickly settled him.

"Finish that work on that tail, Rocco," Aurelio said. "We must accompany our lady on her most perilous mission, and I wish to appear every inch a suitable escort."

I hid another smile as I turned to take hold of Cardo's saddle and toss it across his back.

"I assume you wish to do this work yourself?" Aurelio asked, watching over the stall wall between us.

"Unless time is short, I do." I bent beneath Cardo's belly to retrieve the far strap. "When I was quite young, I accompanied my father on a hunt and saw a nobleman fall and break his neck because his groomsman had failed to properly buckle his saddle strap. Ever since, I have saddled my own horse."

He winced. "That is a tragic end to a life."

"Indeed. A terrible, senseless waste. I imagine that groomsman still thinks of his fallen lord every day."

"And likely had to find a new trade," he said with grim humor.

He moved off, then, to assist Rocco with the saddling of his mount, sending the boy off to see to his own horse so he could accompany us too. I couldn't help but think he wanted me to see he could do it on his own, and he did, in sharp fashion. In short order we were off, with Cook's wide berry basket tied and bouncing at Cardo's side.

I led Lord Paratore and Rocco north, across the creek, and skirting the edge of Castello Greco, up a narrow boar trail through the thick woods. This was prime hunting land for boar, because they loved the acorns the downy oaks all around us provided. Jays and doves preferred the acorns of the neighboring turkey oaks.

"Gall wasps nest in those turkey oaks," I told my companion. "My grandmother periodically leads us to harvest their cocoons to make ink."

"She is quite resourceful, your grandmother," he said.

"She is. She knows a great deal about the healing arts and history. And she has a fascination with Etruscan art."

"Etruscans, eh? I myself favor the Romans," he said. "I have obtained a few fine sculptures over the years for our palazzo in Firenze, as my father did before me."

I nodded amicably but hid my expression. I found the white, sightless eyes of Roman sculptures rather unsettling, but 'twas not a popular opinion. There were many men in the old city who salvaged and sold pieces of the ancient art, often grafting the head of one sculpture to another when it was missing . . . which unnerved me all the more.

"This manna ash is quite lovely come autumn," I said. "It can be anywhere from Forelli gold to Paratore scarlet."

"Then if all goes well, we should plant many more," he said.

I could feel my face heat at my somewhat flirtatious statement—as well as his response—and was glad he could not see it. I tried to imagine riding with him every day, for a lifetime, but could see no further than this day. So this day would have to be enough.

"Manna ash makes for good oars and masts," he said casually. "Has your father or uncle ever had woodsmen harvest it?"

"I am not aware of them doing so. Mayhap when I was much younger they did." Was he calculating his own future profits, should be become lord of these lands? "These woods have been intact for the past two decades, though the local farmers have permission to harvest any of our blackthorn to craft tools for their trade."

"That is generous of your uncle," he said.

"It is a kind gesture, but m'lord makes a good profit from their sharecropped lands. If he helps them improve on their production, he gains too. Adequate tools add to the effort."

He lifted his chin, as if taking in my perspective. "Does he enjoy good relationships with those who live on your lands?"

"Very good. They all attend our feasts, and my father and uncle often go to visit them. Do you have sharecroppers about your estates?"

"Our palazzo is in the center of the city, so nay. But we have two country manors to the north of the city, and I have had the pleasure of supping with each and every one of the farmers and vintners and shepherds that work Paratore lands."

I nodded, gratified to hear it. Again, I recognized why Papa might have entertained this young man's offer to take my hand. He seemed rather . . . honorable.

"May I ask you something, Lord Paratore?" I said, turning in my saddle to look at him.

"Anything, m'lady, as long as you would call me Aurelio." He gave me another gentle, encouraging smile.

I paused, considering this invitation to further intimacy. "How is it that you came to converse with my father, Aurelio?"

"As you know, your father and uncle came to Firenze, endeavoring to create more goodwill between our republics." He inclined his head to me. "Many in Firenze know of you, m'lady. Tales of your beauty and prowess with the bow are reminiscent of your mother's. Fiorentini are ready to vilify you in their tales, but to a man, they are also intrigued. What might the daughter and niece of the She-Wolves of Siena truly be like? That is what one and all wonder."

"And now that we have been well met? Will you vilify me as well?"

"Nay, never," he protested. "I have not detected a single reason to denigrate your reputation."

"You have only been with us a few days," I said with a smile. "Something that displeases you shall certainly arise."

"I find that I have neither friend nor foe that is entirely pleasurable or unpleasurable, m'lady," he replied. "No one is perfect. Or entirely imperfect. Everyone is simply . . . human."

I liked his words. Was he urging me to think the same? We rode on in silence. The man was surprising me, and I admitted to myself at last that I was glad that I had taken the risk to invite him along.

LUCIANA BETARRINI

Giulio and Ilaria Greco had been charged with outfitting us with weapons—a bow and arrows for me, a sword for Nico—and to train us how to better use them, as well as ride horses, somewhere we wouldn't be seen. Oh, and they'd also been tasked with teaching us some medieval dance moves.

Figuring out how to fight? I found assurance in that. Dancing? That made me as nervous as a mouse with a barn cat on the prowl.

Once we reached a secluded meadow about a half mile from the castello, we dismounted and untied our bundles of practice swords, bows and arrows, and a blanket and basket that I assumed was our picnic lunch. Or at least I hoped it was a picnic lunch, because my stomach was rumbling. Back home, I usually cruised through the NYU cafeteria for a *real* breakfast. A piece of whole wheat toast, some avocado mash, a couple of eggs, and some fruit every morning. Maybe some bacon, too, if I was going to practice. Here, they were clearly more about lunch and dinner. Breakfast had been nothing but some crusty bread and watered wine. "Breaking your fast" was clearly just a break. No full-on brunch.

"*Venga*," Guilio said. *Come.*

Nico and I followed Guilio and Ilaria to the far side of the meadow, near a border of trees, where we could set our supplies in the shade.

"You see to his initial training with the sword," Guilio said to Ilaria, "and I shall see to her initial training with the bow."

"Uhhh . . . I outweigh her by a good forty pounds." Nico's glance at Ilaria was appreciative, but kind of disparaging too.

"My sister could kill you in under three strikes, and that short sword is not even her preferred weapon." Guilio laughed. "Be on your guard. She is swift. You would do well to listen to her every instruction."

Nico lifted his hands. "Hey, I . . ." He began in English, apology written on his face. He switched to their Italian. "I meant no offense."

"None taken." Ilaria brushed past him with a mischievous smile. *"Prendi la spada, straniero." Pick up your sword, foreigner.*

He watched as she strode to the center of the meadow. Thigh-high grass waved in a light breeze and somehow made the summer heat a bit more bearable. Wisps of her brown, curly hair danced around her pretty face.

"M'lady said you were a decent shot. Are you?" Guilio turned to me, handing me a bow and quiver.

I pondered how to respond. "My ladies and I—back in Britannia—have been practicing for a while every day to pass the time. But I have never considered shooting in battle. It was only for . . . pleasure."

His eyes narrowed as if my response puzzled him. Belatedly, I realized that everyone in this era would have at least thought about using their weapons in battle. Because, sooner or later, it seemed everyone was at war. "By the time we are through, you might not consider it a pleasure." He turned to pick up the extra quivers and tossed me a leather wrist guard.

I caught it. "What do you mean?"

"Archers who draw and shoot as many as we are about to do oft find themselves with a sore shoulder, arm, and fingers, come nightfall."

Yeah, well, I'm tougher than I look, buddy. "We shall see."

Without another word, he turned and led me toward a tree that had split into two trunks at the level of his chest, then conjoined again above at about the height of his head. I noted I was not the first to use it as target practice. The tree had born the piercing of many arrows.

Guilio patted it. "As you can see, 'tis a perfect target. Many a man's chest is about right here," he said, gesturing to the hole. He moved toward me. "Now let us see how many of your ghostly foes you might dispatch to heaven or hell."

I strapped on the wrist guard, picked up my bow, and drew my first arrow.

"Shoot your first ten, m'lady," he said gently.

But I could feel his eyes, studying my stance, the way I drew my arrow. It made me nervous. Back home, at work at Castello Forelli, I could hit the center three rings of our painted-hay targets ninety-percent of the time. But as I let my first arrow fly, I groaned inwardly. It went high and to the right.

Guilio said nothing.

The next went low and left. *Overcompensating.*

Again he said nothing.

My third-through-seventh arrows hit various parts of the trunk. My eighth went through the hole, and I breathed a sigh of relief, even as my face flamed with frustration and embarrassment. But then I got another through. Overconfident and wanting to impress him, I sent the last winging through the air without giving myself enough time to properly aim. It made it through, but only because it bounced off the edge of one side.

I dared to look at him.

His hand stroked the stubble of his dimpled, well-formed chin, as he seemed to be considering me. Everything about me, it felt like, from head to toe. "Good," he said. He picked up the other quiver and brought it to me, even though I wasn't through with the first. "Resume your stance," he said, taking a few steps back.

I did as he bid.

"Down a bit on your left hip," he said, and it was as if I could feel his eyes on my hip like it was a touch. "Are you lifting to your toes?"

"Uh, mayhap."

"Keep your foot flat and bend a little at the knee. Keep loose."

"I shall."

"Now draw."

I nocked an arrow and pulled back on the string. He came closer, his body and head six inches from mine—terribly close, and yet consciously not touching.

"Hold it," he instructed, clearly about my stance even as I had a hard time thinking about anything but his, shadowing mine.

I tried to keep my position, but in seconds it was obvious I was struggling. My arm trembled.

"Release a bit of pressure," he said, still clearly concentrating, a foot away, his eyes tracing my body again, clearly utterly unaware how his attention was undoing me. "You only need to get the arrow through the hole, not send it all the way into the woods beyond."

I did as he bid.

His fingers tapped my right scapula, with all the interest of an eighty-year-old professor. "Your shoulder is almost in proper position, but not quite right. Lower it a bit."

I shifted, chastising myself for being so affected by his touch. How many times had my master touched and moved me physically in order to show me the nuance of a jiu jitsu move? Thousands. It only took a fraction of an inch to be off, to fail. And yet the master's touch had been perfunctory, all business. With Guilio, while he seemed entirely on task, there was something so warm between us, it was hard to ignore.

"Now," he said, and I released the arrow.

It went through the hole. High and to the right, but through!

"Good. Again," he said, handing me another arrow. He pointed to my diaphragm. "I want you to concentrate on breathing there. It shall keep your stance steadier. And right before you let your arrow fly, release your breath, rather than hold it." He moved away, while I tried to remember his instructions.

I steadied my breathing, lowered my scapula, and kept my foot grounded. Remembering not to pull back the string so far, I aimed, exhaled, and the next arrow sailed neatly through the hole.

"Well done," he said approvingly. I smiled until he continued, "Now let us do that a hundred times more."

By the time we were through those hundred arrows, I couldn't really tell if Guilio was irritated by this assignment to see to my instruction or if he was kind of into it. I got alternating vibes from him. But as I shifted to Ilaria for some instruction on horsemanship in a sidesaddle—the most ridiculous invention ever—I could tell what was really irritating the sibs. They wanted to know the truth about us.

After circling her twenty times, Ilaria finally allowed me to slow and asked, "How is it, m'lady, that you are older than I and yet not well used to such a saddle, let alone riding a horse?"

I thought about that. "In Britannia, our village is very small. We can walk to the—the *market*, church, and our friends' homes. If we cannot walk, we ride in wagons, as we did here, before we were robbed."

She looked at me, puzzled. "But wagons are most uncomfortable for a great distance."

I uttered a laugh, trying to buy myself some time. Were there alternatives? "Indeed. If only I could be borne on a litter, as Cleopatra once was! As much as I tell my brother I should be treated as a queen, he fails to oblige me."

She smiled at me, all dimpled, olive-skinned beauty, but I could see it didn't add up in her head. She suspected I didn't tell her the truth. As did her brother. He'd asked me more about me and my ladies shooting for "pleasure." I'd tried to pass it off, playing the All-Girl card. "Do ladies here not do the same? Leaving warfare to their men?"

But those dark-blue eyes had shifted over mine for a moment, measuring me, penetrating to my soul—as if he could see that I neither trod in the light of truth, nor the dark of a lie, but in the gray between. I'd had to concoct a reason to move away before I was telling him the whole crazy story.

Because the temptation was real. I knew, inherently, that I could trust these two. Guilio and Ilaria were willing to give up all for the Forellis, do anything they asked. Such soulful friends, I'd never encountered. Later, as we ate our picnic lunch of preserved meats, cheeses, bread, and dried fruits, I looked over at Guilio.

I gestured in the direction of Castello Greco. "So Aurelio Paratore's bid for Tiliani's hand might require you to give up your claim to your father's castle? Are you willing to do that?"

Guilio bit into a hunk of bread and chewed. Swallowing, he said, "I am. As are Chiara and Ilaria." Ilaria nodded in assent.

"Why?" Nico asked.

"Might you tell us?" I hurriedly added, trying to soften some of his blunt question. "It seems a great deal to relinquish."

Guilio cocked his head and thought a moment, then looked to Ilaria, as if seeking her permission. "We have long resided at Castello Forelli. Our elder sister too. It simply seemed . . . better to be with the Forellis."

Ilaria finished a dried apricot and smiled. "A castle is only a home if it is filled with family, friends. Without them, it's but a fortress. We have a life with the Forellis, in their castello. They are ours, as we are theirs."

I thought about that for a moment. Of a home filled with family and friends. Of making a life with them forever. Of claiming others as my own, and them claiming me. But the thought of it left me feeling depressed. Because here, now, seeing what they all had together?

It seemed farther from my reach than ever.

9

LUCIANA BETARRINI

For the fifth straight day, we rode to the clearing in the woods and commenced practice on mounting, dismounting, walking, and trotting. Then we spent an hour practicing with our weapons. And finally, we finished with an hour of dance lessons. Because we were all apparently heading out to Siena in a few days, where there'd be a lot of dancing, and even our Britannia-born cover story would not excuse us for not knowing rudimentary steps.

Not that I was complaining about all this time with Guilio. One-on-one time with one of the most intriguing knights in the castle? It was every medieval-major's dream. The fact that he was dreamy to look at was just an added bonus. And yet I got the sense that while they seemed to like us, they kept us at arm's length. As Tiliani's closest guardians, they clearly didn't like being out of the loop. Not that they could deal with it if they knew. No one was really prepared to hear that someone they were hanging out with was from another time, let alone another country that hadn't even been discovered yet. While the Vikings had likely made landfall by now, Columbus was still about a hundred-plus years from his voyage.

Nico and I had a hard time believing it was real ourselves. That we were here. Talking and interacting with people who'd been dead for seven hundred years.

But today, as Giulio took me in his arms and looked so intently at me, stubble accentuating his square jaw and the shadow beneath his defined cheekbones, I decided he was *very* much alive. I smiled as we moved through the steps, Ilaria counting loudly, and I succeeded in not messing up until we were halfway through. "All right, all right," I muttered to myself in English. "I've got this."

"*Ancora*," I said, quietly demanding we go again.

Ilaria had just resumed her counting when Lord Paratore came riding into our clearing, followed by Valentino and their young squire.

"What is this?" Aurelio asked, pulling up on the reins of his horse. The big stallion danced beneath him, as if eager to move on.

We all looked at one another.

"A picnic," Ilaria said casually, stepping forward. "Why are *you* here, m'lord?"

He squinted at her. "We heard the noise and came to investigate." He clearly wasn't fooled. His green eyes flicked over each of us.

"We thought to teach a few of our local dances to these northerners," Giulio said lightly. "We do not wish for them to embarrass the house of Forelli in Siena."

Seriously. The capacity for embarrassment might be epic, I thought. But I was unnerved by Aurelio's suspicious look. His eyes roved over our weapons, including the wooden sparring swords, by the horses.

"Do the Forellis know this is transpiring?"

Giulio cast him a half smile. "We do nothing without our lady's permission or direction. But man to man, would you want everyone to know of every enjoyable interlude you had, m'lord?"

My heart fluttered—actually fluttered—at those words. *Nah, he's just saying that to throw the guy off.*

"Nay, I think not," Aurelio returned with his own half smile.

He nodded at us. "Carry on." He wheeled his stallion around to depart.

But just then a warning trumpet sounded from the direction of Castello Forelli.

As one, everyone with us pivoted toward it.

"Is it Firenze?" Giulio barked at Lord Paratore, striding toward him, his face a mask of fury and suspicion.

"Upon my life, 'tis not the Fiorentini," he said, fist to chest.

"Then 'tis likely the Perugians," Giulio said tersely to Ilaria. He grabbed my hand and hustled me to my mare. There, he took my waist in his big hands and lifted me to the sidesaddle, then swiftly set my slippered feet in the stirrup and passed me the reins.

"Mayhap our lords' negotiations did not go as planned," Ilaria said, holding Nico's mare's reins while he mounted.

"Or enraged them," Aurelio put in. "The Perugians know that if Siena is in peace talks with Firenze, then the battle lines might eventually draw closer."

Neither of the siblings responded. They turned to Nico and me.

"Return to the safety of the castello at once." Giulio's tone was a blend of plea and demand.

"Do not tarry," Ilaria added. "They shall close the gates in short order."

And then they moved to their own horses, swiftly mounted, and disappeared among the trees and brush, Aurelio, Captain Valeri, and the squire right behind them.

"Whoa," Nico said.

I didn't know if he was managing his horse or commenting on what had just gone down.

Three more trumpet blasts sounded, in quick succession. Calling others back to the castello? Did everyone but us know what it meant, like some sort of medieval Morse code?

I glanced around the clearing and the woods, with afternoon sunlight streaming down, penetrating the dense upper tree canopy.

The sudden quiet was more than a little creepy. Even the birds were silent. My mare pranced left, then right, as if unnerved too.

"This is our chance, Nico. We could make it to the tombs now and hightail it home."

"No, not yet, Luci. It's too soon. There's too much I want to see, learn. Don't you?"

"I don't know," I confessed, a shiver of fear running down my back. There was an odd pull for me to stay. The startling clan-like connection between the Forellis and Grecos that drew me. As soon as Gabriella and Evangelia knew who we were, we became theirs, in a way. And as fellow time travelers, we were connected in a manner that I'd never experienced with any other family member, even Mom. It was in their eyes, their touch. I *did* want to know more of their story and what they had learned over the years. Why they elected to remain.

But as the horn blared again, I realized we were in danger. As in, *you-could-die* danger. I remembered Giulio's stern warning as well as Lia's reminder that this was a time of hand-to-hand, mortal combat. "If we're not going back home, we should at least get back to the castello," I said, urging my mare forward.

"Or . . ."

I knew that tone. I glared over my shoulder at him and pulled up on the reins. "No. Absolutely not. Four-and-a-half days of training does not make us ready for the dance floor, let alone real battle."

"Come on, Luci. Wouldn't you just like to see what this is all about? And if they do go to battle, what it's like?" he cajoled. "Think about it. Watching would be kind of like continuing our training. There's nothing worse than a surprised soldier. We need to know what we'll be facing."

"No, Nico. We can go to the castle and see what we can see from the walls. That's it." Since he wasn't moving, I headed off in the direction of the castello, hoping he'd give in and follow. "Come on, Nico. We need to hurry!"

I glanced back at him, and for just a sec, he looked as good as any of the knights—until the mare began fighting her reins, and he got a little wobbly in his seat.

But his attention was not on his mount. It was on me. "You go back. I'm going to find a place where I can watch." He held a palm up. "From a safe distance."

"Absolutely not!" I circled my mare back toward him. "You know as well as I do that where you go, I go too. Together is the way we got here. And it's the only way we're going to get out."

"You can't be ready to leave yet," he argued. "What about the fact that you've ditched the headaches since we've been here? How you wanted to figure out why? What about all the things we haven't explored yet? *Living* medieval history rather than just reading about it?"

"I am," I admitted slowly. *And more than a little interested in getting to know Giulio of the Big Blue Eyes better.* "But I don't want to die either."

"Yeah, I'm not so much into dying," he said with an irritatingly cavalier smile. "But what if we don't?" He edged his mare closer. "We've learned the basics with our weapons, but we didn't show the Grecos what else we could do if we added some of our jiu jitsu."

"Not that we will," I rejoined. "Because we're not actually going to enter hand-to-hand *combat*. That would be idiotic, Nico. These guys have been training since they were kids. We have half a summer's acting experience 'using weapons' and four days of actual training."

"Right. But what if we went and saw what hand-to-hand combat looked like? A little live history lesson? And don't you kinda want to see Giulio and Ilaria in action? They've been holding back on us. What would they be like going full-out?"

I heaved a sigh and looked to the woods. "From a safe distance?"

"Definitely," Nico said, a grin splitting his face.

I hated giving him this. Knew, deep down, it was probably a mistake. But he'd landed on the last thing I thought would change my mind.

Giulio in action.

"I have zero willpower," I muttered to myself, following Nico out of the clearing and down the road. Because despite my best intentions, I wanted to see all six feet of that man doing what he'd been trained to do since he was three feet high.

10

TILIANI FORELLI

Aurelio pulled alongside as we cantered down the road.
"M'lady, would you permit me to move in your stead?"
he asked.

I tried to stifle a laugh. "And what? Return to the castello? Pick up my needlework?"

He bit back a look of irritation. "I merely seek to ensure your safety."

"M'lord, you have much to learn of our ways," I said. "I suspect that my mother and aunt shall meet us ahead. You suggest I not join them?"

His face slackened. "Even in their advanced years?"

"I would not doubt it." I moved into a gallop, finding any further word with the man agitating. My skin prickled as we saw clouds of dust rising in the distance and heard another warning trumpet. Troops were amassing along our southeast border.

Over the years, Giulio, Ilaria, my cousins, and I had experienced our fair share of skirmishes. But primarily with the Fiorentini, riding south to seek us out as if dared to do so. 'Twas like a rite of passage, to face Castello Forelli and live to tell about it. They seemed to particularly relish meeting me or Ilaria in battle. She and I became more adept in our fighting skills because of it, and I was thankful for all those trials now as we crested a hill and pulled up.

Because there were close to two hundred men on the Umbrian hills. Far more men than we had ever encountered. A mile out, dust rose. How many more Perugians approached?

Fortino and Benedetto rode up with six other knights.

I eyed Fortino briefly before turning back to the troops before us. "Mama and Zia Gabi?" I asked.

"They shall arrive shortly," he said, a little breathless. "Keep your patrol on my left flank, Tiliani, no matter what happens. Benedetto, keep yours on my right. And follow my lead. Lord Paratore, please stay on my cousin's far flank."

"You may count on me, sir."

It agitated me, hearing Fortino assign me "protection," but as Marcello's heir apparent, 'twas his duty to lead us all in our fathers' absence. I turned to see who was rising to the trumpet's call. The castello's contingent of sixty knights had mustered and were already in line, looking formidable, with many riding destriers and in metal armor and helmets. But the others who were gathering were mostly local farmers and vineyard keepers, loyal to us. Some carried swords and wore old leather chest armor, but a fair number carried pitchforks or sharpened lances, as well as crudely made wooden shields. The nearest allied castle—Monteriggioni—was several hours' ride away. Siena was almost a day's ride.

"Our mothers dispatched riders to Siena, as well as Monteriggioni, to aid us," Fortino said as if reading my thoughts.

I hoped that no Perugian spotted them. Killing scouts and messengers was a swift way to assure victory.

Mama and Zia Gabi arrived then, looking regal in matched battle finery that I had not seen in years. They wore split skirts—wide enough to almost appear as one when they rode astride—ivory shirts made of the finest silk, shimmering in the sun, and dark-blue tunics, heavily embroidered with gold. Against the blue backdrop was the image of a wolf. Together, they were magnificent, and it thrilled me to see them take command. Looking about, I knew I was not alone.

But then I hesitated and looked to the crowd of enemy soldiers.

"M'ladies, where are m'lords?" Giulio asked, edging closer and voicing my own thoughts. We'd expected them to be riding to join us, as was customary.

"They have yet to return," Mama said grimly, her blue eyes shifting over to the men amassing on the far hill. Between us, the valley floor was our border.

A chill ran down my back, and I searched the Umbrian hills for any sign of what she and my aunt did—prisoners.

"Do you see a flag?" Mama asked quickly. "Any sign of a nobleman?"

"There!" Fortino said, pointing.

The crowd of knights split, and eight horsemen moved forward in pairs. Six knights. And at the end, two men, hunched over, barely keeping their seats.

Zia Gabi's face twisted with rage. She tugged her gelding into a tight turn and came alongside Aurelio.

"The Fiorentini have nothing to do with this?" she bit out, leaning toward him.

"Nay, m'lady!"

"They are not planning an attack in concert with the Perugians?"

"Nay!" His nostrils flared, and a blush of frustration rose at his neckline. "Upon my life, I am here to secure peace."

Her eyes shifted over his for a moment. Then she turned to the men on her right. "Francesco and Agostino, take four men and ride for our northern border. Get to the heights and make certain we do not have other enemies closing in on us while we are distracted here. Lord Paratore may have been purposely duped, and we do not want any surprises."

"Yes, m'lady," Francesco said, immediately turning to do as she bid.

I swallowed back my fear. I hated to see six men go when we were so outnumbered. But I could see the wisdom of it. We had to know exactly what we were facing.

"Gabi." Mama drew her sister's attention.

The men in front had lifted a white flag. They were ready to talk.

"Tiliani, Fortino, you ride with us," Zia Gabi said swiftly. "Keep your eyes on me and Lia. Do not look at either your father or your uncle. We shall attend them when we can. But this enemy means to use them to dissuade us from fighting. Remember that battle is as much a mental game as a physical one. You must pretend that no matter what we witness—*no matter what we witness*," she repeated, "it has no effect on us. Do you understand me?"

"We do," we said together.

"Lord Paratore, Captain Valeri," she said, turning toward them, "if we are attacked, follow Lord Greco and Sir Benedetto's lead. Is that clear? You follow and come to their aid. They will best know how to proceed, knowing our unique battle strategies."

She did not wait for them to give her their assent. She wheeled her horse, and Lia, Fortino, and I fell into formation with her, with two knights—Mama and Lia's principal guardians, Celso and Lutterius—behind us.

"Have they killed the men who accompanied Papa and Zio Marcello?" I asked tenuously. I knew the kindly, silver-haired Captain Mancini had ridden out with them. As had Carlo. Armando. Benito . . .

"Let us hope they were taken prisoner," Mama said, her face lined with consternation, "not killed."

I blanched. Papa and Zio Marcello had ridden out with but twelve knights, given that it was a diplomatic mission, approaching a relatively peaceful neighbor. But among them were six of our most senior, seasoned fighting men. I tried to imagine them being taken. Had there been a fight? Or had they been forced to relinquish their weapons upon arriving at Castello Fortebraccio and then been overtaken?

I tried not to look at their hunched forms. The way Papa began to slide off his saddle, as if he fought to stay conscious. Or how Zio

Marcello reached out to right him. I remembered Mama's words and stared at the two men in the front of the group, Lords Fortebraccio and Belluci. Those with Perugian estates closest to our border. Lord Fortebraccio was older than my father, Lord Belluci about ten years my senior, his father having passed a year ago.

Mama and Zia Gabi pulled up. Fortino and I rode forward to flank them.

"You have committed an act of war, attacking our husbands," Mama said.

Lord Belluci said nothing, merely untied a bundle and let it unfurl in his hands. It was bloody, but clearly it was a horse blanket with the emblem of Castello Forelli—a triangle of gold. "My men were attacked on the Western road two days past. All six were murdered, but they managed to take down two of your knights. So you can imagine we were not eager to welcome your lords with open arms."

I frowned. No men had been reported missing and all patrols had reported on time for the past week.

"We faced similar losses," Lord Fortebraccio declared. "Six men on patrol, brutally slain. They managed to kill only one of yours, but we, too, have evidence."

Zia Gabi was shaking her head, looking to Fortino and me for verification. "We have lost no one. No patrols have returned with any reports other than peace."

"'Tis impossible," sneered Lord Belucci. "Twelve men do not go down without a significant fight. There had to be Forelli men returning, injured. Three who did not return at all!"

"It is possible if they were not our men at all," Mama said evenly.

"They were yours," Lord Fortebraccio said. "The patrol that came upon our slain brothers said Sir Ercole was among them."

I felt the blood drain from my face as Mama paused. When the fierce, young knight had cornered a maid in a turret and made untoward advances, I had gone to my parents. He was a valuable man, but such action was never tolerated at Castello Forelli.

"Sir Ercole was dismissed a sennight past," she said. "As I am certain my husband informed you."

"He did," Fortebraccio allowed, lifting his chin. "But we found the claim rather . . . convenient."

"By rights, we could have taken your husbands' lives," Lord Belluci said.

"But we elected to spare them as an act of mercy," Lord Fortebraccio's tone was almost pompous.

"Sorely abusing innocent men is not *mercy*," Mama said, her gelding sidestepping, agitated. "'Tis torture. An act of war."

Zia Gabi lifted her voice. "As is assembling en masse."

"We cannot abide such atrocities," Lord Fortebraccio said.

"And we hear that you are treating with the Fiorentini," Belucci looked up the hillside to where Aurelio remained, his scarlet horse blanket and tunic easily seen. "You intend to pledge your daughter's hand?"

Mama raised her chin. "That remains our daughter's choice."

"If Lady Tiliani is to wed, I again offer my son's own hand," Lord Fortebraccio said. "Let us sit and discuss."

I bit my lip. He'd been one of my first suitors—on behalf of his young son. I found him overbearing. And more than a little interested in proving his masculinity by reminding me of my proper place, which he'd told me in no uncertain terms would be in the castello, bearing as many babes as the Lord chose to grant us. At least Aurelio was not like him . . .

"Lord Fortebraccio, you have severely beaten her father and his cousin," Mama said. "We would not pledge our daughter to your house, even if your son was the last man on earth."

The man's eyes shifted to me as I gave him a glare that I hoped echoed every one of her words. "And yet you would ally with Firenze? After all your family has endured at *their* hands? How many hundreds of your people were lost to them? How many thousands among the Sienese?"

There was a moment of silence before Mama spoke. "We have been at peace for some twenty years."

"And yet surely it has not been forgotten."

"There remains the fact that our men were murdered—" Belucci persisted.

"By an interloper," Zia Gabi interjected. "One who wished to sow unrest between us. A vindictive act. Show us the bodies of those you killed. We shall see if we know any of them."

"The survivors carried off their bodies," Lord Fortebraccio said. "We only managed to capture the horses of those slain."

"And they have the Forelli brand?" Zia Gabi said.

"They did," Belucci said.

She shook her head and glanced at Mama, then back at him. "'Tis a forgery. There is no other explanation. Again, we are not missing any men or horses."

"Mayhap it was not your own, but an act designed to divide us and force you further into the Fiorentinis' arms," Belucci allowed. "Are you certain there is not a new wolf abiding in the She-Wolves' den, m'lady?"

Zia Gabi followed his gaze up the hill to Aurelio. I fought not to do the same. She returned a cold stare to the younger lord. "There is not. I give you my word."

His jaw muscle tightened as his stallion danced beneath him. "Alas, m'lady," he said, "we can no longer take you at your word. We must act on evidence. And evidence tells us that Castello Forelli must be put back in her place."

I grimaced. Belucci was as vindictive as Fortebraccio. I'd spurned his suit as well, finding him mean-spirited. My eyes ran across the men beyond and around us. These were not merely Perugian forces; there were mercenaries among them. Someone was backing them. Venezia? Pisa?

"'Tis time for someone to remind Siena that her outposts are not invincible," Lord Belluci declared. "Take your wounded and prepare yourselves. Today, we fight. May God's hand be upon the favored."

LUCIANA BETARRINI

Nico and I army-crawled through the grass to a small cliff near where most of the action seemed to be going down.

"Do you think that's . . . ?" I said.

"I do," he returned.

Frozen, we watched as Fortino and Tiliani led their fathers' mounts slowly down the hill, away from the attackers, back to the assembled knights. Evangelia and Gabriella followed behind, looking as regal and fierce as the old tales made them out to be. The two men were bloody and barely keeping their seats. Marcello clutched his belly, while Luca leaned over and bounced with each step his steed took. Lady Adri and Chiara made their way to the center of the mass, and the group conferred. We watched as they each took one of the mount's reins in hand and led the wounded men out, clearly taking them back to the castle where they could see to their injuries. No others rode with them; not another knight could likely be spared, facing the masses across the valley. On the far hills, the enemy rumbled to a roar, their captains apparently psyching them up for go-time.

Without further pause, men began to run down toward our side—*when had I started to think about these people as ours?*—and Evangelia shouted, bringing archers forward. They knelt in a line, pointed their bows upward and, on her mark, loosed their arrows as one. The arrows had not yet reached the apex of their arc when they again drew, letting another volley fly, and then still another.

I watched in mute horror as the arrows, gaining velocity as they fell, pierced shoulder, eye, and leg of more than thirty of the charging soldiers. Lia's archers drew again and again as horsemen charged, making their way around and between the foot soldiers. Horses were pierced as well as their riders, sending them stumbling and tumbling, tossing up great clods of dirt.

Our knights ran down to their attackers, never pausing, meeting those on the ground. The clash of swords, war cries, and shrieks of pain filled the valley. Castello Forelli was outnumbered at least two to one. "Nico . . ."

"I know!" he interrupted. "We have to go help them, Luci."

"No! That's not what I meant," I said, watching as one knight whirled and cut off another's head. I turned away, fighting the urge to vomit. Had I really just seen *that*? "We need to go, Nico. And I mean go *home*. Right now," I told him. "No one is watching us."

"What?" He gaped at me. "We can't leave now! They need help!"

I gripped his arm. "We aren't ready for this!" I grimaced as I heard a man scream in agony. He sounded close, but I could not bear to look. "This isn't a history lesson anymore! There is no get-rich-quick scheme for you here. We have to get out of here!"

He stared at me in disappointment. "Luci, this is family. *Our* family."

"They are not really our family," I returned. "Distant cousins, if that." The words felt hollow in my mouth, and I admitted the lie to myself. But I was desperate. If we were dead, what good was discovering some semblance of family ties?

"And yet we're close enough to share the special gene that landed us all here," Nico said, voice taut. "That's close enough for me." He moved as if to rise, and I yanked him back down. He pulled away and looked back at the battlefield. "How can we not help them? Look at them, Luci! Look at what's happening!"

Taking a deep breath, I followed his gaze. Knights were down across the field. Some were dead, many more wounded. I had to swallow back bile when I saw a man clutching his midsection, intestines spilling to the ground.

This was not the era of drone bombers, strategically taking out key targets. This was the era of slow annihilation, one terrible blow or strike at a time. Or horrifically slow bleed-outs.

"Look over there."

I saw where he pointed. Tiliani and Giulio were back-to-back, fighting off two men. Evangelia had moved to a higher point and still directed archers about her, even as she herself aimed, taking one enemy after another down. But I gasped as I spotted Gabriella, not far below us, and saw an archer rise from behind a boulder and pierce her shoulder at close range. The force of it sent her flipping over the back left flank of her gelding.

"We did not come here to die!" I tried once more, clinging to Nico's arm as he bolted to his feet again.

"Then let's not." He shook me off and drew his sword. "Cover me?"

"You overestimate my aim," I growled in half desperation, half fury. But I had no choice other than to follow him partway down the bank, hurriedly drawing on my wrist guard and nocking an arrow.

He was moving through the rocks, dagger in hand, intent on sneaking up on two knights fighting a soldier from Castello Forelli. I figured he was going after the closest, so I aimed at the other. My hand trembled, and I bit back a curse. If I trembled too much, would I pierce the wrong person?

Who was I kidding? I was not Evangelia Forelli, She-Wolf. I had maybe a tenth of her skill.

But there was no further time for doubt. Nico leaped onto the back of the closest knight, hooking his arm around the guy's throat. Surprised, the man hesitated, and a Forelli man stabbed him in the leg.

My arrow was already in flight. It glanced off the other knight's thick, leather arm pad.

"Well, that's just going to make him mad," I muttered, angry at myself for missing.

He shouted to his right, gesturing up at me, calling for someone to kill me. I nocked another arrow as Nico took care of him with a basic takedown. But my eyes were on two men, already making their way up the boulders, and an archer, kneeling to take aim at me. I got a little lower between the rocks for cover, waited for one to reach for the next handhold, and let my arrow fly.

This one hit its target. The man stumbled to his right, hand clutching his neck.

My mind was trying to register what I was doing, but Ilaria and Giulio had drilled me well. I immediately drew another arrow, concentrating on my next adversary still running in my direction, his face a grim mask of determination.

I sensed the arrow a second before I heard it, narrowly ducking in time. I tried to rise, take aim again, but yet another arrow was flying my way. It whizzed past my head, so close I felt it part the air. I forced myself not to obey instinct and cower, focusing instead on shooting my own arrow. I saw it glance off my attacker's metal helmet—now just thirty feet away—before I ducked back down. I winced and shied as an arrow struck a rock a few inches to my right.

I crept around the boulder, well aware I needed to find a new position or the archer would just keep me pinned until the other was on me. I slid through a narrow crevice, pulling my quiver and bow behind me, trying to stay low. Nocking another arrow, I moved around the giant rock, listening for telltale sounds of the knight's approach over the din of the battle below. Another arrow skittered to the rocks where I had been before. Heart pounding, I moved around the far side, getting ready to fire as soon as I had a target—

And discovered a man three feet away, trying to sneak up on me.

I had two choices—fall back and try and fire or go on the attack. With so little room between us, my self-defense training kicked in. *Sometimes, the best defense is offense,* my coach had always said. With the fiercest cry I could muster, I dropped my bow and sprung at him, grabbing hold of the wrist of his hand that held a dagger.

I crashed into him, and with a grunt, he fell back against a mid-sized rock, his momentum slamming his head hard enough to send his helmet rolling off. I turned and rammed my elbow under his chin, sending his head back against the rock again, and he slackened and slid to the ground. Sliding his dagger in my belt, I searched for my brother, ducking as another arrow came my way.

When I dared to take another look, I found him and gasped. A huge knight had Nico by the throat and was choking him. Try as Nico might, the other had him by weight and position. I started running, sliding, crawling across the rocks, ignoring the arrows that continued to whizz by my head, concentrating only on my brother.

No, no, no!

There were but several strides left between us. I hopped from one boulder to the next, letting gravity aid my momentum, and went flying, catching the man around the neck and dragging him off Nico, even though he probably was twice as big as I was. He landed on top of me and continued rolling, but I stayed with him, arm around his neck. He got to his feet, and I clung to his back, monkey-like, squeezing his neck as hard as I could between my bicep and forearm, willing him to unconsciousness.

"Nico!" I ground out. "A little help!"

I glanced back, but Nico was on his hands and knees, still gasping for breath.

The big man was clawing at my arm. If I hadn't had the protective arm guard on, he would've likely drawn blood. Finally, he passed out and crumpled, landing partially on top of me again.

With some effort, I pushed him off, ran back to Nico, and helped him to his feet. I grabbed his sword and placed it in his hand—watching with rising concern as he still gasped for breath. Had his attacker damaged his windpipe? I turned quickly, putting myself between anyone else and my brother, but for the moment, we were not the target. Valentino and Tiliani were clearly under siege, however. Each was fighting off two men.

I looked up to the rocks, where I'd left my bow and arrows, but knew there wasn't enough time. Wrapping my fingers around a dagger, I charged toward Tiliani, screaming at her attackers to leave her alone, only dimly registering I did so in English. It was basic trash talk, but in a universally understood tone.

One of the knights turned from Valentino, stepping into my path and wiping his lip of sweat with the back of his gloved hand. He huffed a laugh as he circled me.

"*Piccola ragazza,*" he sneered, "*vuoi morire o qualcosa?*" *Little girl, do you want to die?*

With that, he swung his giant sword.

I leaned back, and as soon as it passed, I straightened and charged into his chest, hands up before me like a boxer.

My move startled him. I grabbed his sword arm and rammed it—hyperextending the elbow—forcing him to drop the sword, then slammed my head back into his nose. With my other hand, I plunged my dagger beneath his leather chest shield. "*Non oggi,*" I said under my breath, pulling the weapon loose, trying to ignore the warmth and wetness that came with it. *Not today.*

I didn't wait to find out how badly he was injured. I concentrated on Tiliani, who had taken a blow to her chest shield, slicing it almost in half, and had staggered back. Again, I ran toward them, calling to them, trying to get one of them off of her, even as she belatedly raised a sword, narrowly parrying her attacker's blow. He struck again, and she was a half second late in her defense.

That was when Valentino reached her. It was he who blocked the next strike, bending backward against the force of it. He who drove her assailant back a few steps. The other Perugian knight moved to take his place, but I rammed into his ribcage at the same time as grabbing his legs, which brought him down. I scrambled to lean all my body weight into my knee, now atop his neck, while twisting his arm behind him, so that he couldn't use it to rise.

Panting for breath, I took stock. Our forces were waning, and still the Perugians came. We weren't going to outlast them. Three advanced on me now, and for the first time, I wondered if I had the strength to take them on. The adrenaline was fading. But then, in quick succession, they were each pierced by an arrow. I followed the arrows' path to Lia and another archer, who stood partially behind a boulder, continuing to fire as a squire handed them arrows. I stared at her, stunned.

She really was like some sort of freakin' medieval warrior queen. She-Wolf? More like She-Lioness! But at some point, the arrows would run out. Her blue eyes met mine, and she seemed to be of the same mind. We were outnumbered. Arrows were running short. And our strength even shorter.

Nico was beside me as Lia called for retreat—for everyone to fall back to the castle. He kicked my captive's nose, and I cringed as I heard it break, though I recognized the importance. We needed as few chasing us as possible. "C'mon, sis." He grunted, grabbing my arm and yanking me to my feet. "Time to go."

"*Now* you want to go," I quipped.

I hoped this meant he was done—that we were heading back to the tomb and our real home, but as men limped and ran toward Castello Forelli, I realized most were already ahead of us. Nico and I were essentially on the front line, among the last to retreat. Tiliani was on the back of Aurelio's horse, her dark-blond hair streaming behind as the mare struggled to run up the hill, carrying two. Lia was gone. Fortino and Benedetto too.

I fought panic as Nico and I began running in earnest, well aware that fresh forces had arrived, chasing after us. For the first time I wondered: if we were taken, what would become of us?

But then Giulio and Ilaria came back down the hill on horseback, each of them extending a hand for us. Giulio's blood-spattered arm reached for mine, and I did not hesitate. Could I really feel the breath of our enemies breathing down my neck? I swung up behind him and hadn't even quite landed before he urged his mount up the hill.

"You came back for us!" I cried, still trying to get a better seat without squeezing my legs too much. "Grazie!"

"Do not thank us," he replied. "Thank Lady Tiliani."

He sounded a little disgruntled, and my romantic dreams

disintegrated to a crashing, burning heap. *So much for the hero riding in for the rescue,* I thought. Not that I ever wanted to be the whole damsel in distress, but well, whatever. Nothing about medieval battle had been anything like I had imagined anyway. It was not neat and orderly, the *Three Musketeers* sort of swordplay I'd imagined. It was all guts and blood and sweat and panting and dirt and fight-to-the-death.

I looked over my shoulder, clinging to Giulio as tightly as I dared, trying not to squeeze his gelding with my legs and yet not fall off either. Men limped along, hurrying through the underbrush of the woods, all trying to reach the sanctuary of the castle before they would have to bar the gates. Perugians were already clearing the top of the hill and tearing through the woods behind them. How many would make it in time?

C'mon, you guys! I thought desperately. *Faster!* And in that moment, I was taken aback by how much I cared. How worried I was about them.

Because somehow, in battling beside them, I had sort of become *one* with them.

11

TILIANI FORELLI

"Take those men down!" I screamed to every man in sight. "Those without bows, throw stones!"

I ran down the alure, keeping the parapets between me and enemy archers already returning fire, repeating my commands over and over. "Give our people time! Keep the enemy back! Drive them back!"

"Be ready at the gates!" bellowed my cousin Benedetto, on the opposite wall across the gate. With some relief, I saw my mother was with him, the only one of our elders still standing. Fortino was with them too. Below, men assembled at either one of the massive doors, ready for their lady's command to shut and bar them.

If we were too early, we'd lock out some of our people.

If we were too late, the enemy might gain entry.

I pulled up at the end of the alure, crowded with knights, arrows drawn. I gasped for breath, watching as our people streamed through. *Please, Lord. Mercy! Mercy!*

"Make haste!" I cried. "Make haste!" I turned back, searching among them for Giulio and Ilaria, who had gone back—on my command—for Luciana and Domenico, but could not find them. The crowd of fighting men slowed to an agonizing mass on the path that circled the castle, bottlenecked at the gates. "Spread out!" I yelled. "Run through the underbrush! You must get inside! They come! They come!"

We could hear their battle roar as the next wave of enemies crested the hill, running in our direction, only a minute or so away.

There. Noting the blocked entrance, Giulio and Ilaria had gone wide, the Betarrini twins riding behind them. I breathed a sigh of relief, seeing them so close. But they went wide in order to go faster—could they complete that arc and get inside before my mother issued her command?

Mama lifted her arm. "Get everyone to the back of the courtyard to allow more in!" she ordered. "Able men, take position! Prepare for attack within!"

Fiore and Gaspare led the others, taking knees and nocking arrows in front. Behind them, a line of swordsmen formed.

"Get inside!" I shouted. "Make haste! *Make haste!*"

The bulk of our men had made it through the gates. I met Mama's gaze and together, our eyes moved to Giulio and Ilaria, still two hundred paces away. They turned on the main road at last and galloped toward us. But then the first of our enemies arrived at the gates, some cutting down the closest wounded Forelli knights, some daring to attempt entrance—and swiftly dying. But more were right behind them.

Giulio and Ilaria split and arced back through the underbrush in separate directions. They had seen it and known what must be done.

"Shut the gates!" commanded my mother.

Nay, Mama! I cried out silently, knowing I could not argue aloud. To tarry longer would certainly see our gates breached.

I flung myself to the wall and watched as Giulio and Luciana, Ilaria and Domenico moved into the forest, a group of men running after them.

Valentino was at my side. "Might they make it to Castello Greco?"

As four men on horseback tore after them, I shook my head. "'Tis not likely. Bearing the weight of two slows their mounts."

"They know the wood well, yes?"

"Yes," I agreed, clinging to that slim hope.

"They shall use it to their advantage, then."

Or perish within it, I thought grimly, as our men slid the iron bar into place, just as the Perugians pressed against it en force.

Please, God, I prayed, *do not let them perish.*

LUCIANA BETARRINI

"Can we get closer to Ilaria and Nico?" I called out to Guilio as we raced through the woods.

He did not answer, clearly concentrating on simply finding us some place to either hide or take our stand. A place that might give us an advantage. We'd gained some distance and the knights on foot were no longer visible. But as we pulled up, we could hear the sound of horses in pursuit. He cocked his head, and I realized he was holding his breath, listening. "Four, mayhap five. We cannot outrun them. And if we do, 'twould be straight into Fiorentini territory."

"Might our time with Lord Paratore—"

He was sliding out of the saddle, ignoring me. He reached up. "Come," he demanded.

In my rush, I awkwardly slid down off the back of the horse, landing kind of lamely in his arms. He gestured behind me to a narrow crevice in the rocks. "Go! In there!" Then he turned and slapped the rump of his mare, sending her running toward the river.

I made it through the crevice and saw that it widened into a larger crevasse, maybe big enough for two. Giulio hurried after me, brushing his boot over the dirt to erase our footprints and pulling tumbleweeds in front of the crack in the rock as he eased inward. Then, with some effort, he squeezed his considerably bulkier body through the passage and eased in to face me. We were impossibly close, but all I could think was that I was so, so glad I wasn't alone. He could have dropped me, told me to hide, and went on. But he'd stayed with me. Was Ilaria with Nico? Were they trying for Castello Greco? Were the Perugians attacking the castello, too, even now?

The first two horsemen raced past us, and my knees seemed to turn to jelly.

"*Stai benne?*" Giulio whispered, catching me as I partially slumped and tried to right myself. *Are you all right?*

No! No, I wasn't all right. I wanted to laugh, in a losin'-it sorta way. Would they kill us if they found us? Had I really killed a man, maybe two, down in the valley? All at once, it came rushing back, one scene after another rapidly unfolding in my brain like someone manically flipping through Insta-reels. I began to tremble all over.

His brows knit together, and he lifted a hand to my cheek, urging me to meet his gaze. "'Twill be well," he whispered. "I am here, m'lady. I shall not leave you."

I tried to focus on the promise in his tone, the confidence, but all I could think about was the blood, the sounds of battle, the feel of the dagger as I plunged it into that man's belly . . . how oddly easy it was to pierce someone's flesh and organs. A deep chill settled into my bones. A knot built in my throat. Tears streamed down my face.

"You are overcome," he said soothingly. "'Tis common, after one's first battle." He wrapped me in his arms as the next two horsemen passed us, cradling my head with one arm and pulling me close at the waist with the other.

At first I thought it was a sweet, kind, comforting move. But as knights began trotting past, I realized he was probably trying to muffle my chattering teeth. Or maybe it was both. I didn't care. I clung to him, hot tears now coming, in spite of my best efforts to keep them back. I'd killed people. Killed them.

People who had parents, maybe siblings. Maybe wives and kids.

I buried my face in his chest, feeling his sweat-dampened shirt become wet with my snot and tears, but now I was fighting to keep back full-blown, ugly sobs.

What had I done? What was I doing, killing people? What was happening? What was about to happen? Nico! Where was Nico?

"Shh, shh," he was murmuring in my ear, stroking my back now. "Courage, m'lady, courage." He leaned closer and brushed his lips past my cheek—was that the barest of kisses?—and whispered, "Dig deeply." His breath was warm on my ear, his lips so close. "You are a warrior, at heart. I saw it in you this day on the battlefield. Find her again in your mind's eye."

But it was he who was holding me together, not memories of my own strength. I pulled him closer still, praying his courage, his sheer might would enter into me. *Become* mine, somehow. He smelled of sweat and leather and pine and soil and blood. I concentrated on that, taking deep breaths and identifying more about him, bit by bit, rather than my memories on the battlefield. I concentrated on the feel of his touch and his warmth, the heat of him easing away the chill inside me. Lord Guilio Greco embodied assurance. Will. Strength. And freely loaned a portion to me as if he had plenty more to spare.

Even as more men passed us, my trembling began to ease. I knew he felt it, too, because he loosened his grasp on me. We drew slightly apart, and I stared at the leather-covered holes and bone "buttons" of his vest. One was broken. I reached up and touched it, unaccountably sad and overwhelmed about it, distantly wondering how difficult it might be to fix it, and who made buttons like that? Where did you shop for a replacement?

He covered my hand with his, and slowly, I dragged my eyes up his chest, his neck, to his square, stubble-covered chin, past his full lips and into those deep-ocean eyes, laced with dark lashes. He stared down at me, his eyes shifting back and forth over mine. For a second I thought he was going to kiss me, but then his head slowly turned to the opening crack, and I realized he was just being quiet, listening. Because there were knights turning back. Horsemen nearby again. Shouts.

What an idiot I was. This knight was just trying to keep us hidden, his mind on escape, survival. And here I was, like some silly twit that I myself chided when watching suspense movies. *Now is not the time for a kiss, you idiots! There's no time for that!*

But then, I'd never seen a couple crammed together in the center of a cracked boulder . . .

As we heard knights come down the path directly before our rockface, the creak of the saddle leather, the clipped strike of hoof against stone, I pulled Giulio closer, in spite of myself. His hand pressed against my back, and we remained utterly still, our shallow breaths our only movement. Crazily, I wondered if the one who paused nearby might hear my pounding heart. To my ears, my pulse was a rush of water, waves that anyone else should be able to hear too. I closed my eyes, unable to stand the suspense of our enemy looking back down the path and forward again, as if puzzled.

"All'ariete!" cried someone in the distance. *To the battering ram!*

They were storming the castello gates?

"Ne abbiamo due!" cried another. *We have two of them!*

I bit back a gasp. The man hovering near our crevice moved to mount up, heading toward the castle. But my mind wasn't on the castle. It was on my brother and Ilaria.

They had them? Or *had*, had them?

"Giulio," I whispered desperately.

"Come," he said, scraping by me and taking my hand. He eased through the narrows with effort, and I followed.

12

TILIANI FORELLI

"Ramparts in place!" ordered my mother, joining me in the courtyard below. "Pelt them with arrows!" she called to the archers above, already on task.

The sound of another strike of the battering ram rent the air, and the doors bounced with the impact. In all my life, nothing like this had ever happened. I wished that Papa and Zio Marcello were here in the courtyard with us, as well as Zia Gabi. But Mama was firmly in command as men came with long wooden beams to bolster our gates. I did not think they could crack the iron-clad crossbeam, but I worried about the ancient wooden doors themselves. How much abuse might they withstand?

Aurelio, Valentino, and their men brought three additional support beams and set them in place, cantilevered against the gate. Aurelio came to my side and looked up the fifty-foot-tall gate, hands on his belt. I chanced a second glance at him, wondering how he had managed in battle. Blood spattered his face and neck, his shirt, but from the way he moved, I guessed it was solely our enemy's.

He caught my gaze and took my hand and gave it a brief squeeze. "Take heart, m'lady. The gates appear strong."

I thought it kind of him, his attempt at assurance, as well as the brief length of it. I was not in the mood for romantic gestures, but it *had* given me a small measure of comfort, him trusting the integrity of the gates. Mayhap he had been a part of other sieges and was a good judge. Papa had said he'd proven himself in battle, time and again. Something in his tone, the tilt of his square chin, made me believe him.

My cousin Fortino moved through the crowd to us. Benedetto, I saw, was behind him. "Tiliani, m'lord is asking for us. And my mother wishes for a report."

I nodded and followed him back at a trot toward the family quarters, watching as men moved all around the alure that circled the castle, shooting arrows.

"Ladders!" shouted one on the southeastern face. "They bring ladders!"

Mama sent more men to the turrets to climb to the walls and join the defensive line. The gates would hold or would not. She left but ten men with Benedetto below to look after the bolstering beams, driving pegs into the dirt at their base to keep them from sliding, putting others back in place when they shook loose. Numerous young boys and girls scurried around the yard, picking up errant enemy arrows to resupply our own archers above. Everyone else was sent to the walls.

I followed Fortino through the turret door—short enough that he had to stoop to get through—and gazed down the hallways to my left and right. If we were breached, the turret doors themselves were reinforced and could hold for a time. Servants were bringing in supplies. This wing had a second reinforced door on either side, providing perhaps another hour's time before an enemy could breach it. Had our messenger made it to Monteriggioni yet? And was the other even halfway to Siena? How soon until reinforcements might arrive?

A good while, I thought grimly. *Unless they burn us out first.*

But that would be their last resort. 'Twould benefit Perugia if they captured Castello Forelli whole. Then they could utilize it to expand their own borders.

We entered my parents' room and went directly to the massive four-poster where my aunt—her bare shoulder bandaged, her arm in a sling—stood directing servants attending my father and uncle, who had been laid upon the bed. Seeing her pale complexion and sweat on her brow, I took her elbow. "Zia Gabi, you must sit before you faint. Tomasso, a stool, please!"

The man set down his bucket of water, grabbed a stool from a corner, and brought it to us. I helped Gabi to sit and felt her trembling, the uncommon weakness in her, her unspoken gratitude at me seeing what she might have been too late in recognizing. Never had I felt anything but strength from her.

I gazed from her to my father, stripped to the waist, his midsection and chest a mass of bruises and bloody strikes. Were those whip marks?

"Papa," I groaned, tears rising. He moved his head slightly, as if he had heard me, but his eyes did not open. I drew in a shaky breath, hearing the distant sound of the rhythmic beating of our enemy's ram against our door. I looked over to Zio Marcello, his shoulder and arm swaddled in one cloth, his face as ashen as my father's.

A bright-red bloodstain spread across the cloth, but he looked at me and Fortino with steady, weary eyes. "What is happening out there? Report."

"They are attempting to break through the gates as well as breach us with ladders," Fortino said, running an agitated hand through his thick curls. "I must return to them, m'lord."

"What of the Betarrini twins?" Zia Gabi asked.

"Away. They were with Guilio and Ilaria and escaped into the woods as we closed the gates. They could not enter in time."

Gabi blinked several times, then glanced at Chiara Greco, who was bandaging a knight's bloody head. I knew my aunt now not only fret for the Betarrinis, but also for our beloved Ilaria and Giulio. The thought of anything happening to them made my mouth go dry. I had sent them after Domenico and Luciana. Had I sent them to their deaths?

My cousin shifted, his agitation increasing in tandem with the number of cries and shouts we heard outside.

"M'lord!" he begged Marcello. "Papa! I must . . ." He gestured over his shoulder, his face awash with frustration and fear.

"Go," Zio Marcello said. But as Fortino turned from his father, my uncle grabbed his wrist. "But if we are overrun, Fortino, be certain that you and Benedetto make it back to our quarters. I will not have you captured, ransomed, or worse."

Fortino's eyes shifted to his father's bloody shoulder, then over to his beaten, unconscious uncle. "Yes, m'lord."

"I must go with him," I said. "I can aid him and the others."

"You shall remain here," Zio Marcello returned steadily, and I recognized that determined, decided look. It brooked no argument.

I swallowed a ball of frustration. If my cousins were to defend the castello until they could do no other, why was I not? But I could see it in my uncle's eyes. I was Lia and Luca's only remaining child.

I had to survive. For their sakes.

I bit my cheek and glanced over at two knights on blankets in the corner, groaning or crying out in pain. There were eight others in the room. With some relief, I found Nona approaching, directing Padre Giovanni and servants to administer a tincture to one and prepare a poultice for another.

She paused before me and took my hands in hers. "God be praised that at least one more of my family is *not* wounded. See that you keep it that way, *intesa*?" She gave me a brief, weary smile and touched my chin.

"Understood," I promised.

"And your cousins too?"

I gave her a rueful smile. "That I cannot promise."

"How does my Lia fare?" She turned to take a poultice from a servant.

"She is well," I said quickly. "She is directing the men from the southern side of the gate. Benedetto is on the north. I have never . . . never seen her so *fierce*."

"There is more to your mother than you know," Nona said. "And a reason she is called She-Wolf," she added, moving on.

Two more knights were led in, an arrow through one's shoulder, another with a sword wound, and Nona turned to them, coming up under the second man's arm to help him to a blanket in the corner. A sword wound . . . from men on the ladders? Were some reaching the top? Or was this still from the battlefield down in the valley?

I hurried over to my father as he roused at last. "Papa, I must return to the courtyard," I said, taking his palm in my own, interlocking thumbs. I sat down on the edge of the bed and brought his hand to my chest and looked over to Zio Marcello, knowing I was attempting to gain permission from the only one able to best my uncle's decision here. "I belong with Mama, my cousins, in this fight."

"Nay," he said, still looking terribly pale. Dark bruises were gathering on his cheeks and neck, and one eye was swollen shut.

I swallowed back my frustration.

"Why, Papa?" I asked, gently stroking his cheek. "Why did the Perugians do this to you?"

"'Tis all in error, Tiliani," he said, speaking each word as if it pained him to do so, and I saw then that his lip was split too. "Or an error they wish to believe."

"So they beat you?" I asked. "To force you to admit to wrongdoing?"

"They attempted it, yes," he said. "But Marcello and I . . ."

I could plainly see what had transpired. My father and uncle had refused to capitulate.

We heard a trumpet blast, this time, one long one. The walls had been breached.

"Stay with us, Tiliani!" Zia Gabi cried as I leaped to my feet, ready to go, with or without permission. "Behind the barrier! Siena shall come to our aid."

"Zia, if you were whole and hale would *you* remain?" I asked, glancing to the door and back. "They shall need every sword, every arrow. My cousins are out there. *Mama* is out there. *Without you.* Has she ever been in battle without you?"

She paused a moment, silently recognizing the truth of it. Then she uttered a soft, reluctant, *"Andare,"* overruling my father and uncle. *Go.*

And in that one, small word, I heard the whisper of her prayers that we would all live to come together again.

LUCIANA BETARRINI

Giulio paused at the mouth of the crevice as more men rushed past, heading toward Castello Greco. He took my hand in his and we waited a moment. A long trumpet blast sounded from the direction of Castello Forelli.

Giulio tensed. Apparently that was bad news. What, exactly?

We waited as four more horses galloped by, followed by about twelve men, all headed toward the castello, all in good cheer. Like sharks smelling blood in the water.

I need to grab Nico and get out of here, I thought. We were somewhere close to the tombs now. As much as Giulio was kind of my dream guy, and we'd shared a moment and all, I'd pretty much had my fill of medieval mayhem. It was time to get back to our own time, where most people I knew didn't kill each other. Or try.

Giulio led me out, and we found ourselves on the road, no more soldiers in sight. I suddenly noticed that he was unarmed, except for a dagger at his belt. As was I.

Fantastic, I thought. *Unarmed in woods full of soldiers who will shoot us or cut us down on sight.* We heard them, then, even over the war cries and pounding happening at the castello, in the distance. Ilaria's cry of rage, Nico's yell. Somewhere close.

We hunched over and moved through the thick underbrush, ready to drop where we were if any other soldiers came down the road. Giulio pulled me along, pausing here and there to take stock, his handsome face etched with grim lines. He was clearly torn—the castello was under siege and maybe losing ground. But our sibs were first on our list. If we could help them at all, weaponless.

I took heart in what I had learned already on the battlefield. Those fighting in this time knew little of martial arts. Handholds. Wrist turns. They were used to straight-forward fighting. Sword to sword, with an occasional punch or headbutt or stranglehold. They were unused to the moves that Nico and I had become adept at deploying.

Not that I didn't wish I had a bow and arrow—or even one of those gargantuan swords—but I particularly wished Giulio had one. We cleared the next hill, and what we saw made my blood run cold. Six knights encircled Ilaria and Nico, who stood back-to-back. The knights were laughing and taunting them. Taking turns nicking them with their swords and drawing back, making jokes.

"Giulio," I whispered, then winced as he squeezed my hand tight, utterly absorbed in the scene before us.

Belatedly remembering it was *my* hand he was trying to squish into paste, he let go and splayed his fingers wide, eyebrows arched in brief apology. But then his blue eyes were on his sister again, and his cheek muscle pulsed in silent rage.

I took his arm. "We can handle this," I whispered, eying the smallest guy in the circle, two to our left. "But first, we have to get you a sword." I moved out, knowing he would have no choice but to follow, giving him no opportunity to debate. There was only one way this was going to work—and it was to surprise this group of jerks who were abusing Nico and Ilaria.

Shock and awe, I thought, repeating my jiu jitsu professor's favorite war slogan. From twenty feet away, I dropped beneath the covering of thick ferns and brush and cupped my hands to make the bird whistle we'd learned as kids. I prayed Nico would hear it over the fray.

I figured he did. He started shouting, in English. Calling them names and taunting them in a tone that they would understand in any language. I immediately began army crawling through the brush. Or more like bear-walking, I thought, with my irritating skirts. After a second's hesitation, Giulio followed suit.

Nico kept it up, screaming at them now, God bless 'im. He knew I was coming. Giving me cover of noise. A chance at this crazy plan.

I glanced back at Giulio. *"Pronta?"* I mouthed. *Ready?*

I didn't wait for his response.

I was up and running, going to my hands and turning, leaping, my skirt lifting to my thighs, my legs wrapping around the poor, hapless little guy who could never have imagined me coming. We fell on top of the next one, and I left Bully Number One—and his sword—to Giulio, picking up Bully Number Two's fallen sword and tossing it to Nico, while immediately preparing for Number Two's first blow. In my peripheral vision, I saw Giulio finish One. Behind me, I felt Nico and Ilaria surge into offense again.

But my stomach felt Two's fist. I'd been too late, getting my arms up, preparing. I'd call it a rookie mistake, but I'd succeeded in the greater mission of arming Nico. I took a defensive posture again, trying to hide my need for air.

At that moment, Giulio spun and sliced through Two's arm, just as his fist was coming to meet my face.

He turned and went after Number Three, leaving me to finish Two, who stood before me, gaping at the stump of his arm. Trying to ignore the ghoulish, squirting blood flow, I bounced on my toes twice—my signature centering move—and then jabbed at his nose as hard as I could. When he wobbled backward, I turned and sent him to the ferns with a spinning roundhouse kick, where he collapsed, unconscious. I stayed low, instinctively knowing another now had me in his sights.

I turned to face Number Four, who was stocky with shoulders like a champion wrestler, about my height and age. We circled each other, his sword held high in both hands over his right shoulder. Watching his eyes, I knew where he was going before he brought his sword down, shifting to my left to avoid it. He did not stop his swing, bringing it down to my right. His fatal mistake was continuing the pattern, not using his shield to mix it up. On the next arc, I dodged, but then grabbed hold of his right wrist—clearly his dominant—and held tight. I pressed my hip into him, pulling away.

Stunned by my foreign actions, he hesitated. And in that moment, I got my elbow between his wrist and ribcage and twisted, forcing his hand back in an excruciatingly painful move. His sword clattered to the stones below us.

"Ilaria!" I shouted, making the final move to break his wrist—a move I would've never ever done in competition—while kicking the sword toward her, praying she could reach it. I leaned my full weight into my enemy and heard—and felt—the sickening pop of his bones breaking beneath my hands. He screamed and fell to his face.

Without pause I turned and side-kicked the man who was now taking on Nico—I think maybe catching his eye—before charging into another who was coming my way. Again, my unexpected move seemed to utterly surprise him, allowing me to grab hold of his arm and wrist, curve into his chest, and drop my body. I pulled his arm over my shoulder and drove my hips in the air, sending him to his back.

The sword in his right palm clattered to the ground.

I glanced around and felt a surge of relief. We had the upper hand, only two Perugians yet on their feet and armed.

I faced them full on. *"Andare!"* I spat. *Go!* "Tell your friends there's a new She-Wolf in town, and you do not wish to face her!" I announced loudly in English. The two glanced at each other and then turned and ran pell-mell through the woods.

"You know they don't understand English, right?" Nico said, panting and wiping his forehead with the back of his wrist as he gazed about. It was so good to hear his voice.

"Oh, they got it," I said, trembling. But this time it was with righteous anger, not dissolving adrenaline . . . like it had been in the crevice.

My eyes went to Giulio and Ilaria, his arm draped around her shoulders, uttering quiet, reassuring words.

I shook my head, as if to clear my fuzzy, cobweb-filled brain. "Nico," I said, forcing myself to turn from Giulio and lowering my voice. "We are right by the tombs. I think we've seen enough. We're not supposed to be here. You didn't land in the time of the Renaissance, where you can get rich quick with the whole Medici-treasure scheme. You're a century off. And I've gotten my share of historian fodder. And this kind of battle . . . the blood . . ." I shuddered. "It's time to go."

I turned and stalked off, but in seconds, knew Nico wasn't behind me. Out of my peripheral vision I could see a couple of the Perugians try to rise, but Ilaria and Giulio took care of them.

I stopped and turned, glaring at Nico. "What? C'mon!"

I turned and started walking again. Eventually, Nico caught up, and I took my first, relieved breath. He was coming! We were finally in agreement! I felt the relief, the hope of returning to our own time. To cars. And people in regular clothes and hospitals and cell phones and sanity. But then Nico grabbed my wrist and pulled me to a stop.

I glanced behind him. Even from here, it was clear in Ilaria's and Giulio's expressions that they realized we were running. Leaving. Ilaria briefly raised her hand in farewell to us. Giulio's face was a mask, devoid of emotion. They turned and started running toward the castello, where they belonged. And as they disappeared over the rise, it oddly stole my breath.

I wondered over the sudden sensation of loss, which felt like a gut punch, stealing my breath again.

Loss? I thought. *I barely know them!* Can a person really feel pain over losing someone they've only known a week?

But we had fought together. Trained together. Danced together.

"We still can't go, Luci." Nico gestured back toward Castello

Forelli. "It's not any different from when you wanted to leave before. We can help them."

"Right," I said. "Or be killed."

"We've made it this far, right?" he said. "Maybe we can't be killed, because we haven't been born yet."

I lifted my arm, showing him the bruise and cut there. "Does this look like I can't be hurt, Nico? Or does this?" I said, gesturing to my cheek, where I'm sure a solid shiner bloomed. "Because I'm totally feeling every blow I've taken here! Aren't you?" I stepped closer, really getting in his face. "Aren't you?" I gave a dramatic pause. "Oh, I'm sorry. Mayhap you need medieval-speak to get through to you here. Are you not feeling every blow, Domenico?" I pressed. "Are you not?"

We stood there, nose to nose, but he remained still. "Of course I am," he said patiently. "But Luci . . ."

And it was then that I saw Giulio and Ilaria had not run for the castle. They stood on the crest of the next hill in silhouette, glancing back and forth, every muscle tensed. Torn between their duty to the Forellis and their duty to look after us.

"Look at them, Nico," I pled. "They belong with the Forellis. We are holding them back. And what? Changing time? Futures? Lives? History? For what?" I turned in a slow circle, palms to the sky. "This is a world of hurt, Nico! This is not our time. But it *is* time to go back."

I started again toward the tombs. When I looked to the hillside, I noted with a pang that our guardians had disappeared. I shoved down a tinge of fear and regret. This was right. This was our path back.

We just had to get to the tombs. Fast.

Nico ran after me. I heard the lashing of the damp brush, the clatter of the gravel beneath his boots.

I looked back his way, but then faltered.

Because beyond him were twelve soldiers, spreading out. Half had bows, stretched taut, arrows nocked. The other half had swords in hand. I turned my head and saw twelve more had appeared before us too.

Surrounded. And so outnumbered that we didn't stand a chance.

I looked frantically for Ilaria and Giulio, but they were gone. We'd dismissed them when we turned toward the tombs for the second time, away from Castello Forelli. Appearing like deserters in their hour of need. Deserting the castello—their family, our distant kin—when they needed us most.

We were surrounded, and jiu jitsu wouldn't save us now. There were just too many.

And so *that* was how we landed in a wagon, tied up and getting pelted by rotten fruit, on our way into a town full of people who hated us, even before we arrived.

13

My mother was firing arrows as fast as she could at men below. Fortino and Benedetto had taken up guard for her, knocking back Perugians who streamed up and over the southeastern wall.

"Push that ladder down!" I cried, fighting my way forward. I had run out of arrows and picked up a fallen enemy's small shield with my left hand and his short broadsword with my right. Valentino and Aurelio were ahead of me, fighting two newcomers, giants of men with more vigor than I feared we had remaining to us.

I had to get to that ladder. If we didn't get it down, we would soon be outnumbered. But I was blocked by the men ahead of me.

Aurelio swung his sword, narrowly missing his adversary. The big man stabbed at him, and Aurelio turned aside just in time. But in that second, I rammed my sword into our enemy's belly. He gasped, reached out, and grabbed his companion, and in that moment of startlement, Valentino struck, nearly decapitating his comrade.

I winced as hot, wet blood spurted across my face, but I could not pause. I wiped it away from my eyes and tore down the alure to my mother and cousins, who now battled a greater number of our enemies. I could feel Aurelio and Valentino right behind me and breathed a silent prayer of thanks.

Benedetto took a stabbing blow to his midsection, and I

prayed it had not penetrated his chest shield. I dodged a strike from another, slipping under his arm, and left him to the knights behind me. *I must get to the ladder.* And if not the ladder, at least to my family to lend them aid.

Hard-pressed and out of arrows, Mama abandoned her bow and took turns with my cousins in parrying, striking and blocking their opponents. Locking eyes with me for a moment, she gestured with her chin. "Go!" she gritted out, knowing I was after what she'd been endeavoring to do. But even as we made that brief exchange, three new men had clambered over the parapet.

I charged, blocking the first's strike with my small shield and then again turning to lift my sword against the second's. Valentino came charging past, driving the third to the wall, punching him, then picking up his legs and sending him screaming to the rocks below. I had to admire the decision—and wished I had the strength to do the same. He caught the first man's strike with his sword, blocking it before it hit my neck. I rammed my shield up at the interloper's face, catching him on the nose. He reeled backward, and given the space, I jabbed, managing to pierce his leg, given his scream.

I ran on and reached the ladder just as a new man grasped hold of the wall. I stabbed at him and sent him windmilling back, taking grim satisfaction when he clutched at the next man and pulled him down too. I pushed on the ladder, but it was already heavy with six more Perugians below. I dodged as an archer sent an arrow my way and looked madly about for a forked pole. Dead men lined the alure— so many of them ours, my heart sank.

Valentino ran past me, knowing what I sought. Twenty paces farther, he rolled a man off of the pole and came running with it as I dispatched the next man to reach the top of the ladder. More arrows whizzed by our heads. Valentino pulled a dagger and sent it into the throat of the next man. Then he hooked the top rung of the ladder and pressed forward. I joined him, and soon Aurelio behind me. Together we finally edged the ladder upright and then backward, sending twelve men toppling to the ground.

I flashed a grin at Aurelio as Valentino ran to a new ladder, just now set against the stone. And for the first time since he'd arrived, it struck me. I was glad—genuinely glad—Aurelio had come. Where would we be without these two and their men?

Other knights along the alure cheered and, with the stream of enemy knights temporarily dammed, renewed their efforts to dispatch the remaining enemies among us. Still the pounding continued at our front gates, a sizable, splintering hole on one side. How many more strikes could it take?

Mama had picked up her bow and was returning to the gate with haste, calling for other archers to aid her. I moved in the opposite direction around our quint-faced wall, picking up arrows and a bow as I ran from an archer, who had been shot through the eye, praying to God that I would not end up the same. At least it would be swift, I surmised. But my parents . . . my younger brothers had only passed four and five years ago. My grief over them was a quiet sorrow, a distant memory. But for my mother and father, the loss remained a gnawing wound to their hearts. I knew if they lost me as well—

But I could not afford to think of it. I had to remain on task, focused on what was to be done next if I was to be most effective in my aid. I ran past Valentino, and clenching my teeth, I alone sent the next ladder to the ground before too many were atop it.

"More arrows!" I shouted to the children in the courtyard below, still collecting those that had missed their mark. My mother and I—and the six or seven archers still standing—would need them.

I dragged two wounded archers from the parapet nearest the front gate, helping them to sit against the far wall of the alure, promising I'd get them help soon. Then I took up position and began firing as my mother was doing from the other side, aiming for that tender, brief exposure beneath the men's armpits, where their protective armor gapped when they leaned into the massive battering ram, still repeatedly striking our gate. I managed to hit two, then a third above the knee, but new knights simply moved to take their place.

Valentino joined me with a bow in hand, three quivers full of arrows.

"You do know the way to a woman's heart," I quipped, taking a basket from him. I immediately regretted it—given his half-second's hesitation as if he did not know what to do with my jest—but I had more pressing matters on my mind. Together with the remaining archers, we settled into a rhythm of drawing and shooting in opposite beats, creating a constant barrage of arrows. My mother and her group did the same, and in seconds, we had slowed our enemy's progress. Too many of them were falling.

"Return fire!" screamed a captain below, and twenty-four new knights moved to take a knee, aiming at us.

We ducked as their volley came flying past. But then they deployed our own tactic back upon us, shooting in rounds, so we never had a chance to rise, take aim, and shoot. We heard the sickening crunch of more of our gate splintering with the next ram.

But then, the most beautiful sound I believed I'd ever heard.

A *Sienese* trumpet.

Reinforcements had arrived from Monteriggioni at long last.

LUCIANA BETARRINI

After grueling hours of travel, we finally reached the walls of Perugia. The hilltop town's road wound higher and higher until we reached the main square, with a massive church on one side, two palazzi flanking either side, and a fortified castello on the far end. We were dragged inside, our hands still tied behind our backs. Nico and I had not attempted escape—having been surrounded by far too many to hope for success, nor wishing for them to know of what we might be able to do. The last thing we needed was our feet tied together too.

But as we were dragged before a grizzled, balding knight and asked for our names, we saw that we were not the only prisoners taken that day. Other men—some of whom I recognized from Castello Forelli—were being led down a long hallway and what appeared to be a set of steps. The dungeon? My heart was racing like mad.

"Name?" asked a secretary, sitting beside the grizzled knight, dipping his pen in the inkwell.

"Domenico Betarrini," Nico said.

"Domenico *Betarrini*," the knight repeated, straightening in his chair and looking more closely at my brother.

I groaned inwardly, wishing Nico had thought to lie. Because the man clearly recognized the name.

"Nay," Nico tried. "I said Domenico Benatini."

The knight's eyes slid to me. "And yours?"

"Luciana Benatini," I said swiftly.

"Husband and wife?" he asked, rising.

"Brother and sister," I said, not seeing a reason to lie about that.

"Take him to a cell." The knight gestured two knights toward Domenico. He gestured to the next two. "Take her to my quarters."

"Wait—what?" I said in English, attempting to process what was happening. To his quarters? "*Fermare!*" I cried, digging my heels in. *Stop!* I tried to wrench my arm free from the smaller knight but failed. "If my brother is going to your prison, send me there too!"

"Lady *Betarrini*," said the knight, coming around the table to face me, eerily never blinking. "Surely the She-Wolves prepared you for this."

"Prepared me for what?"

"Given your position as kin, your brother's life shall be traded for ten of our own, held by the knights inside Castello Forelli. But *your* life," he reached up and put a finger under my chin, looking me over like he might a fine horse, "shall benefit us in other ways."

I froze. What other ways?

"Take her. See to it that she is closely guarded, even as the maids get her out of that foul mess and into something suitable. She shall be presented to our lord and lady before we sup." He dismissed them, and the guards ignored me as I cried out and protested. I met my brother's anguished gaze one last time as he looked over his shoulder and his captors bodily hauled him down the stairs, while my own took me up the opposite flight.

When we reached the third level, we moved through a wooden door and down a beautiful hall in the palazzo, the stone beneath our feet a masterful mosaic of mixed granite and porphyry. Whoever owned this place was incredibly rich. Even Castello Forelli—held by one of the Nine—had nothing so beautiful in decor. Such floors were typically reserved for churches, not private homes . . . even if they were palaces.

"*Venire!*" said the bigger guard to two maids at the end of the hall. *Come!* "Send for water and a tub! And fetch a suitable gown for this lady."

They looked confused. Probably because they weren't used to a "lady" being escorted by armed guards—nor dressed in the dirty, torn remnants of clothing suited for a common maid. I glanced down. *Or covered in the remains of sticky, rotting fruit.*

The knights brought me inside and closed the door. "Do not attempt escape," warned the bigger one, and the other moved behind me to untie my wrists.

I eyed him as I rubbed my skin, red and raw from the rope, and slowly rolled my aching shoulder, thinking through the moves that would bring these two down in under a minute. But I doubted I could escape. Especially with Nico down in some sort of dungeon. How was I going to get him out?

I wavered on my feet, overwhelmed, my mind spinning.

"Careful, m'lady," the nearest knight said, taking my elbow with a steadying hand.

I turned to him hopefully, feeling a kind of wild desperation, and reached out to grasp his arm. "Please, I must see my brother. We must remain together, even if it means I must sleep in the dungeon."

"Put thoughts of the dungeon aside," said the bigger one, brushing my hand off his comrade's forearm. "You, Lady Betarrini, shall be a captive of an entirely different sort."

I looked at him, trying to keep the fear from my eyes. "What does that mean? Speak plainly!"

But he only gave me a lurid smile as the maids arrived carrying pails full of hot water. A manservant set the tub before the window and settled a screen around it as the maids dumped the water inside. Then I was ushered behind the screen and stripped, one maid wordlessly working on the laces of my bodice, another yanking off my boots. In short order I was naked, foolishly wishing I could hide. The maids grabbed my wrists and hurried me into the tub.

A middle-aged one turned to the knights, who'd sauntered a bit too close to the screen. She crossed her arms. "Turn around," she demanded.

"The captain instructed us to not look away from our charge," said the bigger one.

"She is in a bath, not on her way out the window," returned the woman.

She made a twirling motion with her finger, and the knights reluctantly turned their backs. But as more water was poured over my head and my hair lathered with lavender-scented soap, I looked to the window. Was it actually a way I might escape?

But what about Nico?

I could not leave without him. I would need to see this—whatever *this* was—through. And hope to God that the Betarrinis and Forellis would somehow help us find our way out.

14

TILIANI FORELLI

There was much celebration as the Perugians retreated and our Sienese brothers were welcomed into the castello. Repairs began at once on the gates. My aunt and uncle were brought to the Great Hall and made comfortable in their chairs, with added blankets and pillows, in order to receive Lord Fabbri, who had ridden to our aid with a hundred knights at Monteriggioni. Had they not arrived when they did—and Siena herself five hours later—I feared what might have become of us.

Papa now rested in his own quarters, the barber-surgeon advising strict bed rest for three days as he recovered from his head injury, as well as others to his body. It still was difficult for me to look upon my father, his bruised face and swollen eyes testimony to the beating he had taken, refusing to capitulate to the Perugians' demands. Zia Gabi sat beside Mama, taking over command, as was her custom as elder. Asking Lord Fabbri questions, while Zio Marcello demanded an accounting from each captain, but with slightly slurred speech because of his aching head.

It unnerved me. I'd never witnessed Zio Marcello—or my father—with less than their whole faculties.

Cook and the servants were well into preparations for a feast—two whole hogs already upon spits above open fires—when Giulio and Ilaria made their way to the front of the line to report. Immediately,

I knew something had gone desperately wrong with the way Guilio shifted nervously and Ilaria looked about the room. I searched the hall for Luciana and Domenico and my heart sank. They were not to be found.

"God be praised," Zia Gabi breathed. "I am most pleased to see you whole and hale, my dear ones."

"As are we to see you," Giulio said. He cleared his throat and glanced at me, standing between my mother and aunt. "M'lady, I regret to report that we lost our charges in the melee."

Gabi stilled and frowned. Mama stiffened. "You lost them," Mama repeated, each word a broken piece of glass.

"Yes, m'lady," Ilaria said. She, too, glanced my way, eyes full of regret. "We had fought our way free and had turned toward the castello . . ." She gave Mama and Zia Gabi a long, meaningful look.

"But they did not," my mother said, her words barely audible for those beyond our inner circle. This time, there was a bit of relief to her tone. Why?

She sank back into her chair as she and Gabi exchanged quick glances. "So they . . . they elected to return home."

"'Tis understandable," Zia Gabi said, nodding slowly. "Given the circumstances. They had done what they came to do and saw an opportunity—"

"Which is what we believed, too, m'lady," Giulio said, running a weary hand through his dark hair.

"Believed," she repeated.

"We thought all of our enemy had convened here, intent on overcoming the castello, and we rushed to come to your aid. But when we spotted two patrols, heading north, we circled around to try and intercept the Betarrinis again. I regret to report that they were surrounded before we could get to them." He straightened, face grim. "They were captured and carted away."

It was Gabi's turn to sit back heavily in her chair. Mama closed her eyes and tightened her fists.

Zio Marcello's attention had turned from another conversation in time to catch the end of Guilio's report. "You are certain?" he asked Ilaria.

"Yes, m'lord. We followed at a distance for some time. The company is en route to Perugia. We assume to Palazzo Fortebraccio."

My uncle looked to my aunt and mother. "They shall offer them in trade. Or ransom."

They nodded, seeming to take hope in this. Clearly Zia Gabi had told Zio Marcello of their arrival . . . and who they were. She reached out to take his hand. "We must get to them. Before . . ."

Before they were beaten like he and my father had been.

"They shall be spared," Marcello said confidently. "They have no power to cede."

"Unless it becomes known that they are kin," Mama observed.

Papa considered that, then turned to Ilaria and Guilio. "Bathe and change," he instructed. "Then make your way to Palazzo Fortebraccio, as my emissaries. Take a patrol with you—also in clean dress—and funds to meet the ransom price of our prisoners."

"Or negotiate a trade for some of our own prisoners who now eat from our storehouse," Zia Gabi said.

"We shall at once," Giulio said with a bow.

He and Ilaria turned to go, but Mama spoke up. "My friends."

They turned back.

"Do not return home without the Betarrinis. They are . . . foreigners in our land. Not accustomed to our ways. To leave them in the hands of the Perugians could bring us further trouble."

Giulio and Ilaria gave her a slow nod.

"Take heart, m'lady," Ilaria said, stepping forward and dropping her tone. "They have learned a peculiar manner of fighting in Britannia. 'Twill benefit them in what is to come, I believe."

"But fighting prowess shall not aid them if they are chained," Mama said under her breath.

Ilaria straightened. "We shall bring them home, m'lady."

"See that you do."

LUCIANA BETARRINI

After my bath, they wound a forest-green silk skirt around my waist and an impossibly small, matching bodice around my torso, lacing me so tight that I blushed at what could be seen at the edge of the wide neckline. The bodice scooped up to the edge of my shoulders and descended in sleeves so skinny I had a hard time getting my wrists through.

Seriously? I thought, looking down, wondering how they possibly thought this was appropriate. But they all went about their business as if this was the norm, dipping pails to empty the tub and carrying them out as swiftly as they'd brought them in. I had changed behind the screen. The knights stood on either side of the door, arms crossed and eyeing me, the hint of a leer in the big one's eyes.

I looked away from him in disgust but then caught sight of myself in a speckled looking glass and did a double take. The gown accentuated the narrowing of my waist, the flair of my hips, and made me look like I had a model's bust. And did the green make my brown eyes more golden? I was startled, in spite of myself. I'd been wearing medieval costumes all summer, but I hadn't been wearing *this*.

One maid gestured me to a stool and began combing through the ends of my long hair, working her way up until it was all smooth and free of tangles. As much as I was having a hard time breathing, I had to admit that it felt good to be clean and in clothing that did not smell like old sweat and dried blood. She twisted and braided, working in a strand of freshwater pearls through my hair, pinning again and again. Another brought in a pair of embroidered slippers, but they were too small. With a sigh, she departed again to go in search of another pair for my big feet. At five-eight, I was practically an Amazon in this era, looking most men in the eye. Gabriella was the only other woman I'd seen that was taller than I was. I thought about the men who had some height on me . . . Aurelio's captain, Valentino Valeri. And Tiliani's cousins, Fortino and his younger bro, Benedetto. But Benedetto was tall and gangly. Even though he was a couple years older than I was, he still looked more like a teen. Not like Guilio Greco.

I thought about guys back home in the States. Guys who were working with us for the summer at the castello. How at twenty-one, men were still mostly boys.

But not Giulio.

I thought about him again in the crevice. The feel of him pulling me close. His confidence. How I felt secure, protected, beside him. The feel of his whisper at my ear. The heat of his breath near my neck.

And the look on his face as I turned away, intent upon running toward the tombs. How he'd probably believed we were abandoning the fight. Cowards. Traitors, running away when their people needed us most.

I swallowed hard. I couldn't regret that, I told myself. I couldn't. If Nico had just come with me, not argued, we might have made it to the tombs in time. Even if the Perugians had seen us, chased us, couldn't we have made it? And be home by now? Be dressing in our old castello costumes, rather than this? And yet . . . if the Forellis' plan to marry off Tiliani to Aurelio and fortify relations with Firenze failed, would Castello Forelli even be there to return to? Would we return and find it in rubble, ourselves out of a job in the worst way possible?

It was enough to make my head spin. I felt the dull throb of a migraine gathering at the base of my neck, the first I'd experienced in medieval Italy.

Again, I glanced down and tried to take more than half a breath. If I took a whole breath, I thought I would burst the seams. The second maid returned with another pair of slippers—sadly not matching my gown at all. But as she and my hairdresser conferred, I gathered it was all they could find. They looked at me for a moment in consternation—as if it was my fault I was so tall—but then quickly turned to admiring my hairdresser's work.

And her work was amazing. Never had I had such a fancy updo of coils. The strands of pearls woven through them made me look like some sort of princess, and the two maids were all congrats-way-to-go behind me. You know, in a medieval-Italian sort of way. *Some things never change,* I thought.

A knock at the door brought the twittering maids to attention. The guard slouching against the wall hurriedly straightened. He opened it a few inches, then flung it wide. "Come in, m'lord. The lady is presentable."

I stiffened and turned on my stool, bracing myself for what was to come. But then I had to swallow a laugh. Because in walked a pimple-faced kid of perhaps seventeen. This, *this* was the heir apparent of Palazzo Fortebraccio? But by his demeanor—and that of the maids and guard—I knew that to laugh at him would be a really bad idea.

He strode over to me and let his hazel eyes slide down my body from head to toe. I fought the desire to stand and strike him. How dare he? But then I reminded myself of where I was, *when* I was, and remained still.

"Lady Betarrini," he said with a courtly bow. "I am Franco Fortebraccio, the future heir of this grand palazzo," he said, with a flourish of his hand. "And I understand from my father that you are a captive of this latest battle."

"I am," I said, unwilling to sit a moment longer. I rose, took my skirts in hand, and gave him what I hoped was some semblance of a curtsey.

Trust me, it was awkward. I'd really only seen them in movies and at Castello Forelli, not tried one myself. But I pressed on, hoping to win his favor. "I am honored to meet you and grateful for the courtesy of this fine gown."

He looked up at me—he was maybe five-six, and his boots had a chunky heel—and then slowly circled me. I ground my teeth, pushing down the urge to side kick the little jerk, sending him flying to the wall.

"You are . . ." he began, searching for words, "quite tall," he finished.

"I am." I gritted out, waiting him to finish his perusal.

"I hear tall women fare better with childbirth."

I blinked at him. What? Was that true? My mind flitted off for a second. I'd never heard that. But in contemporary times, people didn't really fear childbirth. "Oh?" I managed.

"And while you are overly tall, you are quite beautiful."

Again, I blinked at him. "You are most kind."

"'Tis how my father's captain knew you were lying about your name," he chided.

"Oh?"

"Yes. The captain well knew that any woman as tall and as beautiful as you—and with uncommon fighting skills—must share the She-Wolves' bloodline. You were foolish to try and pretend to be another."

I faked a smile. "One is never foolish when trying to maintain an edge in the house of their enemy. When they are held captive. Or when they have arrived in a cart, bound and pelted by rotting fruit."

He shook his head. "Yes, well, I am sorry for that unfortunate greeting. The people did not know." He gave me a gap-toothed smile.

"Did not know . . . what?"

"That you, m'lady," he said, taking my hand in both of his, "could be my future bride."

I stared at him, fighting down revulsion. And panic. He was so earnest and trying to appear all manly, but his hands were cold and clammy, and the whole idea made me feel sick to my stomach. "I-I, uh, you do me a fair honor, sir, even considering me, but I do not intend to remain in Toscana."

"Not remain?" he scoffed. "Why, where else might you go?"

"I hail from Britannia. I must return to my family there. My father would not look kindly upon me taking a husband without his blessing." I silently congratulated myself on that idea. I was pretty sure that in medieval times peeps didn't just up and go to Vegas to get hitched.

"Give me his name and town, and I shall send an emissary, bearing gifts and a formal request," Franco returned breezily. "If we take to each other that is," he added, giving me a briefly irritated glance, as if to ask why I would ever, ever do anything but leap at the chance to marry him. "Now come, let me show you the beauty of my home. What could be *your* home in time, if God so favors you." He gave me another slight bow and then offered his arm.

Stifling my bewilderment and rising concern, I laid my hand atop his arm and allowed him to escort me from the room and down a long hall. I could hear the hum of a crowd ahead of us, laughter, and braced myself. Would they sense my distaste for their young lord and begin pelting me with rotting fruit again? I had to put my best foot forward. If I could find a place with these people, some semblance of honor, maybe I could negotiate Nico's return to my side. Or maybe just find a way to slip him a get-out-of-jail-free card.

The Great Hall was encircled with rich, vibrant frescoes from floor to ceiling, and dimly, I remembered Perugia had been the home to some sort of school of art in medieval times, hearkening back to their Etruscan roots. I fought between the urge to stare and study them and dissolve into a puddle of tears at the thought of being surrounded by my enemies. These men had probably tried to kill people at Castello Forelli over the last days—maybe they still intended to kill them. But now, each was clean and dressed for a formal dinner, with richly embroidered tunics, their wives in lovely gowns.

Though in time, with a closer look, I saw a man limping, another cradling an arm, and many others with cuts and bruises at eye or lip. They stared at me through slitted eyes, as suspicious of me as I was of them. Their women were even more so.

I did my best to ignore them as Franco escorted me through a gradually appearing path, toward a dais where a fat man in his fifties and a woman two decades younger sat in very fine dress, drinking wine and idly eating grapes. A trio of instrumentalists continued to play in the far corner—made more obvious when the people in attendance gradually hushed, pressing closer to hear us.

In time, even the musicians grew quiet.

"M'lord, I present to you Lady Luciana Betarrini. Our captain deserves an honor in capturing her and her brother this afternoon. And Stefano deserves another for discerning that they were not who they declared themselves to be."

"Ahh," said the older man, who had clearly enjoyed his share of wine and grapes, judging by the thick ring of fat around his neck. "So this is your captive bride?"

"Mayhap," Franco returned. "We shall see if I take to her."

"Indeed," said Lord Fortebraccio, looking me over, as apparently every man in this era felt he had the right to do. His eyes hovered at my cleavage, and I fought the urge to turn and walk out. "A beauty such as this, the newest of the She-Wolves, would be a fine choice for you, my son. She would bear you fine, strapping sons! 'Tis a pleasure, m'lady, to have you in my home. We shall give you the opportunity to flourish at my son's side. Surely in Siena, you would wither in the shadow of the elder Betarrinis."

I struggled for a response. "Mayhap, m'lord," I said with a slight curtsey, opting for ambiguity. "As I told your son, 'tis an honor to be considered a potential bride. Unfortunately, my brother and I are due to return home to Britannia." I shook my head sorrowfully. "Our father expects our return."

Lord Fortebraccio steepled his fingers. "Travelers do well to stay out of the fray when neighbors fight," he said. "But you were not some innocent avoiding battle, were you, m'lady?" He then took a long swig from his goblet and stared directly at me through narrowed eyes. "Some say that you even killed a few of my men. Mayhap more with your arrows. And many saw you bring down several others with a most curious fighting prowess."

I lifted my chin. "We merely came to the aid of our hosts. Would you truly not expect the same thing of any capable person abiding in your home, were you to be attacked?"

He sat back in his chair and lifted his goblet to his wife. Wordlessly, she picked up a pitcher and refilled it. The crowd behind me stilled, as if scared that he was about to order my head to be chopped off. And for the first time, I worried about it too.

But instead Lord Fortebraccio laughed. Just a little at first, and then with a great guffaw. Around us, others followed his lead, until every single one seemed to think I was totally hilarious. When it waned, the fat lord said, "I like you, Lady Luciana. I believe that having you in my court shall be . . . entertaining, regardless of what my son decides about your future." He rose and lifted his goblet. "To the newest She-Wolf, now abiding among her future comrades."

"To the She-Wolf!" cried a man behind me.

"To the She-Wolf!" others returned.

15

TILIANI FORELLI

I was sitting at my father's side, helping him drink a cup of water, when Captain Valeri knocked on the open door. Six men still laid on blankets about the floor of my parents' bedroom, twelve others in the adjoining rooms—all recovering, post-battle—and Nona and Chiara were tending to them all along with two maids and Padre Giovanni, the Forelli chaplain. The barber-surgeon from Monteriggioni had departed with the knights.

I watched as Captain Valeri's sad eyes took on an even greater sorrow to see his friend, Salvatore, absent a leg. The man was still blessedly unconscious after my grandmother had amputated his leg last night, explaining that it was full of infection, and his only chance at survival. I was thankful for the poppy tincture she'd given him. I didn't relish the idea of being in attendance when the man awakened.

Valentino's eyes found me, sitting on the edge of the bed, and he gave me a slight tilt of his head in greeting.

"Captain Valeri, please, come and meet my father."

Papa tried to lift himself up, but I gently pressed his shoulder back to the pillows. "You must remain still, Papa," I reminded him in an undertone.

He let out a resigned sigh. "Here am I, advancing in years, and women are still directing my every move."

"There are worse things, I hear, m'lord," Valentino said with a slight smile. "I am relieved to see you recovering."

"As am I." Papa grasped Valentino's arm with what weak strength he could muster. "I understand that you fought bravely alongside my daughter."

"Seeing your daughter fight would inspire many a man," Valentino said, giving me a slight smile. I liked it when he smiled. It made his sad eyes more wise than sorrowful. As if those green-brown orbs held a hundred stories he was bursting to tell.

"You saved my life, more than once, Captain," I said. "I thank you."

"As did you, mine," he returned. "I thank you in kind."

Papa lifted one brow. "Sounds like you two were quite the formidable force."

"Oh, no," I began as Valentino responded, "'Twasn't quite like that."

"The battle was long and we all worked . . . together," I said, faltering with that last word, recognizing how inadequate it was, remembering how Valentino had stopped that knight's strike just before it had reached my throat. I lifted a hand to my neck, belatedly realizing what I was doing.

Valentino clearly remembered the same moment. "God was gracious, to spare us both. Apparently, we have yet to do all he bids us."

His tone was reverent, not glib. So he was a man of faith, no matter what he'd said about prayer. I tried to swallow but found my mouth dry. I wished I could take a drink from my father's cup but resisted the urge. My father's keen eyes were already taking in too much.

"Why have you come, Captain Valeri?" I asked abruptly.

His eyes widened slightly. "To bring you this." He took a wooden chest from beneath his left arm and set it on the ground. "I thought these herbs I have collected might be of aid to your grandmother."

"You are a healer?" Papa asked.

"The cook at Castello Paratore was," he said, a slight blush rising on his neck. "I learned to spot different medicinal herbs at an early age. And traveling so widely with Lord Paratore, I oft find unique, rare ones. In the field, far from home, I've utilized this chest to treat our own wounded. But now . . ." he paused and looked at Salvatore and the others. "I knew Lady Adri and Lady Chiara might have immediate use of them. Your grandmother permitted me to attend her last night as she took my friend's leg. She is a most knowledgeable surgeon."

"Mayhap you should abandon your knightly duties and attend the university in Bologna," Papa remarked, "to gain further knowledge of medicinals and treatment of the wounded."

Valentino's smile grew. "You and I both know that at present, a Fiorentini would not be welcome in Bologna."

Papa flung out his hand. "Last month I would have wagered a bag of gold florins that a Fiorentini would never dare come and sup with a Sienese. Mayhap we have a new world on our hands, where everything is on shifting sands. If my daughter accepts your master's hand, Siena and Firenze may take on Bologna—or Perugia—together."

I stilled, recognizing his not-so-subtle reminder about Valentino's subservience to Aurelio.

But I had to admit I was taken by Valentino's thoughtful gift. I was taken by him. There was something between us, some sort of visceral pull that I'd never felt with anyone.

And yet Papa was right. He was Aurelio's captain. And it might appear I was behaving like a hapless consort. I had to get past my romantic notions and this gift to us. Was it not logical, that he would offer such a bounty? Mayhap he did so in order to increase our favor for his lord. And yet . . . I sensed that this was his idea alone. And the gift *was* most generous. How long had he been collecting these precious herbs? A year? Two? And to so freely offer it to us!

I hurriedly rose, clapping my hands as if to slap some semblance of reason into my head and heart. "Come, Captain, let us find my nona. I want to see her face when you give her your gift." I started to leave.

But my father's voice called me back. "Tiliani."

I turned and went back to him, leaving the captain at the door. "Yes, Papa?"

His keen eyes shifted back and forth over mine. "Remember yourself," he said softly. "If you are going to give a Fiorentini a chance at claiming your heart, be certain that it is Aurelio."

"Of course, Papa," I said, feeling the heat of a blush on my cheeks. This potential union between Siena and Firenze was precarious enough. We did not need any complicating factors. I gave him what I hoped was a reassuring smile, but felt it fade as soon as I joined the captain in the hallway. "This way," I said, leading him to the next room.

We found my grandmother wringing out a wet cloth and placing it on the forehead of a man who was spiking a fever.

When she was finished, I cleared my throat. "Nona, Captain Valeri has brought us a gift."

Valentino lifted the box toward her as she rose, wiping her damp hands on her skirt. The shy smile he gave her threatened to melt my heart a bit more, so I swiftly concentrated on my grandmother. But as she set it on a side table and opened it, sifting through the neatly boxed herbs inside, I was undone by her tearful expression as she turned to Valentino, hand over her heart. "Captain, 'tis most gracious of you! It has been some time since I have had bindweed, and I have never found mullein or bluebell. And with this last battle, I have used all of my alkanet!" She went up to him and took his hand in both of hers, lifting it to her cheek, tears in her bright, blue eyes. *"Grazie, grazie mille."*

My mouth fell open. My grandmother was a loving woman, but she was strong and, most of the time, largely stalwart. To see her tearful thanks, her subservient action with his hand, took me aback, as it clearly had with Valentino. It came to me, then. She had been desolated, facing the fact that her most-needed herbs were gone. In desperation over the need of all these wounded men. Valentino had arrived like an angel of hope, bearing gifts.

"You are most welcome, Lady Betarrini," he said gently. "I know you shall make the best use of them."

"But then your own chest shall be empty when your men have need of it."

He shook his head. "I shall begin to search for replacements at once."

"Tiliani is a good herb hunter," Nona said, looking fondly at me. "You must go with our friend at once," she directed, "to begin rebuilding his own medicinal stash."

I paused. "I do not—"

"Do not argue with your nona," she said with a playful frown, putting her hands on my shoulders and turning me around, as if I were still a girl of ten rather than two-and-twenty. "Show the good captain the glen, where we oft find hawthorn and mallow. And fennel might be sprouting by now in that meadow nearby. 'Twill be good for you both to get some sunshine and quiet after these last days full of such strife."

"Yes, Nona," I said, awkwardly leaving with the captain, hoping my father wouldn't spot us as we went out.

We paused out in the hallway, separating to make way for two maids carrying buckets of hot water to my father's chambers.

My father wanted me to mind myself about the captain. I knew he truly thought I should keep a distance. And my grandmother was pushing us together—intentionally or not.

"So, m'lady?" Valentino said, a hand resting on his wide, leather belt. "Might you show me the way to the glen? Or tell me how to get there?"

I wondered if I could direct him. But there truly was no way to describe it. It was a hidden space, a place few ever reached, because one had to climb. I looked him in the eye, wondering if he was concerned about the same thing I was, but his expression was guileless, and the only thing I sensed was his earnest intent to find more herbs to fill his empty chest.

"I shall show you," I said resolutely, "then leave you to hunt."

That, I thought with some satisfaction, was the best solution. And a way to obey *both* of my elders.

LUCIANA BETARRINI

With the crowd's cries of "She-Wolf!" still ringing in my ears, I allowed Franco to usher me to the table at the far end of the hall to dine with his parents and four curious younger brothers. The youngest, Gregorio, a child of about five, sat across from me, beside his mother. The next eldest, about fourteen, was by my side, Franco on the other.

"Why do they call you She-Wolf?" the child asked me, then took a big bite of lamb.

"Gregorio!" chastened his mother. "That is not appropriate."

But I liked little kids. "I think it's because I have hair and fangs that come out at night while you sleep!" I said with a wink.

Gregorio's eyes grew wide, and he looked worriedly at his mother. But she was laughing at me, her eyes warm. She was maybe thirty years old. Lord Fortebraccio's second wife? She wasn't old enough to be Franco's mother, was she? And yet I knew they began birthing babies earlier in this era. It was common to be married by sixteen and a mother by eighteen. It was the reason that Lady Tiliani was considered an old maid and had fairly resigned herself to never getting married at all. Until Aurelio arrived. And now she was facing as unwelcome a prospect as I—an arranged marriage on behalf of the republic.

Franco poured more wine into my goblet. "So you have a good

sense of humor," he said approvingly, seeming to mentally check off something pleasant on his Could-She-Be-the-One list.

"My brother keeps me laughing," I replied, then took a breath. "Speaking of Domenico . . . sir, since you have esteemed me worthy of consideration as your bride, would it not be appropriate to release my brother and have him with us as well?"

Franco gave me a sidelong look, stabbed a piece of meat with the tip of his knife, and bit off a chunk. "Rest assured, your brother is not suffering mistreatment. You have no cause to fret."

"I fret because he is in your dungeon at all. 'Tis not the sort of treatment that I expect for my family members."

"Yes, well, that particular family member murdered one of my finest knights."

The table grew still and quiet.

I took that in, not allowing myself to look away. "It was a battle. Your knights were killing as many of us as we were of you. That is hardly murder."

He looked up, and for the first time, I saw that he was battling tears. Nico had killed someone dear to him. Truly dear. Inwardly, I groaned.

His father gave him a stern look, as if to say that if any tear fell, he'd be in big trouble. And for the first time, I felt a measure of empathy for the kid. But he took a swift breath in through his nostrils and leveled his gaze at me, pulling it together.

"I shall consider releasing your brother in the coming days." He lifted a finger, shushing me, when I began to protest. "I believe that leaving him where he is for now is most prudent."

His father grunted in approval and took a sip of wine.

I took a moment to deal with the fact that this man—boy, really—had lifted a finger to quiet me, and I had done as he silently demanded. But this teen held my brother's life—and mine too—in his hands. Despite the dress, despite the fancy hairdo, despite the subtle offer of marriage, I was a captive. *And this is not contemporary America.*

"You must, at the very least, allow me to visit him," I dared to press. I summoned my years of Jane Austen character study and lifted a hand to my breast, mentally cursing myself for using my body, sort of, to get what I wanted.

I know, I know. It was lame. But I was pretty desperate. "I do so worry over his well-being," I said, trailing my fingers across my chest.

Franco paused, mid-bite, clearly irritated—and unaccustomed—to a woman pressing him at all. But then his eyes were drawn to my figure, and he smiled, all hundred-percent lordly lord. He waved his beringed fingers in an elegant oval. "You may see your brother. But he shall remain inside his cell and you outside it, and a guard shall remain with you at all times. Understood?"

"Yes, yes," I said, utterly relieved at the thought of at least getting a chance to see Nico, speak to him. "Grazie."

"Sup and drink, my friends!" cried Franco, lifting his goblet and rising. "We shall mourn our lost friends and family members in the coming days. But tonight, we shall celebrate the memory of their lives with good food and good drink and a fine round of dancing. For though we did not gain the territory we sought, we proved ourselves a worthy adversary, a republic who is to be taken seriously by her neighbors. And we gained admirable captives—" He paused to gesture to me. "One that might gain us access to fortunes untold."

I froze. I was a captive worth access to fortunes? What was that about?

But I was more chagrined over his mention of dancing, shallow as that was. Because it was about to happen. Had I learned enough from Guilio? Would I remember the steps in the heat of the moment? And if I blew it, what would happen? What would they know about me? What would they suspect? Could I pass it off as your average cultural divide, given that we were from "Britannia"? Or had they known many English travelers and merchants who would make me look like a fool if I didn't figure it out? I could only be thankful that Aurelio Paratore wasn't here, because if they put together all my medieval social faux pas and his testimony of us arriving near the tombs and not being adept at dancing—

"M'lady?" Franco inquired, refilling my goblet, a fact that I distantly decided was not a good idea. The last thing I needed was to get drunk. "Are you quite well?"

I took a deep breath. "I am well and yet I feel somewhat weary. It has been a day, a day like no other." Maybe that would get me out of it.

He studied me, and for a moment, he looked older than his seventeen or eighteen years. Because he seemed to really see me, remember what I had been through in these last days. The battle. He had been there, I'd gathered. But far from the front lines. He'd heard of my fights, but not seen them himself. Nico had killed his friend—but the young lord hadn't been there to see it himself. I'd told him of the cart. Of the townspeople pelting us with rotten fruit. He'd already returned home.

But then he sat back with a close-lipped smile, as if he knew every thought in my head. All of what I had experienced. He folded his arms. And in that action, his smug expression, thinking he had me, I knew I had to find a way out sooner rather than later. This was a guy who thought he could use me. My stature. My name. My capture. My body.

And God help me, in that moment, I knew that even if I had to stay in medieval Italy forever, I was *not* going to stay with him. I wasn't going to be his wife. Even if I had to fight my way out of here.

We could hear the musicians tuning their instruments, apparently the sign that dancing was to begin, and my pulse picked up. Guilio had taught me four different dances. Would they be the same? *At least I have some idea,* I told myself. It wasn't like I was going in totally cold.

We proceeded, my arm on Franco's, to the far end of the Great

Hall and separated into lines of men and women. My mind spun, trying to figure out by the opening notes what was first, and with a whoosh of relief, I recognized the steps and rhythm, an easy country dance that drew together couples in a cross-handed grip, where the "maid" traditionally looked away for the first circle, and then to her partner in the second. We separated, joining hands in a hop-and-skip pattern for a circle, then dove under the opposite line for a figure-eight formation before creating a new circle.

I was so intent on following the closest woman's moves— rendering me a half second to a full second behind most of the time—that I was late in recognizing the slowing of the music, the dancers, and the change in focus. I turned. And what I saw took my breath away.

Giulio, Ilaria, and twelve knights strode into the end of the Great Hall, taking position in an arc of six, with the other six behind them. They had been stripped of their weapons. But there was no denying their power and stance. Giulio and Ilaria stepped forward, their Forelli-gold embroidered tunics glittering in the candlelight.

"Good evening, Lord and Lady Fortebraccio, Sir Franco," Guilio said, nodding to each of them. "We are here as emissaries from Castello Forelli, come to reclaim Lady Luciana and Lord Domenico Betarrini, as well as negotiate a trade of prisoners."

But even as he spoke of others, his eyes were solely on me. His word, *reclaim*, oddly stirred me. Reclaim. Had I been claimed in the first place?

He wanted to free the other captives. But his eyes seemed like he wanted only one—me.

Claim.

It echoed inside my head. *Claim, claim, claim.* I wondered what it might be like to be fully claimed by Lord Giulio Greco.

Franco noted Giulio's proprietary gaze. His hands went to his belt, and he squared off with Giulio, not nearly big enough to really take him on, but this was his home turf. And he clearly didn't like what he was sensing between the two of us. I fought for breath. Was this really happening? Two guys going toe to toe over me?

I'd never felt before like I was the only one someone wanted. Someone who seemed to see me, look into my soul and know me, and still want me, despite my failings. Was that what I noted in Guilio's gaze? Or was he here just to get us back on behalf of the Forellis? Regardless, I was overwhelmed in seeing them here, hope rising that they would take us back home. To Castello Forelli.

My pulse seemed to pound everywhere through me. I could feel my life force, in total. I was absorbed, hearing a far-off, ethereal *humm,* like I'd heard in the tomb when we were catapulted through time. The tomb. The handprints. The path Nico and I must take to get back.

But now there was Lord Giulio Greco. All manly and handsome, his eyes piercing Franco, practically daring him to make a move. His hands went to his own belt.

It was then that I finally admitted to myself that I was crushing on him pretty hard. For someone seven hundred years older than I was. Just as Gabi had for Marcello. Lia for Luca. I was on the precipice of something monumental. Something that could change my whole life's trajectory. Exactly as it had for them.

But did I want that? Really? Did I want Giulio Greco to truly claim me? Relationships in this era were different. What would Guilio think I should do as a girlfriend? Act? Would I be free to be me?

What was I thinking? I had no business falling for anyone here. Now. I had to talk to Nico. He'd help me figure it out. Shake some sense into me. He wasn't ready to leave yet. But he also hadn't said he wanted to stay forever. Neither of us wanted to stay here forever.

"We hold thirty-two of your men in our dungeons," Ilaria said. "You hold . . . ?"

"Twelve, aside from the Betarrinis," Lord Fortebraccio supplied from his chair atop the dais beside his wife.

"We shall return twelve of your own in exchange for our dozen in your cells now," Giulio said. "And the remaining twenty in exchange for Domenico and Luciana Betarrini."

Twenty?

Ilaria's eyes sifted through the crowd, looking to me and then for Nico, and her eyes narrowed. "Where *is* Domenico?"

"He remains in our dungeon," Lord Fortebraccio said. "We have found that 'tis best to keep sister and brother separated. They are quite formidable when fighting together, and we wished to enjoy a peaceable eve." He leaned back in his big chair. "While we can arrange for an exchange of prisoners, man for man, we shall take the remaining twenty in exchange for Domenico Betarrini alone. Luciana shall remain in our keep."

The muscle in Giulio's cheek pulsed. "That is unacceptable. Lady Luciana must be returned home as well."

"My son has done her the honor of considering her as a potential bride," Lord Fortebraccio said, ignoring how Guilio and Ilaria stiffened. "We have learned that Lady Tiliani is considering a union with a Paratore." He lifted his hands. "Would this not be another fortuitous alliance? A nuptial bond with both Firenze and Perugia would only strengthen Castello Forelli's—and Siena's—fragile hold on peace. All of Perugia would celebrate. 'Twould go a long way in soothing our pain over the men your knights murdered."

But it might be a pain for me and Tiliani, I thought.

Again I wondered if this all could really be happening. Would the Grecos consider it?

Thankfully, I saw both Giulio and Ilaria slowly shake their heads. "As my lords told you, we had nothing to do with your murdered patrol. You attacked us for false reasons. And Lady Gabriella made us foreswear we would return with both of their cousins," Giulio said. "We cannot leave here without them. If young Lord Franco wishes to vie for the lady's hand, he may do so. But her bride price shall not be negotiated here, by us. You must make your bid to the Forellis."

He didn't look my way. How I wished he would look my way again. So easily he said those words. *Bride price.* Did he not care if Franco tried to marry me?

What was I thinking? This was all crazy—so crazy. I wasn't getting married. To *anybody.* I was twenty-one. I had two semesters left to get done and nab my history degree. Then I would go get a job. A real job, where I'd have a cell phone and fancy heels and Starbucks in my hand all day long.

Except . . . Giulio. He was looking at me now, those dark-blue eyes silently asking me how I fared, taking in my fine gown, my hair . . . and with that one glance of admiration, my heart fluttered again.

"You misunderstand us, Lord Greco," Lord Fortebraccio said. "There shall be no bride price. She shall be freely given to take my son's hand, or she shall be ransomed for a thousand florins."

Women gasped. Men murmured. How much was a thousand florins? A thousand bucks? I glanced around. No, more. Much more.

"That is a king's sum," Giulio countered.

"Yes, well, we would have claimed two castelli in the last days had not Siena arrived to aid you." Lord Fortebraccio's voice was like steel. "Worth far more than a thousand florins."

So this was it. I was some sort of human bandage for his wounded pride and disappointment. As well as a human tie between Perugia and Siena.

"'Twould take months for us to gather such a sum," Ilaria protested. "Mayhap a year!"

"You may not need to do so," Lord Fortebraccio said with a shrug. "Over the next weeks, my son shall determine if he favors Lady Luciana. If he does, then you shall be spared gathering that fortune. And if he does not, then you may have the lady with our blessing . . . once we have the florins in hand."

"You sorely abused our lords, Marcello and Luca. You exacted anything *due* you from the wounds on their persons," Giulio bit out, taking a step forward, one hand in a fist. "My lady told you that action alone is grounds for war. And then you dared to attack the castello. Keeping Lady Luciana captive is yet another reason for us to draw swords."

Lord Fortebraccio leaned forward, expression set. "I believe we have proven ourselves in battle. If Siena comes behind you again, other Umbrians shall rise to back us. But would this not be best settled in a more peaceable way? See if my son takes to this lovely, intriguing girl. In a fortnight or two, you and the Forellis could return to help celebrate their nuptials. Would that not be a far better conclusion for all?"

Guilio held his head high. "Not for all." But what I saw in his eyes made my heart sink. He was running out of arguments.

"Come, come," Lord Fortebraccio lifted his goblet. "Castello Fortebraccio is a fine place for any lady to settle. Would you not agree, wife?"

"Indeed, m'lord," his wife returned, with a demure nod.

"Rest assured that Lady Luciana shall not want for anything," Franco spoke up. "I shall see to it."

Giulio gave him a cold stare then, jaw muscles twitching, but said nothing.

"You must be weary from your ride," Lord Fortebraccio remarked, his tone changing. "Let this be an evening of healing and goodwill. Come, join us." He raised a hand. "Food and wine for our neighbors. Ready some rooms." He turned back to the Grecos, all *host* now, as if they hadn't just had the most unsettling throwdown. "You shall partake of our fine victuals and sleep before you return to the Forellis. As a sign of good faith, we shall even send our prisoners home with you, trusting you shall return our thirty-two in two days' time."

Lady Fortebraccio clapped her hands toward the musicians, and in moments, music again filled the air. Stiltedly, the group separated, most of the knights going to the table that Lady Fortebraccio led them to, but Giulio and Ilaria moved directly to me, ignoring Franco's outraged expression as they brushed by either side of him.

Giulio led me to the side of the room as the people prepared to dance again. The feel of his hand—big and warm at my lower back—sent shivers up my neck. He searched my eyes. "Are you well, Luciana? Are they treating you properly?"

Ilaria stood close, glaring with fierce eyes at the nobles in their finery, as if every one of them was a threat.

"I am well enough," I said in a hushed tone. "Other than the fact that somehow, I've ended up a potential bride of a boy. And my brother is still in the dungeon. Please, please tell me there's a way out of this. Other than sending the Forellis into debt?"

Their grim faces made my heart sink.

"So I am to remain here? Alone?" I hated how small and whiny I sounded, but for the first time—thinking of even Domenico far away—I felt pure panic.

"Nay, m'lady," Ilaria said. "I shall insist I remain. As your companion. Your chaperone."

I wanted to hug her. "I believe I can handle that one," I said, glancing over to Franco, who stood with a friend, staring furiously at us, his cheeks red.

"Undoubtedly," Giulio said. "But if he—" He rubbed his face in agitation. "If he tries anything unchivalrous, my lady, you must inform me. I shall exact punishment from him. I already ache to take my revenge on these people who so sorely mistreated Marcello and Luca, as well as wounded and killed so many of our friends."

"Watch yourself, brother. Remember, we are emissaries," Ilaria warned. "They could toss us out, here and now, without even those in the dungeon. We owe it to their families to free them. We shall find a way to rescue Luciana as well."

"I could make myself thoroughly disagreeable," I said, at last alighting on an idea that was solely in my power.

A slow smile spread over Giulio's face. "That is a fine idea. If you are a shrew, the boy may abandon his pursuit."

"Mayhap," Ilaria said benignly. "She could try. But then they shall insist on those florins."

Giulio's face fell and, with it, my spirits. "It is a terribly large sum?" I asked meekly.

He gave me a puzzled look.

"I mean . . . I do not know how it compares to our form of currency," I added hurriedly.

"'Tis a terribly large sum indeed," he said, still puzzled how I might not know this. "Luca might appeal to the Nine, to see if Siena might contribute. But Castello Forelli . . ."

"We rarely have more than a hundred florins in our chests, even at the height of harvest," Ilaria supplied. "It costs a great deal to run the castello, man it, feed our people, pay the knights."

Her eyes flickered, and I saw what had drawn her attention. Franco approached. "M'lady," he said, giving me a bow. "May I have this next dance?"

"I fear she has already promised this one to me," Giulio informed him with a curt nod, offering me his arm.

I set my hand atop his, but seeing Franco's fury, I paused. "Mayhap the next one, m'lord?"

Franco straightened and then lifting his chin, permitted us to pass.

"That is not the way of a shrew," Giulio said under his breath.

"Yes, well, I shall at least see you, Nico, and our men to safety before I begin my campaign," I said. I tried to act normal as he stood beside me and placed his arm across my lower back to my hip, then held out his other. I did as the other women were doing with their partners, placing my right hand gently over his on my hip, and crossing over with my left to take his other.

The steps came easily, with him leading me. It was a basic box with three other couples, *three steps, pause, three steps, pause,* and as we returned to our original position, Giulio let go of my hip and lifted our enjoined hands to lead me in a three-step-pause circle, and then again, and again. We had practiced it every day in that meadow. But there, it had simply been practice, and I'd worked so hard to learn the steps. Now, with the music, and the candelabra casting such a warm light about the room, making his black hair glisten, his dark-blue eyes appear like mountain pools, I felt something shift in my heart. We turned, looking into each other's eyes, and I glanced at his lips, wishing we were alone. Wishing he would kiss me.

"What of your father, Luciana?" he asked quietly as we resumed our original position.

I blinked. Had he not just felt that crazy moment like I did? Was I losing it? "My-my father?" I stammered.

"Could we send him word in Britannia? Might he have access to a portion of the sum?"

Part of me was heartened that he was at least still thinking how to free me. But the other part was ashamed at the lie he believed true.

He paused, frowning. "Are you well? You look pale."

"It's this dress," I said quickly. "I can barely breathe."

He led me from the floor and toward two chairs near a table, where a sweating pewter pitcher of cold water beckoned. "While I wish for you to breathe freely, I must say . . . you are the most beautiful woman in this room," he said in a low tone, his eyes steadily holding my own. "I wager you are the most beautiful in all of Perugia."

It was my turn to blush. "Nay. You flatter me, m'lord."

"'Tis not idle talk." He poured me a goblet of water and offered it to me. "When we return to Castello Forelli—"

"Is it at last my turn, m'lady?" Franco interrupted Giulio. "I believe I have been most patient."

"The lady is feeling a bit light-headed," Giulio said gruffly. "She needs to rest."

"Nonsense," Franco brushed him off. "She has now sated her thirst. I have come to claim what she promised."

I rose, wanting to break these two up before it got ugly. Giulio was so on edge, it wouldn't take much more. "I am much improved, Lord Greco," I said, placing a gentling hand on his forearm. "Thank you. And I did promise Sir Franco this next one." I turned to Franco and allowed him to draw me out on to the dance floor, feeling Giulio's eyes on me with every step.

But as Franco took my hand with his, so slim and cold in comparison to Giulio's warm, firm grip, I fought the desire to shiver. The way he looked at me—as if I already belonged to him, as if I truly had no way out other than to become his bride—filled me with ice-cold fear. We began to dance, and as we did so, the room began to slowly spin. I faltered.

"Come, m'lady," he chided. "Surely even the English know this step."

"What? Oh, yes," I said, trying to catch up with him, still a half step behind. But as we completed the first round, the room began to spin faster. I panted for breath and felt the first pang of queasiness. Sweat beaded on my forehead, and belatedly, I felt my knees buckle.

But it was Giulio who caught me as I fell. Franco had stepped back, perplexed.

Giulio picked me up in his arms. "The lady is plainly overcome," Giulio gritted out. "I told you she was light-headed. She has endured much and needs to rest."

"And a dress that allows her to take a full breath on the morrow," Ilaria said. "Kindly direct us to her quarters."

16

"Shall we fetch horses?" Valentino asked.

"Nay, the glen is only over the next rise," I said, pointing my chin to the hills to our southeast. "And it is too steep and heavy with wood for horses to manage well."

"Making it a fertile place for what we seek."

"Indeed." I stopped by the kitchens and took two gathering baskets, as well as two pruning knives. I paused. "Shall you don a weapon?" Our morning patrol had not detected any new interlopers within miles, but that could swiftly change. While Perugia had been sent home with their tails between their legs, and Firenze would not wish to begin anything new with Lord Paratore pursuing my hand, brigands oft roamed the roads. And if they knew I was out and about, I would be an enticing target. My aunt and uncle, as well as my parents, had drilled that into me since I was a child. It had taken years before they allowed me to take part in the morning patrol, and only if Ilaria and Giulio or my cousins were at my side.

"Aurelio would skin me alive if he learned I had escorted you outside the gates, unarmed. Let me get my broadsword. And four of our men ready to keep watch over us. They shall alert us if anyone approaches."

Aurelio. He had left that morn to return to Firenze for a few days, declaring that he would return with the promise of aid, should Perugia rise against us again. His eyes had glittered with excitement at the opportunity to bridge our divide in yet another way. And truthfully, if he could secure what he hoped, mayhap we truly did stand on the edge of an entirely new era of peace between our republics. He had taken some of his men—two patrols had arrived to aid us after they learned of the attack—but left his captain and four behind. "I shall leave my best at your side," he had told me, taking my hand in his. "To stand in my stead." With a kiss to my knuckles, he had departed. And for the first time in a week, I found I could take a full breath.

I watched as Valentino approached the four men, who were already mounted and ready. Captain Valeri went over to one, and the man passed his captain his sword. Valentino slid it over his shoulder and into a sheath at his back. Though I felt well protected and didn't intend to stay out long, I fetched my bow and a quiver of arrows from the weaponry room. I always felt more secure with them on my shoulder, cumbersome as it was when carrying a basket. I would simply set them aside once we reached the glen. Echoes of the battle just days before still rang in my head like I was standing inside a massive cathedral bell having tolled its last, yet still humming.

The gates were opened for us, and we walked outside, our guardians following behind on horseback. "Would the lady care to ride with me, Captain?" called one cheekily. "I would not wish her to weary herself."

Valentino cast a wise eye over his shoulder. "I believe the lady wishes to walk. I already offered her a mount."

I heard another grunt something bawdy under his breath, and the others laughed. Valentino stopped and turned. "We head to the glen just over the saddle of those hills to our southeast," he said sternly. "Head out, now, to surround it and keep watch. If you see anyone, known or unknown, approaching the glen, ride immediately to us. I shall give you the signal when we are ready to return to the castello."

All smiles disappeared from the knights.

"Sí, Captain," said one.

"Sí, Captain," echoed the other three. They edged past us and then galloped to take their stations. I had to admire his command. As well as their obvious respect—and the comraderie they all shared too.

"Are they men Aurelio recruited?" I asked. "Or did you?"

"I recruited every one, as well as the other twenty-six who reside at Palazzo Paratore in Firenze. I insisted upon it. If I am to rely on a man—as well as rely on him to protect my lord—I must know him well."

"Tell me of Palazzo Paratore. How did you come to abide there and be in Aurelio's service?"

He paused a moment. "Eighteen years ago, I was a child of the streets, and very ill. 'Twas my good fortune that Aurelio's mother found me and took pity on me. She brought me to her home and allowed me to sleep in their stables. Gave me food, medicine. And then convinced Lord Paratore, Aurelio's father, to make me a squire."

I raised a brow. Squires were usually children of other nobles, fostered by allies' families. To become a squire, and eventually a knight—especially a knight with a destrier suitable for battle—took a fair amount of funds. Or had he earned his armor, his horses, by his impeccable service to the Paratores? Been given them as rewards? I noted he rode a gelding, not a destrier; mayhap he'd yet to find the funds for a warhorse or had left it behind in Firenze.

"What of your parents?" I asked.

"I never knew my father. And my mother . . ." He looked up to the canopy of trees. "She was no lady." He flushed. "But she loved me, until her last breath."

"She died when you were quite young, then," I said gently, his sad eyes making more and more sense.

"When I was but five. Taken by a round of plague that ravaged

Firenze. I was on the streets, begging and stealing for a year before Lady Paratore took me in."

I absorbed that and allowed the Paratore name to be redeemed just a bit more. Mayhap they were not all villains. Mayhap 'twas only one branch of their family tree.

"Are you older or younger than Aurelio?" I said.

"A year younger," he said. "We were raised together. Became like brothers. When it came time to name a captain, he turned to me first. He honored me."

I nodded. But the knowledge that they were so close—and that he was beholden to the Paratores for his very life—made me feel a little sick to my stomach. Was he feeling this growing pull between us like I was? How was I to truly consider Aurelio's bid for my hand when I was drawn threefold to his captain?

We fell into an uneasy silence.

"You have no siblings, m'lady?"

"I did. Two younger brothers, Dante and Rocco, both taken to heaven."

His eyes grew even more grave. "How old were you?"

"Fifteen when Dante died, when he fell from his horse. Eighteen when Rocco passed in a fever."

We walked for a bit in silence. Our mutual losses of family members bound us together all the more. Moving our way through the rocks, he took my elbow, assisting me. Though I needed no such solicitous care, I allowed it. Whereas I might've shaken off Fortino's or Guilio's hand with irritation, Valentino's hand warmed me.

"I shall always miss my brothers, but their faces are fading in my memory," I confessed. "That is the worst part. How can we lose the visage of someone who was so dear to us?"

He nodded and clasped his hands behind his back as the path straightened. "I oft try and remember my mother. All I can remember is her hair." He paused and looked at me, eyes widening. I turned slightly toward him. "Mayhap that is why I was so taken aback, the first time we saw you." He lifted his hand, and I tensed when I realized he meant to touch an errant strand that had fallen by my cheek.

"May I?" he asked, his hand hovering precariously close to my hair, my cheek, so close I could feel the brush of them.

"Yes," I breathed, partially drawn, partially perplexed.

He took the strand of my sandy-blond hair between his fingers and thumb, stroking it, utterly intent. But his sad eyes told me he was not thinking of me. He was thinking of his mother. He had cascaded almost two decades back. "Mayhap this color, with streaks of sunlight. Or mayhap it was just a bit darker. And her eyes . . . Nay, I believe they were brown, not like yours. Yours are like a summer sky at noontide. Such an ethereal blue. Hers were . . ."

He stared at me, and I held my breath as he searched my eyes, as if he could plumb from the depths something of her. Recall something of her, in me.

He startled and abruptly took a step backward. "Forgive me, m'lady. I utterly forgot myself."

"'Tis all right, my friend," I said, forcing a swift smile to my face and turning to resume our walk as if immediately forgetting what had just transpired. "I am honored that you would allow me such an intimate glimpse into your past. And if there is something in me that helps you recall the mother you loved so dearly, then I am glad. I oft gaze after boys in the village or Siena who remind me of Rocco or Dante."

"Your parents did not have any other children?"

I shook my head. "The Lord did not bless them with more. Truth be told, losing my brothers almost broke my mother. In that last battle with . . . Firenze," I said, seeing no way to avoid it, "my mother and Zia Gabi lost their father, as well as their dear friend, Lord Greco, Chiara's adoptive father. Chiara's mother was pregnant with Giulio when he died. Their losses—as well as so many others—sent my mother into a period of darkness. She has a tender heart."

He cocked his head. "I saw nothing but a warrior in her during the battle with the Perugians."

"Nor did I. Clearly, she can still rise to the challenge. But my mother feels things intensely. All things. My grandmother says it is what makes her a good artist."

"Do you feel things so deeply as well?" he probed gently.

I smiled. "I believe I am somewhat like her, and yet somewhat like Zia Gabi too. I am not as given to melancholia. For months and months after her father and Lord Greco died—after we lost so many in the battle and plague—she did not draw or paint. It was like she had died herself. Finally Zia Gabi set her down before a canvas. She put charcoal in Mama's hand again and told her to draw everything ugly and dark that was inside her. To get it out and onto the parchment. Out of her heart and mind."

"What did she draw then?" he asked. "Scenes of battle? Death masks?"

"Nay," I said, tears rising unexpectedly in my eyes, the story meaning even more to me now after our battle—after losing people I cared for too. I had seen the drawings, now curling and molding at the edges in the library box. "She drew all the people she loved and had lost. But when she drew them, she drew them laughing. Or hugging. She drew Lord Greco, cuddling Chiara and her mother. Knights we had lost, as she longed to remember them."

He gave me a low, thoughtful *hmmm*. "I had heard that the Ladies Forelli were unusual. I am glad that she found a way through her grief. Some never find their way past the dark veil again." He was silent a moment before speaking again. "Did she do the same after your brothers passed?"

I thought about that. How Mama had disappeared from us again for several years. But how she had fought her way back. "She suffered a dark period, for certain. And when she returned to us, she was not as tender as she once was. She is far more fierce now than she ever was. Still loving," I assured him, "but guarded now. As if she shelters her heart."

He nodded. "Loss does that to a person. One must don new armor in order to not be so hurt again."

"Indeed. But I do not believe that is how our Lord wishes us to live. Armored, on the inside. If we are to grasp—fully grasp—the bounty he has offered us, we must be willing to risk, do we not? If we cannot open ourselves to the width and breadth of what he offers, then we shall narrow what can be taken in."

He gave me a sidelong glance. "Perhaps you are correct. But believing and acting on said beliefs are oft separate things."

"My Zia Gabi, Lady Gabriella," I amended, "has told me that our world is as full of life as it is death. That it is like a ripe pomegranate, with one seed after another to be popped and tasted, both piquant and sweet."

His eyes held a smile. "As I said, the Ladies Forelli are most unusual. And wonderful," he quickly added.

"That they are."

"They have done well, raising you," Valentino said. "You are a combination of them both. Fierce and tender. Wise, yet aware."

I bit my lip. Never had I had such a conversation with a man outside of my family. Never. Why was this so easy, conversing with him?

He cleared his throat. "Forgive me, m'lady. I have again forgotten myself." He lifted a branch from our path for me as we entered the heavily wooded glen, rife with ferns, and began making our way upward. "There is something about you that seems to make me . . . forgetful."

"Indeed," I said, lightly. I forced myself to try to begin our hunt in earnest, to ignore his proximity. I began listing in my head what we were to find. "Here, before we get much higher," I indicated, "should be some mallow. As well as some fungi, among the fallen wood near the creek."

"Indeed!" he said, stooping and cutting several stems with

their signature pink flowers. I know Nona and Chiara used the leaves in a poultice for wounds.

"Well done!" I turned in a circle and then set my bow and quiver of arrows against a tree. "There should be more about," I muttered. I brushed one fern back and then another. "Here!" I cried, glad to have matched him. I used my small knife to cut the stems free and proudly placed them in my basket.

"Bracket fungi!" he called, excited by his next discovery. "Mounds of them by this tree!"

I hurried over and crouched to help him harvest the orange-brown mushrooms, sneaking glances at him as I did so. All traces of sorrow had briefly left his face—only joy remained. Remembering my father's warning, I forced myself to look away and rise, making my way up the path again. I had to keep my distance from him, even in my thoughts.

Farther up the path, I found a small patch of gentian, with its little blue flowers. As soon as Valentino reached me, I left him to harvest the bitter herb, endeavoring to keep more distance. Ahead, I found a hawthorn sapling and swiftly stripped the bark—used for sedation—before moving to pluck the flowers. Chiara frequently had long rows of them out and drying to preserve them. I couldn't remember how they were used.

Valentino moved closer and lifted a branch, heavy with the blossoms. "Did you know the Greeks used these in wedding ceremonies?"

"I can see why," I said, gazing at them. "They are beautiful."

Weddings. Why could I not consider Valentino as a potential groom? I dared not meet his gaze and continued to trudge up the hill.

"And here is mulberry!" He brushed past me to cradle the fruit in his hand and smile back at me, victorious. "Your grandmother was quite right in sending us here. This glen is a veritable treasure trove!" Again, there was no trace of sorrow in his eyes, and his smile . . . his smile took my very breath. This was where the man belonged. As mighty as he was on the battlefield, this was what brought him joy. Amongst nature, harvesting medicinals.

"What is it?" he asked with puzzlement.

"What? What is what?"

"You gaze at me in a most curious fashion."

"Do I?" I felt the heat of a blush at my cheeks. "'Tis only that you look . . . well, for the first time, you look at peace. And so glad to be out here in the woods."

He gave me a quick smile and then turned to cut the clump of berries and place them in his basket. "It reminds me," he said, "of hunting for herbs and medicinals with Cook. She was like a mother to me."

"I thought it was Lady Paratore who took you under her wing."

"She saved me. Gave me a life. But it was not proper for her to do anything more. It was Cook who raised me."

I understood but was curious. "If you'd had the opportunity, would you have liked to go to Bologna? To study? Or have your own apothecary?"

He drew slightly back, and the sorrow returned to his eyes. "What good is it," he said softly, "to wonder after paths we cannot take?" He leaned an arm against a tree, looked down, and kicked at a loose rock.

But as he lifted his eyes to mine, I knew he did not speak of Bologna.

He spoke of us.

I swallowed hard. So he *did* sense this draw between us.

All at once I was aware of how close we stood. So close, the folds of my wide skirts surrounded his legs. I abruptly stepped backward. "Well, you are firmly established here now," I said brightly. "My basket is already full." I lifted it up in evidence, despite the fact that there was still room. "I shall leave you to fill your own."

I turned to go.

But he reached out and gently grasped my arm.

I paused, waiting for him to release me. But he did not.

Slowly I turned toward him.

We stood there a moment in silence. Never had I wanted a man to kiss me as I did in that moment. And the look in his warm, hazel eyes . . .

Suddenly, he let go of my arm, and we both startled back to ourselves. Our places. "Forgive me," he said, horror in his voice. "M'lady, we cannot—"

"Nay, nay!" I said, forcing a laugh, the sound hollow. "We cannot. Pay no heed to this, Captain," I said, turning to resume my retreat. "Nona always said there is something magical about this glen. That 'tis the fae-folk themselves who planted so many things we can make use of. And we all know that faeries like to sprinkle their confusion-dust around their human adversaries."

"Oh?" he asked, following me. I could hear the hint of a smile in his tone, but dared not look, dared not stop and let him come near again. "In order to do what?"

"To do what faeries do! Create mayhem. Twist coils in our minds." *And our hearts,* I added silently.

"Troublesome sprites," he remarked. "You might have warned me."

"Indeed. I was negligent, Captain. Hereafter, I shall give you ample warning before we forage again."

The words were out before I had thought them through. And they hung there for several seconds as we tromped through the wood.

"So we shall forage again?" he asked tentatively.

"Mayhap," I said overly brightly. "Or now that you know this place, you can come any time you wish. Rest assured, we shall send you home to Firenze with your chest amply resupplied."

This time, I noted he did not respond. Because the thought of leaving troubled him? But at that moment, I wished he would leave and take Aurelio with him. Because they both had tied my mind and heart in far more knots than any faerie might.

✤   ✤   ✤

LUCIANA BETARRINI

I came to in my room, with Ilaria fiddling behind me, trying to unknot the ties that held my bodice together.

"Get her out of that thing," Giulio demanded, his back turned to give us privacy. "She cannot breathe."

Someone pounded at my door. "Lord Greco! Open this door at once!" It was Franco. Giulio had locked him out.

"In a moment! My sister is seeing to our lady!" Giulio called.

When Ilaria still struggled, Giulio let out a low growl, strode over to us, and before I knew what was happening, heard the cutting sounds of knife on cord. All at once I felt the blessed relief of being able to take my first full breath in hours.

"M'lady?" Giulio said, kneeling when he discovered my eyes were open. He nudged his sister aside in order to allow me to turn to my back, and then took my shoulders in his hands. "Are you recovered?"

"I am, partially," I panted, "thanks to your blessed knife, freeing me."

His face grew ruddy, suddenly aware that what he had done was rather inappropriate. "Forgive me. I could not stand it a moment longer."

"Clearly," Ilaria said dryly. "Now you best let the young lord in before he breaks down the door."

Giulio cast her a furious glance. "He is a child. A blind child. Any fool could see Luciana was about to faint. And it was *his* servants' doing, putting her in that tight bodice. That, after all she's endured."

Ilaria placed a steadying hand to his forearm as Franco again pounded on the door and bellowed his demand for entry. "You served our lady well. Now you must serve her by endeavoring to retain what tender hold we have here. Would you have them toss us out this very night? At least one of us must be allowed to remain as Luciana's companion."

He frowned, then glanced at me and leaned close. "We shall see you freed of this place, Luciana. I promise you."

I nodded wearily. "I hope you are right."

"And though they must return to Siena, I shall remain with you," Ilaria said, leaning in from my other side. "Together, we shall find a way for you to escape." She looked at her brother across me, brooking no further argument. "Allow him entry. Now."

"Remember your inner shrew," Giulio whispered to me, giving me a quick smile and a surprising wink. Then he rose, strode to the door, unbolted it, and allowed the blustering young lord in, followed by two maids and four knights who took their stations— two inside the room, two out—ensuring that their young charge would not again be barred from the room.

Ilaria helped me sit up and covered me with a blanket, the back of my open bodice hidden between me and the headboard of the bed.

Franco gave Giulio a furious look. "What right have you to bar any door to me? This is my home, not yours." He poked him in the chest.

I held my breath. But Giulio lifted his hands in a placating manner as he looked down at the younger man with nothing but deference in his expression. "The Ladies Forelli charged us with looking after Lord and Lady Betarrini. To see m'lady falter, faint . . . I could do no other than what I just did—swiftly bring her to a place she might recover. I did not wish to cause you umbrage, m'lord. But see for yourself. She is better." He gestured toward me.

Franco, somewhat mollified, straightened his tunic and turned to me. He moved to the bed and took my hand. "Forgive me, m'lady. I forced you to dance when you were plainly weary. I forgot myself, so taken was I with your beauty."

He waited expectantly. For what? *Oh.*

"I forgive you. The last two days have been . . . momentous. Much has transpired. Between the battle and our *introduction*." Could he not see it? How maxed out I was?

"You merely became a candle at the end of her wick," he supplied. He lifted my hand and bent to kiss my knuckles. "We shall leave you now, in the hands of your maids. They shall see you changed and put to bed. On the morrow, your wick shall be whole again."

"I hope you are right," I said, feeling every word like a weight on my tongue. On the morrow. Tomorrow.

Tomorrow, Giulio and my brother and the knights were going to leave us here in the hands of our enemies. And that thought left me feeling more weary and frightened than ever. I wanted to go with them. To return to Castello Forelli and the Lords and Ladies Forelli, to find out if they were all recovering. To Tiliani and Benedetto and Fortino. To the knights who were gradually becoming familiar friends. Knights that had fought alongside us. Saved us. Sacrificed for us.

Franco stepped back and waited for Ilaria to rise.

"I intend to remain," she said resolutely. "My brother shall go with you, but I shall remain to attend our lady."

Franco clearly did not like it—did he really think he could cut me off from everyone familiar to me?—but he soon realized she wasn't going to back down. With a stiff bow, he turned on his heel, waited for Giulio to exit first, then followed him out, his knights behind him.

Ilaria looked at the maids when the door shut at last. "Is your young lord always so . . . overbearing?"

The maids shared a look, eyes wide, and then they burst out laughing, covering their mouths.

I took that as a yes.

And in that moment, laughing with them and Ilaria—laughing until I cried, because I so desperately needed to laugh—I loved her all the more.

17

TILIANI FORELLI

I spent the following days studiously avoiding Valentino. Ignoring him in the yard, stripped to the waist, sweating and sparring with his men—and ours. Well, fairly ignoring him. Just now I was about to enter the armory, intent on doing inventory, when Nona, emerging from the Great Hall, met me at the door.

"*Buongiorno*, Nona." I greeted her with a kiss to both cheeks. *Good morning.* She looked weary and wan, after caring for the wounded these long days. I felt a measure of guilt for not having assisted her of late. But I had not wanted her knowing looks. She had always known me in ways I did not yet know myself. And I was fairly certain she had noted the draw I felt toward Captain Valeri—and he to me—and had sent us on that medicinal hunt together on purpose. It unsettled me.

I moved to go past her, but she laid a hand on my arm. "*Bella bambina*," she said quietly. 'Twas a pet-name from my childhood, one she had not used in many years. *Beautiful child.*

I turned toward her. Hesitant. Knowing she would not use such tenderness unless she meant to say something I did not wish to hear.

"We are in need of mullein for our medicinal chests. Your father is improving, but he has a troublesome cough this morning. Might you not ask Captain Valeri to take you to the valley to retrieve some? It should be blooming by now."

"Nona." I took a deep breath. "I fear I must be off to fetch supplies to forge more arrows, not medicines. Our stores are severely depleted. My father would expect me to have this done already. I have no time to search for herbs."

She gave me a cat-like smile. "Benedetto and Fortino saw to that two days past. Have you not noticed the young arrow makers in the villages at task as you patrolled?"

I was caught.

I had not noticed. My mind had been . . . elsewhere.

She reached out and cupped my face. "You do not bear the full weight of this castello atop your shoulders, my girl, despite what you feel. Your cousins, and the Grecos, share the weight."

Her words melted me, as I was sure they were meant to do. I fell back against the stone wall and glanced around to make certain we were alone. "Then why do I feel that weight, Nona? Why, with elder cousins—male cousins, at that, in line—must I bear the burden of considering a marriage I do not want?"

She leaned against the opposite wall and crossed her arms and looked to the light of day. Giving me the distance I craved yet remaining near. She was glorious, still, despite her advancing years. She was now six-and-sixty. An age few reached in Toscana. Fewer still reached seventy. And precious few, eighty. But there was something about my nona that was timeless. Vital. And I believed it reached far beyond the fact that she had come to us from another time.

Her gray-blond braid rested over her shoulder. Well-earned wrinkles were at her eyes and cheeks. But she was as beautiful as her daughters. A She-Wolf in her own right. She was the Mama-Wolf that had held her daughters through the most momentous years of their lives. Through peace. Through war. Through loss. Through gain.

"You feel the weight," she said at last, looking to me with those clear, blue, Danish eyes, "because your brothers are gone. And you are your parents' sole remaining hope. But dear one," she stepped toward me, placing her long, slender fingers on either side of my face, "you are *not* their sole hope. Their sole hope is in God. What he wills and what he doesn't. You cannot bear that weight. And if they thought it through, they would want you to choose what makes you happy." She ran a light finger down from my temple to my chin. "They themselves made that choice once," she said, kissing me gently, "at great peril for us all." She took my hand and held it outstretched between us as she stepped away, turned back, and covered my hand with her other. "Go to the valley with Captain Valeri on the morrow—"

"No, Nona. I do not believe it wise. I-I—"

"Go, bella bambina. You must go. See where your heart takes you. Not where the republic directs you." She gently released my hand.

I struggled with my words. "Nona. To do what you suggest may unravel all that my parents wish to knit."

Her eyes and lips lined in an irrepressible way that made me think of the impish faerie-folk.

"Sometimes, we must unravel a few rows in our knitting to get to an errant row and get the stitches right. Go to the valley," she said over her shoulder, as she moved away. "Tell Captain Valeri I have need of mullein and damson, too, if you can find some," she said.

She did not look back as I watched her go. She was not like my friends' lady relations. Indeed, she had never been anything like the rest.

She dipped in, she dipped out. But what she left was formative. Solid every time.

And so now when my Nona directed me, I decided 'twas best to follow.

That eve, I met Captain Valeri in the stables, for the first time in five days. I had positioned myself to be brushing down Cardo and pretended not to notice when he entered to groom his mare.

I resumed my efforts, double-time, as he drew closer. We had not truly spoken since our time in the glen. Certainly, over the last few days we had passed good tides and well-wishes at the table, or in the halls as we passed, but we had not truly spoken.

"M'lady," he said, giving me a stiff nod, and took a brush from a shelf.

"*Buonasera,* Captain," I said in greeting.

We worked in silence, each on our own steed, the tension building. After a time, I cleared my throat. "My grandmother would like us to fetch a few more herbs from a valley five miles distant. My father is in need of a particular poultice. Would you and your men be available to attend me?"

I watched as he paused, a hand on his mare's chestnut side. "We are at your service, m'lady. We had intended to do an exercise on the far field on the morrow, anyway. Mayhap we might do both?"

"Of course," I assured hurriedly. "I do not wish to inconvenience you." I turned from him, continuing to brush down Cardo, then laid a blanket across his back.

"M'lady."

I stilled. Not wanting to face him, but unable to do any other. I slowly turned and found him hanging his arms across the stall wall in such an earnest fashion, it made me want to withdraw. Despite his gentle, warm smile, the sorrow had returned to his eyes.

"I shall be your escort. Nothing more. No more than a steward. To go and do your bidding. To fetch, retrieve, cut, harvest." He bowed his head, lifted a hand, as if in pledge. "No more than that, m'lady. You shall be entirely safe with me."

Safe with him? Outwardly, mayhap. But my heart? *I do not believe it true.*

Truth be told, I did not wish it to be true. But I forced my lips to form the words. "Very well. I shall meet you and your men after morning patrol. And I shall bring some men of my own, given our increased proximity to Firenze's borders."

"No Fiorentini shall trouble you with us in attendance." He gave me another smile that changed his expression to wisdom and hope.

I chose to draw confidence in his promises, his men, and the relative peace that had permeated between our republics, with Aurelio courting me.

And that had been a mistake.

Oh, how that had been a mistake.

LUCIANA BETARRINI

Giulio and his men prepared to leave. It was only when we gathered in the courtyard that I at last saw my brother.

After fainting the night before, Ilaria forbade me from even entertaining the idea of going to the dungeons. "The last thing you need is to take in that foul stench or to catch a chill. You shall see your brother come morn."

And so when I finally, *finally* laid eyes on Nico, I ran to him and hugged him. He had clearly been given access to a bucket of water and a change of clothes—maybe a gesture of kindness from Franco or his parents. But his hands were still tied behind his back.

"What is this?" I said to a nearby guard. "Release him at once."

"Not until he reaches our border," returned the middle-aged man. "M'lord's orders. That will be where the others receive their weapons back as well."

Half-a-dozen wounded knights were in a wagon, and I was so glad they would be returning to Castello Forelli, where Lady Adri could see to their care. With her knowledge of modern medicine and ways with herbal remedies, she was their best chance to find healing. The remaining knights were mounted and ready to go.

We took a few steps away to talk. Domenico looked into my eyes. "I hate leaving you here," he whispered.

"I hate being left. Just promise you'll be back."

"I will. We will find a way out of this."

"What if . . ." I looked away but couldn't keep my voice from quavering. "What if they force me to marry him, Nico?"

"They can't do that. If you refuse to say the vows, they cannot force you. We will return with the ransom money, or we will return to help you fight your way out."

"Or maybe I can make Franco hate me so much they'll pay you to take me away," I said, half testing this on him.

"That would work," he said with a smile.

"Don't do anything stupid while we're apart, Nico."

"Like what?"

"Like get killed. This place is all kinds of dangerous. You understand me? Take care. Please. Because you're my twin. And because neither of us is going all the way home to *Britannia* without the other. I need you alive, for multiple reasons."

"You do the same." He leaned down and touched his forehead to mine. "We'll find a way, Luci. I promise."

I soaked in his words, then pulled him close and kissed his cheek.

"Hey, how's your head been the last couple of days?" he asked.

I blinked. "It's been . . . okay." The thought stunned me. *How, through all we've encountered over the last few days, had I still not had a migraine?* "I thought I was starting one, but then it just kind of faded."

Nico gave me his sidelong smile. "It's kind of weird, huh?"

"Weird," I repeated, resting my hand on my head. "And fabulous."

"You see? It's not all bad, being here."

My eyes moved past him to Giulio, speaking with Ilaria. "No. It's not all bad, for sure."

He followed my gaze. "Something tells me you're not going to be marrying Franco," he whispered.

"I'm not marrying anyone," I protested. "Here. In this time. We're going to make it back to Castello Forelli, and we're going to say our good-byes, and get back to Britannia."

Because I had no business falling for Guilio Greco. The dude didn't even know the truth about me yet. And when he found out, he'd probably freak.

My brother hesitated. "Maybe," he said slowly.

"Nico—"

"Just give me a few weeks. I have a new plan."

"Nico!"

"It'll be okay," he said, backing up from me. "See you in a fortnight, sis."

A fortnight. Fourteen days. It sounded like forever.

Only the sight of Ilaria walking my way brought me any sort of comfort.

But Franco approached too. "You look as if you might faint again, m'lady."

"You are sending nearly everyone I love away and holding me captive. I do not wish to remain here. If you wish to court me, why not do so at Castello Forelli?"

"I fear that is not my father's plan." He took my arm. "Come. I shall provide you with distraction. Let us play a round of backgammon."

I pulled away. "I think not." *Let the shrew-games begin.*

Giulio had mounted up and caught my action. He swallowed a quick smile, waved to his sister, then turned to lead all our knights out of Castello Fortebraccio's gates.

"Come, Ilaria," I said loudly. "Let us retire to my quarters. As the young lord noted, I am not feeling my best."

18

TILIANI FORELLI

It was with some trepidation that I moved out with the others, crossed the river, passed Castello Greco, and began climbing into the hills beyond it. Not only because it drew us precariously close to Firenze's border. But because of who rode beside me.

We barely spoke, yet I could feel Captain Valeri's hazel eyes on me. I found myself sitting a little straighter in my saddle, as if wanting to look my best for him, and then silently berated myself for it. Should Aurelio return to find us together, where would that leave Valentino? 'Twould be devastating for him. Did he not think of Aurelio as a brother? Himself beholden to the Paratore clan for his very life?

And my parents were counting on me to consider Aurelio's suit. Was he not, even now, seeking to further ally Firenze with Siena? Persuade them to come to our aid, should Perugia attempt another attack? Mayhap aid us in securing Luciana and Domenico's freedom?

It did me little good to indulge in idle fantasies about Aurelio's captain. *Valentino is not mine, nor will he ever be.* He knew it as well as I. Even if my grandmother had tried to persuade me otherwise.

At last we reached the far wood. I ducked as we rode under lower, long branches of trees and then finally pulled up and wheeled Cardo around. "Otello and Falito, patrol our southern flank. Baldarino and Iacapo, take Captain Valeri's men and keep close watch to our north. There have been some reports of brigands on the road up there, robbing travelers. Should they get wind of our presence here . . ."

"Yes, m'lady," Otello said immediately. "They shall not get past us."

"We shall climb the hill to the west," Captain Mancini said, gesturing to three of the men.

"And we shall climb to the east," Lutterius said, leading several more.

"Good. We will swiftly see to our task. Return in an hour's time, and we shall likely be ready to ride for the castello."

"Yes, m'lady." They turned and rode away.

Valentino came to hold Cardo's reins as I dismounted. He did not offer to assist me. And somehow—knowing he dared not touch me—heated my skin as much as if he had done so.

I hopped to the ground and settled my skirts, then reached for my bow and quiver. "With luck, we shall find that patch of mullein just over that rise," I said. I hadn't bothered with a gathering basket this time, only a sack, tied to my belt. Valentino had two more at his own belt, as if he hoped to find even more herbal treasures in this new patch of wood.

I was tense, at first, as we climbed, but he did not engage me in conversation. We stayed a few paces apart, wordlessly gathering more hawthorn. It was not what Nona sought, but we knew it was foolish to pass it by when it was so ready for the taking. I could hear the pounding sound of the small waterfall up ahead, where it fell to a small pool. It was around those waters that we oft found the elusive damson.

The sound of the falls became louder, drowning out the birds twittering and squirrels chattering in the branches above. I had always loved this pool. The cool it brought even on the hottest summer day always restored me.

"Can you swim in it?" Valentino finally said, hands on his hips, taking it in.

"It's deep enough," I allowed. "When we were children, my cousins and Giulio and Ilaria and I would often steal away to take a dip."

"You had to steal away?"

"Given our proximity to Fiorentini territory, our parents thought it foolish."

He thought on that for a moment. "But not once you were grown?"

"Not of late," I said, shaking my head a little. Why had we not been swimming in the last few summers? Because we thought it childish?

Nay, because we have been too weary. Our days were filled with patrols and duties at the castello now. Even in the midst of relative peace, there were countless things to be done. Supplies to be fetched. Taxes to collect. Trips to Siena to attend my father for his meetings with the Nine.

"Sometimes I wish I could return to the more carefree days of my younger years," I admitted. Then I inwardly winced. My companion had likely never had a carefree day in his entire life.

But it did not appear to rankle him. "With a pool such as this within reach, I can well understand it." He looked around. "The damson should be about the water. It favors the damp."

"Yes. 'Tis a little early in the season for it, but with luck . . ." I turned to search for the berry tree—Nona used the roots to treat fevers. I set aside my bow and quiver, finding them catching in the dense brush. Valentino moved ahead of me, hopping from one boulder to another in the shallows to reach a promising, damp cliff.

He was light on his feet, with impeccable balance. 'Twas part of what made him a good swordsman. I resisted the urge to follow behind him, even though my competitive spirit wanted to. He was likely to find it first, and that galled me. Was this not my wood, my pool?

And yet if Aurelio was given Castello Greco, would it not soon become theirs? I thought about that for a moment. Would returning the castle to the Paratore clan be enough to settle a more long-term peace between our republics? Was it *truly* necessary for us to wed in order to bridge the gap?

I wished it had been Valentino who was the Paratore heir. I wished he had grown up here in this valley and met the Grecos and me to swim as children. I wished he hadn't lost his mother at such a tender age, suffered as he had. How was it that I was so fortunate, blessed, when others were not? He had managed to become such a fine man even after such a rough beginning.

I found myself grateful to Lady Paratore and their Cook for rescuing Valentino. For redeeming his future. "Is Lady Paratore still alive?" I asked. "Or your dear Cook?"

He was crouching and digging away in a crevice and glanced back at me in surprise. "Lady Paratore and Cook? Nay. Cook died of old age a few years past. Lady Paratore the year before with the ague." He lifted a brow. "What brought them to mind?"

"Oh, nothing," I said, embarrassed that he would know I had been thinking of his past. I hurried over the rise, heading to the second pool.

I walked past a broad, ancient oak. Suddenly, a man leaped out and grabbed hold of me, wrenching me to his broad chest and covering my mouth with a meaty hand. Another faced me and put his finger to his lips, warning me to remain quiet.

I tried to push and pull my way out of my captor's arms, my muffled cries likely drowned out by the sound of the rushing water. I dug my fingernails into his arm until I heard him grunt. But he did not release me. They were obviously waiting to surprise Valentino too. A fire had been hastily doused, three feet away. Grimly, I saw two other men hovering beside a boulder to my left. And two more higher up. Brigands, below.

I'd sent my men to the hills to watch the roads for men such as these, and instead we'd stumbled upon their very camp. With the noise of the stream and falls, it had been impossible to hear them. But somehow, they had heard us.

"M'lady?" called Valentino. "Lady Forelli!"

I saw the men share a gleeful look at my name.

Valentino paused, as if listening. I tried to cry out and struggled to get free. The man moved his hand over my nose, mayhap to suffocate me into a faint, and I eased, recognizing the threat.

"*Tiliani!*" Valentino shouted. "Where are you?"

He came around the tree and stilled for but a second before reaching for the sword on his back.

But the first man had already brought the tip of his blade to Valentino's throat. "Uh, uh, uh," he warned. "Leave it sheathed, and your lady just might live."

Four more men emerged from among the trees. A total of twelve?

"We mean no harm," Valentino said, raising his arms. "Release the lady and we shall go in peace."

"Nay," said the man with a laugh. "We shall release the lady when I have a fat bag of silver in my hand." He looked me over. "If I am not mistaken, Lady Tiliani Forelli shall be worth a tidy sum."

"Mayhap we should extract the price from that lovely body," leered another. "She and her patrols have kept us from a good deal of profit of late. I believe she owes us her father's silver and a little sugar to boot."

"Touch her and you shall die," Valentino growled.

I bit my captor's hand, and he dropped it from my mouth, letting out a curse, but still held me with his other burly arm.

"We have men on every hill around us," I said. "You cannot escape."

The first laughed, with little mirth. "Ahh, but if you speak the truth, you shall be our letter of safe passage."

"She speaks the truth," proclaimed Otello, rising from the ferns twenty paces away and loosing his arrow.

I leaned my head to one side, feeling the heat of the shaft as it flew past my neck and pierced my captor's neck. I felt the splatter of blood, the sudden release of my captor's hands, heard the gurgle that signified he would soon be dead. More arrows flew, men shouted, swords were unsheathed, and we were surrounded, both by our own men, who had stolen closer, and even more brigands than were first apparent.

There were more than twenty of them.

"Come." Valentino seized my hand and thrust me behind him. He turned to face a swordsman, and I kept close, knowing he was my only true shield. I had my dagger in hand. It was something, but no match for a sword. I glanced down the streambed. If I could only reach my quiver and bow . . .

Valentino grunted at the force of his opponent's strike. The man was as big as he was and coming hard. Another circled around a boulder, likely intent on trying to capture me. I could not remain where I was. Another headed in the opposite direction, bent on hemming me in. My only chance was to reach my bow.

I did not hesitate another second. Grabbing my skirts in hand, I hopped over the same rocks in the water that Valentino had—my slippered feet nearly sliding from one of the last—and on to the farthest stone before stopping. With a glance back to my startled enemies, I ran, half sliding through the slick, damp ferns and mossy banks, hearing the tear of my skirts, and, in relief, finally reaching my bow. But as I did so, another brigand appeared, grabbing my quiver and tossing it into the wood.

"Not today, Little She-Wolf," he said, advancing on me. "Our men are quite weary of your arrows."

I stood on the balls of my feet, gripping my bow, waiting for him to come, but I pretended to be frightened. "Please, sir, you must let me go," I said in my meekest voice.

"In time, in time, we shall," he said, giving me a smile devoid of several teeth. "Just as soon as we get that bag of silver. Or other payment," he said, sliding his eyes down my body. "You shall find us to be reasonable men."

He pounced then, reaching for my arm, but I brought my bow up under his chin, clipping him with the point, then whirled it around and cracked it over his head. Bright blood emerged from both points of contact, and he staggered a moment before growling and coming after me again, this time with full force.

I fell backward, with him partially atop me, my bow pinned between us. Fury laced his face as blood dripped off his head and onto me. He called me a foul name and punched, but I dodged at the last second, and it just grazed the side of my jawbone and ear. He leaned down with one forearm across my throat, angrier now. I managed to get an arm free and reached up and pressed my thumb into his eye. He tried to bite at my wrist, but he could not keep pressure on the arm that held me as well as reach me with his teeth.

It was a battle of will. Would he release me because of the driving pain to his eye—the threat of losing it—or would I pass out first?

Lord, Lord, help me! I cannot breathe! Do not let me die this day!

I shifted my hips, trying to get my other arm loose, and pressed harder with my thumb.

The man let out a scream of rage but would not let up.

Gasping and pressing, I heard the footfalls through the forest before my captor did. Belatedly, he glanced up only as Captain Valeri rammed into him, driving him off of me. I weakly rolled to my knees and checked to make sure no other enemy was close, sucking in the tiniest breath even as I heard my attacker exhale his last.

Valentino stood up, panting, and wiped his lip of sweat. He turned to me and offered his hand. But I could not rise. I was still having trouble getting enough air. I closed my eyes, trying to calm myself. My windpipe must be bruised. I'd seen it before. After skirmishes and blows, men found it hard to breathe, swallow, or speak, oft for days.

Frowning, the captain knelt and took my face in both his hands, scanning every inch of it, trying to ascertain where I was wounded. I gestured to my throat. When I tried to tell him, it only came out as a gargled whisper. Worse, I was growing dizzy.

He gathered me up in his arms and rose. "Fear not, m'lady. I shall get you to your grandmother at once."

I nodded, grateful that he understood my need—and his best course of action. Men were gathering about us, and it was with great relief that I saw they were all *our* men, the brigands either dead or fleeing.

"Take her a moment," Captain Valeri said to Iacapo, passing me into his arms. He swiftly mounted. "Now up to me." He set me before him on his gelding, encircling me to take the reins with one hand, the other strong arm holding me about my waist to keep me steady. I gratefully leaned into his strength.

"Half of you accompany Lady Tiliani and Valentino back to the castello," Captain Mancini directed. "Half of you with me. We are going to find the last of those brigands that escaped us and clear these woods once and for all."

We set off then at a gentle trot, Captain Valeri clearly concerned about me. Even at that speed, I struggled to breathe. By the time we reached our gates an hour later, I was feeling light-headed. And what greeted us inside the castello made my head spin all the more.

Aurelio had returned, along with a contingent of twenty-four Fiorentini knights, setting my men immediately on edge. Riding in behind us were Guilio and Domenico, with twelve freed prisoners in tow from Perugia—some of them wounded. The castello courtyard was a cauldron of horseflesh and humans, cries of command and tearful reunions. Aurelio and Guilio both caught sight of us and immediately hurried toward us, as did my cousins, Benedetto and Fortino.

"What has transpired?" Aurelio said, his brow lowered in deadly fury.

"We were attacked in the woods by brigands," Captain Valeri reported.

"Let me take her," Giulio said from our other side, reaching out his arms. "I shall get her to Lady Adri."

"*I* shall take her to Lady Adri," Aurelio countered. He raised his own arms.

"She is my charge. I am her captain," Giulio said stubbornly.

"I do not care who takes her, but someone must at once," Captain Valeri interrupted. "She's suffered a trauma to her throat and struggles to even breathe." Even so, he passed me to Guilio, rather than his lord. That would not settle well with Aurelio, but I was relieved to rest my head against my old friend's chest, rather than a man I was not entirely glad to see again.

And as he carried me toward the turret, I guessed why Valentino had chosen Guilio. Here and there were pockets of Forelli knights, fairly squaring off with Paratore knights. With such tension, 'twas best our own observed me in Guilio's arms, not Aurelio's. Benedetto ran ahead and opened the door for us. Fortino and Aurelio followed behind.

"Take her to her room," instructed Fortino. "Benedetto, go and find Nona."

When we reached my room, Guilio gently set me on the bed. I saw that his face was streaked with road dust and sweat, and for the first time realized that I'd seen Domenico, but not Luciana. "Lu-Lucia," I rasped.

His jaw tensed. "We had to leave her behind for a short duration, but Ilaria is with her. I shall tell you all of it in time. For now, you must rest your voice."

Mama and Zia Gabi were first to arrive, then Nona. In quick order, they shooed all the men out. Nona examined me, had me try to speak, try to take deep breaths—listening intently with her ear close to my mouth—then tenderly probed my neck. I winced and tried to swallow, desperately thirsty.

She looked into my eyes. "Let us try a sip of water."

Mama hurriedly poured a goblet full and brought it to us. Nona helped me sit up slightly. "Just a small amount. Let us see how it goes down."

I nodded and winced again, realizing that I probably had several strained muscles in my neck. I took the goblet and took a tentative sip. It was with some relief that I felt it slide all the way down. I gave Nona a little smile.

"Good, good. Take another."

I did so, and her long fingers traced the muscles on either side of my neck. "Do these hurt?"

I nodded the tiniest bit.

"They must have gotten strained during the attack. That is half the trouble. They shall heal in a few days, as will your windpipe. 'Tis bruised, but not broken."

I thought back to how I had tried to get out from under the man. Thrashed back and forth until he had laid his arm across my neck. And even then . . .

"'Tis a great deal, to suffer at the hands of such a foe," Zia Gabi said, brushing back the hair from my face. "'Tis your first real experience, these last days. With battle. Hand-to-hand combat. Before this, you have sparred with your own men, driven brigands from our woods and roads, shot arrows at them. But few have dared to turn and fight."

I nodded and closed my eyes. For the first time, I realized what Zia Gabi and Mama had gone through to become the She-Wolves of Siena. They had fought this way, time and time again. For months, even years. Until they had finally experienced a measure of peace with Firenze. In that moment, it helped me better understand their desire to hold on to it.

"Tiliani," Mama said, "why were you in the north woods?"

"I sent her for herbs," Nona intervened. "Luca is in need of a poultice that requires mullein. And we were in need of more damson for others."

"Why not send some of the men? There are certainly enough of them idling about."

"She went with ample guard," Nona said. "And our girl has an eye for finding what I need. Bumbling, bored men would not."

"You sent her into the lion's den, Mom," Mama said in English.

"You know I would never intentionally do so," she returned. "How was I to know the brigands were there?"

"She sent her with Captain Valeri," Zia Gabi said, lifting a brow meaningfully at Mama.

Both women looked at once to their mother.

"Tell me you aren't matchmaking," my mother said.

I struggled to keep up with their English.

"We don't need to make this any more complicated than it already is, Mom."

"Is it my problem that Captain Valeri is as good at hunting medicinal herbs as your daughter is? And you cannot deny that our need for herbs and remedies are at a fresh height. 'Twas a true need, not a device. And I wanted her protected."

"But you didn't really need to send Captain *Valeri* with her, did you? Others could have protected her."

"You two followed your hearts," Nona said to them and folded her arms, lifting her chin. "At great personal cost to our family."

"And gain," Gabi countered. "Had we not, we would not have had those years with Dad. We might not have found such love. Or had our beloved children."

"Had children and lost children," Nona said gently, reaching out to lay her hand on Mama's shoulder. "This land . . . and time . . . is extreme. On all fronts. So you cannot blame a grandmother for doing what she can to ensure every one of her children and grandchildren lives lives to the full. And that includes who they give their hearts and futures to, regardless of how it might impact their family or the future of Castello Forelli."

Mama sighed. "You know it's different here, Mom. It's a different time. I had hoped . . ." She turned to me, and her eyes were so full of quiet pleading that I could not look away. She placed her delicate fingers against my cheek. "Tiliani. If you cannot give your heart to Aurelio, you cannot," she said, returning to our native tongue. "But for us, could you not try?"

I nodded, wincing as I did so.

"Come now," Nona said in irritation. "Do not make her try and speak or move her head. The girl needs a good poultice of her own and rest. Let me see to her. Off with you now."

My aunt and mother reluctantly retreated from the room, and Nona closed the door behind them and came back to my bed, taking my hand. "Your mother has lost so much over the years. The losses of my Ben and your brothers makes her want to protect you and those in her family all the more. It is entirely understandable. Grief is a cruel sculptor at times. But my sweet child," she tightened her hold on my hand, "the future of this family and the republic cannot be laid solely at your feet. That is a burden we all must share together. Do you understand me?"

I gave her a soft smile rather than nodding. She leaned in and kissed me, satisfied that I had heard her. And I had. But my mother's earnest words rang in my ears too: *For us, could you not try?*

LUCIANA BETARRINI

I did my best to dissuade the young Franco over the course of the next week. Awkwardly spilling on my lap and over the table when we were at dinner, wearing dirty gowns rather than donning a clean, new one. But by day five, he sent maids up to see to me

before our afternoon stroll, either clearly on to my game or intent
on teaching me what he expected of "his lady."

They arrived en force and did not even respond to Ilaria when
she tried to block them. I was again subjected to a bath, dressed
in a beautiful golden skirt and bodice—though laced more loosely
this time—and my hair wound into coils and knots at the base of
my head, a netting cover pinned over it. When they left, I looked
to Ilaria, who stood against the far wall, arms crossed, with the
face of a dismayed Roman goddess.

"That bad, huh?" I asked in English. When she frowned, I
translated. "They did not do well?"

"Too well," she groaned. "You look beautiful. That dress,"
she gestured helplessly, "it makes your eyes all the more golden-
brown." I thought of her brother, with those beautiful blue eyes,
and his jet-black hair. I was just reaching for my skirts, wondering
if I could somehow tear the fabric, when Franco knocked on my
open door.

He was dressed in a finely embroidered tunic, clean, flowing
white shirt, and leggings. Soft, leather boots and a floppy hat. "At
last," he said, giving his hands a clap, "you appear as you ought.
Come, m'lady. We are to stroll the town so that my people can get
a good look at you."

"The last time I was on the streets of your city, they pelted me
with rotten fruit," I said.

"They did not know you might take my hand in time," he said.
"Trust me when I say that not a one of them shall attempt such a
thing again."

Not seeing a way out of it—and frankly needing any excuse I
could find to escape the palazzo and stretch my legs—I agreed. I
awkwardly placed my hand over his, and he led me through the
hall, down the stair, and into the foyer, where eight guards waited
on us. Four led the way and four followed behind us and Ilaria,
who resolutely stayed behind me.

I didn't know how I would be handling this without her. For the hundredth time I wondered how Nico was faring. How everyone at Castello Forelli fared. How I would get home and how we might make our excuses and get to the tomb . . .

What had Nico been saying about a few more weeks? A new plan? I shook my head and rubbed my temples.

"M'lady?" Franco asked, obviously annoyed because it wasn't the first time.

"Forgive me," I said. "My mind was elsewhere."

"As it oft is, it seems. But should not your mind be best kept here with me and our courtship?"

"Mayhap it would be if I were truly a woman free to choose her suitor, rather than a captive."

"Yes, well," he sniffed, "my mother tells me that love has oft been discovered in time, even when thrown together for less auspicious goals. Can we not hope for the same?"

I looked at him. He was serious. And maybe it really did happen sometimes for people in an arranged marriage. After all, in my own time, more than half of marriages failed. Maybe the odds were better in medieval times. Maybe after a while, people just gave up and decided they may as well embrace it rather than fight it. Divorce was a rare thing, given that the Church wasn't a fan. And most people wanted the Church on their side.

He was still looking at me, awaiting an answer. It obviously irked him to find me with my mind still wandering. Which was perfect. "M'lord?" I asked blankly, as if I had forgotten his question.

He let out a sound of frustration. "I asked if we cannot hope for the same."

"The same?" I asked, blinking my lashes slowly, as if I had no idea of what he was talking about.

His arm stiffened under mine, and he took a long, slow breath. I think he muttered something about not marrying a simpleton to the guards before us. Red splotches appeared on his pimpled cheeks.

"I have heard tell that simple women make the best wives," returned one, daring to look me in the eye.

I resisted the very serious urge to bring him down then and there and make him cry for mercy.

"Or she feigns simplemindedness," Franco's eyes studied me anew, "in order to dissuade me from my pursuit."

"Mayhap she is simply a better soldier than a general," put in the other guard. "I heard tell that she was quite the fighter in our battle. Mayhap once she has direction, she can follow orders with the best of them."

"Which might make her the very best of wives," said the first. "She simply needs a strong hand, strong direction."

Now I really wanted to take that one down.

"I do *not* take direction well," I said. "I prefer to keep my own counsel."

"That she does," Ilaria dared to confirm. "Her own brother cannot keep her in line."

It really was the other way around, but I knew she was just helping me build my case. If it had been up to me, we would have escaped this place—and time—at least on three different occasions. Yes, my migraines were gone. No, I would not have met the very handsome and intriguing Guilio Greco. But I'd landed in a place that was going to give me a new sort of forever-headache. And with the last guy I'd ever pick in the world to be my potential hubby—Franco Fortebraccio. *So, no, Domenico, this whole medieval thing is not working out for me.*

He had to find that chest full of gold florins to buy my freedom. Or help me escape.

"We have been invited to Siena," Franco was saying. "There is to be a great feast at the home of Lord Angelo Santini, one of the Nine, who is friendly to my father. And he has insisted that we escort you there."

"Me? Why?"

"Because Sir Luca Forelli is one of the Nine as well, and he claims we kidnapped you and refused to exchange you for an ample number of prisoners."

"You did kidnap her and refuse that offer, m'lord," Ilaria said.

He frowned. "We captured an enemy on the battlefield. And we merely made a countermove because the Forellis endeavored to bring Firenze to our very door. You, my dear," he said, turning to me, "are but one piece on a complicated chess board. The Nine shall decide your fate."

I didn't know what I disliked more—this pipsqueak calling me *my dear* or referring to me as a chess piece or these Nine "deciding my fate." But I did like the idea of getting to Siena. And having more of the Forellis and their people around me.

19

As my grandmother suspected, I made a swift recovery over the next few days. And I had to admit, Aurelio had been solicitous in his care, attending to me every afternoon after he had run through the daily sparring exercises with his knights and washed. He brought in a chess board and then backgammon and let me choose which we played. When I beat him for the third time in a row, he sat back in his chair and smiled, with a small shake of his head. "You are a canny adversary. It behooves me to make an ally out of you for more reasons than one."

I smiled back at him. Mayhap the man did not have the outsized ego I had assumed from the time we met. It truly could have been more bravado or a tactic to try and take the upper hand, by surprising me with the news of our potential bond.

His eyes moved to the bruises at my neck and then further to my scabbed-over ear, where it had torn when the brigand punched me. His fist clenched. "Had I been there, m'lady, I would have killed your assailant."

"Captain Valeri did so in your stead," I said soberly. "He kept watch over me and came to my aid, just as you bade him. Had he not, I might have perished."

"Captain Valeri should never have escorted you into that wood," he ground out, snapping the chess pieces into their places in the storage box.

I paused. I had feared that he blamed his friend. "He did everything he could, m'lord. It was my grandmother who sent us out, and I agreed to it, because we needed an herb for my father's care. I am only thankful that the captain and your men doubled my guard. We were more worried about coming across Fiorentini than brigands. We've chased our share of robbers from the wood in years past."

"But not cleared them," he said flatly.

I took a breath, ignoring the slight. "Now we have, at least for the time being. We merely had the misfortune of stumbling upon their camp. Had Captain Valeri not have the foresight to send some of the guards to watch our flanks from the heights, they would not have seen the smoke of their campfire and come riding to our aid."

He stared at me dolefully, clearly having heard this before. "You shall have nothing to fear from the Fiorentini or brigands, if you choose to take my hand," he said gently.

"Nothing to fear from the Fiorentini—as long as I have you or your men with me. For forgive me, m'lord, but no one can promise freedom from brigands. As soon as we clear one group, another takes its place. Surely it is the same in Firenze as it is in Siena. And do your people truly favor our union?" I pressed, leaning toward him. "Truly?"

He tucked his chin. "I believe my visit here is changing the thinking of my people," he continued, hope warm in his eyes as he met mine.

"Or are they as divided as our own?" I returned. "Papa said we have been summoned to Siena. That some believe this is a wise course, and others, a fatal turn."

"I am aware. In order to bolster our aim, I have asked that several friends among Firenze's Grandi attend our gathering there."

Fiorentini Grandi in *Siena*? "And they agreed to your request?"

"They have," he said, a smile on his lips.

He had an engaging smile, with that small gap between his

front teeth. He lifted my hand to his lips and kissed it, gazing at me all the while. "It truly is possible, Tiliani. Our union might go far in building bridges between our two republics. 'Twould bring greater fortunes to our households. Help us each to secure greater power. And together . . ."

His green eyes held mine, and I tried to decipher all that was within them. Hope? Greed? Desire? Dreams? Intention? Power?

Mayhap a measure of all of them.

But did not his words bring up the same in my own mind and heart? I startled at the thought that we may be unified in this. Then scrambled for a change of subject. "Do you have siblings, m'lord?"

He paused, likely wondering over my chain of thought. "Please, might you finally call me Aurelio?"

"If you shall call me Tiliani."

"With great joy," he said, giving me a slight bow at the honor. He then went on. "Like you, I had two younger brothers who perished in the plague."

My heart sank. Oh, how I knew his pain. How was it that we had both suffered the same losses? Was that part of why my father opened his mind, heart, and life to a Paratore?

"As well as three sisters and my mother," he said.

I gasped. I knew of entire families losing their lives to the plague. But most of the others were more in keeping with our own losses. One-in-three for every village or clan. "Oh, Aurelio. I ache for you." His name came easily to my lips in my compassion. Here was a man who also knew the pain of losing little brothers— but he had lost sisters too. "Were you the eldest? Did any other sibling survive?"

"Nay. 'Twas only my father and I who survived. And I was fourth, in birth order." He moved to the window. "I will tell you that I was not my father's favorite, nor my mother's. But now the whole of my father's intentions rest on me. And I feel my dead siblings' expectation to do my best on their behalf."

I considered him. "That is a great weight to carry on one's shoulders."

He gave a slight shrug. "One does not argue with fate. God cast my family into shadow during the plague. Now he appears to be casting me into the light, with this hopeful new road before us." He put a hand to his chest and bowed toward me.

I sighed, both because of his words and how it piled further weight upon my own back. "I do not believe God casts anyone into shadow. Not your family, nor mine. Almost all were dealt hard blows with the plague. Some suffered more than others. But 'twas not God smiting them. 'Twas simply sin and our fallen world."

"So you believe the Almighty is punishing us all, pell-mell?"

"I believe we are all sinners and very far from the Eden. And sin, run amuck, shall continue to haunt and threaten us with various means of destruction. But my God is one of light and hope and life. He is with us and for us."

He let out a scoffing sound and rose to look out the tiny library window to the woods and opened it, as if needing air. "God has thrown us into a gauntlet. And only the canniest of knights shall make their way through alive."

I considered him. Was this what plagued him, drove him? Sent him to mass every day? Did he think he could work his way toward God's favor and grace, and therefore extend his own life?

"Everyone meets their Maker at some point, Aurelio. It may be as a babe or as an old man or woman. The point is to make the most of the time we have here. That's what my mother, aunt, and grandmother have taught me. Padre Giovanni too. We must live life as our lost loved ones would have us do." I paused. "What would your brothers and sisters want for you?"

He said nothing but glanced back over his shoulder at me, and in that moment of shared, remembered grief, I felt closer to him.

I lifted my hand. "Mine would want me to embrace joy and hope. To embrace all that makes our lives worthwhile."

He turned toward me, folding his arms. "So you are as wise as you are beautiful," he said, giving me a small smile, and when I shifted uneasily, looked out the window again.

"Captain Valeri told me that you are more like brothers," I said lightly, hoping to ease the discomfort.

Aurelio gave me a curious look. "Did he? I suppose we are. He never had any himself, and we were playmates as children, sparring partners as squires. I trust him with my life, which is why I entrusted you to him."

I tried to swallow and found my mouth suddenly dry. What would Aurelio have done had he seen the captain touch my hair? Or take my arm? I had seen how agitated he was when we rode into the courtyard, Valentino's arm about my waist.

I reminded myself to not entertain any further imaginings about Valentino Valeri. Aurelio needed him—as Valentino needed Aurelio. As employer and friend. And brother.

The last thing I wanted was to destroy their relationship.

Nay, my focus needed to remain on Aurelio.

No other. *No other.*

LUCIANA BETARRINI

I was returning from my walk with Franco along the streets and piazzas of Perugia—where I felt more like a chained cyclops on display with everyone gawking and whispering, than a fine lady on Franco's arm—when Lord Fortebraccio intercepted me and Ilaria.

I had tensed up the whole time, bracing myself for a blow or a flying, rotten piece of fruit. I could feel Ilaria's wariness, too, as well as the chill of the villagers' judgment, the heat of their wrath. Who knew how many had died in the battle with the Forellis? Had I killed any of their loved ones myself? Were some of the people dear to them even now in the Forellis' dungeon, yet to be returned home?

I couldn't blame them, really. I'd feel the same. *I just wanted out.*

But when Lord Fortebraccio spied us walking by, he halted our escape to my quarters. "M'ladies! Please. Join me for a moment."

Franco inclined his head and stepped back as Lord Fortebraccio turned and led the way in, not inviting him to join us, nor allowing us a moment to make our excuses. Ilaria and I eyed each other, took a breath, and warily entered what appeared to be the elder Fortebraccio's office. The door had always been shut when I'd passed before—because he feared we might spy?

He gestured to two chairs before his desk and took his seat beyond it, then put his elbows on the table and folded his hands. "How did you fare in the square?"

I looked to Ilaria.

"As well as a fat hen before a starving group of jackals might," she returned.

He chortled, then let out a real belly laugh, making his fat neck and jowls jiggle. "You women are most . . . unusual."

Dude, you have no idea. It'd blow your mind if you knew how "unusual" I really am.

He sobered. "If you think we are fooled, please know we are not. No woman could be as clumsy or as ignorant as you pretend to be, Lady Betarrini."

"You may be surprised," Ilaria murmured, trying to keep up our charade.

"Little surprises me," the fat lord responded. "You are clearly a lady of breeding," he said to me.

Breeding?

"And you wish to discomfit my son to the point that he dismisses you."

I stared at him as if I had no idea what he was talking about.

"'Tis best that you abandon your campaign." He leveled a gaze at me. "We shall not be dissuaded."

"I hear tell that we are to go to Siena," Ilaria put in. "The Nine shall take issue with this forced courtship."

He grimaced and sat back. "I have my own inroads with the Nine. I do not fear Luca Forelli's position among them."

"But what of Lord Marcello Forelli and the She-Wolves behind them?" she asked quietly.

He shrugged like it was no big deal, but there was a flicker in his eyes.

It gave me hope that he was worried. The Nine might be my way out. The Forellis held some serious sway there.

"Or we could bring in a priest tonight and all would be resolved," the lord rejoined.

My heart sank. *Or not.*

"I do not believe the young lord truly favors me," I tried. "Nor do I believe that he is . . . uh, what I mean to say is . . ."

"They are ill-suited, m'lord," Ilaria filled in.

"If you would cease your ridiculous pretense, which he finds embarrassing, he might regain pleasure in the fact that we captured a great beauty."

"And if he does not?"

He paused and his jowls quivered. "Then you had better pray the Forellis are able to gather that ransom. Otherwise, you shall find yourself thrown from your very fine quarters and into our dark dungeon, your companion," he said, nodding at Ilaria, "outside our walls."

I gaped at him. "You would do such a thing?"

He looked straight at me. "You have value to me in two ways. Either woo the favor of my son or help him forget his wounded pride with a chest full of gold. If you can do neither, why should I provide for you in luxury?"

"Thank you, m'lord," I said coldly, "for making it abundantly clear."

"Of course, my dear." He waved a hand of dismissal. "Now go to your rooms and rest before supper. I am expecting company.

However, Lady Betarrini," he said, his eyes hardening, "see that you do not spill or insult my guests this night, or you shall suffer my wrath, as well as my son's."

20 ✦

TILIANI FORELLI

While eating naught but soup and porridge was still uncomfortable for me, I knew I must dress and get to the Great Hall to sup that night. After all, on the morrow many would be traveling to Siena, and if my father did not see me among those at table, he would likely insist I remain home. And if he was well enough to be up from his sickbed and ready to travel, I was determined to be the same.

Though Zio Marcello and Zia Gabi looked a great deal improved when I entered the hall, Papa still appeared pale. But it comforted me to see all three of them with my mother, up on the dais. 'Twas as if normalcy had returned. Domenico Betarrini, sitting across from Marcello, was speaking urgently with my uncle, inquiring about the ransom request in order to secure his sister's release, as I passed.

"Luca has sent an appeal to the others among the Nine," Marcello said. "We are certain the majority shall demand that Lord Fortebraccio lower his ransom demand."

"Can they not force him to drop it all together?" Domenico pled.

"Nay," Marcello said wearily, leaning back in his chair and rubbing his sore shoulder. He lowered his voice. "'Tis a common aspect of battle here—the 'fruits' of war. Even if one does not conquer one's enemy, securing valuable captives can make the whole skirmish worthwhile. And Lord Fortebraccio lost many men—from the patrol of which we are falsely accused, as well as those in battle. He needs your sister's ransom to assuage his people."

"Or his coffers," Papa said.

Belatedly discovering I had joined them for the first time in days brought Aurelio and Captain Valeri to their feet, drawing the others' attention. All males rose—from my uncles to cousins to every knight at our table for twenty —and gave me a slight bow. "'Tis a fine honor to return to sup with you all," I smiled. "I grew weary of being abed."

"Agreed," Papa said, raising his goblet to me. "To the fact that no Forelli ails abed."

"To the Forellis and their health!" seconded a knight down to my right.

"To the Forellis and their health!" bellowed everyone in the hall.

I felt more at home and more like myself than I had in days. Aurelio helped me move my chair in and then sat down beside me. "Here, allow me," he said, pouring wine into my goblet.

I thanked him, while carefully avoiding Captain Valeri, sitting next to my mother, who was directly across from me. I had not seen him since that day he'd rescued me in the woods, but I was as inherently aware of him as I had been that day. Hurriedly, I took a gulp of wine, glad that the rest of the castello's people were settling at tables behind us, and maids and servants were already bringing in the food, providing distraction.

"'Tis a fine day indeed to have you up and about again, m'lady," the captain said, lifting his goblet.

I forced a cordial smile and raised my own, but not at a modest height. "I have you to thank, Captain. Had you not intervened, I might not be here at all."

"To Captain Valeri!" called my father, lifting his goblet.

"To Captain Valeri!" echoed the hall.

I felt Aurelio stiffen beside me.

"You look quite well, Tili," Papa remarked, leaning toward me. "Other than the bruising?"

"I am quite recovered, Papa. And ready to take up my bow and accompany you all to Siena, come morn."

Papa glanced at Mama, then back to me. "Oh? We thought it might be best for you to remain here. Zio Marcello and your nona intended to remain with you."

I shook my head. "There is no need. I am well enough to travel. I loathe the idea of you all riding off without me."

His brow furrowed.

"And Lord Paratore must go," I hurriedly added, nodding deferentially toward him. "He has friends from Firenze arriving. Would it not be best if I was there to greet them as well?"

My parents shared another brief look.

"Very well," Mama conceded. "If you are certain you are up to it."

"And if you are certain it shall not overtax you," Aurelio said, boldly taking my hand and lifting it to kiss as he looked into my eyes.

For a moment, it seemed as if the entire table paused and took note. I could feel a hot blush rising and I narrowly resisted the urge to pull away. But Aurelio was releasing me, moving as if it had been the most natural thing in the world to do. As if he had done the same for years before it.

I steeled myself, trying to still my whirling thoughts, feelings. "I am certain."

And I was certain that I could go and fare well enough. But of him? I did not know what to think. Our conversations over these last days had warmed me.

But then I remembered Captain Valeri's touch, our own conversations and moments in the wood. How even a long look from him sent little tingles up my arm and neck.

Why could I not respond in kind to Aurelio?

Luciana Betarrini

Never had I been happier to leave a place than when I exited Perugia's gates. I glanced at Ilaria and we shared a relieved smile. Because while we were miles from safety, we were finally out from under total captivity. Here, in this wide, sprawling valley full of vineyards and olive groves, rich pastures boasting cattle and a winding river—sparkling under the mid-morning sun—I felt like we could make a break for it.

Other than, you know, that we were both riding sidesaddle and in full skirts. And neither of us had a weapon, so we'd probably get recaptured in minutes.

But *still* . . . it felt good to have even a tiny bit of hope for the first time in weeks.

And we were heading toward people I knew—my brother, the Forellis, Guilio, and more. Somehow, they would surely help me find my way out of this mess.

Despite his father's warning, I had kept up my campaign with Franco. Ignoring him when he spoke. Wearing dirty dresses when he insisted I accompany him. Whining when he wished to walk too long. And when he tried to kiss me, wriggling out of his embrace. Operation Shrew was rather effective, I thought. The boy's interest was clearly waning.

On the downside, I doubted the Forellis had a pot of gold waiting at the end of this rainbow. But if I could somehow get back to their castello, I'd grab Domenico, and we could get out of their hair forever, resolving everything.

Yet even as I thought it, a pang of sorrow went through me. Leaving Ilaria and Giulio? *Giulio. Ilaria.* She'd given up a lot to remain with me. I shook my head when I found myself thinking about her brother's piercing, blue eyes.

"What do you love most about the Forellis, Ilaria?" I asked quietly.

She glanced at me in surprise.

"I mean, you and your brother have chosen to abide with them rather than at Castello Greco. You said they are more like kin. How so?"

She cocked her head in thought. Watching her—all adorable Tuscan beauty against the lush landscape, brown hair glistening in the sun—I could see why Nico had a serious crush. She was small, but she was powerful. Even at nineteen, Ilaria was more mature than the college seniors I knew.

"A true woman knows where she's going, where she belongs," Nico had said to me once, when I asked why he didn't have a girlfriend. *"Girls look at me as if I'm going to show them the way."*

Which was fair. Most of my friends back home kept looking to guys as if they were going to be The Answer. As if finding the right guy would make their whole lives right. But the women here among Castello Forelli? *Notsomuch.* These girls knew what they wanted and were not willing to settle for less.

"The Forellis are our family," Ilaria said. "I would die for any one of them. As they would for me. Why would I want to live apart from them?"

I considered that. "How do you feel about them giving your castello to Lord Paratore?"

She raised a brow. "I *feel* nothing about it. I *think* that if Marcello and Luca believe it a sound course of direction, I trust them. They have said we shall be compensated. And as you noted, our home is with them. The other castello has always been ours in name only. 'Twas my father's, but my father and mother have long been buried. Our people are the Forellis."

Our people.

Did I feel like I had "people" like she was talking about? Nico was one. But Dad . . . Uncle Vinny . . . they felt more distant than what she described, by tone. It was a conclave. Connection like I'd never known. And I had to admit, I was drawn to it. If Ilaria, not born of the Forelli clan, was made one of them in time . . . could I? Could Domenico?

I pulled back, frightened by the thought. Was my longing for family, community, so deep that I was willing to remain in medieval Italy to find it?

Yes, my daily migraines were mitigated, maybe even eradicated. Because of what? The food? The lack of additives? Preservatives? Or had the time tunnel somehow healed me?

I thought back to Renato, about his stories of the Betarrini girls showing up, their demand to get to their father, and yet Gabi suffered nothing but a pretend bout of appendicitis, even though I'd heard whispers of poisonings and stabbings. I was sure of it. I'd have to ask her and Adri about it.

Because being without a daily headache? Even with everything else here?

It felt miraculous. I could think clearly. I wasn't chained daily by pain.

Could it be that traveling through time healed me forever? Or would my headaches resume as soon as I hit the twenty-first century again?

21

TILIANI FORELLI

I tried not to pay attention to Captain Valeri. God help me, I
did. But every time he galloped by to see to his men or watch
our Western flank—as assigned by my father—all I could see
was the fine line of his shoulders, his flawless command of his
mount, and how the men responded to him with utter respect
and devotion.

I also tried to be more attentive to Aurelio, filling the long
seven hours of travel time to Siena with talk—both idle and deeper.
Aurelio Paratore had the position, the authority, the stature to
be my husband. But with a sinking feeling, I understood that
Valentino Valeri was more my match. I thought back to our time
side by side on both the battlefield and gathering herbs for my
grandmother. It had felt both natural and yet with a heightened
awareness, as if God was directing me toward him—as if I could
sense exactly where he was at any time, and he, me.

But he had been studiously ignoring me in these last days. Not
coming to inquire as I convalesced. Meeting my gaze but once at
table last night.

Mayhap he sensed his lord's jealousy and censure and felt
chastened. Or he had examined that moment in the wood when
his hand took my elbow—and recognized that he had likely
intended to kiss me.

But could he know how I longed to kiss him back?

I had to cease such idle thoughts. If he were to pursue me—truly pursue—he would have to renounce Firenze and Aurelio, whom he treated as both lord and brother.

Renounce. That brought me up cold.

And for me to welcome such a pursuit? 'Twould destroy all my father, uncle, and the Nine hoped our union would accomplish in creating ties with Firenze. Deep within, I knew that Papa would not force this marriage upon me—after all, Zia Gabi had drawn Zio Marcello away from his own marriage-pledge. And Mama had been allowed to choose Papa for love. But 'twas also easy to see how pleased all four were, every time I seemed to welcome Aurelio's company. They held such hope in their eyes. If love could blossom between us, I knew it would be an answer to prayer.

Mama and Papa, as if sensing my restless thoughts, moved to ride beside me, flanking me. Those before and behind us separated by about ten paces, sensing our need for privacy.

"'Tis been a great deal for you to absorb, Tiliani," Mama said quietly. "Aurelio's arrival, and his bid for your hand."

I nodded.

"But it seems as if you are not entirely against the idea of it," Papa observed.

"Nay. Not entirely," I said. "As suitors go, I must admit, he is one of the best. Clever enough, socially well-placed. Handsome."

"Yet?" Mama asked.

I squirmed a little, then glanced over my shoulder, making certain no one was within hearing. "Is there not supposed to be something more? Zia Gabi calls it a 'spark.' Should there be stirrings of love?"

"Mayhap that shall come in time," Mama said. "You have only known each other for a sennight. Love rarely happens all at once; more often it builds over time."

"Do you realize how long it took me to convince your mother she was in love with me?" Papa asked, leaning forward to smile across me at my mother.

She flashed a smile. "'Tis true. For a very long time I simply wanted to return to . . . Normandy." She glanced around, again making certain we could not be overheard. "But Gabi fell in love with your uncle, and when we considered that we might be able to return to Normandy and save your grandfather, we knew we had to try."

"Wait," I said. "You saved Nonno?"

She nodded soberly. "Before we first traveled here, our father had died. When we returned the first time, we found your nona and came back here for Gabi because she had to see Marcello again."

"Come now, admit it," Papa put in. "You felt a keen urge to see me too."

She gave us a cavalier smile. "I was not against the idea of it."

Papa snorted and looked to me. "You see? To this day, she still makes me pursue her."

Mama ignored him. "But then we wondered if we traveled back to just the right place in *Normandy*, we might be able to find our father and bring him here, before the accident that took his life occurred. Miraculously, we were able to do so. It gave us four more years with him that we might never have had. And from then on, the die was cast."

"And obviously, she could no longer resist my charms and handsome visage," Papa interjected.

"He *was* fairly handsome and charming," Mama said, smiling over at him.

"Was?" He gave her an indignant look.

"You are *still* handsome and charming, Luca," she laughed. "And I have never met a finer man than you."

I loved their banter. Moreover, I loved how they loved each other. Could I find that with Aurelio in time?

"Can one marriage and the Paratores reclaiming the castello truly accomplish all you hope?" I asked. "We build one bridge with Firenze, but it seems we have burned another with Perugia and beyond them, greater Umbria. Do we not create more trouble for ourselves trying to control what only God can truly control?"

That silenced both my parents.

"Domenico and Luciana said Castello Forelli was still whole in their time, as it was when we returned," Mama said slowly. "And yet it was naught but rubble before we traveled the first time. Clearly, we accomplished something that changed the outcome for our family. As *you* shall."

"Could it not already have been accomplished?" I said. "Mayhap it was how you were able to anticipate the plague and save so many of us." I fell quiet for a moment, as we all thought of those lost, as well as my brothers. "Nona told me you are doing your best to not change history at all. Is that so?"

"Indeed," Mama nodded.

"And yet you have already." We rode for a time in silence.

"We are doing our best to protect the Forelli descendants, and Siena at large," Papa said. "Mayhap if we can build some bridges, fewer shall die when Firenze overtakes the republic."

"Thousands die, Til," Mama said softly. "*Thousands.*"

"But that is not for more than a hundred years," I said, shaking my head. "A thousand things could happen that would bind or break these ties we attempt to forge."

Again, they were both silent.

"God moves as he sees fit, does he not?" I pressed. "He saw fit to bring Mama and Zia Gabi from Normandy. To have them fall in love with two of the finest men I know and to lead our people in battle after battle. He had to have had a hand in bringing you here, Mama. As well as allowing you to return. He had to have had a hand in allowing you to change some of what is to come. Shall we not allow him to move in my heart too? If I find that spark, that stirring of love with Aurelio, then we shall know. Because I doubt either of you truly wish me to marry a man I do not love."

Mama exchanged a long look with Papa.

"You are right," he said to me, while looking to my mother.

"Your mother and I want you to know a love like ours," he said, reluctantly glancing back to me like he didn't want to look away from my mother. As if it was as much a pledge to her as it was to me. "I believe it would be a blessing if a love blossomed between you and Aurelio. But if it does not, we shall not force these nuptials upon you."

I heard the words he did not say too.

He and Mama wondered if I would *ever* find love or bear children. I was becoming too old for most suitors, my most fertile years rapidly disappearing behind me. Nor did many approve of me on patrol or taking up arms. It would take a very unique man to be my mate.

But if the She-Wolves had found my father and uncle, could I not find love too?

And with someone who wouldn't destroy all my parents hoped for?

LUCIANA BETARRINI

I breathed a huge sigh of relief when Ilaria and I rode through the Porta Camollia—the northern gate of Siena. Although it looked far different in the interior than the modern Siena I knew, there was a familiarity to it. For the first time since I had time traveled, I knew where I was, exactly where I was. The road before me was the same I would walk in modern times, though the cobblestone had probably been replaced somewhere in between. The shops were different, but they varied only a little in structure. Up ahead, we would reach il Campo—the broad, shell-shaped piazza, so unique in Toscana. The Palazzo Pubblico would be there, as well as all the fine palazzos that flanked her, flanking her gloriously wide shell.

After all I'd experienced that was so different, the promise of some semblance of familiarity was more than welcome. And to even be in the same room as my brother? I would be able to take my first, full breath in two weeks. It comforted me, too, that Franco was steering clear of me. He hadn't even come close to us on the long road from Perugia to the city and appeared to be arguing with his father at one point. "He is likely seeking relief from his courtship responsibility," Ilaria said under her breath. "Well done."

"Why does his father continue to press him?"

"Because he knows you have tried to dissuade the boy from his pursuit. That you are not nearly as clumsy and untidy as you have led him to believe. And if the Sienese catch wind of the fact that the boy is not truly interested, then they may have additional power in negotiating a lower ransom for you."

"Then you shall inform them of this fact immediately, yes?" What did I care for my reputation here, if I might aid the people I cared about?

"Indeed," she said, giving me a cat-like smile. "One way or another, we shall see you to freedom, even if it is to fight our way out," she added in a whisper. "You shall not be returning to Perugia."

"But we are attempting to negotiate first?"

"Leave it to Lord Marcello and Sir Luca, as well as m'ladies. They are a force, between them, and have many friends in the city."

Hope swelled in my heart. I wanted to urge my horse into a gallop, even at the risk of falling out of the stupid sidesaddle. Our procession had taken up a dreadfully slow, stately pace that I was sure was meant to show off the Fortebraccio herald and colors—as if he had no fear of entering Sienese gates and wished to flaunt it.

"He is more swagger than sword." Ilaria followed my gaze. "The Nine shall soon put him in place." She ceased speaking as four Fortebraccio knights closed in around us. They separated me from Ilaria and held up a rope.

"Forgive me, m'lady, but it must be done," said one.

I glanced over at Ilaria, who was facing her own captor with her chin lifted. "'Tis not necessary. If we wished to fight you, we would have already done so."

"Not so," said the knight. "Here you have many more allies than enemies. 'Twould make more sense for you to attempt to escape here. We know that you are both capable fighters, skirts or no. M'lord insists you both be tied. Once you dismount, you shall each be tethered between two of us as well."

I frowned, pretending dismay. But I was already thinking about how I might use our bonds to my advantage as a man tied my wrists behind my back. They would not consider me a threat, bound this way. Only my skirts were truly an impediment. But if I could slip the knot at my wrists . . .

"Ouch!" I cried loudly. "Not so tight! I do not wish to lose use of my fingers forever."

But the man did not ease up the pressure. "You broke my friend's wrist on the battlefield," he growled. "I shall not be the reason you break another's."

Inwardly, I groaned. *So much for that idea.*

Well, it would just be up to Nico to get me out of this mess. Or Guilio. My heart skipped a beat at the thought of him.

Meanwhile, Ilaria wasn't trying her feminine wiles like I had. "How dare you escort me into my city as if I were a common prisoner!"

"You are our captives and could fetch a fine ransom price, though I doubt anyone will bid for you," he said to her. "No man wants a woman who is more manly than he is."

My eyes widened. Did he say this because she was a warrior?

Because Ilaria Greco was one of the most sultry women I had ever met, and her strength made her all the more beguiling. She already had my brother wrapped around her little finger. But maybe that was because we lived in a time when women were permitted to be strong. Nico lived in a time where he had trained with women in jiu jitsu. Including me.

As we resumed our progress along Via di Citta, I pondered that. I liked that women had few obstacles in my time. That we could choose our profession. Stay single if we wanted. Have children or no children without scorn. Let alone survive childbirth at a far better rate than in medieval times. I shuddered at the thought of giving birth here, now.

No, when I have a baby, I want a clean, white hospital room, a bunch of nurses, and a nice, fat epidural.

And yet Gabi and Lia had managed to get through five births between them. I knew Adri was a decent homeopathic doctor of sorts, making use of all the herbs she could get her hands on. For the hundredth time, I wondered how she'd treated Marcello and Luca and Gabi and others after the battle and how they fared now. I wanted to see all of them, but I guessed that my friend was five-times as anxious for that moment than I was.

"Ilaria," I said, looking over my shoulder at her. "Thank you for staying with me. I do not know how I might have made it through these last weeks without you at my side."

Her chocolate-brown eyes smiled at me. "You are welcome. You are a Betarrini, as our ladies are. So you are kin to me. A sennight of serving as a lady's companion was but a trifle."

Kin, I thought, the word sticking with me. A sister? I'd always wanted a sister. Again, I was taken by their deep love for one another, the tight bonds that existed between them all. Was it forged by battle or this place? I'd observed enough Italian families in Tuscany to know they were tight. Expressive, demonstrative, often confrontational. All fire and fierceness, but also ferociously loving. Uncle Vinny's family was that way . . . we just didn't quite fit with them.

And now Ilaria seemed to be saying that by name alone, we were already one of the clan.

Looking to her, so fierce and fervent—serving me selflessly these last days—I dared to face the question for the first time.

Could I bear to leave people like these behind?

22

It infuriated me to see Ilaria and Luciana led into the Hall of the Nine in the Palazzo Pubblico like common prisoners. Their hands were tied behind their backs, and a leather belt around their waists was linked to a knight on either side of them. Those knights were allowed to keep their swords—the only four men in the hall who were visibly allowed a weapon, as keepers of the captives in question.

Not that I doubted that every other man carried a dagger or two beneath the folds of their tunics. And I knew every woman of Castello Forelli had one strapped to each calf.

"Lord Fortebraccio," my father said, stepping forward from his place among the Nine. "There is no reason to bind our women so. We shall not take them until we conclude our negotiations."

"Forgive me if I do not take you at your word, Sir Forelli," said the lord with a curt bow. "After all, 'twas your men who murdered mine while on patrol."

A murmur rolled through the crowd of hundreds. We had brought thirty with us from Castello Forelli, leaving thirty behind to guard her. Fortebraccio had brought forty. The others were nobles or friends, curious to hear the outcome. The majority were Sienese. The remaining were Fiorentini.

"I told you before, and I shall tell you again—we did not move against you," Papa said loudly, as much as for the crowd as for

Fortebraccio. "We formerly dismissed a knight for untoward behavior, and he is clearly bent on revenge, framing us for his misdeeds."

"So you say," Lord Fortebraccio sniffed.

"As I said, and my cousin said," Papa returned, "through every lash of your whips or strikes to our flesh."

"We were sorely abused," Zio Marcello put in. "Tortured because of conjecture, not solid evidence."

"We had evidence enough," Lord Fortebraccio said brusquely.

"Evidence enough?" Papa raised a brow. "Was any knight who moved against your patrols present on the battlefield? Did any of your knights recognize them among us?"

"The heat of battle hardly allows time for such things. And most of our men were *murdered*."

"What if I invited survivors among your patrol to come to Castello Forelli and examine every one of our men? Would that not have been a more humane option than an outright attack on us? Or our castello?"

Fortebraccio scowled. "Ferocious attacks invite ferocious responses. And you could send any of your knights to the hills before we came for such an inspection. Nay." He sliced his hand through the air. "We shall abandon such frivolous talk."

"It is not frivolous." Lord Enici stepped forward. He was a slim, tall man, one of the most senior among the Nine. "I know you have friends among us, Lord Fortebraccio. But when one of our principal castles is attacked, no part of the matter is frivolous. You should have come to us, here, to demand recompense from the Nine. Come to me! Or to your friend, Lord Santini. To attack the Forellis was to attack Siena herself. Surely you knew that. 'Tis only because we do not wish to destroy our slim hold on peace with all of Umbria that we did not immediately turn and decimate Perugia and take your castello down to the foundation. By rights, we had the excuse when we learned of your sore abuse of our brothers—even more so after we learned of the many losses on the battlefield. Your refusal to set Lady Betarrini free in the prisoner exchange is yet another."

Lord Fortebraccio reddened and turned his pig-like eyes toward Lord Enici. "I knew I was poking the wolf. But between the Nine entertaining an alliance with Firenze, and the attacks we suffered at the hands of—by all appearances—*Forelli* knights, we believed there was no other option. We wanted Siena to know, without a doubt, that we are not only strong enough to defend ourselves, but also strong enough to attack. And we only beat Lord Marcello and Sir Luca in an attempt to exact the truth." He shrugged. "When they refused, we took our pound of flesh in honor of *our* fallen brothers."

Lord Mori, another of the Nine, spoke up. "I believe the Forellis must more clearly state their case. Who are these knights who masquerade as Forelli guards, killing others? They are clearly enemies of the republic now."

"It was a knight named Sir Andrea Ercole," Zio Marcello said. "He is about two-and-twenty in age, my height, and carries a battle axe as his weapon of choice. He was dismissed from Castello Forelli when he made improper advances on one of our maids. While every man is informed that we shall not permit such actions when they swear fealty, some are feeble-minded. But we allow no grace on this front. To a man, they know that to make an advance on a servant is the equivalent of making an advance on Lady Gabriella or Evangelia."

"And we never allow them a second chance," Papa added. "Therefore, Sir Ercole was immediately put out and told never to return."

"He was dismayed," Zio Marcello went on. "Clearly, he stole several of our castello tunics and horse blankets, items which he has used to frame us in attacking Lords Fortebraccio and Belucci's patrols. Mayhap a brand as well, since Lord Fortebraccio found horses with our marking, and we have yet to note a lost mare."

"Rest assured," Papa's eyes flashed, "when my cousin and I are fully recovered, we shall be hunting Sir Ercole and his mercenaries ourselves."

Lord Enici lifted a finger to Lord Fortebraccio. "If you ever so sorely abuse one of us again, we shall come for you. And you shall beg for death before we grant your wish. If you have a complaint, you come to us, here in Siena, and we shall see it resolved."

Lord Fortebraccio snorted. "Forgive me if I doubt it would be resolved to my satisfaction."

"Nevertheless, m'lord, consider yourself warned. Tell others among your Priors—and the pope himself, if need be—that we shall not tolerate another attack on our people or our properties. Or shall I send a missive to each one of them?"

"I shall pass it along," Fortebraccio replied shortly. "Now what of this one's ransom?" He gestured to Luciana. "Do you have my gold?"

Lord Enici pursed his lips. "You have asked for an unreasonable sum. One that only a king or queen would fetch. We shall give you two hundred florins."

Again, Lord Fortebraccio gave a scornful laugh. He looked to Papa. "My son shall wed her, then. The Forellis shall grant us fifty hectares of land as her dowry. And a bridge shall be built to Perugia, just like you consider building between you and Firenze." He spread out his arms and smiled, but there was no joy in his eyes. "Then we might all be one, big, peaceable family."

It was Lord Enici's turn to snort. "We all know alliances built upon marriages seldom hold."

"And yet sometimes they do, so we continue to attempt them. Women bind us, whether we acknowledge it or not."

"Three hundred florins."

"Nay. Lady Betarrini's price is one thousand florins or her hand in marriage. This is not a visit for negotiation. This is a visit to collect what is rightfully mine or an opportunity for us all to witness the nuptials."

"Your son does not appear overly fond of my wife's cousin,"

Zio Marcello said, and for the first time, I noted the discomfited younger Fortebraccio, reddening about the cheeks. "Come now, Lord Fortebraccio. You and I both know that three hundred florins is more than fair for a bride your son does not wish to take. It is a tidy sum. You must accept it and go in peace. Others among Perugia's Priors would accept it as fair, too, and see your demand as unreasonable. To hold Lady Betarrini any longer shall be considered another act of war."

I eyed Giulio, and he gave me the barest of nods from across the room. Slowly, steadily we began making our way through the crowd, getting closer to Ilaria and Luciana. It was with some surprise that I noticed Domenico had already managed to get within a few paces of his sister. There was but a single man between him and her guard. I tensed, hoping he would not tip our hand.

"And as I said," Lord Enici said, "we shall not tolerate another move against us. Take the gold and go in peace."

"Nay," Lord Fortebraccio said, a blush of fury rising along his jowls. "You knew my price in advance. I shall not leave without it."

"You have no choice. We have heard you out and found your complaint wonting. We have offered you a generous settlement for your captive. And that is after the Forellis gave you far more prisoners in exchange for those you held!"

Lord Santini stepped forward, arms out between Enici and Fortebraccio. "Your cause is lost, friend. Go in peace or we shall have to insist."

"Nay, 'tis I who must insist." He lifted his hand, and the knights on either side of both Ilaria and Luciana drew their swords. One lifted it to point beneath Ilaria's chin, the other beneath Luciana's. The second guard on each drew their swords, too, watching the crowd for the slightest move against them.

Luciana Betarrini

I froze as I felt the tip of my guard's sword poke at the tender flesh of my throat. But then I felt the slide of metal against the skin at my wrist and the quiet, rhythmic sawing against the ropes. Someone was trying to free me. Nico?

I'd seen him slowly making his way through the crowd while the nobles argued. My pulse picked up, the thrill of hope surging through my veins. I had instantly become calmer, as soon as I had seen Nico in the room. If he could free me, together we could take on my captors, even without swords. But we had to make sure Ilaria was safe too.

"Lord Fortebraccio!" Lord Enici barked. "Tell your men to sheath their swords at once!"

"Give me the sum I demand, and I shall," ground out Fortebraccio.

I felt the tap at my wrists and understood. There was but a frayed edge left, holding them bound—one I could easily break— and Nico moved on to Ilaria. But his motion caught her guard's attention, and he swiftly came around her, threatening my twin with his sword. "Back away!" he ordered.

"Move away from them, all of you!" Fortebraccio shouted.

As the crowd shifted, drawing the guards' attention, I broke free of my bonds, wrapped my hands around my sword-bearing captor's wrist and twisted with one hand while jamming it with the other, instantly breaking it. Once again, it was a prohibited move in competition, but not in combat. And I was intent upon fighting my way out of here, regardless of whether these medieval dudes could negotiate the price of my freedom or not.

Nico had taken down the guard who menaced him. He circled

Ilaria and the guard who now held a more maneuverable dagger to her throat, holding her tighter against his chest.

"Kill them!" Fortebraccio bellowed.

"Stop them!" Enici followed.

I looked to my second captor just in time to see him swinging his sword. I bent back, the slash of it narrowly missing my upper body, then shifted to keep my feet and be ready for his next strike.

But Guilio came behind him and stabbed his calf, sending him crumpling to his knees, crying out. When he tried to rise, Giulio stepped on his sword and placed his own beneath the guard's chin. "Do not tempt me," he growled.

Together we looked to Ilaria and her captor.

"It is over, Fortebraccio!" Lord Enici's voice carried through the room. "Cease this at once!"

Lord Fortebraccio looked furiously at Ilaria and me. With me freed, he seemed to pop like a poked balloon. His shoulders sank, and he heaved a sigh even as he lifted a weary hand, signaling his knight to release Ilaria.

"It is over," he grunted toward the Forellis.

"I believe it is," Lord Enici said, gathering himself. "Escort them to the gates," he said to a formidable knight beside him. "Give Lord Fortebraccio his three hundred florins and then close the gates behind them."

"Yes, m'lord." Hurriedly, others joined the knight, and they led the Fortebraccio crew out of the palazzo. Franco gave me one last, furious glance as they exited.

See ya, Romeo, I thought with relief, as I watched my teenaged almost-fiancé disappear. I turned, and Nico gathered me up in his arms and hugged me tightly.

I melted into his arms. It felt *so* good to be with him again.

We were both safe for the moment. And *free.* I felt like I could take my first, full breath in weeks.

"Thank God, Luci," he said, setting me down. "I was so worried."

He stared into my eyes for a long moment before he gave me another hug.

"Thanks, Nico. If you hadn't gotten to those ropes, I'm not sure how that would've come down." I realized we were speaking in English, and glanced around, wondering who had heard.

Giulio was closest and glanced at us, but I was pretty sure he didn't understand any of it. Besides, our cover story was that we were from Britannia. "And I must thank you as well," I said to him, returning to Italian. "If you hadn't gotten to that man, he surely would have carried out Lord Fortebraccio's orders to kill me."

Giulio smiled, and wow, I'd forgotten how handsome he was when he smiled. He spent a good deal of time looking all tough and don't-mess-with-me, but when he smiled? There wasn't a woman alive who wouldn't take another look at Guilio Greco . . .

Not that they could avoid it, even if he was glowering.

"Something tells me that if I had not come to your aid," Giulio said, "you would have found a way to conquer your second foe, as well as assist Ilaria."

"Well, I am not as certain as you are, but I would have tried."

"How did you break the first man's wrist?"

I felt a little flustered with his full attention upon me. "'Tis not a difficult move. Your hands simply must be in exactly the right position to make it give way."

"Will you teach me?"

I pretended to be chill at the idea of teaching *him* something for once. "Of course."

He continued to gaze at me with such admiration I had to look away. It was unnerving, having a man so handsome stare at you that way. Thankfully, others were closing in then, all praising me and my brother, Ilaria and Guilio. The elder Forellis finally reached us, and after embracing us and being assured that we were not injured—nor had we been abused while held in Castello Fortebraccio—they turned to speak to others in the hall.

But Lia hovered. "May I have a word?"

I nodded, and my brother and I followed her through the doors to a wide verandah, three stories above the street, overlooking a beautiful, wooded valley between two "arms" of the city. Swallows and starlings and martins swarmed, their high-pitched screeching filling the air as they ate their fill of insects we could not see. It reminded me a little of bats, leaving me ill at ease. But then I was a little on edge to begin with, for obvious reasons.

"I am so thankful that you are safe and sound." Lia put her hand on my forearm. "We were praying constantly for you, Luciana."

"Thank you," I returned. "And thank you for coming up with all that gold. My brother and I will find a way to repay you."

She made a dismissive move with her hand. "There is no need for repayment." She switched to English, pausing over the words as if not quite totally remembering. I supposed after twenty-some years of speaking mostly Italian, I'd start to forget too. "This is a big moment for you two," she said quietly. "You have now seen how volatile life is here, among medieval Italians. One can be in control one day and at the mercy of another the next. Conqueror or captive. Our alliances among the Nine and other nobles help, of course. But there is no guarantee."

She looked at me. "You felt that sword barely miss you. As I imagine you felt others that day on the battlefield. Arrows and swords, meant to kill you." She gestured at us both. "You two are able fighters, but you have been sparring in a gym, where people keep to rules or get thrown out if they do not. You have not been fighting for your lives, your friends' lives, your sibling's life." She took our hands, one and then the other. "And that's what this life here, now, entails. Constant fighting to not only survive, but thrive. This is a good time to return to Britannia, isn't it?" She looked back and forth, between us. "Before your hearts are too tied to us or our people?"

We glanced at each other, then back to her. "I-I was thinking that way," I said hesitantly. "But . . ." I glanced again at Nico. "I mean, it makes no sense. After all I've gone through—we've gone through—it's way more logical to hightail it out of here. But . . ."

My eyes went to the bird-filled sky as if I could see Ilaria, who had so faithfully remained with me in Perugia. And Guilio. Tiliani. The other Forellis.

When I looked back, Lia's eyes searched mine and then my brother's. "I know how it feels, the subtle warp and weft of this place as she weaves you in. You must escape before you are so thoroughly woven into her tapestry that you cannot free yourselves. Trust me. The longer you stay, the harder it will be."

"But what if we want to stay?" Nico's expression had become hopeful upon hearing of my change of heart.

For the first time, I didn't protest. I just kept thinking about Guilio, looking at me like I was something special—really special—and Ilaria, so faithful. The Forellis, and how they'd gotten me out of this mess with the Fortebraccios.

"We understand what you are saying," he stated. "These fights are to the death. But surely they can't happen all the time, right?"

She sighed. "Far too often. Even in times of relative peace. Someone, somewhere is always trying to get ahead. And the lack of medical care? My mother is amazing with what she accomplishes with her herbal remedies. But she could not save my sons." Her voice cracked as she looked to the valley below. Then she gathered herself and turned to us again. "She has tried and failed with as many of our friends and loved ones, as she has succeeded."

"That must have been so, so hard," I said, and Nico murmured agreement.

"As it continues to be." She looked away. "One never stops grieving a lost child."

"I imagine that's true," Nico said and went on, impulsively. "But we don't get sick very often. We have good immune systems working for us."

"Your immune system hasn't encountered medieval bugs."

"Your mother, you, and Gabriella survived the plague," Nico said. "Did you get sick?"

She shook her head. "I think some of the vaccinations we had as children helped. But be warned—we've been vulnerable to other things over the years that we thought might kill us. Your system is used to fighting viruses in the twenty-first century. They're very different in this time."

He gave a slow nod, hands on hips, a classic-Nico stance when he was trying to figure something out.

"We will think it through," I promised.

"Good. Because when we return to Castello Forelli tomorrow, it would be a logical time to say your farewells and head for the northern road." Her eyes grew sorrowful. "I wish I could encourage you to stay. But I cannot. It was Gabi falling in love that first brought us back. Our only chance to stay in our own time was to never put our hands on the prints again. After that second time through, we were committed."

"I wanted to ask you about that. Did the time tunnel heal you? The ticket booth guy at the castello said Gabi acted like she had appendicitis, but then you just took your dad and left."

Lia nodded. "That was an act. But it does appear to heal. She was poisoned and stabbed the first time we returned—I myself sewed her up, and you can imagine how that went. And yet the tunnel seemed to completely heal her."

Did that mean that the reverse was true? If I went back to my own time, would my headaches return? Or had I been healed forever? "But when you came back here, she wasn't again suffering from the poisoning? Or the stabbing?"

"No," Lia said. "It was permanent. Her *skin* was healed, like it'd happened years before." She smiled. "It was part of what made the legend of the She-Wolves grow. Rumor had it that you couldn't kill us, no matter which method was tried. Lucky for us, it made men less gung-ho to come after us. They thought they were at a disadvantage."

"So Gabi taking an arrow two weeks ago showed weakness," Nico said.

She shook her head. "We've been wounded before and recovered. I think her recovery and presence here will just add to the lore."

Lia looked at us knowingly. "I realize that's a draw too. The notoriety. Feeling like you're someone special, just because you're doing what you've been trained to do and then getting all the adulation from people. It's hard to ignore, because it feeds your pride."

I began to object but she interrupted. "Trust me. We all have pride. And I've found it is the root of all sin. It gets us in trouble, time and again, so watch out for it." She lifted her hands. "That's it. I've said what's been weighing on my mind and heart. The rest is up to you and God. Enjoy this evening of celebration. You deserve it. Then, please, give serious consideration to returning home. Because honestly? I think it's where you belong."

I pulled back. *Where I belonged?* "But what if . . . what if I feel like I belong here?"

She squared off with me and gave me a long look. "If you remain with us, we shall be your family. But think long and hard, Luci. Nico," she added, turning to him, while taking his hand again. "Because this place can give you much . . . but it also can take more than you can imagine."

23

LUCIANA BETARRINI

We watched Lia disappear into the crowd, and I thought over her words, *returning home* hovering in my mind. And my first thought when she said it was *Castello Forelli*. Not my own time, as she'd meant it. Not New York. Was that my answer?

Did I belong anywhere else, if my first answer was *here*?

I had just turned back to talk it over with Nico when the others arrived—Guilio and Chiara, Fortino and Benedetto, Tiliani. They surrounded us, hugging and patting us on the back and kissing us from cheek to cheek. They brought us goblets of wine as music filled the air. Apparently the hall was transitioning from negotiation-chamber to party-central. More nobles were spilling out onto the wide verandah, celebrating like their team had just won a championship or something.

"So they are happy that they only had to pay three hundred florins for my release?" I asked Fortino and Benedetto over the din.

"They are happy that they sent Lord Fortebraccio home with his tail between his legs," Fortino returned.

"But isn't three hundred florins a small fortune?"

"'Tis worth every bit to have a new She-Wolf amongst us." Benedetto smiled proudly at me.

"Don't forget her twin He-Wolf," Nico put in as he nudged into our circle.

"I do not believe they shall." Fortino clinked his goblet against my brother's. "'Tis a good thing for our enemies to fear our might. And your arrival has reminded everyone just how strong Castello Forelli is. She withstood Perugia's attack—"

"Narrowly," Benedetto said wryly.

"'Twas narrow," Fortino allowed, "but she still withstood it until reinforcements arrived. That is all that can be asked of an outpost. And our two cousins took down man after man with naught but their hands and feet." He looked between us in wonder. "Where did you learn such fighting skills? Are they common in Britannia?"

I eyed my brother, wondering how to respond.

"Nay. We were taught by a master from . . ."

"The Orient," I supplied. "'Tis a technique designed to reinforce a swordsman."

"'Tis most effective," Fortino admired. "Can you train us?"

"We shall learn too," Guilio declared, alongside Ilaria.

"You could train all our knights," added Benedetto.

I bit my lip. *Talk about changing history.* I was pretty sure jiu jitsu didn't really become a *thing* until a couple centuries from now.

"Mayhap you wish to keep it to yourselves to solidify your own reputation," Fortino said stiffly.

"Or mayhap she wishes to keep it to herself so she can continue to take down her adversaries before they know what is to come," Guilio said, slightly chiding him. His subtle defense—even if he was off-base—made me smile a little.

"Keep your own counsel," Ilaria said to us both. "But know we would be eager to learn, should you wish to teach us."

That was it for Nico. "I can show you a basic move right now," he said, giving her his best smolder-look.

She smiled benignly. "Mayhap this is not the best setting. But when we return to Castello Forelli? I would welcome your lessons."

His face fell as she moved away to speak to two young men, who were waiting a few paces away. Fortino and Benedetto laughed. Benedetto nudged him. "Welcome to how Ilaria places an eclipse over every young man's sun," he said. "She is not interested in the affairs of the heart."

I frowned over that. Spending the last two weeks with her, I doubted it was true. Not that we'd gotten into girlish talk about cute guys or what our dream-husband might be like. As I glanced her way, I saw that she did not flirt with those two young men. She conferred. They were talking about some serious matter, and she was as strong and determined here at a party as she was astride a horse, bow pulled taut. Maybe that's why my cousins thought she didn't care about romantic things.

"Mayhap she simply has not found a young man with a bright enough sun," Nico quipped, staring at her too.

Leave it to my brother to consider this a challenge. Given that he was pretty cute, he'd always had girls who were after him. But the girls who resisted his charms? That really got his juices flowing. But the last thing we needed was him seriously falling for Ilaria Greco—or me for Guilio Greco. Not if we were leaving soon, as Lia had encouraged.

But were we really willing to go?

"M'lady, would you care to tour the Palazzo Pubblico?" Guilio asked. "Many like to admire the fine artwork."

"I-I think it would be best if I stayed out here in the fresh air. After these last weeks, held captive at Castello Fortebraccio, it . . . aids me, to see the swallows flitting about."

His dark-blue eyes followed to where I gestured to the swarming birds, still chasing mosquitoes for their evening snack. But then he smiled down at me. "You wish to see a place with even more birds in flight?"

There was nothing for me to say. I'd kind of painted myself into a corner. "I would not say no."

"Come with me," he beckoned.

He led me off the verandah and into a narrow corridor. We crouched through what I assumed was a servants' passageway—avoiding the crowds inside who might waylay us—and out a lattice-covered door to the broader staircase. "We must make haste before someone discovers us." His voice was low. "They shall want you front and center for the night's festivities. But mayhap I can give you what you most need in order to prepare. This shall fortify you."

We hurried down the wide, marble steps and into the open foyer. It was then that I knew where we were headed—Torre del Mangia, the massive tower that overlooked il Campo. He opened the door and, with a furtive look around to make sure we had not been seen, gestured me inward. Then he closed the door and led me up the stairs at a steady clip, just slow enough that I knew he was paying attention to the cloying folds of my skirts, as well as my heaving breath.

We reached the top of the four hundred serpentine steps, and I went to the wall and stared out in amazement. We could see for miles outside the city—acre upon acre of grapevines, divided by neat squares of land growing golden wheat. Here and there were sections of heavy wood or the pale-green groves of olives. In the distance, mountains. But below us, the beautiful, red-tiled roofs of Siena's citizens gathered. Around the piazza, the massive palazzi surrounded the shell-shaped il Campo, nine rays freshly bricked in—spreading out from the base of Palazzo Pubblico in a nod to the Nine. And halfway down, sparrows swarmed and spun, rose and soared.

Guilio looked down with me. "There, you see? Now you have more air than the sparrows themselves."

I grinned, truly feeling freer than I had in weeks—if, you know, the most handsome man I'd ever met wasn't standing to my side, staring at me with mad intensity.

"Was he beastly to you, m'lady? Lord Fortebraccio?"

"The elder or the younger?" I managed.

"Either." All trace of a smile had left his face.

"They were not intolerable," I said, turning to him in earnest, wanting to ease his concern. "Franco pursued me for a time to appease his father, but I followed through with my plan to make myself rather un-enticing."

"I cannot imagine that possible," Giulio said quietly.

I had no reply as I met his earnest gaze.

"You are clever, as well as beautiful, m'lady."

I swallowed. "You are overly kind, m'lord." I said, trying to deflect his praise. What was happening here? I mean, we'd been all flirty before but—

"Overly kind, I am not," he said, looking outward again for a moment, with those earnest blue eyes that could pin a girl to a target, despite her best efforts. "But I am truthful." He straightened, and I did too. He took my hand as we faced each other. "And if I am to be truthful, I must tell you that it rent my heart to leave you and Ilaria behind."

"I am so sorry Ilaria felt like she had to stay with me." Had they ever been separated? "You must have been quite fretful for her safety."

"Nay," he said, slowly shaking his head, "that is not what I meant. Truly, I was concerned for my sister. But I was glad she could remain by your side if I could not myself."

Slowly, tentatively, he lifted his free hand to touch my temple and trace my cheek. "I knew Ilaria would be well. But the idea of another man . . . the thought that someone else might . . ."

He leaned in, and we were so close I could feel the heat of his breath on my lips. We stared at each other. Never had I felt anything like it. I wanted to wrap my arms around him and pull him to me. To stand up on my tiptoes and close the distance between us.

But then we heard them. Men and women climbing up the steps. Laughing and bantering. We quickly separated a few paces. I leaned over one wall, and he leaned against the adjacent one.

"There you are!" Benedetto said. "I told you they would be up here!" he said to the others who followed him. Fortino, my brother, Ilaria, and three young women.

"Father, Zio Luca, and the others of the Nine all wish to speak to you," Benedetto said to me. "We volunteered to fetch you. We saw him escorting you out. Knowing how Guilio favors this pigeon's perch, 'twasn't hard to imagine where you had gone."

"'Tis quite the grand pigeon's perch," one of the young women said, sliding her hand around Fortino's elbow and casting him a flirtatious glance.

I supposed the brothers were hot commodities in medieval social circles. Sons of a She-Wolf. Next in line for lordship over Castello Forelli. The whole nine yards. Quickly, introductions were made between me and the Ladies Cavani, Dondoli and Baldi.

"How many parties have you escaped in favor of Torre del Mangia, Lord Greco?" asked Lady Dondoli with a sly smile.

"Not nearly enough," Lord Greco returned, granting her the favor of a small smile.

Had he brought other women up here? Or come alone? Lady Dondoli looked like she would more than welcome an invitation.

I bit back a twinge of jealousy. I had no right to be jealous over him. I should be cheering any of these ladies on. Because after all, I was likely leaving in a couple of days.

Right?

LUCIANA BETARRINI

My senses were heightened as the dancing began.

My father and the Nine had succeeded in freeing Luciana and Ilaria, and so I was feeling that swell of victory, relief, but there was also the fact that there were twenty-four—*twenty-four* Fiorentini knights in Palazzo Pubblico. In a hundred years, I doubted that had occurred before, so deep was the hatred between us. Visceral was the wariness between us, even now.

"Steady," Captain Valeri said at my elbow. I glanced up to him in surprise. Had he sensed my unease? I looked about for Aurelio. He was on the far side of the room, regaling a group of four with a story.

"As far as I can recollect, this many Sienese and Fiorentini have not supped," he said.

"Indeed." I took a goblet of wine from a passing maid's tray.

"This could be the beginning of something momentous," he said, looking out at the room, hope etched in his handsome face.

"Or the beginnings of disaster," I said, feeling guilty for betraying his hope.

He turned to me, brows lifted. "Disaster? Or not the fragile structure of a bridge?"

"It might well be," I said. "But many men in this room doubt it. 'Twill take a great deal to solidify her foundations, if she is truly a bridge."

"Then strengthen her, we shall." He leaned back and placed a booted foot against the wall, crossing his arms. "Would it not be grand if our republics no longer fought, but rather joined?" he asked.

I paused. "We have long been enemies. Do you truly believe we can get past that and move toward solidarity?"

He leaned slightly toward me. "Would you not welcome it? To sup together rather than attempt to destroy one another on the battlefield? This night together, here in the heart of your city, and your potential union with Aurelio, are vital first steps."

I let a breath, then two, pass. Could I truly wed Aurelio and live with his captain forever in my Great Hall, around my fire, and yet cease feeling the draw between us? Was he not feeling the same? Had he not meant to touch me? Had I imagined he wished to kiss me?

Mayhap I merely had to force myself to act as he was—that I was entirely supportive of these first steps—and mayhap I would start believing this was a friendship, not a romance we were both fighting.

"Do you think, Captain—"

"Please, can you not yet call me Valentino?"

I paused again and searched his eyes, wondering if he was

seeking greater intimacy. But he seemed guileless. I began anew. "Valentino, after centuries of battle, hatred—the desire to return the harm done to us with greater harm to our enemies—do you *truly* believe that we might enjoy peace?"

His sudden smile was almost beatific.

He not only hoped. He *believed.*

Firenze. Siena.

Unified? Truly at peace, not for just a time, but potentially forever?

For the first time, I caught the fish for which my parents, my aunt and uncle, had been angling. The reason we were even in the same room.

"You believe?"

He took my hand. "Truthfully, I do not believe. I *hope.* But would it not be a blessed conclusion?" he asked earnestly. "No more battles, no more war, no more loss? Mayhap I could let my sword rest and spend my days finding herbs and concocting tinctures that heal, as do your grandmother and Lady Chiara."

His hope-filled expression softened my heart even as he dropped my hand, remembering himself.

I wanted to fill those usually sorrowful hazel eyes with a *sea full* of hope. And for the first time, looking into Valentino's face, I thought it might be within our reach.

But the question remained—was I willing to wed a different man in order to aid the effort?

24

LUCIANA BETARRINI

I made my way around the group and had just started down the tower steps when Guilio broke from his conversation with Lady Dondoli to call, "You intend to leave, m'lady?"

Lady Dondoli looked to me with some disdain, clearly unhappy that I had distracted him. Or that he was paying attention to me at all?

"Yes. I must speak to my brother. We have much to discuss after our weeks apart."

"I shall escort you," he said, stepping around his young companion.

I held up my hand. "There is no need. I know the way."

But there was no stopping him. "If you are going to the hall, then you shall soon be invited to the dance floor," he said under his breath, pressing past me in the narrow stairwell. To keep the others from overhearing? I shivered as he leaned even closer to whisper in my ear. "And if I am to claim a dance of my own with you, I had best do so early. Because you, Luciana, have caught the eye of every free man to wed in the room." He stared at me for a meaningful moment and then turned.

I gathered up my skirts and followed him. Every eye? Wed? He was worried about this? Jealous? The others lingered at the top, and their chatter and laughter echoed down to us but gradually faded.

"Are you certain you should not claim a dance with Lady Dondoli?" I forced myself to ask.

"I shall in time," he said with a shrug of his shoulders. "'Tis important to the Forellis that I make some effort with their friends. But truly, the only dancing I have ever enjoyed was teaching you in the meadow." He cast me a mischievous smile over his shoulder that made my knees actually wobble.

Why couldn't I find a guy like Guilio in my own time? I wondered.

Because men are different here.

Or in this time.

Or was I meant for another time?

The thought so startled me I had to force myself to not stop on the stair.

Giulio seemed as capable a dancer as he was riding horses. Effortless in a way. The way I felt when practicing my jiu jitsu moves for the thousandth time. Like it had become part of him. I doubted dancing would ever be that way for me. I'd forever be counting and trying to remember what came next.

"You are a graceful dancer," I said. "Why do you not enjoy it?"

"Mayhap 'tis because I had yet to find the right partner." He gestured about us. "Too much of it is flirtation and decorum, rather than the dance itself. I enjoy the music. The movement. The feel of the music. But not how women second-guess every invitation to the floor."

Is that why he enjoyed our dances in the meadow? Because I was concentrating on learning the steps, rather than on him?

Mayhap it is because I had yet to find the right partner.

Had. What did that mean?

My thoughts were all jumbled. It was with some relief that we reached the bottom of the tower steps and entered the Palazzo Pubblico courtyard. It made my heart glad to hear Marcello telling the story of why the tower had been named *Mangia*—apparently, after an old bell ringer who ate through his earnings—and to see Luca give me an appreciative smile. Ailing as they had been, we had yet to properly meet. Knowing this, and that Fortino had been sent to fetch us, Guilio brought me directly to them. The lords turned and greeted me warmly, kissing me on both cheeks, as Evangelia introduced me.

Marcello tucked my hand around his arm, and Lady Gabriella looped her arm through mine from the other side. "Grant us leave, Lord Greco," Marcello said over his shoulder. "We shall relinquish Gabriella's young cousin's hand back to yours after we have a brief word with her."

"As you wish, m'lord," Guilio said deferentially, half-bowing.

"Are you unharmed, Luciana?" Gabriella asked quietly as we convened in a quiet corner. "The Fortebraccios treated you with respect?"

"Largely, yes," I said. "But I am very relieved to be back with you and the others from Castello Forelli."

"As we are glad to have you returned to our fold." Marcello's voice was strong and warm. "Do you expect to stay long with us, m'lady? Gabriella tells me you might wish to soon return to Britannia."

I eyed him and immediately knew he knew exactly who I was and where I was truly from. "I am . . . uncertain. Domenico and I must discuss our plans."

He lifted one brow, and I could see that he was still handsome, even if he was my father's age. "I have spoken with young Domenico at length and know he desires to remain. But he believes that you remain . . . undecided."

I huffed a laugh. "No one is more surprised than I over that. But there is something about being here that has . . . overtaken me."

"Something? Or someone?" Gabriella asked in my ear.

I dared not look at her. Was that encouragement in her tone? Or simple understanding, since falling for a guy was at least part of why she herself had decided to remain?

But it was both, I thought. Both someone—Guilio—and something—the Forellis—that was changing my mind. Changing *me*, in a way.

We moved toward the dance floor. Music swelled within the room, the air hot with human bodies in movement. "Lord Greco will not be the only man to seek a dance," she said to me. "Remember your story and do not deviate from it. You are from the Cotswolds, in Britannia. You came to bring me and Evangelia news of an inheritance . . ."

"I remember," I whispered in English. "Don't worry."

But as one song ended and another began, and Marcello gently led me to face Lord Greco, I started to fret. Because as Guilio took me in his arms, I wanted to tell at least *him* the truth. Well, he and Ilaria both. Did our agreement to the cover story extend to them too?

And if we did tell them, would they totally freak out?

TILIANI FORELLI

It was with some delight that I watched over Aurelio's shoulder as Guilio took Luciana in his arms. Never had I seen him look at a woman the way he did now. He tried to disguise his interest, of course. Maintain a polite distance. But I hadn't missed how he'd prowled the ramparts until the moon began to sink each night, in her absence. He'd claimed it was concern over his sister, and undoubtedly, he had been concerned for Ilaria.

But now, seeing him with Luciana, I knew it was *she* who had truly driven him to pace the walls. This cousin of ours from the future was quickly capturing his heart. I frowned. Would she break it when she left us? And I knew Ilaria was rather taken with Domenico, despite her protestations. Would they both be devastated when the Betarrinis returned to their own time?

"What is it?" Aurelio asked, as we came side by side in the dance and clapped twice.

"I am uncertain of what you speak," I feigned, as we switched sides and clapped again.

"You appear vexed," he said, placing his hand on my hip and turning in a circle, stopping for a beat at every quarter. "And I have yet to step on your toes."

"Forgive me, m'lord," I said with a smile. "I confess I was thinking of my friends, not your toes."

"Oh?" He glanced about. "What is there to concern you? Your lovely cousin Luciana has been freed, and your friend Ilaria returned to you."

"You are quite right," I said. "Mayhap 'tis simply the carryover of weeks of concern."

"Best set that aside, my dear," he said, turning me in another circle. "This night should only be filled with joy. After all, we have much to celebrate. You have recovered enough from your attack to be here, dancing." His eyes slid down to my high-necked gown, covering the bruises, and he seemed to visibly shove away the memory in order to continue. "Perugia has been sent home, our captives reclaimed, and for the first time in decades, Firenze and Siena sup together."

"Indeed," I agreed. He was an adept dancer, and I felt the admiring glances of more than a few as we moved across the floor. He was not only good at leading, he was also careful not to overshadow me. 'Twas as if he wished to show me off to every man in the room.

Which should have felt like a compliment, of sorts. He was clearly proud of me. Proud of being my escort. But why did it chafe rather than soothe?

"My friends shall wish to meet you, and some might wish to claim a dance," Aurelio said. "Would you be willing to accept their invitations?"

"Of course," I said, yet hearing my own tone as wooden. To dance with one Fiorentini after another? It seemed forced, as if I only continued to play the role that my parents wished me to play. When there was only one Fiorentini's hand I would truly welcome.

I startled at the thought of Valentino, missing a half step.

"Careful," Aurelio said, catching me and easily moving me back into rhythm. He cast me a curious look, but I ignored it. After a few more steps, I dared to look about the dance floor, half wishing to see Valentino, half fretful I would. For I did not want to see another woman in his arms and wish again that it was me. At some point this evening, would Aurelio send Valentino to dance with me in his stead again? And what sort of traitorous heart wished for just that to occur?

I remembered the hope in the captain's eyes. His quiet dream of retiring his sword in favor of seeking out herbs, looking after others, as my grandmother did. And how he believed that a union between me and his lord would help him make it a reality. My mind raced as I thought about taking up residence in Castello Greco—soon again to be Castello Paratore. How it would feel to see Castello Forelli in the distance, not abide within her walls. Mayhap Valentino could go foraging with Chiara for the herbs they all needed. They might fall in love, sharing their passion for healing. She was as lovely as he was handsome. They were both fine people, people who had survived much. Deserving of love, peace.

It was a pretty vision. But then why did the thought of it make me feel so sick?

25

LUCIANA BETARRINI

My dance with Guilio ended far too soon, and I endured one dance after another with eager Sienese and a few Fiorentini alike. It made me happy that I only saw Guilio dance a few times. Instead, he conversed with other knights from Castello Forelli and a few from Siena I did not recognize, all the while keeping his eye on me. I tried to pretend I did not notice. But again and again, our eyes met.

At long last, he returned to my side. "May I have this dance?"

"Might you escort me outside instead, Lord Greco? I need a bit of air."

"Gladly," he said, offering his arm. I placed mine atop it, and we moved out of the crowded, hot room, down the wide stairs, and into the piazza.

I sighed with relief as the cool of the evening air washed over me, drying the sweat on my brow and neck. "Oh, it feels so much better out here."

He gave me a smile as he led us around various sculptures that dotted il Campo, up to Fonte Gaia, the big fountain that had totally been redone in my day. Or somewhere in between his day and mine, anyway. But fresh water still flowed, and I leaned down to cup my hands in the water, drinking deeply, as Guilio did beside me. Torches lined the fronts of the palazzi that circled the piazza, casting dancing warm light across us, as well as deep shadows. I straightened and traced my damp fingertips across my clavicle and back of my neck, belatedly sensing his gaze. He watched me intently with those deep, blue eyes.

I slowly turned to face him. "My lord?"

He turned to more fully face me too. "My lady," he whispered. He lifted a hand to my cheek and cupped it, gazing down at me. "Oh, that you would be my lady." He leaned his forehead to touch mine. "Luciana, I have never met a woman like you."

"Nay?" I whispered, my heart galloping.

"Nay. May I . . . may I kiss you?"

"I would like that. Very—"

Before I could utter *much*, his lips covered mine. In a moment he deepened his kiss and pressed me closer. My arms encircled his neck, loving the feel of being as close to him as I'd wanted to in the meadows. I reveled in the smell of him—the clean scent of lavender and leather. I reveled in the strength of his arms, remembering how easily he lifted me to his horse or to carry me to safety. I reveled in his lips, so seemingly hungry for mine.

Abruptly he pulled away. "Forgive me. I forget my—"

But it was my turn to cut him off, reclaiming his lips again.

Long moments passed before he slowly eased away again. "We must . . ." he panted, hands on my shoulders, "stop."

Reluctantly, I nodded. He was right, of course. I looked about and saw couples walking about the piazza. Fortunately, no one glanced our way.

"I shall speak to your brother on the morrow," he said, fingers brushing my cheek.

"Speak to Nico?" I asked blankly. "About what?"

He gave me a curious look and charming smile. "About my intentions," he whispered, lowering his forehead to mine again. "For us."

"Us," I repeated, feeling his warm breath on my face, half wishing he'd kiss me again—make me forget all my objections about how this wouldn't work—and half wishing I could disappear through the time tunnel right then, before I was completely lost.

But he'd said *us.* The word echoed through my mind, like waves upon a distant shore as I stared up at him. Beautiful, glorious, him. *Us, us, us . . .*

TILIANI FORELLI

I was making my way back from the garderobe to the main hall when Flavio Bartolini intercepted me.

"*Buonasera*, Lady Forelli," he said, stepping into my path.

"Good evening, Lord Bartolini," I returned formally, trying to sidestep him. We had known each other since we were children, and briefly, he had attempted to court me.

I had always found him overbearing, as I did so now. He placed an arm before me, halting my progress. Two of his friends—Andrea Donati and Stefano Rondelli—stood behind him, hands on their belts. What was this?

"May we have a word, m'lady?" he asked, gesturing toward an alcove to our right.

Refusing to be cowed by them, I nodded, led the way into the alcove and turned, arms crossed. "What is it? What can you not say to me in a proper meeting?"

"Why are you doing this, m'lady?" Flavio asked. "Truly? Why take up with a Fiorentini when you could have your pick of Sienese noblemen?"

I stared at them. "So this is why you waylay me? Because I have wounded your pride? What I do or do not with courtship is not your affair."

"But it *is* our affair," Andrea said, leaning toward me. "Because what you endeavor to introduce here—between you and Paratore—might forever change our republic, as well as the Fiorentini."

"If it progresses," I said, leaning toward him, "'twill be for the benefit of one and all, not the detriment. My father and uncle hope that a union between our houses might improve commerce as well as promote peace."

"You cannot trust the Fiorentini," Andrea growled. "Everyone knows that."

"Many Fiorentini say the same of the Sienese. Is it true?"

"Of course not."

"Mayhap it is time we give our neighbors a measure of grace, as I pray they will for us."

"Such is the thinking of a female," sniffed Flavio. "She looks every inch the warrior from the outside, but on the inside," he edged closer, "she is but a woman."

"Sometimes it takes a woman to think beyond what a man has created. And it does not escape me that your family is best served by continuing warfare." The Bartolinis had made their fortune producing some of the finest arrowheads available in Toscana. "You place your coffers ahead of the men, women, and children of Siena. Take a breath and consider your fellow citizens rather than the coin in your purse."

He let out a dismissive sound. "Every man in this building considers his purse first."

"My father and uncle have not. They encourage this courtship out of a sense of duty to Siena. They want to see peace settle over our lands for decades to come. They want many to prosper because of increased commerce, not only a few."

"Forgive me if I doubt you," Flavio said flatly. "The Forellis always take care of their own first. Everyone knows that you all had ample supplies during the plague. And yet you kept your gates locked up tight when your people came to you, begging."

I bit my lip, refusing to rise to his bait. It had long been our battle, fighting this rumor. But I knew my father and uncle had passed out many, many crates of food to those in need. They had only refused to open our gates to the pestilence, trying to keep us all well, until we were breached by the Fiorentini. "We took care of our people. None who relied on Castello Forelli went away hungry. We simply could not welcome them in. To do so would have been inviting death itself."

"I do not fear death," Stefano said, straightening.

"Then you are a fool. You shall likely meet your Maker, earlier than he intended."

Fortino and Benedetto were passing by when they caught sight of me, behind the wall of men. They pulled up short. "Cousin?" Fortino's voice hardened. "Stand aside, you louts. How dare you waylay a lady!"

Reluctantly, the men stepped aside, allowing me to pass and step between my cousins.

"We merely wished a word with her," Flavio said, crossing his arms.

"If you want another," Fortino said, poking him in the chest, "you come to Castello Forelli, or ask for it when she is in the company of one of us. Understood?"

"Fortino—" I tried. My cousins were more protective than ever since my attack. But these were not brigands in the woods; they were Sienese we wanted on our side.

The young nobleman bit his cheek, then gave him the slightest of nods. "Forgive me, m'lady. We meant no harm."

"You did me no harm." I lifted my chin. "I do not fear an honest dialogue."

"But a dialogue is between two," Benedetto said curtly. "Next time, leave your henchmen behind."

"As you say," Flavio said, with a more deferential nod.

My cousins ushered me away. "Are you well, Til?" Benedetto asked.

"Well enough," I assured him. "But it seems not all are at peace with this idea of a bridge forming between Firenze and Siena. If I choose to wed Aurelio, there may well be repercussions against us among the Sienese, as well as between Siena and Perugia."

26

I stepped away from Guilio after our kiss. It was the last thing I wanted to do. But I had to gain some physical separation so I could think. Speak. My hand went to my head, and I turned from him. "Guilio, there are some things you do not know about me," I began.

He wrapped his arms around me from behind, nuzzling his head beside mine. "As there are things that you do not yet know about me. That is what courtship—"

"Nay," I said, turning miserably around to face him, wanting to make him drop his arms and yet lacking the willpower to ask him to do so. It simply felt so good, so right, to be held by him. I sighed and lifted a hand to his cheek this time, looking into his eyes. "Guilio, I am not from here."

He squinted at me. "I know that. You are from Britannia."

I shook my head slowly. "I am from farther than there."

"Farther? Are you Norse?"

"Nay. Farther."

His frown deepened and he eased slightly away. "There *is* no farther than that, Luciana, other than the Orient. Or Africa. And you are plainly from neither place."

I looked around, making certain no one was still within earshot. "I am from a place called America. I was in Toscana for the summer." I laid a hand on his arm. "But this will be the most challenging thing for you to understand, since I do not quite understand it myself." I took a deep breath. "Guilio, Domenico and I are from another *time*. Another year. Far in the future."

He stared into my eyes, as if checking to see if I might be joking. "The . . . future," he repeated.

"Yes." I swallowed. "A very different time. Nico and I . . . when we went into that Etruscan tomb . . . there is something magic about them. Mysterious." I sighed and rubbed my temple. "It's very hard to explain. There were two handprints, and when we touched them, we found ourselves here. In your time."

He frowned and slowly shook his head, backing away. "You speak of witchcraft."

"Nay," I hurriedly assured him, tentatively following him, fearing he might actually bolt. "There were no spells. We did not ask or seek to come here. We were simply . . . brought. As if God himself wanted us here."

He blinked in bewilderment again, then his eyes grew distant, clearly remembering the day they discovered us near the tombs. In our strange clothing, with our unique fighting skills. The reasons why I was unlike any girl he'd ever met.

He ran a hand through his dark hair, then rubbed his cheek, staring at me. "So then you intend to return? From whence you came? Through the tomb, back to the time in which you were birthed?"

I shook my head slowly. "I do not know. I did not expect . . ." *You*, I finished silently. *This family.* "The Forellis. Castello Forelli . . ." I hugged my arms around myself, looking about il Campo. "Siena. I did not know I could come to love a place, a people, so quickly. I did not know I could feel so much like I was a part of something, like a missing puzzle piece finally in place." I took a deep breath. "Guilio, when I was held at Castello Fortebraccio, I spent a great deal of time thinking about getting back to Domenico and returning home, to our own time. But," I had to tell him, let him know, "I also spent a great deal of time thinking about you, and how I missed you." I paused. "I know this is a great deal for you to consider."

"Indeed." He laughed mirthlessly. "'Tis sore luck for me to be in the midst of giving my heart to a woman who might be nothing more than an apparition."

I frowned. "Guilio." I stepped closer, and he allowed me to place my hand on his cheek again. "Does that feel like the touch of a ghost?" I whispered.

"Nay," he said miserably.

I drew his forehead to mine. "Does my breath have the chill a spirit's would?"

"Nay, 'tis warm."

"And my kiss?" I whispered, lifting my lips toward his.

His lips hovered over mine, so close I felt the brush of them. "'Tis otherworldly," he whispered back, but didn't give in. "And yet very present." Tentatively, he placed a hand on each of my hips.

"Would your hands not brush through me, if I were not real, Guilio?" I persisted.

"Sì," he said. "But you are very much . . . corporeal."

I didn't know what *corporeal* meant, but Guilio uttered it in a way that made me feel more desirous of him than ever. And yet despite our nearness, we did not kiss again. There was too much in each of our heads, I suspected. Too much to think through.

But what I hated most was the disappointment I sensed in him. Like I'd crushed his hopes and dreams by telling him the truth.

"There is a great deal for us both to consider," I said gently. "For me and my brother, truly. Together we must decide to either remain here or return to our own time. Whatever we decide, it must be together. And if we wish to remain," I lifted my eyes to his, "then 'tis your turn to again consider me, if you truly wish to pursue me. You said I'm unlike any you have met before. And now, you know why."

His expression—his bewilderment, his consternation, his frustration and fear—well, it was liable to break my heart. I wished he knew that Gabriella, Evangelia, and Adri were time travelers too—because undoubtedly, it would aid us—but that was not my secret to share.

I stared up at him, miserable, a lump forming in my throat. "Mayhap 'twould be best if you escorted me back to the Forellis?" I managed.

He remained still a moment, then gave a single nod.

I turned quickly because I did not want him to see the tears that were now streaming down my face. Hurriedly, I moved down the slope of il Campo to the palazzo, fervently hoping that someone would be able to take me wherever we were staying that night in Siena.

He followed me, close enough to protect and yet distant enough to give me space. But we both halted when a woman screamed, and then another. The shouts of men rose and increased in number. Inside Palazzo Pubblico.

"Stay here," Guilio demanded as he passed by, running into the fray even as people began rushing out of the building.

27

TILIANI FORELLI

It was late, and many were deep in their cups when the assassins struck. Aurelio had only just introduced me to the kindly, elderly Lord Gubbioti, one of the Grandi of Fiorentini, and he'd bent over my hand. "'Tis very good to make your acquaintance at last," the man said, smiling into my eyes and then over to Aurelio.

He suddenly shuddered, and with a gasp, his mouth fell open. Alarmed, I drew back.

A woman screamed across the room. I glanced wildly around as Lord Gubbioti crumpled to his knees. Behind him, I caught sight of a man who was pulling up a hood as he melded with the crowd.

Aurelio had caught Lord Gubbioti as he sank and slightly turned him to reveal a dagger in his back. I was horrified to see it. The kindly man would be dead in minutes.

"Valentino!" Aurelio shouted. "*Valentino!*"

I again searched the crowds, trying to discover the assailant when another woman screamed. From the center of the dance floor there was more shouting. What was happening? Assassins? Amidst this crowd of two hundred or more, how many were bent on creating mayhem?

Valentino shoved his way toward us, looking with consternation to Lord Gubbioti, now breathing his last. He was armed with but a dagger—as were most around us, given that all other weapons had been checked at the door. He slowly circled, keeping me behind him, looking at everyone as potential enemies. "Take Tiliani!" Aurelio said sharply. "She may be as big a target as we are. Get her to the corner where you can more readily guard her!"

"What? Nay? Nay!" I protested, as his captain fairly dragged me toward the corner of the room. I tried to shake him off. "I need no guarding, Valentino. I can protect myself!"

He did not release me from his iron grip, clearly as fearful for me as Aurelio was. "Make way, *make way*," he barked to everyone we met, waving his dagger threateningly. We made it to a wall— the corner already filled with a group—and Valentino turned to stand in front of me. "Keep watch to your left and right," he said over his shoulder.

"I will for both of us," I returned, bending to retrieve my own dagger, irritated that Aurelio and he had conspired to treat me like I was incapable. But to my left was poor, old Lady Tolani and her ladies' maid, and to my right, three simpering girls. I could help keep them safe too.

Lord Enici was calling for more candles.

Another man shouted from the staircase, and right after, another woman screamed from the adjoining room. How many did our enemies intend to take down?

"More candles! We must have more light!" shouted Lord Enici.

To what end? I thought. *To better see our fallen friends?* For I could fairly feel the threat leave the room as men and women swarmed for the doorways, all bent on escape. Surely, the assassins were escaping with them.

In minutes, the cavernous room had but fifty people left within. Here and there, groups hovered around the injured or dead. "They have fled, Valentino," I said quietly. "Let us return to Aurelio."

Without a word, he took my hand in his—all ceremony lost in the chaos of the moment—and led me back to Aurelio, who had left the body of Lord Peligrini to his wife and now cradled a dying

Lord Bianchi in his arms. Aurelio briefly looked up at me, a tear streak on his face.

Tears instantly rose in my own eyes, seeing his grief. Glancing around, I took in the full truth of it. Every one of those fallen—other than a couple of Sienese women who had stumbled on the stairs and were trampled as people rushed to exit—were Fiorentini.

Nay! Nay, nay, nay . . .

My uncle and father drew near first. Then my aunt and mother.

I looked to Valentino, horror flooding my mind, my heart. By my count, more than a dozen people, decent people, friends to Aurelio, had died this night. The assassins had clearly intended to kill as many as they could.

And when Firenze learned of it?

They would blame Siena. Accuse us of inviting peaceable ambassadors into a bloodbath.

I panicked at the thought of all that my father and uncle had sacrificed in order to make this possible. The memory of my mother and aunt's hope that this was the beginning of a new day between our republics, which would help ensure the safety of any future Forellis, as well as Siena itself. And I panicked at the thought of Aurelio needing to flee . . . and taking Valentino with him.

I rushed over to a young man, struggling to breathe, his family holding him as blood gurgled to his lips.

"Stay away!" choked his grief-stricken father.

"Yes! Keep clear!" cried a younger man—the victim's brother?—waving a dagger at me.

I knelt and set my own dagger on the marble floor, hands raised, tears in my eyes. "Please. I only wish to try to find out who did this. I am so desperately sorry. I want to know. May I ask?"

The father, in his finery, rocked the young man slightly, as if he might soothe an infant. It made me weep all the more. But at last he acquiesced, gesturing me forward.

I inched closer on my knees to the young man's side. He was gasping for breath, blood on his lips.

"Please. What is his name?" I asked his father.

"Vanni."

"Vanni," I said urgently, taking the young man's hand in mine. "Did you see who did this to you? Did you know his face? Was he Sienese?"

Cloudy eyes tried to focus on me, and I could see he was about my age. I fought back my tears as I strove to keep his gaze, willing him to tell me.

"'Twas a . . ." he gasped, choking on his own blood. "A woman," he managed. "I did . . . not . . . know . . . her."

Luciana Betarrini

I watched Guilio fight to enter Palazzo Pubblico as men and women streamed out, running away. He wanted me to stay here in the piazza? For how long? I rubbed my arms as people passed me, parting around me like a river around a stone. Was I any safer here than inside, where I could see my brother and the Forellis? I thought not.

I ran into the crowd as Guilio had, squeezing past people, dodging others. I helped a woman who'd been knocked down rise to her feet before she was trampled. After watching her limp away, I turned and ran smack-dab into a hooded man and woman. The man gruffly set me aside with a muttered apology, but not before I got a good look at his face—half-illuminated by the torchlight.

Their deep hoods captured my attention, as well as the embroidered gold thread along the shoulders. *Gold like the Forellis use on their tunics.* I stared after them, watching as those threads glinted in the torchlight.

Before I could think about it further, I turned and followed them. It was as if I could do no other. *These two had something to do with the chaos inside.* Their whole vibe was remarkably different than the others. Their actions were furtive, while the rest were fearful.

They were trying to hide. Disappear.

I darted quickly from column to deeply shadowed doorway. The tall man frequently looked backward, checking for any who might be following. The woman did not.

I was at the top of the piazza when my brother emerged at the entrance of Palazzo Pubblico. "Luciana!" he called, his shout echoing briefly. "*Luciana!*"

I half grimaced, half rejoiced that I might not be alone in this. Observing my targets turn a corner, I came out and waved my arms. "Nico! *Sono qui!*" *I'm here!* I gestured to where I was going, hoping he could see me in the flickering torchlight. While the entire Palazzo Pubblico was glowing and bright at the bottom of the piazza, up top, it was more intermittent. But I couldn't wait for him. The couple I trailed was already, what . . . a block down the neighboring street?

I ducked into an alcove and hurriedly pulled my skirts from behind me and up between my legs, tucking the bulk through the wide sash of my bodice. For the first time in days, I felt mobile. Free. Or at least free-er. I took off in a run toward the corner and down the street, looking for the two in hoods. I just barely caught them taking a left, down an alley, and glanced back, hoping Nico was about to appear.

He still wasn't in sight.

I ran down to the next corner and cautiously peeked around it—ignoring a small cluster of women gaping at me and how I'd arranged my skirts—and saw the couple striding down the narrow lane. She had taken his arm, and they had slowed their progress, as if consciously easing their momentum to avoid attracting attention. She pulled her hood back, and I noted she was about Ilaria's height, with dark-brown hair.

Great. Like ninety-percent of this town's population. That'll narrow it down.

I glanced back, hoping to see Nico, and spotted him rounding the corner. He saw me and pointed left, then ran down an adjacent street. I figured he was trying to cut them off at the other end of the alley.

No one was ahead of me.

I felt my pulse double. Had I lost them?

I pressed into a run, hoping I might outpace them.

And ran straight into a clothesline that caught my chin, rammed into my throat, and sent me skidding to my back.

On the ground I gasped for breath, feeling the slow burn of the cobblestones at my calves, my bare shoulder. *A ball gown really isn't the best for fighting garb,* I thought.

Dimly, I realized that there were people on either side of me. They were little more than silhouettes, here, in the star-lit alleyway. But I immediately recognized them. The hooded man and the woman. I fumbled for my dagger, before realizing I had lost it.

I gasped for breath that would not come.

"Forgive me," crooned the woman.

Apologizing in advance?

Instinctively, I rolled to avoid her strike, surprising them both. Her dagger crunched into the cobblestone and skittered from her hand. The woman, hunched as she was in skirts, lost her balance and tilted backward. Snarling, the man grabbed my hair, hauling me upward.

But Nico was there, then. Striking the man. Turning and kicking him, narrowly avoiding my head. I'd dodged at the last half second, years of training setting in. I heard the man gasp, grunt, swear. But Nico was relentless, striking again and again.

I scrambled to my feet and grasped at the woman when she tried to run. But she slipped from her cloak which I held and took off. After making certain Nico was holding his own, I looked for her again and discovered she'd disappeared down another alley. I ran after her. But when I reached the corner, nothing but darkness greeted me.

Was she hiding?

Tentatively, I moved down the tiny lane, where people had built overhangs for their houses—keeping to their allowed footprint while expanding their inside space—which blocked any light I might have gained from the night sky. I paused and held my breath, wondering if she was hiding nearby. Wondering if she had reclaimed the dagger I'd seen fly from her hand before fleeing.

My pulse pounded in my ears as I eased in, arms raised. Ready for attack.

One step. Two. Four. Ten.

"Luciana!" Nico cried at the tip of the alley.

As I turned back to look his way, I heard the telltale signs of flight a half-block distant. Now too far for me to chase down. I sighed in frustration.

"Did you get him?" I called in English, hoping against hope the guy was hog-tied or held somewhere by someone coming to our aid.

"No," he panted in frustration, as he arrived by my side. "He got away! The dude had *skills.*"

I groaned inwardly.

"Yours?" Nico asked, hands on his knees, still gasping for breath.

"Gone."

Gone, gone, gone.

And what secrets with her?

28

TILIANI FORELLI

They wished to create bedlam. And they had succeeded.
Come morn, we understood that twelve indeed had died, and eight more fought for their lives.

All Fiorentini.

All Fiorentini.

And time and again, those who had been near the victims reported a man or woman in cloaks of blue with gold embroidery at the shoulders. A few reported a howling wolf in the decorative embroidery.

My father and uncle had been called into council with the Nine at dawn's light. We called our own with the twins.

We went through their story a second time, along with Aurelio, Valentino, Benedetto, Fortino, Guilio, and Ilaria. We were all exhausted, having not slept. But had anyone slept in Siena last night?

"They were clearly assassins," Luciana declared. "Could they be part of Ercole's crew, since he seems bent on making you out to be the villains? Mayhap it was even Ercole I saw last night."

"He was a good fighter," Domenico said, half in admiration, half in disgust.

"Tall? Longer, lighter-brown hair worn tied at the neck?" I asked, remembering him in our Great Hall, our courtyards.

Luciana nodded. "Mayhap. It was dark, and he was hooded

most of the time. He was in the company of a woman about Ilaria's height, but with curlier hair."

I thought through the female servants that resided at Castello Forelli. Rosa, the sister of a groomsman in the stables, had left her post as a maid without a word, right around the time Ercole was dismissed. Her brother had said she was homesick and assumed she had left for their village. But what if she had fled with Ercole instead? Mayhap she had welcomed his advances when the other girl protested?

Quickly, I shared my thoughts with the others.

"I might have seen her with Ercole once or twice," Fortino said slowly, thinking back. "He flirted with her in the Great Hall as we supped and she served."

"And I may have seen her on the dance floor," Benedetto said. "I remember seeing a woman that I thought I recognized but could not place."

All eyes turned to him.

"May have," he reiterated. "The candles were few and far between on the dance floor."

Aurelio caught my gaze and inclined his head slightly. "I fear the shadows are against us," he murmured.

"Indeed," I returned, feeling overwhelmed and anxious.

"Could Flavio Bartolini have been behind it?" Benedetto asked, eying me. "He and his friends made it clear that they were not supportive of your potential union with Lord Paratore."

"And they are not alone," Fortino put in. "I had another conversation like it with a friend."

"Or could it have been Lord Fortebraccio?" Luciana suggested. "He was most displeased when he was escorted to the gates."

"I would not put it past him," Benedetto said tersely.

Aurelio stood. "You must find who was behind it. Uncover the entire viper's nest. Because we shall need to accompany our dead home to Firenze. And if you do not soon arrive with an explanation and proof of intrigue, then any hope for a union between our families is over, let alone our republics. These men—those who have died and those still fighting for their lives—are important to many at home. These attacks, and their losses, shall not be readily soothed."

I wondered over the partial horror—and yet partial hope too—his words brought to my heart. Would this put an end to our somewhat-forced courtship? I dared not glance in Valentino's direction. But if Aurelio left to return home, so would he. The thought of it made my heart stop a moment and then pound, almost painfully.

If Valentino left with Aurelio, he would likely never return.

Aurelio went on. "As miserable as this last day has been," he said, reaching down for my hand to draw me up beside him, "I fear there shall be worse days ahead."

"If we do not turn up these assassins and uncover their entire scheme," I finished for him, nodding grimly, "Firenze shall declare war."

LUCIANA BETARRINI

Guilio was avoiding me. If I went into the dining hall, he left it. If I went to the city stables, he muttered an excuse and exited. So I stopped seeking him out. It just hurt too much to have him basically reject me, over and over.

He couldn't deal with it. Who I was or where I was from. Would he ever?

Sensing my loneliness, Nico invited me out for a morning walk along Siena's market streets. "We can keep an eye out for Ercole and the girl," he said. But we both assumed the couple was long gone, slipping out of the city from one of the six gates. Unless they had other plans to further sabotage the Forellis . . .

The city seemed pretty normal, even after the massacre last

night. Maybe some were quieter or on edge. But life went on. A fishmonger moved toward il Campo with a cart full of eels. A cloth merchant set out rolls of colorful silk. A baker opened his door, and the heavenly smell of yeasty loaves drifted out. My stomach rumbled, but I ignored it. The thought of really eating after the horrors we saw last night made me feel a little sick. I supposed I would have to make myself eat eventually. Just not yet.

"Maybe when we get back," I said to Nico, "we should just go all the way back. This place . . . this time . . ."

He shook his head. "I don't know. I still feel like we need to help see them through this mess. See if we can find out who is setting them up. And I feel like it's us, too, who have been falsely accused. The Forellis—all of Siena could be in serious trouble. To just abandon them now feels wrong."

It was the same refrain, but with even more at stake. I agreed with him now, though. Somehow, we had become a part of the family. Last night, when so many were attacked, I'd felt fear for each and every one of them. When we'd gone after Ercole and the girl, I'd wanted to capture them and bring them to justice—on the Forellis' behalf.

Among the crowds, we spotted Lady Adri ahead with Chiara. Their baskets were full of herbs and bottles, likely medicines, but they had paused at an antiques shop. But "antiques" in this century were portions of Greek and Roman statues, as well as Etruscan ossuaries and pottery. We paused beside them.

"*Buongiorno*, Lady Adri," Nico said.

She glanced up at us in surprise.

"Good morning," she returned. She lifted a cracked vase and smiled at us. "I can't help myself," she said in English.

"I imagine not," I said, glancing over all the other Etruscan pieces the merchant had displayed.

"It soothes us," Lady Adri commented in English, "to return to what we know best. Things we can control, when other parts of life seem out of control. Medicinals to aid us. And art that distracts the mind." She held the vase out to the merchant and asked how much he wanted, bartered with him a moment, then handed him a few coins. "In our time, this would be priceless. Here, not so much. But I can't get over how much is here." Her smile broadened. "I have a hard time not buying it all."

She turned to Chiara and asked her to return to the palazzo with their supplies. "I think I'd like to walk with our young cousins for a while."

Chiara obediently accepted her basket and nodded at us. Coils of her curly hair escaped her low knot, framing her pretty face. "Of course, m'lady." She turned to weave her way through the crowds.

"She is far quieter than her siblings," I observed.

"Chiara is an introspective soul," Adri said. "But little escapes her. She went through a great deal as a young child. Such trauma changes a person."

"This place is full of trauma, it seems."

She glanced at me with her Danish-blue eyes, knowledge deep within. "Indeed. Staying here is not for the faint of heart."

"And yet you did."

Those eyes grew soft. "Gabi and Lia found love, chose to stay. And we had Ben with us for a time." She looked up to the sky, cradling the Etruscan vase in her hands. "It became home for us, like we'd never had before. And we became family with those who were not even Forellis or Betarrinis. As you say, these are traumatic times. But enduring trauma together, healing together, tends to either divide people or make them one." We passed a silversmith. "Take that man's craft," she said, gesturing back. "He uses extreme heat to refine his silver. And it eventually becomes purified, beautiful." She glanced at Nico and me. "The question for you is if you can withstand such heat."

"Is it always so *hot*?" I asked, as we walked through the city gate to look across a verdant valley that stretched out for miles. In the distance we could see mountains.

LISA T. BERGREN

"Nay. We have enjoyed decades of peace. And when those years come, we do not ignore them. We relish and celebrate them. That is different from our own time as well, where many can take good years with an apathetic spirit. People from our time often get absorbed in work or, when fearing the lean years, work even harder during the good times. Right? Here, we move from one feast day to the next. It forces us to pause and celebrate what we have, regardless of whether it's just enough or a bounty."

She gave us a brief smile. "Last night shall not be the last feast you experience. And the next will not end in such a tragic way."

"It was awful."

"Horrific," she said, her face sobering. "I loathe the thought of parents, siblings, and friends in Firenze hearing the news."

"What will they do?"

"I do not know. I hope we can find who is behind all of this and force them to confess. I believe it is our only hope. But God has brought us this far. Why would he abandon us now? That's what Padre Giovanni tells me," she said. I'd seen Aurelio and some of the Forellis enter for morning mass each day, and the priest seemed friendly, but we'd never spoken. "If you're struggling about whether you should go or remain, you might seek out his counsel. I find him a good listener."

"I don't know. I'm not Catholic. Is that allowed?"

Her eyes twinkled at me. "There is nothing but Catholics in this time," she said kindly. "Therefore, no matter your faith background, you fall under their umbrella."

That made sense. "Were you Catholic, before you came here?"

"I was agnostic. But living here, now, encountering death like we have . . ." She gazed off into the distance. "It forces a person to think more deeply about what lies beyond."

"So does traveling," Nico said, referring to the tomb.

She smiled. "It does indeed."

"Do you think all Betarrinis can travel?"

"No. I believe only those who are supposed to, do."

"But what about the others? The brothers who came and left?"

Lady Adri lifted a shoulder. "Who knows? Maybe they regretted their return. Or maybe they were supposed to come to meet us, so we might learn something new. All I know is that God has a hand in it all. And perhaps if he allowed you two to travel, you ought to stay long enough to find out why."

⁜ ⁜ ⁜

TILIANI FORELLI

Aurelio found me on the rooftop of Palazzo Forelli at sunset. I saw that Valentino accompanied him, but remained at a discreet distance. After last night's attack, they were taking extra precautions, no matter where they went. And I could not blame them.

"My lady, we must be off in the morn," he began. "There are fourteen now dead, and we must return them to their families before their corpses . . ." His voice trailed off. In the summer heat, I knew decomposition came quickly.

Tears pricked in my eyes, thinking of all those families mourning their dead. It was all so senseless, so terrible.

"And I must do my best to stay the Grandi's hand against Siena," he said, gathering himself.

"How long do you think we have until they demand vengeance?"

"I told your father and uncle that I shall be fortunate to waylay them for a week. 'Twould be best if we are presented with evidence exonerating your family within the next few days."

I glanced at him quickly. "You do not suspect—"

"Nay," he stated firmly. "But the only evidence we have is one witness after another who saw a cloak with Forelli markings. I can clearly see how someone is seeking to destroy your reputation, make your family appear the villains. But in the end, 'tis the only evidence that has been presented at all."

"But it would make no sense," I protested. "Why would my family seek to build this bridge only to tear it down?"

Aurelio appeared to have aged years over the last two days. "There will be some in Firenze who shall say that they drew us in, only to cut down the best of us. All my friends were warned of the risk before they came. Just as you have nobles against us, so do I in Firenze."

I swallowed and nodded. Together we gazed out for a moment at the sunset. In the golden light streaming across verdant, green hills, it was difficult to imagine that anyone had murderous intent for another. That anyone had political or financial aspirations great enough to set forth such a scheme. "I feel deeply for your losses, Aurelio. I know many of those who died were friends. Had I known about it, I would have done anything I could to stop it."

"I know." He nodded, paused. "M'lady . . ."

I turned to face him.

"This may well be the last time we see each other. At least, in private."

"I know," I said quietly. He was saying farewell.

"I shall do my best to argue your case, preserve hope, but I confess my hope is rapidly dwindling. I know my people. And I have come to know yours. They are equally as stubborn."

He thought our courtship over. I was torn between relief for myself and grief for my republic.

I laughed mirthlessly. "I appreciate that you were ready to forge a new path, Aurelio." Because I sensed he had been. Yes, he had had Castello Paratore in mind too. But I'd come to know him well enough to know that more than riches drew him.

"As I appreciate that you"—he said, taking my hand and lifting it to his lips—"were ready to consider a union between us. I know that you did so solely on behalf of your people, your family."

"At first it was," my lips curled, "but I did not find you entirely reprehensible."

He laughed at that, and it did my heart good to see smile lines overtake his consternation.

"If we get through this, clear the Forelli name, the Fiorentini—"

"Would still stand against our union," he said. "'Twas a battle to find enough to support my cause here, vying for your hand." He shook his head sadly. "To contend for your hand, after this, might be considered a form of treason."

I squeezed his hand. "Even if we are never to be together again, Aurelio, I hope we can be friends. From afar, if necessary. Mayhap in time, we can find new ways to build bridges between our republics."

"Know that I shall do my part in that endeavor."

I leaned forward and kissed his cheek, then the other. "Go with God, my friend."

He turned and walked to the stairwell door and disappeared inside. Valentino did not look back as he followed his master inside. And it was then, at last, that I gave my grief—and my tears—free rein.

29

TILIANI FORELLI

An hour later, the peach-toned sunset had given way to shades of teal and purple, signaling nightfall. But still I remained on the rooftop, thinking. Trying to find a way out of this terror for my family, fighting an unknown enemy, and my republic, potentially on the brink of war.

I heard the wooden stairwell door squeak and turned my head to see who joined me.

My breath caught.

Valentino.

He hovered there in the doorway, looking at me, then somberly closed the door. He stood for a moment, facing away, as if asking himself if he truly ought to be here. And I knew then, why he had come.

I went to him without thinking and wrapped my arms around his middle and settled my forehead between his shoulder blades. For several moments, neither of us spoke. We simply were together, truly together, for the first time.

"I could not leave without . . ." he said and then seemed to lose heart for his words as he turned to me.

"I am glad you could not," I whispered, looking up at him.

We stood there for a few more moments before he took a deep breath. "My lady, did I understand Aurelio right? You are no longer courting?"

I gazed into his beautiful, hazel eyes. "Neither of us believe it is possible to continue. The odds are against us. But Valentino," I touched his cheek, "while I grieve what that does for my parents' dreams of building a bridge with Firenze, I cannot mourn the fact that Aurelio will no longer be courting me. I know now why he is your friend. He is a decent man, a good man. But there is another who seems to be rapidly stealing my heart."

He held my hand to his face, clearly glad for my words. But his eyes held questions for which neither of us had answers: How? When?

"We must get through this mess," I said. "And then . . ."

"And then?"

I smiled at him fondly. "Mayhap you shall come south to search for herbs and medicinals in the woods that border Castello Paratore. And mayhap I might be on an errand for my grandmother at the same time. And given that it's the height of summer, we ought to do our very best to collect the most herbs possible before fall closes in."

He leaned in. "Promise me you shall not enter those woods without guard."

"I promise," I whispered.

He took my other hand and searched my eyes. Seeing my invitation, he bent and kissed me so softly, so reverently, that I was utterly taken up in the moment.

Valentino. The right man. The right *soul*.

He slowly drew away, eyes closed, as if wanting to memorize our kiss.

"You, Valentino," I whispered, "are the one I have been waiting for all this time. 'Twas because we had not yet met that God kept me from giving my heart away. 'Twas you. All this time," I repeated in wonder, squeezing his hand.

"Could it be?" he breathed. "That God would so utterly grace me?" There was glory in his eyes. Pure celebration and praise, and in it, he honored me.

But as we forced ourselves to break our embrace, as he reluctantly turned toward the door, I wondered.

How was it possible for us to ever be together? He would leave come morn, and once he was behind the border, would I ever truly see him again?

Direction, Lord, I prayed. *And mercy. Please, Lord. Mercy!*

LUCIANA BETARRINI

The next day, Guilio would still not even look my way. He rode past us as we traveled toward Castello Forelli, two by two. My brother and I followed Gabriella and Evangelia, but they, like all of us, were rather somber. Marcello and Luca had ridden out to rally friends to their cause, as well as to try and gain any information they could on who might be setting up the Forelli clan.

It was basically a hot mess.

Behind us, Lady Tiliani and Ilaria rode, uncharacteristically silent too. Was she sad about saying good-bye to Aurelio after all? Or was it more his somber captain? For the hundredth time, I wondered if I was the only one who saw the two trail each other with their eyes every chance they got. And then I wondered if anyone else saw me and Guilio do the same thing. Until, you know, he learned the truth about me.

My answer was Gabriella. She watched Guilio ride wide and then glanced over at me, as if reading my thoughts. She pulled up on her reins until she was beside us. "Domenico, would you mind?" she asked in English, nodding toward Evangelia.

I don't know what it was. But hearing English was some sort of balm to my soul. As well as the fact she wanted to talk with me. Because I'd totally been dying to talk with her.

"Sure," Nico said easily, urging his mount forward to ride alongside Evangelia.

"This way, Cousin," Gabriella said, leading me out of the line so we could ride alongside the Forelli caravan, but at twenty paces, affording us a bit of privacy.

I was a little tongue-tied, with this sudden intimacy. Because after all this time, we had done nothing but speak as part of a group.

"I imagine you're a little overwhelmed," she said softly.

"You could say that."

"And wondering what you should do now?"

"Pretty much."

"And Giulio's behavior has changed because. . ."

"I told him," I blurted out. "Who I was. Where I'd come from. Two nights ago, the night of the ball. Right before . . ."

She nodded in understanding. "And how did he take it?"

"Not well." I gestured helplessly toward him. "As you can see, he's pretty freaked out." I looked at her. "How did Marcello take it when you told him? And Luca?"

"They were pretty *freaked out* too," she said with a grim smile. "But then I was poisoned, and I had to return to our time. It was my only chance. Marcello carried me to the tomb and put my hand to the print himself . . ." She looked off to a neighboring cliff face, as if remembering, and I again noted her beauty, even as a middle-aged woman who had survived battle after battle. Still all She-Wolf, from her head to her toes.

But I was going back over her words. "You said you were poisoned?"

She gave me a rueful grin. "Not everyone likes strong women here. Especially if they draw the eye of a powerful man." Together, we looked Guilio's way. "It's a little more cutthroat than contemporary America."

"I've gathered that." I laughed, then grew serious again. "But you chose to return?"

"The time tunnel heals," she told me. "And I had fallen for Marcello. As I left, he asked me to return. I really couldn't do anything else." She eyed me and smiled. "But I had to convince Evangelia, which wasn't easy."

"This whole two-fer thing is a challenge. I mean, Nico seems to want to stay right now, thinking he can make some sort of financial killing—knowing what we do, in advance—but what if he wants to leave later?"

"Exactly. You have to agree, together, on *forever*. Here. There. But you have to be of one mind, or it will tear you apart."

"Your sister seems to think we should go home," I said bluntly.

Gabriella considered that. "She has lost a great deal," she said, gazing at Evangelia. "But gained too. I think if you pressed her, she would admit to the gains. The losses though . . ."

"Are sometimes overwhelming," I finished.

"Sometimes."

We rode on in companionable silence. "Why is it," I asked hesitantly, "that you have waited until now to speak to me?"

She waved her hand across the horizon, then over our caravan. "Because I wanted you to experience this, know it for yourself, before I influenced you."

"Influenced me?"

Her gelding danced around a prickly bush and came alongside mine again. "Yes. I know my sister spoke to you earlier. She felt the need. Grief can make you guarded. Wary. It can build walls, as it has for my sister. I felt it was important to give you the chance to open your mind—and heart—to this place, time. To give you time to experience it for yourself, without undue influence from me. I'll ask you what I asked myself, Luciana. God saw fit to bring you here. Why do you think that is?"

I thought about it. "I ran across a quote right before we traveled."

She waited for me to go on.

"It stuck with me, maybe because I still so miss my mom and

gramma. It said, 'There are four things in this life that will change you. Love, friends, family, and loss. The first three will keep you grounded and yet free. May you allow the last to make you brave.' Being here, with you all, it seems like I'm experiencing all four things at the same time, and it's changing me. Somehow, it's making me stronger. More brave, as I realize what I can survive.

"I lost my mother," I went on. "And my grandmother. We never really had my dad. He finances us—our education and, you know, things like jiu jitsu. But he wasn't ever really my *dad*. Girls talk about having such a special relationship with their fathers. I—" I stopped, abruptly, remembering too late that Gabi and Lia had lost their father, and then lost him again. "I'm sorry." I swallowed. "You were probably close to your dad."

She gave me a kind smile. "It was not always so. When we were growing up, our parents really only had eyes for each other and the Next Great Etruscan Dig. It was only when we went back for him that we got to know him well over those awesome, precious years. And he, us." Her eyes caught mine. "Maybe your dad just needs another chance too?"

I considered that. But I just couldn't see it happening. "My dad left when we were little. He's really into real estate. Not history. Or us, at all. I don't think there's ever a chance we could nab him and bring him here and he'd be happy about staying. Or that we'd be happy to have him." My eyes suddenly widened. "But my mom!"

I looked to Gabriella. "Do you think . . . if we went back before she got sick with cancer, we could bring her here? Would the time tunnel heal her?"

"I don't know." She hesitated, clearly thinking. "You need to know that what my mom, Lia, and I did was extremely risky. Pulling off the prints at the wrong time could mean the difference of a decade or ten. We were trying to return to Marcello and Luca then. And we'd been gone so long, Marcello had almost given up on me. And Dad was in Tuscany. Your mom lived in America?"

I nodded, understanding. It'd take us a while to get there and get back to the tomb.

She looked toward her sons, deep in thought. "For a while, I thought that every minute back in our time seemed to be about a day here."

Things fell into place for me. The reason why they'd been in such a rush to get out of Castello Forelli, nab their dad, and escape. Because Marcello and Luca had been waiting . . . and waiting. "You said *for a while*."

"Yes, now I know that it is an inexact science. Because you said we disappeared about a year ago, right?"

"Right."

"Well, a year is made up of about five hundred twenty-five thousand minutes, and that many days would mean it was about fourteen-hundred years here. And since we're not dust in our graves by now, I'm thinking my calculations no longer hold." She shrugged. "It seemed the same each time we traveled. But something has clearly shifted."

"Or it is all in God's hands," I said, then paused. "And if he smiled over your efforts to save your dad, why would he not do the same with my mom?"

"He very well might," she allowed, "but consider the fact that in the end, my dad died anyway," she said. "We did get a few years with him that we never would have had back home. But Lia and I realize you can't play God. He might have granted us time with Dad for a few more years than originally planned—*here*, in *this* time—but in the end, he was gone. We were so glad for our time together. But in the grand scheme of things—with the time exchange as it is—did we lose him really when we lost him before?" She shook her head. "We're not sure. We've come to think that God knows how many days we have on this earth, and that alone is all that can be understood."

I sighed, gradually giving up on the hope of seeing Mom again, talking with her, living with her. "I see." I sighed again. "I'd give an awful lot to hug my mom again. Even just once. But losing her again?" I shook my head. "I do not know if I could handle grieving her all over again."

"Believe me, I understand."

"But even after your dad's death," I said, "you stayed."

She looked almost surprised. "Well, yes. Because I had Marcello, and Lia had Luca. And babies on the way." Her eyes moved to Guilio again. "What made you decide to tell him?"

"Things were—I just had to. It's not like you can keep it a secret forever, right?"

"Not when things get serious," she agreed. "And I've never seen Guilio get serious with anyone."

"Anyone?" I blinked. How had he avoided the throngs of medieval bachelorettes? He certainly had the land, title, and looks to attract many.

"Nay," she said. Her eyes grew distant. "He is single-minded, much like his father. Focused."

I studied her. "How else is he like his father?"

She continued to look at Guilio. "In their refinement, their leadership. Guilio is as gifted a tracker as his father was. And he is just as handsome, if not more so. If that were possible."

"He is like, umm, crazy handsome," I blurted. "And he seems to be into me. Or at least he *was*. I kind of keep thinking I imagined the whole thing."

She smiled at me. "He's real. Just as real as his father was."

I got the sense there was more to that story.

"His father was Fiorentini," she said.

I started at that. "Really?"

"Really," she said, smiling, looking to the horizon now. "And he was dear to Marcello. They had been friends as boys. It carried over into adulthood. Even when things got . . . rough."

"Rough?"

"Yes. We were constantly battling the Fiorentini. At one point, I was captured. They hung me up on a cage on a wall, and I thought

I was going to die. But then, Rodolfo Greco saved me. Well, Rodolfo, Marcello, Lia, and Luca did," she amended quickly.

But I wondered about how she had phrased it. Her tone. It didn't take much to realize there had been some sort of love triangle at some point. I went back over what she'd said. "They hung you up in a *cage*?"

"Yeah," she said, arching a brow in my direction. "It's a thing here," she said, almost lightly. "Robbers, murderers, traitors. They get hung up in cages to die a slow death. When I was captured, they strung me up as bait, wanting to force Marcello's—and Siena's—hand. With no food or water."

I thought about that for a minute. "How many days?"

She squinted, as if trying to remember. "I think it was three. I was at the end, almost dying of thirst. But then Rodolfo made a way for my escape. He and Marcello—along with a number of others—had taken an oath as boys. They carried a tattoo on their inner forearm of a triangle as a sign. Once there were twelve. There are only a few left now, alive. The rest . . ."

She looked to a vineyard, sloping off and down to our right. I assumed she meant the rest had died. From plague? Battle? I wanted to ask but didn't feel like I should. My mind was already spinning.

Gabriella brought her eyes back to me. "You stand at the precipice, Luciana. I know the feeling well. Guilio is a good man. But I do not want to see him hurt. Please do not press forward unless you intend to stay."

I nodded. "But how do you know? How did you know?"

She leveled her chocolate-brown eyes on me. "Think of yourself as an estuary. Partly of the river, partly of the ocean. Dig deep, Luciana. Ask your Maker where you belong. Do you go back upriver? Or release yourself to the ocean? Whatever you decide, settle on it. Don't second-guess it. But"—she gestured with her head toward Guilio and lifted a brow—"if love has found you, is that not answer enough?"

I startled. "L-love?"

Now both her brows raised in question. "Did you not just say that you have experienced all those things here, all at once? Family, friends, love and loss?"

I stared past her to Guilio, on the ridge, still conferring with the scout as we passed.

And for the first time, I recognized what I was feeling. I wasn't just crushing on him. I wasn't just into him as a boyfriend.

God help me, she was right. I was falling in *love*.

30

TILIANI FORELLI

I went about my tasks at Castello Forelli as if I were a wooden puppet. We moved through patrol, exercises in the courtyard, and followed through with missions to neighbors to seek what my father and uncle sought—answers. But all the while, I could not get Valentino out of my mind. When might I see him again? How?

Two days after returning home, we had made no progress. The interlopers had disappeared, as if they had been apparitions, leaving naught but air behind them. If it was Sir Ercole, he was long gone. The Fortebraccios? There was no evidence. The Bartolinis or their ilk? We could not find a way to connect them to the murders four days past.

And we had to travel to Firenze on the morrow and report what we knew, scant as it was. If we could convince them of our innocence, we might avoid war. But if we did not try, we knew the Fiorentini were bound to extract vengeance, no matter how long and hard Aurelio pled our case.

Solemnly, my parents, aunt, and uncle conferred with us. "Prepare to depart," Zio Marcello said. "We go to Firenze, not with the information that would exonerate us, but with what little we have. We shall present this truth: we, too, seek what they want—knowledge of who is responsible for these murders."

Fortino stared at him. "But if we walk in there, we may well be walking into a death trap. They shall demand retribution."

"And that is why you shall attend me," Marcello returned, "but Benedetto shall remain behind."

"But—" Benedetto began to protest.

"Nay." Marcello lifted his hand. "I take my eldest, to show I have no fear of the truth. But I leave my second-born behind, in case the worst happens."

We all fell silent.

"You all need to know," Papa said, mostly to me, "we've faced dire straits in Firenze before."

Zia Gabi nodded. "And came out on the other side."

"We may be old," Papa added with a sly smile, "but do not count us dead yet. This is not the first circle of intrigue we have encountered, nor our first battle. And we shall have the She-Wolves by our side."

It heartened me, to see Mama tentatively return his smile. Again I glimpsed the warrior I'd seen on the battlefield with the Perugians.

Zio Marcello lifted his chin. "I do not believe this shall be our end. But regardless of what becomes of us, Castello Forelli and her people must carry on."

I blinked, trying to take it in.

"We leave come morn," he said. "But this night, I must speak to Lord Greco." He looked down to the far end of the table. "Guilio, walk with me. Tiliani, come also."

Surprised, I rose from the table, and in response, so did all my male counterparts. Together, my uncle, Guilio, and I moved out the door and then into the courtyard. He lifted a hand, not uttering a word, and men ran to slide back the guardrail, opening the freshly repaired gates. We walked out as though this was completely ordinary.

But nothing about this was ordinary.

Still, my uncle strode forward. Guilio and I followed him around the outer, high walls of the castello. We moved out into the vineyards beyond, then up the far hill.

He came to a halt, finally, surveying our westward boundary. Another sunset was upon us. He seemed to sense me, as I came up on his right shoulder, and raised a hand for mine.

Curiously, I took it, but while he grasped my fingers, he did not turn.

"This is your land, Tiliani," he said. "Your future."

I frowned. "What do you mean?"

"If the worst happens, you and Benedetto shall carry on in our stead, seeing to the castello and her people." He did turn, now. "Guilio shall see to Castello Greco."

"Yes, Zio. Of course," I said.

"As you say, m'lord," Guilio said, and we moved onward.

I puzzled over the fact that he had not invited Benedetto along with us. Did my younger cousin not need to hear these words too?

When Zio Marcello reached the vines, he lifted a hand to a young bunch of grapes, holding them for a moment as if weighing them. Behind him, we waited. He lifted his head and looked about the valley, as if appreciating it for the last time. A shiver ran down my back.

Zio Marcello was saying farewell. Putting things in order. For all of my papa's brave words, my uncle clearly thought that this may be their end.

He turned to Guilio. "I understand that Lady Luciana told you from whence she came."

I froze. She had? I looked to Guilio, who had gone rigid.

"Y-you know?" he stammered. "All that she claims?"

"I do," Zio Marcello replied. "But I knew the truth of it from the start. Because I have seen others arrive through that time tunnel."

Guilio's forehead wrinkled in confusion. "What do you mean?"

"Lady Gabriella and Lady Evangelia are much like your Lady Luciana and her brother," he said. "Their mother came with them. Years ago, there were two other Betarrinis. Brothers. But they elected not to stay."

I watched Guilio as the meaning sank in.

"What is it you are saying? Do you mean that—"

"Yes," Marcello said. "They are of the same bloodline. And what you struggle to accept is significant indeed. I struggled with it myself." He placed his hands on Guilio's shoulders. "But I shall tell you this. God gifted me Gabriella, and she *is* a gift, no matter how she came. When she arrived it was providential. Never, ever have I met a woman like her. Nor Evangelia. And Luciana is of their bloodline. Just as fierce and strong." He raised his finger in Guilio's face. "That does not mean her heart is less vulnerable than another's. Do not tarry if you feel moved to pursue her. Do you hear me? Do not tarry. Time is of the essence. In more ways than you can imagine."

As Guilio absorbed my uncle's words, they seemed to give him new strength. Permission, of a sort. Mayhap it was knowing he wasn't the first to fall for a woman from another time.

He straightened. "Do either of you know where Lady Luciana is?"

I hid a smile. "I think she and Domenico were headed to the meadow for some sparring practice after we supped," I said.

"Go," my uncle said with a smile.

Guilio turned and hurried down the path.

My uncle turned to me. "And you, sweet niece? A man has stolen your heart, too, has he not?"

Tentatively, I lifted my eyes to meet his. "And yet not the man you and my parents hoped."

He nodded. "I thought as much."

"You did? Do my parents know too?"

"We are your elders, but we are not yet blind." He smiled.

I sighed. "But now it is impossible. He has returned with Aurelio to Firenze, and he owes Aurelio's family a great deal." I shook my head. "I do not see how we can ever be together."

He placed an arm around my shoulders as we walked back toward the castello. "Give it time. Let us see what we discover in Firenze."

"May I come with—"

"Nay," he cut me off. "We do not know yet how we shall be met. And as I said, I need you and Benedetto here. It is of great importance that we know you are both safe, that the castello is in good hands." His face softened, seeing my disappointment. "But if this is love, dear one, trust me when I say that Sir Valeri shall find his way back to you."

LUCIANA BETARRINI

It felt good to be sparring with my brother, going through the moves we'd learned over the years. We took turns twisting and turning, stopping just shy of landing each other on our backs or breaking the other's wrist. We reviewed illegal moves too and began to practice them. Because here in medieval Italy, there were no rules.

We took a break after twenty minutes, each of us sweating and panting. Nico plopped to the ground, and I sat beside him. "So," he said. "Are you still thinking about going home?"

"Kind of. I mean, Guilio seems pretty spooked about the truth. I'm not sure we're ever going to get past it. Have you told Ilaria?"

"Nah. I mean, she's totally my kind of girl, but I didn't want to pursue it until I knew if you wanted to stay for sure."

"That's smart. I kind of wish I hadn't. It's all so . . . complicated."

"Life is complicated, Luci, no matter the year you're living it. I think the trick is figuring out your map so you can find your way through the passes."

I glanced at him in surprise and huffed a laugh. "That's pretty deep, Nico."

"Yeah, well, there's something about facing mortal danger a few times that pushes a guy to dig a bit deeper." He plucked a long blade of grass and began tearing off pieces, letting them flutter away in the golden afternoon light.

"True," I agreed. A thought struck me. "Hey, what's your new idea? If we stay, what are you going to do?"

"Well, if we're staying, I'm going after Ilaria, if she'll have me. But my big idea was to pursue banking. Start small, do the microloan kind of thing and build from there. I was going to talk it over with Marcello, but I'll wait until we're through all this. The Medicis made a killing in banking, and there are already a few banks in Siena. Why not join them? Get in early?"

I nodded. It was a brilliant idea, actually. "So if you can't steal the Medicis' treasure, you're just going to beat them to their riches."

"Basically," he said with a cheeky grin.

"Where would you get your money to start?"

"Well," he said, rubbing the back of his neck, "that's why I need to chat with Marcello."

"Ahh, I see."

He rose and gave me a hand up. We took up our positions again, slowly circling each other, each of us getting ready to make a move.

"Luciana!" called a voice.

We straightened and I shaded my eyes.

It was Guilio.

Guilio.

Through long grasses blowing in the breeze, he strode directly toward me.

I took a step and then another, wondering what he wanted. Why he dared to call my name, after days of the silent treatment.

We got closer and stopped, six paces apart. He looked at me, taking in my man's tunic and leggings—the only thing I could freely spar in. Did he disapprove?

Instead, he raised his voice. "Domenico! May I have a word?"

In my flustered state, I didn't quite hear Nico's response, but within seconds he was beside us.

Everything about Guilio's stature, his tone, as he addressed my brother was formal—almost rigid. "Domenico, as Luciana's closest male relative, may I have your permission to court your sister?"

I stifled a gasp. The wobbly knees became a thing again.

Nico grinned. "Well, you see, brother, in our day, we don't do that sort of thing."

"Nico," I growled in English, "just tell him it's okay or I swear I will take you out."

"All right, all right," he said. "Settle down."

He was enjoying this way too much. "*Nico.*"

He lifted a hand to me and switched to Italian, every bit of levity leaving his face.

"You may court my sister. But," he pointed at Guilio, "if you ever just ignore her again for days on end, you and I will be meeting here in the meadow for our own sparring match. And I will not hold back. Understood?"

Guilio's eyes flickered, and then he smiled. "I understand. But that shall not be necessary." He turned to me and took my hand and tenderly kissed my knuckles, all the while staring at me like I was some kind of miraculous gift. "I do not want to miss another day with your sister."

Nico cleared his throat and took his leave. Guilio and I stood looking at each other, and it was as if I couldn't *see* him enough. My eyes traced his dark hair, shining in the sun, his dark lashes, lacing those gorgeous blue eyes.

Twenty paces away, Nico turned around, walking backward. "I assume this means you're voting to stay?" he shouted in English.

I glanced at him but then returned to focus on Guilio, who seemed in no way bothered by not understanding our exchange.

"I might've just been sold on the idea," I called back. "Is that okay? Do we need to discuss it or anything?"

"Are you kidding?" Nico threw out his arms and grinned. "Let the Medieval Games begin!"

He turned and disappeared into the woods, and I was free to continue gazing at Guilio, and he at me.

And when Lord Guilio Greco kissed me, I couldn't imagine ever leaving his side again.

31

TILIANI FORELLI

We waited for word from our family in Firenze. But it was now three days after they had left, and no scout had returned to report. And in the meantime, it seemed the Fiorentini felt they could poke at us, again and again. We doubled the number in our patrols and tripled the number of patrols per day. We found Fiorentini hunting in our woods. We skirmished with Fiorentini, who shot arrows and then ran. Three of our knights had been wounded.

I was walking the ramparts with Benedetto, wishing my mother, father, aunt, uncle, and cousin would appear on the road south from Firenze, when a knight on the east side of the castello shouted, "Fire! The fields are on fire!"

We hurried down the alure to see. From the east? Were the Perugians tormenting us again now too? The eastern fields of grain—almost ready for harvest—were indeed aflame.

"Everyone get sacks from the stables!" Benedetto cried. "Fire! Everyone to the fire! Bring pails of water!"

We raced down to the courtyard, handing out sacks and pails of water. Almost every able man, woman, and child ran toward the billowing smoke. I was at the gates before I realized our mistake—in an effort to save the harvest that would see our people through the winter, we were leaving the castello vulnerable. Guilio and Benedetto saw it then too. They began calling back some of the knights. We still had the assigned guards on the alure keeping watch, but almost everyone else was outside, some without a weapon.

We managed to get twenty back inside.

"Frederico!" Benedetto called to the knight. "Keep watch! This may be a diversion—beware a new attack!"

"Understood!" The man ran down the alure to pass the word.

"Otello, Falito, gather twenty quivers of arrows and twenty bows and ride out to our people," I directed. "If we are attacked, they shall serve as the first line of defense. Baldarino and Iacapo, do the same with swords. I saw some knights leave armed, but a number were not."

"As you say, m'lady," came the quick reply.

Giulio was at my side. "The Betarrinis are out there. As well as my sisters."

"I know," I said grimly. "We shall have them protected in—"

"On your guard!" bellowed a knight, watching those fighting the fire. He did not call down to us, but rather to our people. "Knights at the ready! Enemies on the rise!"

"Tiliani," Guilio growled. "Allow me to go at least."

"Nay. We *all* shall go." I turned to the men returning from the armory, arms laden. "'Tis too late!" I informed them. "Take an extra weapon to arm a fellow knight but make haste! Let us get to our people!"

They dropped their burdens, each took up an extra sword or quiver of arrows and bow, and together we ran out the gates.

"Close the gates behind us!" I cried to Frederico. "Bar the doors!"

But we could already hear screaming and shouting as we ran.

LUCIANA BETARRINI

I was just admiring the effectiveness of our work—with the help of an already-present irrigation ditch, we'd collectively beaten out half of the advancing line of grass fire—when we heard the knight on the wall shout.

We followed to where he pointed and saw them. Twenty-four men on horseback, bearing down on us. Belatedly, I realized we'd run out of the castle with nothing but sacks as our weapons. I didn't know where Nico was—I'd lost him in the smoke-covered crowd of about seventy fighting the fire. But I knew he was here somewhere. As was Ilaria. But where was Guilio? Tiliani?

About ten knights drew swords *they* had remembered to bring and moved to create a line before us. But I'd seen enough of battle to know that those on horseback had the advantage of height and momentum.

"Run!" commanded Captain Mancini, over his shoulder. "Back to the castello!"

The women and children did as he said, as well as the unarmed male servants. The rest of us stood our ground. Adri had taken up a fallen vine, like some sort of lance. Chiara kneeled, and I saw she had a bow and quiver of arrows, as did Ilaria. I still held the soggy sack in my hands. I felt the heavy weight of it and watched as a knight focused on me. Could I use it somehow? Throw it into the front legs of his charging horse to bring it—and its rider—down?

My heart pounded as I watched them get closer.

Chiara and Ilaria let their first arrows fly, but I had no time to see if they met their marks. The knight coming my way was swinging one of those spiked metal balls on a chain, and it felt like I was the only one in the fields that he could see. Worse, twelve more enemy knights emerged from the woods, all armed with bows. They began shooting at the innocents—the women and children running toward the castle. I could hear their screams behind me.

But I kept my eyes on the knight heading my way. He was now just five horse-paces away, three, one, when I at last dived to the right.

His weapon caught the edge of my gown as I jumped, and he dragged me across the blackened soil for thirty feet, until he could get his mount to stop.

I cursed the skirts that were now tangled around my legs—and his heavy, spiked ball—as he dismounted. I could see one of our knights running toward me, bent on coming to my aid, but he was too far away. I tried to roll to my back, to at least see my opponent, but he grabbed my legs, bound in the skirts, and laughed. I felt the pain of one of the cruel spikes against my calf.

I was on my belly and could only twist halfway around, but I recognized him. Zinali, I thought his name was—one of the noblemen who had accompanied Aurelio Paratore to Siena. He drew a cruel-looking dagger from his belt. "This will be for my friends, who died in your cursed Palazzo Pubblico," he hissed.

He seized hold of my hair, yanking my head back to expose my throat. I had but a second, and as I kicked to unravel my legs from my skirt, I tried to grab hold of his wrist, but my fingernails only grazed his skin.

I tensed, waiting for the slice of the knife across my throat. Wondered what it would feel like to die on the field, as I had seen so many others do.

But then the man suddenly gasped, and his chest thrust forward. He sucked in a shuddering breath as Guilio lifted him upright and sank his sword deeper. My assailant gasped his last, and Guilio shoved him roughly to the side.

He bent and freed my skirts from the spiked weapon, then offered a hand. "Are you harmed?"

"Nay," I said, gasping for breath. "Just . . . shaken."

"Stay behind me," Guilio said, shielding me as he turned to face the fray again.

I saw that the knights still on the castello's wall were shooting arrows at the archers who had been attacking our people. But now those enemy archers advanced toward us, shooting at every Sienese they could. Did they mean to kill us all?

"Come!" Guilio urged. "Make haste!"

I ran after him, feeling the vulnerability of the two paces between us. But I could see where he was heading. Lady Adri was trying to fight off a knight with nothing but a stick. In two strikes, it had broken apart. She turned lithely when he stabbed at her, and it was surreal, watching her skirts billow out as if she danced for her very life.

Guilio stepped in between the two as the assailant whirled to slice her through.

He grunted, taking the Fiorentini's full force and momentum, but then flung the knight backward. His opponent only smiled and wiped his upper lip, coming back after him as if it mattered not who he killed this day—only that he killed. I grabbed Adri's hand, and we moved back-to-back, watching for any who might have us in their sights next.

My eyes caught movement, and I dropped to the ground, dragging her with me as two arrows sailed over our heads. I didn't know which was best—to stay hidden in the golden wheat or to rise and be able to see who might be coming our way. I could hear Guilio still battling with the knight, their swords clashing again and again. Their low grunts and labored breath.

The enemy knight was formidable, and Guilio had clearly met his match. Each were slowing, becoming more weary. And they were getting closer to us. I urged Adri to crawl away, distance herself, as I peeked up to better see. The enemy knight had his back to me, and Guilio was steadily driving him backward. Without further hesitation, I gathered up my skirts, ran forward, and then skidded into his legs, attempting a scissor takedown.

He staggered and looked down at me in fury. "You insufferable minx," he spat, raising his sword to stab me.

But I'd given Guilio the edge he needed. He slashed at the man's arm, then drove his dagger directly under his chest plate. My attacker sprawled back, hitting his head on a rock and was instantly out.

Guilio reached for me and pulled me to my feet. "Luciana," he panted, "never do that again."

We crouched and looked around. "Do what? Help you?"

"Sí, if it puts you in further danger."

"Would you not do the same for me?"

"'Tis different."

"Nay, it is the same."

"Might we argue about this later?"

"Gladly. As long as we're both alive to argue."

But I could see the numbers of our attackers had greatly lessened, and some were retreating into the woods.

One Fiorentini archer turned as he went and drew his last arrow. When I saw him pull back the string and aim among the crowd, I screamed, "Arrow on the wind!"

32

Tiliani Forelli

istantly, I heard Luciana's cry. I was searching for the archer, trying to figure out where the arrow was coming from, when it passed me and rammed into Ilaria.

She staggered, regained her feet, and then abruptly collapsed into a sitting position, eyes wide. She lifted trembling fingers to the shaft of the arrow, then looked up at me.

"Til—" she whispered, struggling for breath.

"Ilaria!" I cried out, falling to my knees beside her as all other sounds from the battlefield faded.

I forced confidence to my tone. "Steady, friend. Let me see."

I eased her just a bit forward and found the cruel point of the arrowhead pressing against the fabric of her bodice in the back. Swiftly, I took out my dagger and sliced open the fabric.

The tip of it just barely emerged, stretching her skin in ghoulish fashion. Surely her lung had been struck.

"Nona!" I shouted, looking frantically about. Where was my grandmother? Had she been hurt also? "Nona!" I screamed.

Ilaria was trembling so much, it was as if she suffered a seizure. I held on to her shoulders. "Ilaria," I begged, "look at me. You must try and calm yourself. Try and take slow, quiet breaths."

But she was wild-eyed, fighting for air. Clearly losing ground by the minute.

And that's what chilled me to the bone. No matter how the

odds were stacked against us, she had never given me *that* look. "Guilio?" I called tentatively, voice shaking. Then more firmly, "*Guilio*! Chiara!"

Chiara was the first to reach us. "Ilaria!" she exclaimed. Her long fingers traced her sister's face. "I am here, dearest. You are not alone. Both Til and I are here." She gently probed the entry point. Then she looked at Ilaria's back. She stilled for a moment, then righted Ilaria again. She looked to the sky, biting her lip, terror in her eyes.

There was no way to save Ilaria. Neither of us had ever seen a knight survive a strike like this.

Nay, I thought as tears filled my eyes. *Nay!* There had to be something that could be done. I could not let my beloved friend die.

At that moment, I saw Luciana, running toward us.

Luciana had a way out. A miracle-cure.

Dim hope lit. Had not my aunt experienced it herself?

LUCIANA BETARRINI

I had seen Ilaria get hit, seen her fall, and raced toward them. With relief, I found Chiara already by her side, and Adri joining them. One of them would know what to do for her.

Domenico came limping toward us across the field, his nose bloody, but he was whole. He did not look at me; his eyes were on Ilaria alone. Had he seen her fall too? When he got closer, his face grew ashen.

"Ilaria," he choked. Wordlessly, Adri made way for him as he dropped to his knees. "It's okay," he said, lapsing into our English. More tender in his tone than I'd heard him in years. He took her hand in his. "It's okay. It will be all right."

Her head tilted his way, but her eyes were vacant, distant, as she clearly sank into shock.

It was most definitely not going to be all right.

Nico looked up at me, alarmed.

She was dying. I could see it in her face. Adri and Chiara's expressions confirmed it.

There would be no surgery, no treatment. No saving her.

Tiliani sat back on her haunches and looked directly at the two of us as she spoke. "The tunnel."

Nico's expression changed, and his eyes were tinged with hope. "Yes! The tunnel!"

He turned toward me. "The tunnel, Luci," he said in English. "It will heal her."

What? "Nico. We're guessing."

"Think, Luci. Your headaches. Gabi, after getting poisoned. She survived."

"But . . ."

I left the words unsaid. If we left here, could we get back? I remembered what Gabi had said. It appeared more an act of God than science.

"But what?" Nico gazed feverishly at Ilaria as she passed out, and he caught her in his arms. "Are we just gonna let her go?"

"'Tis true," Adri put in. "The tunnel heals."

"It heals Betarrinis," I said. "Will it heal others?"

Nico looked at me more sharply. "If it was Guilio, what would you have me do?"

Guilio had arrived then and instantly knelt beside us. "Ilaria!" He looked up at us in anguish. "Why has she not been aided? Adri?"

Lady Adri laid a gentling hand on his arm. "I cannot save her. But," she added, quickly motioning to Nico and me, "these two might."

Guilio looked to us in confusion.

Ilaria was heaving for breath. Even now, blood bubbled at

the corners of her mouth. I made up my mind. "We can try," I said, standing. "But it has to be now." I looked at Nico. "Can you carry her?"

He nodded, and carefully picked Ilaria up, avoiding the arrow. Adri grabbed Chiara's arm as she began to object and jumped up to stand in our way, utterly confused.

"*È la sua unica possibilità*," Adri said to her. *It's her only chance.*

The two stood for a moment, arm to arm, wordlessly conferring, before Chiara relented, face still filled with confusion and concern.

We all moved across the field, looking at knights aiding other wounded knights, the Fiorentini now gone. It would have been like they'd never been here, if I didn't see some of their dead, among ours.

Guilio bent toward me as we rushed along. "We are going to the tombs?"

I nodded, unable to meet his gaze. "We will need a torch. Can you get one for us?"

Before I was finished speaking, he was off to do so.

Adri came alongside us. "That arrow will need to come out before you travel."

That made sense. The time tunnel might heal Ilaria, but she wouldn't want an arrow forever fused through her chest. "Chiara is fetching what I need."

I glanced at the young woman who had so stalwartly stayed by my side at Castello Fortebraccio. Ilaria's gorgeous olive skin was turning a ghastly bluish-gray.

"Stay with me, Ilaria," Nico pled, holding her close, lapsing into English. "Stay with me," he murmured over and over, holding her closer still.

Guilio returned with a torch, and we moved along a wild boar trail through the wood. Finally, we reached a road, and then crossed the summer-starved river, trickling among the stones.

Nico's muttering continued, "Stay with us. It will be okay soon. C'mon, Ilaria. Stay with us. Stay with me."

Every time he said it, my heart broke a little. What if we were too late?

Guilio took my hand, recognizing what my mind had not yet fully absorbed.

I was leaving.

Leaving.

We had to. If Ilaria was to have half a chance.

But was it really going to work?

Could we really just jump back in time like Gabi and Lia had? Would it really save Ilaria, if we did? And . . . *could we get back?*

Or were we leaving Guilio, only to lose both him *and* Ilaria?

We arrived at last at the tombs. "Please," I said to Guilio, my voice choked. "We need light in there."

He went to his knees and crawled inside Tomb Two. Adri followed, as Nico gently set Ilaria down. "We'll need to slide her in on her side," he said worriedly.

"You go first. I'll hold her legs so you won't have to slide her far."

In short order she was in. It was all happening so fast, my mind, my heart, couldn't seem to keep up.

Adri had spread out a cloth beneath the handprints and now swiftly cut Ilaria's bodice further open at the back. She doused the area with a corked bottle of some astringent and then drew out a razor-sharp knife—the thinnest I'd seen here. She looked expectantly at Nico and me.

Chiara watched nearby, still trying to take it all in, utterly perplexed, but there was no time to explain.

"As soon as I do this," Adri said in English, "you must go. She will have only minutes left. Are you ready?"

I looked to Guilio, who appeared as bereft at me leaving as he was in anguish over his sister. I clutched his hand. "We shall bring her back to you, Guilio. Will you wait for us?"

"Will I *wait* for you?" he asked, as if pained. He brought my fingers, interlocked with his, to his lips. "I will forever await your return," he pledged. "But please. Do not tarry."

"We're losing her," Adri interrupted us, in English. "Ready?"

I tore my gaze from Guilio.

"We're ready," I said.

33

Adri lanced the skin at Ilaria's back, exposing the head of the arrow, and a second later, Chiara shoved the arrow shaft six inches through.

It was brutal to watch. As if Chiara was stabbing her sister. But it was the only way.

Swiftly, Adri grabbed hold of the blood-slicked shaft at Ilaria's back and broke off the head.

"Lift her," Adri told Nico.

He immediately bent and gathered Ilaria up in his arms.

"What are you doing?" Chiara cried. "We must—"

Adri hushed her.

"Let me help," I said, "so you can reach the handprint."

Nico shifted her a bit between us so he could reach up to his print. "I'm ready," he said. "Lady Adri, take out the shaft. As soon as it's out, you put your hand on your print, Luci."

"I will."

"Don't let go of her," Adri warned, sounding every inch the protective grandmother.

"We won't."

"Go with God." She kissed Ilaria on the forehead. And then she leaned over, grabbed hold of the remaining shaft of the arrow, and with both hands, took a deep breath and yanked it out.

I set my hand on the other print even as I felt the warm gush of blood flood from my friend's torso.

I tried to look at Guilio for as long as I could, but the tomb was already swirling, tipping as the heat beneath my palm grew. I felt that odd sensation of my skin fusing with the stone and glanced up, waiting for the hole in the top to emerge, letting us know we were getting close to our own time. I held on to Ilaria as the lifeline she was between me and Nico. Would we have to decide when to pull off the prints? Would we just know when it was right? Or would—

Abruptly the room stopped spinning, and we fell back, as if pushed.

I blinked as I stopped skidding across the floor. Then I laughed, upon seeing Nico beside me, still holding Ilaria. Better yet was when she groaned and moved in his arms.

"Ilaria!" I exulted, sitting up and crawling to her. "*Ilaria!*"

But then a voice behind us growled. "Who are you? Where did you come from?"

I turned.

It was the archeologist—Manero—with two younger men beside him. They stared at us, alternately frightened and furious. Had they seen us arrive out of thin air? Or did they think we'd crawled in?

Manero bent down and looked at each of us, perplexed. "You," he said, glaring at me and Nico. "You were the two who came asking about the Betarrinis. How did you get in here? How did you get past the gate?"

"Doc," said one of the young men, eyes wide with shock. "I was looking that way. It might sound crazy, but I think . . . I think they just *appeared.*"

Ilaria's eyes fluttered open. "What—Where—" She sat up and gazed around. Nico and I beamed at her, then at each other. It had worked. She was well! Healed!

"Grab them," Manero said. "They are trespassers. Call the police!"

"But Doc," it was the younger guy again. "Did you hear what I said? They just *appeared*. It's like they fell through that wall."

Nico and I shared a look as we helped Ilaria to her feet. We had little time. "How do you fare?" Nico murmured to Ilaria in Italian. "Are you well?"

"Yes," she said, gazing about in bewilderment at the men, the tomb. "Where are we? Who are these people?" She mirrored the confused expression of Manero and his men.

"Shall we?" I asked Nico over her head. "Even with them watching?"

"Secret's kind of out," he said, glancing toward the younger man.

They were advancing on us.

We grabbed hold of Ilaria's arms and were reaching for the prints when Manero yanked her back. "Do not touch anything!" he shouted at us. "Hold onto them!"

But Ilaria rammed her elbow into his belly, and he bent over in pain.

If I'd doubted she had been totally healed by our traveling, I doubted no longer.

"Hey!" the younger man shouted, pulling her away from the senior archeologist.

We had to get clear of them all.

We had to go back, but we didn't want any of them with us. And every minute that passed might be a day away.

But now the other guy was trying to grab Nico. I didn't want to hurt anyone, but if this went on much longer, others would arrive, and we'd be sunk. Turning, I brought down the one near Ilaria with a side kick as Nico sent the other into Manero, and both fell to the ground.

"Someone's coming!" I spotted a fourth man crawling through the entrance.

"C'mon." Nico took hold of one of Ilaria's arms, and I took the other.

Together we rushed to the wall and put our hands on the prints, each with a firm hold on Ilaria. I willed the time tunnel to open quickly.

Manero and the other two were rising to their feet, but were wary now. Manero was screaming for the new guy to fetch the guards, but his voice sounded like an echo, from far away. With relief I saw the tomb walls began swirling around us and felt the heat rising beneath my palm.

Take us back, Lord, I prayed. *Take us home. And to the right time, please. Please. Oh, please.*

I didn't know what surprised me more. That I was praying. Or that I had prayed that God would take us *home.*

But I knew now what Guilio had meant when he said their home was with the Forellis. That he did not care about giving up Castello Greco if it was best for their family. Because I felt that way too.

Our time with the Forellis had grounded us, given us what we most needed. Family.

And right now, our family needed *us.* We needed to get back and make sure they were okay in Firenze or find a way to help free them. Just as they would have done for us.

Take us back to them, God, I prayed. *Take us home.*

ACKNOWLEDGMENTS

Many thanks to my editors, Steve and Lisa Laube, Sarah Grimm, Megan Gerig, and the people who helped get my jiu jitsu right: Amy Fisher, Abby and Nick Pugh, and Shane Duffy. Andrew Spadzinski, Cheryl Crawford, and Melanie Stroud helped me proof the final draft. I appreciate each of you and your investment in my book!

About the Author

Lisa T. Bergren is the author of over seventy books, including the River of Time Series, the Gifted Series, and the God Gave Us . . . children's book series. She resides in Colorado Springs, CO, with her husband and gradually graduating-from-the-nest, young-adult children. Learn more about her on Facebook.com/LisaTawnBergren, Instagram @LisaTBergren or at LisaBergren.com.

IF YOU ENJOY

OCEANS OF TIME

YOU MIGHT LIKE THESE OTHER FANTASY SERIES:

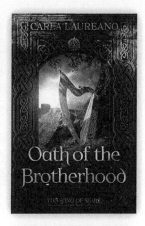

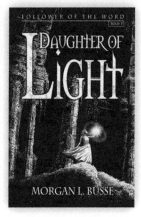

www.enclavepublishing.com